Praise for the haunting novels of Judith Hawkes

My Soul to Keep

"A scary and subtle thriller . . . will keep you up all night." —Lee Smith, author of *News of the Spirit*

"[Hawkes] defines herself as the potential matriarch of a modern genre. . . . Imaginative and satisfying paranormal plot. . . . Rich with promise, enlightening and diverting." —*San Antonio Express-News*

"Clearly delineated characters, moody scene-setting and a perfectly controlled storyline. . . . This is the subtle eeriness of Shirley Jackson transplanted to rural Tennessee." —*Memphis Commercial Appeal*

"Deftly eerie . . . draws the reader into a vortex of haunted events." —*Publishers Weekly*

"It's the best ghost story I have read in a long time. [Judith Hawkes's] sense of atmosphere is beautifully judged and her descriptions lovely."
—Barbara Erskine, author of *House of Echoes*

"A haunting chiller."—*Anniston-Star* (Alabama)

"Steeped in atmosphere that alternately lulls and chills the reader, *My Soul to Keep* keeps the reader enthralled in a story that can't possibly be true, yet must be."
—Marlys Millhiser, author of *It's Murder Going Home*

Julian's House

"Kept me on edge two nights in a row. What a find—what a talent! It's hard to believe this is a first book; the writing is brilliant, the characters are almost too real, and the plot is marvelously crafted. I hope we see a lot more of this writer."

—Barbara Michaels, author of *The Dancing Floor*

"A witch's brew in the tradition of Shirley Jackson."

—*Dallas Morning News*

"A ghost tale . . . a detective story . . . a dazzling evocation of haunting." —*New York Newsday*

"Gripping, readable, and scary as all get out . . . a thriller along the lines of James and Poe . . . a mystery cunningly conceived, wickedly frightening . . . a killer novel that flat out gave me the willies!"

—*Memphis Commercial Appeal*

"A ghost story . . . fashioned of perfect language . . . gives us sensuality . . . apparitions . . . beautiful daytime light and nighttime menace . . . eeriness to creep up your back and break you out in sweats and goose bumps . . . the screws turn even more tightly."—*Baltimore Sun*

Julian's House

"A great ghost story and more . . . will continue to haunt you for a long time. . . . I admire *Julian's House* as literature . . . I urge you to read it."—Annie Dillard

"A modern ghost story . . . spooky, shivery, vivid . . . entertaining terror."—*Louisville Courier-Journal*

"A thinking person's ghost story!"—*Boston Herald*

"Elegant writing and an intricate plot . . . a first-class literary work."—*Atlanta Journal and Constitution*

"Fascinating, memorable, and unsettling . . . an excellent novel in the Shirley Jackson tradition: character-rich, stylish, quietly chilling."

—*Kirkus Reviews*

"The reader gets delightfully sucked into a credible, compelling story." —*Library Journal*

"A chiller for those who like characters who act like adults . . . absorbing, eerie, and profound . . . this book will scare you." —*Milwaukee Journal*

Also by Judith Hawkes

My Soul to Keep
Julian's House

The Heart of a Witch

Judith Hawkes

A SIGNET BOOK

SIGNET
Published by the Penguin Group
Penguin Putnam Inc., 375 Hudson Street,
New York, New York 10014, U.S.A.
Penguin Books Ltd, 27 Wrights Lane,
London W8 5TZ, England
Penguin Books Australia Ltd, Ringwood,
Victoria, Australia
Penguin Books Canada Ltd, 10 Alcorn Avenue,
Toronto, Ontario, Canada M4V 3B2
Penguin Books (N.Z.) Ltd, 182–190 Wairau Road,
Auckland 10, New Zealand

Penguin Books Ltd, Registered Offices:
Harmondsworth, Middlesex, England

First published by Signet, an imprint of Dutton NAL,
a member of Penguin Putnam Inc.

First Printing, April, 1999
10 9 8 7 6 5 4 3 2 1

Printed in the United States of America

For Sharon

It may be objected that the Devil might so harden the heart of a witch that she is unable to confess her crimes.

——*Malleus Maleficarum,* 1484

The *Malleus Maleficarum,* or *Hammer of the Witches,* was the handbook of professional witch hunters during the persecutions of the Middle Ages. Compiled by a pair of Dominican monks at the behest of Pope Innocent VIII, the *Malleus* describes the fantastic evils wrought by witchcraft and offers instructions for identifying a witch, extracting her confession, and bringing her to trial and punishment.

I hereby freely confess my crimes.

No devil will prevent me, for the followers of the Craft have never believed in such a being, however loudly our enemies may insist otherwise. Nor do my crimes bear much resemblance to those described in the lurid pages of the *Witches' Hammer*. I have changed no man into beast's shape. I have stolen no one's wits. I have conjured no tempests, nor have I copulated with an incubus or drunk the blood of any newborn child.

My crimes are of a different nature. Of them, I already stand convicted in the only court of consequence: that of my own heart.

Judge me as you will.

It was Kip who started the ball rolling—literally, as it happens: an official Rawlings baseball, white leather stitched in red. Against the dark velvet of childhood memory it glimmers like a floating, distant pearl—growing rapidly as it approaches, rushing toward me out of the past—and suddenly I'm seven years old again, enveloped by green shadows and dappled sunshine, playing catch with Kip in our front yard. The ball sails over my head; I jump, miss, turn just in time to see it bounce hard in the street behind me.

We knew better than to chase it, of course. It was a constant litany of our parents: never, ever to cross Willow Street by ourselves. Unlike most of the narrow streets in our village, Willow was two lanes wide, divided down the middle by a painted yellow line. Less than half a block from our house it met Main Street at Green Hollow's only stoplight; and to Kip and me the trickle of passing cars, one every couple of minutes, seemed as fearsome as the traffic on a busy six-lane highway. We watched in horror as the ball—the perfect new baseball Kip had received the day before, on our birthday—bounced across the street, heading straight for the Lockley Arms. A passing car briefly blocked our view. When it had gone, we could see the ball lying in the grass on the verge of the Arms driveway, as far beyond our reach as if it had landed on the moon.

We groaned in unison. How many hundreds of times had we been told to play in the backyard, never in front of the house? Mother was forever worrying that our racket would annoy the paying guests across the street at the Lockley Arms. Never mind that the front yard, green and shady in the already hot summer sun, was infinitely more inviting than the treeless backyard with its patches of bare dirt where our games had long since worn away the grass—we had no business playing here.

We knew better. But we had started tossing the new ball around without thinking, and now there it lay on the other side of the street: out of reach and yet so tantalizingly near I could all but read the imprint of the brand name. What would Mother say? She wouldn't raise her voice. But her pained "Oh, *children*" never failed to shrivel our thoughtless, selfish, disobedient hearts.

I looked hopefully at Kip. In some sets of twins, I am told, there is a continuous jockeying for dominance, but in our case he was the undisputed leader, the one who always devised the pranks and schemes into which I was tempted half against my will. His fertile imagination had gotten us out of some tight spots in the past, but in spite of the fact that our predicament was plainly his fault—the throw had been wild—he just stood there with his mouth hanging open. His unaccustomed stillness suspended the whole world in limbo. The wind dropped; the sunlight ceased its dance on the grass. And in that strange lull I registered a kind of flicker inside my head.

Just cross the street. Cross the street and get the ball, and she'll never know.

The leaves stirred again; shadows darted across the grass like schools of swift green minnows. I blinked. The flickering thought had vanished, but the impulse remained. I heard myself say, "I'll go get it."

"Huh?" Emerging from his trance, Kip gaped at me. "Shelley, we can't—"

Can't cross Willow Street without a grown-up. We had been hearing those words ever since we could walk, and even my daredevil brother had never questioned them. Grass is green, sky is blue, you can't cross Willow Street without a grown-up. But what if you did? *She'll never know.* Irresistible, this notion of a second misdeed that would cancel out the first, wiping the slate clean. Only Kip and I would ever know. I took a deep breath and said, "Wait here."

It was not yet nine o'clock on a Saturday morning; traffic was sparse. I waited on the sidewalk while another car went by, heading out of town where Willow Street became Route 23 and wound its way through hilly farm country to the north and west. Once it was past, I looked carefully in both directions, held my breath and darted forward.

The rest of the world fell away during that forbidden journey. I kept my eyes fixed on my sneakers, watching as they sped across dizzying blackness, a yellow line, more blackness. The opposite curb appeared; my left foot stepped up onto it, my right followed—

Safe. I had made it; I hadn't been killed. Exhaling with a rush, I located the ball a couple of yards away in the grass that bordered the driveway of the Lockley Arms. I ran forward and retrieved it, slippery with dew—turned and raised it high for Kip to see, and he waved his arms and cheered.

What happened then I can't explain. Crossing the street had been surprisingly easy, but as I stood looking back across the two lanes of blacktop at Kip jumping up and down under the trees, he seemed immeasurably distant, a tiny figure on the far side of an impassable gulf. The wave of resolve that had carried me on its crest ebbed away as I stood clutching the ball and hearing Mother telling me *never, ever* to cross Willow Street without an adult holding my hand. I had already tempted the fates once. It was too much to expect they would ignore my impudence a second time. Here I was, all by myself, without Kip, on the wrong side of the street. The inner voice that had tempted me was stubbornly silent. My legs prickled. A lump began to grow in my throat as a truck rumbled past and I heard its huge tire hissing that I would never make it back alive.

And then all at once there was a young woman standing beside me. She must have come from the Lockley Arms; maybe she had been out on the porch, watching the whole thing. I was too stricken by thoughts of my own mortality to notice her approach, and to me it was as if she had swooped down from the sky.

"Hi," she said. Her hair was pale brown, spilling loose over her shoulders. A breeze lifted a single lock into the air like a long, glinting ribbon and she reached up to smooth it down. "Are you stuck?"

I squinted up at the shadowy, half-smiling face. Ordinarily I would have been too shy to answer a stranger, but my situation was desperate. And that buoyant, sunlit hair, something in her smile and choice of words, made me realize she was not a great many years older than I was.

"I'm not supposed to cross by myself," I said. We both glanced down at the ball in my hand. For one impossible moment its pale sphere seemed to glow translucent; and in that fleeting interval I saw, at the center, a glimmering scene of dark, hooded figures standing in a circle beneath a crescent moon. I gulped and blinked and the ominous image was gone, in its place nothing but bland white leather stitched in red. When I looked up, dumbfounded, she was smiling at me.

"Sometimes the prize can be worth the risk," she said. The words meant nothing then, but I smiled back anyway. She offered her hand. I took it, and together we crossed the street.

I

All children have an appreciation of the laws of magic.

——Marian Green, *Natural Magic*

Chapter 1

To strangers driving the backcountry of upstate New York just west of the Hudson River, the landscape has a somber feel. The sky is often overcast, and the winding roads are lined with unkempt hedges that seem to obscure the view as if by intention, offering only grudging glimpses of straggling orchards and stretches of bleak farmland above which rise the mountains—dark, silent, aloof. Occasionally the road leads through one of those shabby little villages that clearly knew better days once upon a time, back in the era when this region saw brief service as a playground for the idle rich. Those days are long gone, and their prosperity with them. Now most of the villages offer a depressingly similar aspect: a Main Street with a lot of boarded-up windows, littered sidewalks, no visible population except for one or two incurious locals who watch the infrequent car go by.

Yet once in a while there's one that still shows signs of life—a place where the sun shines brightly and the buildings are freshly painted, where people bustle along a Main Street lined with striped shop awnings and a little park with a bandstand resounds with the shouts of children playing—and that's when it's suddenly possible to sense the charm of life here, the way everyone says it used to be. That's when the urge comes to stop the car right now, pull over to the side of the road and let the pace of existence slow to the measured magic of a long summer afternoon: white wicker chairs, iced tea, birdsong and the sleepy click of croquet mallets audible from the other side of a high green hedge.

Magic. Is there any other word for the atmosphere of such

places? A quality as elusive, as capricious as the enchanted gold hidden in these timeless mountains by the Little People who, according to the tales of Washington Irving, once made their home here. That faerie gold may appear substantial enough, shimmering in the sun. But try to grasp it and it will vanish like wisping smoke.

The village of Green Hollow possessed that intangible magic once, back when Kip and Shelley Davies were growing up. It was a different place in those days, back before the Vietnam War, the birth control pill, and the microchip—a thriving place, confident and serene. The Janicot Company, a mail-order bookseller, provided a livelihood for over a hundred people. The local merchantry flourished—the E-Z Stop Grocery, Main Street Texaco, Purdy's Variety, the Pig & Whistle Restaurant, Duncan's Laundry, Kate's Antiques and Collectibles—and every summer old Bill Garrett drove his Mister Softee truck slowly up and down the tree-lined streets, its mechanical music warbling off-key through the long tender dusks. At the lone stoplight (intersection of Main and Willow) the Town Council offices and local library shared a gabled stone building of the Old Dutch style, with a clock tower that visitors made much of. But the real architectural showplace, several houses south of the intersection yet near enough to shed its glory over the center of town, was an elegant inn called the Lockley Arms.

The Davies family lived right across the street. It wasn't easy for Kip and Shelley, growing up across the street from the Arms. There was Mother's rule about not playing in the front yard, only in the back, and even then not letting their games get too noisy. Her worry was that they might disturb the guests staying at the Arms—those august personages who came and went with mysterious purpose at all hours of the day and night, their sleek cars gliding up and down the driveway, polished surfaces winking in the sun or, as dusk fell, catching a whispery gleam from the old-fashioned lantern that illuminated the inn's sign.The words of that sign were as familiar to the twins as their own names.

The Lockley Arms
Offering Fine Hospitality Since 1881
Everett and Emma Lockley, Innkeepers

The Arms was a Victorian delight, three stories of immaculate white clapboard, graceful and gabled and topped by a tower with a pointed dunce-cap roof. There was a double porch whose lower roof extended out over the driveway to shelter guests arriving in rain or snow, and Elaine Davies had explained to her children that this arrangement was called a *porte-cochère,* the foreign term echoing with mysterious glamour in their small ears. Beyond it, the driveway dipped out of sight to what they knew to be a small parking area for guests, with gardens and grounds beyond. The whole spacious acreage was enclosed by a towering green hedge like a fortress wall.

Although the twins were strictly forbidden to set foot on the Arms property, their knowledge of it was not purely abstract. Benjy Hendricks, who lived down the street and was two grades ahead of them at school, had made several exploratory missions that he was more than willing to describe in detail, down to the moment he was spotted and chased away by the yardman, a hairless giant named Royce who never spoke. From Benjy, the twins knew that beyond the parking lot was an overgrown gully with a trickling brook at the bottom. In the fragrant shade of pine trees you crossed a wooden footbridge—stopping a moment to look down at the brook and watch the shadows of minnows flicking through sunny patches on the bottom—then you went on to emerge in bright sunlight onto a lawn like velvet. After the shade, the sunshine made you blink. To your right stood the old carriage house, where the inn's staff lived on the second floor above Royce's well-kept equipment. To your left was a high wall of leaves. You crept closer, found a gate of slender iron bars set between stone pillars. Beyond the gate a rectangle of clear turquoise water sparkled in the sun—the swimming pool, surrounded by little tables with umbrellas and striped canvas chairs.

If you happened to notice, Benjy said, there was another gate at the far end of the pool. This was a double gate, and on each half the delicate bars had been curved to incorporate a circled pair of letters—*L* and *A*—into the design. Listening to his description, Shelley could see that far gate in her head—the sun shining through the spidery bars, the circled *LA LA* casting its shadow on the grass like the nonsense syllables of a soundless song.

The swimming pool was as far as Benjy ever got before being discovered. And it was almost as if discovery, and the chase that followed, were his favorite part of the whole adventure—what kept him coming back, even more than a taste for forbidden exploring. His eel-thin body seemed fashioned for narrow escapes. The twins pictured him running, his blond hair flying back, as they listened breathlessly to his account of tearing around a corner of the carriage house with Royce in voiceless pursuit—of realizing the giant was gaining on him and knowing he would never make it as far as the footbridge—of diving into a tiny hole in the high hedge and wriggling through its scratchy thickness to emerge at last in the prosaic back parking lot of the E-Z Stop on Main Street.

It was a tale that gave Shelley a stomachache just listening to it. But glancing over at Kip she saw his eyes were shining.

"Let's sneak over there," he said later, after Benjy had gone home. Nearly three years had passed since the incident with the baseball. If they remembered it at all, it was with a kind of wondering disgust that they had ever been naive enough to believe their parents' warnings about the hazards of traffic on Willow Street. Now they crossed it half a dozen times a day—on the way to school or the library, to run errands or visit friends, almost never bothering to use the traffic light at the corner. But the Arms itself was still off-limits. Mother was adamant about that, and her strict rule had so far managed to restrain them.

I think Mother would have died rather than offend the Lockleys in any way. They were the most respected people in Green Hollow, aristocratic and distinctly benevolent, possessed of the tall, icy elegance of a royal pair in a fairy tale. Mrs. Lockley was from England, which in Mother's view was roughly the same as hailing from heaven. The happiest I ever saw her was on the rare occasion when she encountered one of them by chance (they seldom left the Arms, and I myself could remember seeing them only once or twice) and garnered a nod or a gracious word. After such an event there would be a glow around her for the rest of the day, while Dad watched her with a rueful look on his face.

He was a disappointment to her. I grew to understand that sad fact long before I was able to articulate it. In the life of our family it was an aching undercurrent so constant that Kip and I were never consciously aware of it; we simply accepted the tension between our parents as natural, as we accepted the constant feather-smoothing efforts of Aunt Marty, Dad's younger sister who lived with us, paying for her keep out of the salary she earned as a nurse/receptionist for Green Hollow's only doctor.

In Mother's view, Dad had let her down. She had married a young man with a future, a brilliant English teacher (who else, I ask you, would name his children Shelley and Kipling?) destined to rise through the system to an important administrative position. Instead, fifteen years later, he was still in the classroom, brilliant as ever but recognized by the school board as a scholar and dreamer who had best remain there. A disastrous stint as principal had proved him incapable of coping with administrative business—crucial deadlines slipped past him; he muddled paperwork, forgot meetings, failed to control an unruly new teacher. The board eased him out of the position at the end of a year, to the relief of everyone but Mother—I can still remember her shock and hurt at his "demotion" and how for months afterward her eyes would redden and she would abruptly leave the room, Dad looking guiltily after her.

Yet who can blame her for wanting success on her own terms? She had expected it, planned for it, and seen her hopes come to nothing. A schoolteacher's salary wasn't much, and in those days it was virtually unheard of for a married woman with children to hold a job—so we were always just scraping by, Kip and I pricked with obscure guilt every time we outgrew our clothes and shoes, always anxious about showing the proper appreciation for every birthday or Christmas gift. We wanted to please her, to try and make her happy, and perhaps that is why it took us so long to violate her rule about staying away from the Lockley Arms.

Because the place tempted them mightily. Forbidden by parental decree, guarded by the fearsome Royce, it possessed a beguiling air of separateness that Benjy's tales of narrow escape served only to enhance. The world as the twins knew it—the routine world of family and school, friends and homework and chores—stopped abruptly at the border of that high green hedge, and whatever lay beyond was lost in the haze of their imaginations' far horizon. For the uncharted places inside each of us, is there some piece of the external world that provides a reflective surface? Late at night, when he was supposed to be asleep, Kip had a habit of sitting on the windowsill of his darkened bedroom, watching the house across the street. Shadows moved on the curtains; faint music and laughter floated on the night air as the moon rose in the sky. Once a huge white owl, with eyes yellow as doubloons, silently floated down to roost on the tower roof. Once a woman came out onto the second-story porch and spoke to a cat crouched there on the railing, and the cat answered her with a human voice.

Or so Kip claimed. Was he falling asleep as he sat there, weaving bits of reality into the fabric of his dreams? Shelley herself preferred a more mundane reconnaissance. On the way to school in the morning, passing the Arms driveway, she had discovered it was a simple thing to drop her notebook in such a way that the loose pages spilled out of it. While gathering them up, she could surreptitiously survey the realm inside the bastion of the hedge, and using this approach she had managed to collect a few fragments of her own.

Once she saw a brown and topaz tabby cat dash across the grass and heard a voice inside the house call, "Rowan, that's your last warning!" The cat flirted its tail and kept going, but as it passed Shelley she thought she saw it wink. Another day the yard was deserted, but she could hear voices from an open window, and a few scattered notes from a piano. All at once the melody unfolded and a man's voice came floating out across the lawn.

How many moons be in the year?
There are thirteen, I say,
And the midsummer moon is the merriest of all,
Next to the wooing moon of May.

Once, peeking around the hedge, she caught a glimpse of three girls in pale dresses dancing in a circle on the green lawn, hands joined and laughter light on the spring air. But when she blinked, they were transformed into three apple trees growing close together, their spindly branches veiled in pink blossom.

And then there was the time she glanced up from retrieving her geography book (she wasn't such a fool as to drop her notebook every time) to see a man standing on the front porch watching her. With a qualm she recognized the hawklike face and fair, silver-streaked hair: Everett Lockley himself, dressed entirely in black, down to the gleam of a black feather in his soft felt hat. As she knelt transfixed at the foot of the driveway, caught in the act of snooping, he touched his hat brim and smiled. Shelley looked down to fumble the book into her bag. When she glanced up again an instant later, he was gone. But there was a sudden flutter of wings as a large black crow lit on the edge of her book bag and perched there, head cocked coyly to one side. Its bright little eye met hers briefly before it squawked and flew away.

When Kip made his proposal about sneaking over to the Arms, her heart gave a little jump. It was May; the end of the school year was in sight and the warming weather had penetrated her bones and made them itch. She desperately wanted to investigate the provocative domain across the street. To make in reality the journey she had made already in imagination—pass beneath the porte cochere, cross the footbridge over the brook and see for herself the swimming pool and the silently singing gate beyond. But the rest of Benjy's tale—pursuit and near capture—was a powerful deterrent. Benjy had no father (a mysterious deficiency he flatly refused to explain) and his mother, who suffered from chronic migraines that Lisa Bryant had overheard her mother saying were really hangovers, presumably did not care if her offspring trespassed on the Arms' property. But the twins' mother felt otherwise.

"Mother'll *kill* us."

"She won't find out."

"What if Royce catches us?"

Kip snorted. "He won't."

"Why not?" It was her turn to sneer. "We'll be wearing our invisible suits?"

"No. I've got a plan." He was too intent on it to acknowledge her sarcasm, and Shelley looked uneasily at him. Above bright hazel eyes his dark brows formed a line of fierce concentration. "We'll go at night," he said. "When everyone else is asleep."

Chapter 2

I opened my mouth to protest and then shut it. To be a twin is to be half of a whole, to form a kind of intricate knot with another being, and Kip's thirst for adventure defined not only his existence but mine as well. Somewhere in my nature there existed a vague trope toward propriety, a wistful ambition to meet Mother's standards for being a good girl—someone who never dirtied her clothes or behaved in a way that might cause talk among the neighbors. But whenever this inclination ran up against the temptation to follow Kip's lead, it never stood a chance. If he decided to ride his bike no-hands down the steep hill behind the Janicot Books warehouse—if, in the way of boys everywhere, he deemed it necessary to bellycrawl through the slimy culvert at the far end of Willow Street, or teeter along the top of the stockade fence behind the Leonards' house—I was right behind him every time, teeth gritted and heart thundering beneath my ribs. With every skinned elbow, every torn garment, the sorrowful specter of the good girl would rise up to reproach me. I thought I wanted to become her. But time and again I found myself diverted from this abstract goal as if by some internal compass needle irresistibly drawn by the golden glint of mischief in Kip's eye.

When his stealthy tap came on her door that night, the luminous hands of her bedside clock read midnight. Shelley was ready and waiting, dressed in jeans and a sweatshirt and her new red sneakers—bought a size too big because they were supposed to last all summer and into next fall. Closing the door quietly behind her, she followed Kip on tiptoe toward the stairs. Their parents' bedroom door was shut, silence behind it; still they held their breaths as they passed, casting nervous glances toward Aunt Marty's room at the far end of the hall. Sometimes she stayed up late reading her favorite murder mysteries, but tonight there was no line of lamplight beneath her door.

Creeeeeak. The top step of the dark staircase gave beneath Kip's tentative foot, freezing the two of them in place as they waited for doors to fly open and accusing voices to ring out. But there was nothing—only the measured ticking of the clock on the landing below, like a mockery of their scurrying pulse. At the bottom of the stairs the darkened house was an unfamiliar nightscape of black and gray, inhabited by looming shapes they couldn't identify. Could that humped mass be nothing more sinister than Dad's armchair? The floor was not quite solid beneath their feet. Windows floated dim as phantoms in the invisible walls. In the moonlit kitchen Shelley whispered a reminder to set the back door on the latch: no sense in completing their mission successfully to find themselves locked out on their return.

Outside, leaves rustled in a chill spring breeze as they hurried side by side through the wash of silvery darkness beneath cavernous trees. Shelley's feet seemed to move of their own accord, determined to keep pace with Kip's. Willow Street was empty, two lanes of smooth blacktop gilded by the streetlamp. And on the other side, rising pale in the moonlight beyond the dark barrier of its hedge—the Arms. A few windows were still lit, upstairs and down, but both porches were deserted and there was no one to see two small figures dart across the street and melt into the hedge's deep shadow. The whispered conference there could have been audible only to themselves.

"Stay close to the house when we go past it. Duck when we pass a window. That way, even if somebody's looking out, they won't see us."

"Where exactly are we going?"

Their heads were so close together that the bill of his baseball cap poked her temple. "I want to see the swimming pool," he said.

Shelley knew what he was thinking. That soundlessly singing gate, the syllables *LA LA* wrought in graceful iron—what lay beyond it? In her imagination she had already glimpsed the gate itself, but whatever it guarded lay hidden in a mist of possibility.

"I want to get farther than Benjy did," Kip said, and she felt her head nod like a puppet's.

They stole up the driveway, crouching low to the ground, seeing their shadows momentarily darken the band of light cast by the lantern that illuminated the inn's sign. The smooth lawn was frosted here and there with brightness from the windows; they skirted those areas and reached the porte cochere without incident. In its shelter Shelley stopped to lean against the house, her heart pounding and her throat so dry she couldn't swallow. Glancing up toward the dim ceiling of the porte cochere she could make out an unlit bulb at its center—could imagine it suddenly flaring into brightness to pin the two of them against the house. She squeezed her lids shut. There was a burst of light inside her head, as if her guilty fantasy had come true; then she opened her eyes once more on reassuring darkness. Kip had started to creep forward, and she followed so hurriedly that she bumped into him. He stumbled, caught himself and favored her over his shoulder with a look she was glad she couldn't see. Moving with more caution, they reached the back corner of the house to see the ground ahead sloping to the guest parking lot, more than half full. Shelley was counting the dark gleaming outlines of the cars when Kip's tap on her shoulder interrupted her.

He was pointing to a flight of wooden steps that led to a small screened porch at the back of the house. As she watched, his finger stabbed the air four times, his meaning horrifyingly clear.

Let's go up there.

Shelley shook her head violently, but he had already started up the steps. Her heart pushed into her throat as he reached the top and peered through the screen. Had he gone crazy? An assault on the house itself was vastly more than she had bargained for. Suppose someone inside saw him peeking through the screen? Would there be time to run—to escape? Her mind stalled in the midst of its feverish planning, unable to grasp what she was seeing, as he eased the door open and slipped inside.

It shut soundlessly behind him.

Shelley stood staring at the empty spot where he had been, unable to believe her eyes. It had never been part of their plan to enter the house itself, only to explore the grounds without being seen. Now it seemed Kip was begging to be caught. She glanced down the endless stretch of driveway toward the street, then back at the screen door, desperately wishing them both safe home in bed. What now? Wait to hear the uproar of his capture, or abandon him and make a run for it now, on her own?

"Shelley!" Kip's whisper arrested her whirling thoughts. He was poised at the top of the steps, holding the door invitingly open. "There's nobody here. Come on inside. Let's look around."

"No! Are you crazy? They're probably coming right back!"

He didn't answer, just shrugged and went back inside, letting the screen drift shut behind him.

"Kip!"

No answer. She gulped, then gathered her courage to run up the steps and look in. Beyond a back-porch clutter—broom, mop, a ladder, a bucket—a slice of the lit interior was visible. A kitchen. Kip was not in sight. She pressed her face closer to the screen, tasting its metallic flavor. The door seemed to give under her hand then, to open on its own, and she stepped inside.

In contrast to the cool night, the kitchen of the Lockley Arms was warm and glowing with color: polished bricks underfoot, copper pans hanging on the walls, on the counter a stack of red bowls beside a basket of yellow onions. The air smelled of cinnamon and coffee. Shelley stood frozen just inside the door. Something brushed against her ankle and she bit back a scream—but it was only the cat she had seen in the yard, the tabby called Rowan. He rubbed against her leg again, purring, looking up at her with pale green eyes, and she trailed her shaking fingers across his fur. Kip—where was Kip?

As if summoned, he appeared in a doorway to her right, cap pushed back on his head. "See? The place is empty. They've all gone off someplace."

Shelley found her voice. "You've got some nerve, Kip Davies. How do you know they're not upstairs?"

He grinned. "One way to find out. Come on." He disappeared from the doorway. Shelley hesitated, then made her way after him on wobbly legs, knowing she had no choice. He wanted to top Benjy and this was how he planned to do it. A narrow back corridor led her to the front of the house, where she found Kip already halfway up the stairs. There was nothing to do but follow.

Familiar as the house became to me later on, I could never make my knowledge of it match the memory of that first visit. It was as if that childhood prank took me to some corner of my imagination so oblique that I have never again found my way back to it.

Except for Kip and me, the place was empty. It seemed on that occasion to contain countless rooms, many more than could possibly have fit within its physical dimensions. I remember rooms submerged in quivering bluegreen darkness, canopies hovering like restless ghosts above white beds, other rooms warm with lamplight and easy chairs. My trespasser's jitters evaporated as I wandered over polished floors that reflected yet more rooms, lamplit or moonlit, above whose depths I skimmed like some airy inhabitant of a dream. In the darkened top of the tower I stood at a window and looked down on our house across the street, seeing it pale and diminished, huddled in its cluster of trees. It looked desperately far away, like something existing in another dimension.

"Shelley! Come here a minute."

Kip's summons came from across the hall, from a room lit only by a dim golden sphere resting on the wings of a bronze dragon. I wanted to stop and examine this interesting lamp, but he had grabbed my wrist and was pulling me to the open window, where I could see treetops silhouetted against an enormous white moon. His grip was hurting my wrist and I jerked free. "So what? It's just a full moon."

"Not the moon, stupid." The words hissed in my ear. "Listen!"

I listened, at first hearing nothing . . . and then a sound that raised the hair on the back of my neck. A soft, distant, unceasing susurration that rose out of the still night and slowly sank back into it.

Rhythmic. Seductive. Impossible. The sound of waves lapping at a sandy beach.

There were no beaches near Green Hollow. Twenty miles eastward, the broad Hudson River made its way south between forested cliffs toward Kingston, Poughkeepsie, and eventually New York City and the Atlantic—but it was a good three hours by car to those city beaches, and an even longer trip across the width of Massachusetts to Cape Cod, where we had once spent a week's vacation and I had fallen asleep every night with the window open beside my bed, smelling the damp salt air and listening to the sound I was hearing, against all reason, now. I shook my head, but it was still there. I looked at Kip. "What is it?" I whispered.

In his glance I caught a tiny double reflection of the lamp behind me. "Doesn't it sound like the ocean?"

"It sounds like it. But it can't be."

"Look!" He had turned back to the window. "Did you see that?"

"What?"

"There it is again!"

This time I saw it too: a shuddering of the darkness in the distance above the trees, a blue-white dazzle that lasted only an instant and then vanished utterly. If I had been alone I would have blamed it on some vagary of my eyesight, but Kip was right beside me, clutching my arm, saying, "Did you see it? There's something happening out there. That's where they all are. That's why the house is empty."

I strained to look, but it was gone. Yet it had been there: we had both seen it. Abruptly he turned and started for the door.

"Where are you going?"

"I want to see what they're doing. Come on."

Panic woke inside me as I followed him down the long flights of stairs. What if they came back—what if they caught us? All at once the noise of our feet seemed the thudding of an enormous heart. As if he felt it too, Kip started to take the steps in downward leaps, three at a time. The staircase turned a final corner and deposited us in the entrance hall, where a mirror reflected a silver bowl filled with flowers, and our frightened faces flashing past in the background. We plunged through the front door like hotly pursued fugitives, hurling ourselves off the porch to tumble into the safe, cricket-voiced darkness beyond.

I found myself rolling over and over in the cool grass, a tangle of weak limbs connected by my galloping heart. Wild laughter struggled inside me but I hadn't the breath to set it free. I became aware of Kip lying on his belly nearby, feebly smacking the grass with his hands. As breath returned, the two of us surrendered to a paroxysm of smothered giggles that seemed deafening in the quiet summer night.

The crickets' piping stopped abruptly. In the sudden silence my impulse to laugh sank away; I reached out and pinched Kip. "Shut up!"

He rolled over and sat up, and together we looked across the shadowy lawn toward the house. Already the moments we had spent inside were becoming a fantasy, a ridiculous lie not even we ourselves could believe. Certainly Benjy Hendricks would never buy it in a million years. That thought must have occurred to Kip as well, because in the spill of light from the first-floor windows I saw a determined look come over his face.

I grabbed his sleeve. "Let's go. Let's get out of here. We're pushing our luck."

He shook his head slowly. "Remember that sound? And that weird flash of light? They came from somewhere behind the house. I want to see what's going on back there."

"Well, I don't," I said. "I'm going home. Right now." I got up and started across the grass toward the driveway, but I knew he wasn't following me. When I looked back he was headed toward the porte cochere. "Hell's bells," I said under my breath, the way Aunt Marty always said it when she was pushed to her limit. It was the worst curse I knew at that age, but it was nowhere near adequate to express the ferment of helpless dread inside me. I turned back and went after Kip. He glanced my way as I came up beside him, but didn't speak. By then we were passing again beneath the porte cochere—but this time, knowing the house was empty, we didn't bother to be cautious. And so we almost walked right into Royce.

We were halfway across the parking lot when we saw him, a massive black shape guarding the entrance to the footbridge that spanned the gully. Kip grabbed me and we ducked down quickly behind one of the cars and crouched beside a back tire, holding our breath. *Did he see us?* I mouthed the words at Kip, but in the tense darkness he never noticed. His fingers dug into my arm as we heard a rasping cough, then footsteps starting across the paved surface. We should have stayed where we were, trusting the dark to conceal our whereabouts, but we bolted instead—a pair of rabbits flushed from hiding, flying down the driveway at top speed.

Behind us we heard the footsteps quicken, heard the heavy grunt of hard-drawn breath. Was it only imagination that made the ground shake with the impact of Royce's pursuit? We ran, our muscles fueled by pure terror, faster than I could ever remember running before, shoulder to jostling shoulder down the dark driveway, beneath the porte cochere, bursting out from under it into the final stretch toward the street and safety.

And then one of my new sneakers, bought too big because they would last longer that way, tripped me up.

The world seemed to upend and slam into me as I went sprawling full length on my face. I found myself staring at the surface of the driveway a scant inch from my nose. I blinked and tried to catch my breath. There was no pain yet, only shock and disorientation and Kip hauling at the back of my sweatshirt, his pleading voice above me. "Get up, Shelley! Get up!"

Then he made a strangled sound and I became aware of a dazzling light at my back. Royce had switched on the bulb under the porte cochere. Like a fulfillment of my earlier fantasy I found myself frozen within the compass of that light, exposed and helpless. I couldn't move.

"Shelley! Come on!"

My knees and the palms of my hands had begun to burn. All night, it seemed, I had been hearing those words, *Come on,* repeated countless times as Kip goaded me on to each new stage of this adventure for which I had long since lost all taste. At least this time our wishes coincided: at that moment I had no greater desire on earth than to vacate the premises of the Lockley Arms. He hauled on the back of my sweatshirt again, dragging me to my feet, and I stumbled forward out of that paralyzing circle of light without looking back.

Together, into the sheltering darkness, we fled.

Chapter 3

It wasn't until the next morning that Kip discovered he had lost his White Sox cap somewhere over at the Arms.

"You *what*?"

"Shh!" They were doing the breakfast dishes; his eyes darted from Shelley's horrified face to the living room, where the adults were sharing the morning edition of the *Albany Times Union*. "I looked everywhere. It's gone."

"Kip—!"

"I know. We're dead."

It was a day that seemed to last forever, its torment accentuated by how normal things appeared on the surface—a regular spring Saturday, with no outward sign of the disaster hovering over their heads. Once the dishes were done they wandered outdoors, but it was impossible to pretend an interest in any of their usual games. They sat on the back step, weighed down by guilt. How long would it take for a reaction to issue from the Arms? In hot whispers they discussed running away from home, but it was just talk, nothing more. As morning crawled toward noon they watched their shadows gradually shrink and creep closer as if seeking shelter. When would it come—the ring of the telephone or knock on the front door that would spell doom?

The worst thing was that they didn't know exactly where the cap had been lost. Bad enough if it was on the lawn or the parking lot—but suppose it was somewhere inside the house, revealing the full extent of their crime? That cap was as good as a calling card, its leather sweatband bearing the telltale words *Kipling Davies* in permanent marker; Mother insisted on putting their full names in every hat and coat they ever owned.

Yet that day passed, and the next, with no response from the Lockley Arms. Oh, the phone rang, of course, but it was never the call they dreaded. Every knock on the front door made them jump—but it was always a neighbor, or a salesman, or the paperboy. The two of them skulked around the hot backyard, avoiding Willow Street and the sight of the Lockley Arms as the days continued to go by—slowly, steadily, until there was a full week, then two, between them and their midnight escapade. The scrapes on Shelley's knees and palms healed, and still no accusations were leveled. Gradually they began to hope in earnest, to speculate that the cap must have rolled behind a bush in some remote corner of the yard where it would decay unidentified.

As the passing days diminished the likelihood of retribution and summer settled into its usual pattern, the twins began to relax and even take a belated secret pride in their adventure. But it remained secret. By unspoken agreement they told no one else, not even Benjy Hendricks—partly because they knew he would never believe they had ventured inside the house, partly because they had begun to have difficulty believing it themselves. The lack of reaction from the Lockley Arms seemed to underscore their feeling, as if the whole business might never have happened. When they discussed it—the empty house with its myriad rooms, the distant sound of surf and the rippling gleam they had glimpsed in the night sky—it seemed, more than anything else, like one of the dreams they occasionally experienced in common, as once they had shared the darkness before birth.

And like a dream it faded, while summer unfolded at the leisurely pace it reserves for children. The long days were filled with the slap of baseballs into oiled leather gloves and the hiss of bike tires over hot pavement; the piping of crickets blended with the music of the Mister Softee ice-cream truck slowly tracing the streets of Green Hollow at dusk. Kip got a new baseball cap. Shelley grew into her new sneakers. And behind the hedge across the street, its tall white walls dappled by the shade of venerable trees, rose the Lockley Arms—keeping their secret, apparently for good.

Chapter 4

For the past thirty-odd years, Miss Ellie Friend had made it her practice to augment the standard sixth-grade curriculum by teaching her young charges to sing the alphabet backward.

And so that September, like countless Green Hollow school children before them, Kip and Shelley sat at their desks and dutifully repeated: "Z-Y-X and W-V . . ." As the weather grew colder and the surrounding mountain slopes turned bright with color, the sixth-graders made their own leaves out of red and yellow paper and Miss Friend taped them to the classroom windows. These latter leaves floated at the edge of Shelley's vision, falling endlessly but never coming to rest, while the class read the story of Robin Hood, studied the tombs of the Egyptian pharaohs, began long division and continued to sing, "Z-Y-X and W-V . . . U-T-S and R-Q-P . . ."

Early in October, Purdy's Variety mounted its usual display of Halloween costumes, and on their way home from school each day Kip and Shelley made a practice of detouring past the store window on Main Street to ogle them. Not that they had the slightest hope of ever owning one; in their family there was no extra money for such frivolities and their costumes were always strictly homemade. But the ones at Purdy's made their mouths water just the same: the mournful Frankenstein monster, the rotting mummy, the hairy werewolf, the witch with her pointed black hat and broomstick, the vampire with his elegant satin cape. A host of other masks boasted horns, warts, scars, bulging eyes and bloodstained fangs—nightmare faces crowding the store window, staring out as the twins stood staring in.

Christmas may be the runaway favorite among holidays for most children, but for these two it was Halloween. Did they recognize even then something of the true nature of this dark festival, glimmering through its traditional trappings like the bright unpredictable dance of a candle behind a pumpkin's carved face? For those few hours, with the fall of night, the village shed its familiarity to reveal a visage of terror and mystery—the sweet red gleam of a candy apple catching an answering twinkle from the eye sockets of a skull.

Marty helped them with their costumes as usual. Both twins, inspired by the book they were reading in school, wanted to go as Robin Hood, but Mother insisted that Shelley modify her choice to Maid Marian.

"But Kip's going as Robin! I want to be Robin too!"

"Don't be silly, dear. You're ten years old, practically a young lady. You can't go parading around the neighborhood dressed as a boy."

"But Mother, it's Halloween!"

"After all, Elaine . . ." Dad glanced up from the pile of test papers he was correcting at the kitchen table. "It's just a costume. Last year she was a piece of fried chicken."

"Dad! I was Caltiki, the Immortal Monster!"

He winked at her. Mother's lips quivered. "All right, I've said what I think. Do as you like, Shelley. I suppose I'm the only one who cares what people think of this family anyway."

Intimidated by the idea of family disgrace, Shelley caved in and opted for Maid Marian. Marty tried to cheer her glum niece. "They're practically the same anyway, Shelley. We'll just make your tunic a little longer, so it looks like a skirt."

The night before Halloween, the twins were summoned to her room to try on their finished costumes. She had done her best: old pillowcases transformed into rustic tunics by green dye and pinking shears, caps of green felt trimmed with jaunty red feathers—there were even two longbows fashioned from coat hanger wire and string. Once they were dressed, Marty pushed them in front of the mirror on the closet door. "Well, what do you think?"

As they stared at their reflections in silence Shelley bit her lip, fighting to hide her disappointment. She knew Marty had worked hard on these costumes. She knew she should be grateful to her aunt, and she was. But the picture of Robin in the book showed a tall, graceful youth leaning against an ancient oak tree in the Sherwood Forest, wearing a form-fitting green jerkin that showed off his broad shoulders and slender waist. His long legs were encased in green tights, his feet in elegant green suede boots. From beneath his feathered cap, thick honey-colored hair fell straight to his shoulders. However illogically, it had been this image she had expected to see in the mirror—not two kids in shapeless green sacks, sporting what appeared to be squashed melons on their heads. Their longbows might do for roasting marshmallows, but never for shooting arrows. Meeting Kip's gaze in the mirror, she saw him experiencing a similar letdown. And then Marty's face, beaming with enthusiasm, appeared between theirs. "Wow! Don't you two look terrific!"

As in previous years, they went trick-or-treating with the other neighborhood kids their age—Jennifer Moss, Lisa Bryant, Adam Leonard—and this year for the first time, Adam's little brother Alex. In that innocent place and time they were able to wander at will, ringing any doorbell in the village and collecting their booty of bubble gum and cookies, Snickers bars and Hershey's Kisses, caramel popcorn and candy apples with never a thought of a razor blade. Yet for Kip and Shelley the sweets were subordinate to the thrill of roaming anonymously through the crisp October night. A smoky wind shook the trees; dry leaves drifted down and whispered mysteriously underfoot as they made their way along streets rendered magical by darkness. Every house boasted its grinning jack-o'-lantern; the moon itself was a huge orange pumpkin. A taste of wildness sharpened the air; off in the distance they could hear faint shrieks and laughter, catch glimpses of grotesque figures whose paths might unexpectedly intersect their own—ghosts and goblins, vampires and witches and skeletons, denizens of a night in which the dark side of the soul is loosed upon the world.

"Trick or treat!"

"Oh, my! Look at the cute little devil!"

That was Alex, in red long johns, his rope tail dragging dangerously at the seat. Lisa was a gingerbread man (one of Purdy's deluxe costumes), Jenny a witch, Adam an executioner with ax and black hood. To Shelley's chagrin, she and Kip were consistently mistaken for elves.

"We're both Robin Hood," Kip announced the first time this happened, and she winced. What would Mother say? Pricked by propriety, she mumbled, "Maid Marian," and the woman at the door, holding out a plate of cookies, gave a doubtful smile.

Their little band rambled through the neighborhood, kicking through drifts of leaves and chasing each other from streetlamp to streetlamp until they were out of breath. Alex's tail fell off.

The rubber band broke on Jenny's mask, revealing her flushed and freckled face beneath the tall black hat. Carved pumpkins greeted them on every doorstep, grinning or grimacing with flickering light.

"Trick or treat!"

"What darling elves!"

As Kip opened his mouth, Shelley elbowed him and hissed, "Never mind!"

In the stretches of darkness between houses it was easier to leave everyday identity behind. Wind rattled the shedding branches overhead as other disciples of the night passed them: a gang of sheeted ghosts, two arguing cowboys, a fairy princess in a skimpy gown, and something that might have been a lobster. "Trick or treat!" Their bags grew heavier. Five-year-old Alex began to whine that he was tired. Beneath the streetlamp at the corner of Main and Willow, Shelley checked her watch. Mother had said eight-thirty, and the minute hand showed twenty past. Where had the time gone? "We have to go home," she said.

"Shoot." Adam swung his ax discontentedly at a streetlamp. A feeling of anticlimax crept over them as they lingered there, a sense of the night's opportunities slipping away. Halloween would not be back for another whole year. The moon floated above them, enormous in the dark sky. Just last week they had learned in school that its pull caused the ocean tides, and looking up Shelley felt it tugging at her heart, a nameless yearning. Across Main Street the Town Hall clock struck the half hour: Mother was expecting them. She turned reluctantly down Willow Street, the others straggling after her. A gust of wind shook the ragged shadows on the sidewalk and brought a swirl of dead leaves that drifted over them like whispered invitations. Adam slowed to a halt. "Let's do one more house."

Jenny and Lisa were unenthusiastic. But Kip, lagging behind, echoed the words. "One more house." Turning to look, they saw him pointing. "*That* one."

The Lockley Arms, looming white and ghostly against the darkness. Not a single window was lit; no acknowledgment of the holiday adorned the facade, not so much as a lone pumpkin. This aloof and apparently disdainful air provided a deterrent as effective as the stoutest fence, and Kip's suggestion met with silence.

"Looks like nobody's there," Lisa said at last.

"You never know. Let's go ring the doorbell."

The others shuffled their feet. In the dark it looked like a long way to the front door. Shelley knew what Kip was thinking: that on this night, when all rules were suspended by the magic phrase *trick or treat,* he had found the perfect way around Mother's no-trespassing rule. But the clumps of shadow on the moonlit lawn seemed to possess an unnatural density, and the thought of crossing that distance, even in company, sent a wave of misgiving through her. A cold breath of wind hissed along the leaf-strewn sidewalk; somewhere in the distance came a high, faint peal of laughter, trailing off into a silence deeper than before. The night flickered like a somber flame as something momentarily darkened the face of the moon—and glancing up quickly, Shelley caught the tail end of a ragged formation of tiny shapes silhouetted briefly against its glowing circle. No one spoke. Then:

"Geese," Adam said loudly. "A flock of geese."

The others nodded quickly. From behind the gleeful devil's mask, Alex's voice emerged in a fretful wail. "Ad-a-am. I wanna go ho-o-ome."

"Okay, okay." Adam's shrug, more relieved than regretful, broke their trance. "Uh, guess we gotta go. See you guys tomorrow."

"Yeah, see you." Jenny and Lisa, with hurried farewell waves, started down the block toward their homes, leaving the twins at the foot of the Arms driveway. Kip seemed oblivious of their departure; Shelley plucked at the sleeve of his sweater. "Come on, let's go. Mother'll be worried."

He took a step toward the Arms. Then another. Shelley's heart plummeted; that faraway peal of laughter still rang in her ears. She tucked her longbow under one arm and shifted her loot bag to the other hand. "Kip—"

He kept going. As he passed the hedge, something stirred in

its shadow. Just the faintest movement, the softest rustle—Shelley caught her breath—had she imagined it?

A dark, bulky figure leaped out and seized Kip from behind. He gave a strangled squeal and dropped his bow and candy bag. Shelley's heart had time to do a double flip in the instant it took her to recognize Benjy Hendricks, decked out in plastic fangs and a dark blanket for a cape, fair hair plastered stiffly to his skull with what must have been, now that she got a whiff of it, his mother's hair spray. He had released Kip and was laughing hard enough to be in real danger of losing his fangs. Kip muttered a swear word Shelley had heard only teenagers use up to now.

"Shh!" she said. They were making enough noise to broadcast their presence to the entire neighborhood, much less anyone in the house. They subsided. Benjy motioned the twins into the shelter of the hedge, where he took out his fangs and put them in his shirt pocket.

"Get a load of this." He burrowed into the hedge and produced, with a flourish, a brown paper bag.

"Big deal," Kip said. He was still mad about letting Benjy scare him. The older boy opened the top of the bag and a nauseating stench emerged.

"Jeez!"

"Dog turds," Benjy said happily. "From Caroline." Caroline, a stiff and asthmatic lady bulldog, had been Benjy's pet for as long as any of them could remember.

"Hey, Benjy, I got news." Kip's good humor returned with the chance to exercise his wit. "You're supposed to collect candy on Halloween. Not dog turds."

"Think you're smart, dontcha? It's not a treat, stupid. It's a trick. You put this bag on somebody's front porch, see? You light it on fire, then ring the doorbell and run away. They come out and what do they see? A fire on their porch! So they stomp it out, and—whoops! Look what's all over their shoes."

Kip's mouth opened in admiration while Shelley gulped and cast an uneasy glance at the front porch of the Lockley Arms. "You're not going to—"

Benjy threw her a casual glance. "Come on. You can watch."

"We're supposed to be home by now," she mumbled, and he smirked. "This won't take long."

"What if they catch us?"

"They won't. Just be ready to run for it."

Just be ready to run for it. With misgiving Shelley remembered the last time she had run for it—how she had fallen flat on her face, the horror of the moment when Royce had switched on that paralyzing light—but Kip was already stashing his treat bag and longbow beneath the hedge to follow close on Benjy's heels as the bigger boy started toward the darkened house. Quickly she dumped her own burdens, hitched up her sagging tunic and hurried after them up the moonlit driveway.

The closer they came, the less visible the house appeared, its white walls melting into the pale mist that had begun to form in the air. The night seemed suddenly colder as Shelley's trembling legs continued to carry her forward. Near the front porch their stealthy procession halted; Benjy motioned the twins to wait while he mounted the steps. There was a brief flare from the match—a faint crackle of flames—the racket of his fist hammering on the front door. "Hey! Trick or treat!"

Silence swallowed the words; a moment later Benjy's shrouded outline appeared. In his brief absence the fog had thickened so dramatically that the entrance to the porte cochere, close by on their right, was scarcely visible. "Shit," the twins heard him say. "Where'd this stuff come from?"

"Come on, let's get out of here," Shelley whispered. So far there had been no response from the house. The two boys shifted their feet, wanting to watch the outcome of Benjy's prank but hampered by the dense fog. Was the bag still burning? Was anyone even home? All at once Benjy started violently. "Hey!"

A pair of glowing eyes hovered before them. Around the eyes a shadowy outline slowly formed: pointed ears, a sleek body, a long tail curved like a question mark.

"It's only the cat."

"Shit," Benjy muttered.

The cat slipped into the mist and vanished. From somewhere to their left came an eerie, long drawn hoot. Shelley's stomach knotted as a noise of beating wings passed invisibly over their heads, sounding much too large. "What was that?"

Benjy hunched his shoulders. "Just some stupid owl."

She had had enough. "Let's get out of here."

Benjy's grunt sounded like assent, and they started back toward the street. Or so they thought: almost at once it became apparent that in the brief interval they had stopped to confer, the mist had stolen their sense of direction and left them hopelessly disoriented. Benjy, in the lead, blundered into something that turned out to be a car. "Damn! This is the parking lot! How the hell did we get this far . . . ?"

Shelley's heart began to bang against her ribs. "Which way's the street?"

"Must be behind us." Kip's whisper sounded uncertain.

"Yeah, okay. Come on." Benjy turned and Shelley stumbled after him, feeling the car's smooth cold flank glide by her like a passing whale.

"Benjy, wait!" His fuzzy outline had disappeared. A beat of silence passed, then another. Panic flared inside her. "Kip?"

"Shh!" Warm fingers clasped her cold ones.

"Where'd Benjy go?" she whispered.

"He was here a second ago." Kip raised his voice a notch. "Benjy!"

"Come on!" came the muttered reply ahead of them. The older boy sounded breathless, almost scared. As Kip turned toward his voice, Shelley felt his fingers slip from hers. Her seeking hand found only empty air. A sensation like tiny cold claws skittered up her spine.

"Kip?" Was that weak whisper really her voice? There was no reply. By now the moonlit mist was blanket-thick; glancing down, she could not even see her own body. Maybe she was dissolving, disappearing, joining the insubstantial world of ghosts and spirits abroad on this night. The thought sent a violent shudder through her invisible limbs. She stamped her foot hard, received a reassuring jolt and tried again. "Kip!"

"Shut up, I'm right here!" His face swam close to hers. Relief rushed through her—and was transformed the next instant to shock as a fleeting rift in the fog gave her a glimpse of their surroundings.

What I saw made my jaw go slack and my mouth fall open.

The parking lot was gone. Around us in the fog floated an unfamiliar landscape of huge, gnarled trees—eerie silhouettes that loomed and then vanished as the mist closed in once more.

Gooseflesh puckered my skin. It wasn't possible. There were no forests in the middle of Green Hollow. We had taken no more than a few steps in the fog; we couldn't have strayed so far from the Arms. By now everything was hidden once more, and there was only Kip's hushed voice in my ear saying, "What the heck?"

The smell of rotting leaves, always prevalent in Green Hollow in autumn, had intensified a thousandfold. A forest smell. Somewhere an owl hooted as my mind began to babble denials. This is a dream, it kept saying. There's no forest. Any minute I'll wake up at home, in my own bed, with a stomachache from eating too much candy. Mother always says too much candy gives you nightmares. I pinched myself hard. It hurt. Nothing else changed except the fog stirred again, like a gauzy gray curtain thinner in some spots than in others. Through these threadbare places I could make out Kip's dim shape beside me, and all around us, those shadowy but unmistakable shapes of enormous trees.

"Wow," I heard him say. My last feeble hope—that we had somehow wandered into the belt of pines at the bottom of the parking lot—shriveled and died. These were not pine trees. The thick trunks surrounding us, bent and twisted with age, rose into spreading branches already half bare of leaves. My heart gave a sinking, lurching motion like a doomed ship.

"Where are we?" I whispered. Benjy, the Arms, Willow Street—every familiar landmark had vanished without a trace, leaving us hopelessly lost in this unknown forest. How would we ever find our way home? I made a hasty vow that if we could just get back there, I would be content to spend the rest of my life singing the alphabet backward, and I would never disobey Mother again. For I had no doubt this was a punishment for crossing the forbidden boundary of the Arms, for lending our tacit support to Benjy's rude prank. I grabbed the front of Kip's costume. "What are we going to do?"

"How should I know? I don't even know here the heck we are!"

I stared at his indistinct face in horror. Not that I expected him to know what had happened, or where we were—but I was counting on him to have an idea about what to do next. Kip always had an idea. Always. Long seconds passed, in which I could feel my heart thumping in my chest. The mist moved restlessly around us as if possessed of an ominous life of its own. And then, behind the scared *bump, bump-bump* of my heart, I heard a distant sound.

Someone was singing.

Kip heard it too; I saw his head turn. Through the drifting fog we could see almost nothing, only fragmented glimpses of this wild wood—and yet somewhere not too far away, a young man was singing a song. In his voice was an irrepressible cheer that eased my overpowering sense of bewilderment and foreboding. At the center of my fear, a spark of curiosity began to burn like a tiny flame in a dark place. When Kip started in the direction of the singing, I made no protest.

We made our way forward among phantom shapes of trees that emerged from the fog and faded to be replaced by others in a continuously unrolling dreamscape. The bittersweet smell of rotting leaves was everywhere, ubiquitous as the mist that swirled on every side, cloaking us in endless clammy folds, so thick that at moments I could not see Kip in front of me, nor even my own hand clutching his tunic. But the singing was getting louder, and by now I could make out the words.

I cannot eat but little meat,
My stomach is not good;
But sure I think that I can drink
With him that wears a hood!
Though I grow bare, take ye no care,
I nothing am a-cold;

I stuff my skin so full within
Of jolly good ale and old!

As the verse ended, a rough, rollicking chorus of other voices answered the solo:

Back and side go bare, go bare;
Both foot and hand go cold;
But belly, God send thee ale enough
Tho' it be new or old!

The outburst brought us to an abrupt stop. Who were the singers? Had they heard our approach? We stood frozen for a long moment before realizing that there was no need to worry: the invisible gathering was making far too much noise to detect our presence.

A faint radiance flickered through the mist ahead. We could hear laughter, catcalls, a sudden roar of raucous merriment as something happened to amuse the drinkers. A delicious odor of roasting meat reached us, making our mouths water. Whoever these people were, there were a lot of them, and they were having a good time. Kip began to creep cautiously forward once more, and I followed. We moved from one tree to the next, taking shelter behind each mossy trunk to peer ahead. The mist was still thick, but the radiance was growing brighter and we could hear the crackling of a fire. There was another sudden shout of laughter, so loud it made us jump.

"Yon barrel's new enowt, anyway," a disembodied voice said in a strange accent. "Do I no see the mark o'Nottingham Priory upon it?"

"Ay, that you do. A gift from the good Prior himself, from his cellar direct to our bellies. A pity it took a keen arrow or two to remind the fat fellow and his holy brothers of their own doctrine—that 'tis more blessed to give than to receive! Shall we drink to their speedy recovery?"

There was a sound of splintering wood, accompanied by a cheer and a spattering gush of liquid. Someone twanged a raucous stringed instrument and voices joined in.

For sure I think that I can drink
With him that wears a hood—

The words sang in my ears. *With him that wears a hood.* I became aware of Kip's fingers digging into my arm and slowly turned my head to meet his widened eyes.

"Look," we heard someone say. "The moon's up."

The ragged singing broke off. A silence fell, so complete we could hear no sound but the snap and pop of the fire. I held my breath.

"Blessings, Lady," a voice said softly. The fog thinned and all at once they were visible—a ragged company of men dressed in faded green, their gaunt bearded faces lifted to the sky above their firelit forest clearing. My eyes followed their reverent gaze upward, to the moon floating in the vast night. Within its golden circle seemed to hover the shadow of a serene and beautiful face. Vertigo flooded me and I reached out to steady myself on the nearest tree.

Faintly, like an echo from a great distance, came the familiar sound of the Town Hall clock on Main Street striking the hour.

The moon did not change. But where my hand touched the trunk of the tree, I could feel the bark alter beneath my fingers, the rough melting into smooth—and, lowering my gaze, I found myself beneath the porte cochere of the Lockley Arms, grasping one of its supporting pillars. Kip stood beside me, his astonished face a mirror of my own. The mist hung in the air like a ruined curtain; through its rents and tatters we could see the driveway, the boundary of the hedge, and Willow Street.

He grabbed my hand and we made a dash for it, turning to look back as we reached the sidewalk. The windows of the Arms gleamed darkly. Nothing remained of the wild, gnarled wood, the band of green-clad men singing around their fire. As we stood trying to gather our wits, we heard a flurry of footsteps and Benjy came bursting through the remnants of the mist at a dead run.

"Hey, Benjy!"

I saw his white face turn in our direction, but there was no trace of recognition in his glazed eyes. He ran past us without stopping, his cape flapping behind him as he headed down the sidewalk toward his house.

"Benjy, you—" Kip's yell trailed off in weak disbelief. ". . . forgot your candy."

There was no answer, only the sound of fleeing footsteps.

The twins' third and final invasion of the Lockley Arms took place that December.

It was the last day of school before Christmas vacation. When the three o'clock bell rang at last, Miss Friend resettled her glasses on her nose and closed *A Christmas Carol,* from which she had been reading for the past hour in a vain effort to calm her frenzied sixth-graders. "Have a very merry Christmas, everyone. Class dismissed."

Answering shrieks of "Merry Christmas!" accompanied a general stampede for the cloakroom. Shelley retrieved her coat from its hook and struggled through the crowd to wait for Kip in the hall. Kids of all sizes streamed past her toward the stairs, scuffling and jostling one another in holiday spirits. She shifted her feet and looked at her watch. What was keeping Kip? There was no sign of him when she glanced back through the classroom door.

"Still here, Shelley?" Miss Friend, buttoning her coat and shouldering her purse, had seen her.

"I'm waiting for Kip."

"Oh, he's probably halfway home by now. I don't think he likes school much! Not like you, dear. You're a perfect student." She patted Shelley's shoulder in passing, the smell of mothballs from her tweed coat mingling with her old-lady perfume. "Have a wonderful holiday."

"Thanks." Shelley knew Kip wouldn't leave without her, but where was he? Deserted, the classroom looked different: the usually neat rows of desks shoved helter-skelter in the melee of departure, pencil stubs and crumpled paper littering the floor. Gray afternoon sky showed outside the windows, where paper snowflakes had recently replaced the paper leaves; there had been genuine snow last night, and the heavy clouds promised more to come. The ancient radiators hissed and thumped.

Somewhere in the distant reaches of the building some kids were singing "Jingle Bells." And then, close by, there was another sound.

From the direction of the cloakroom, a laugh.

It was a girl's laugh, a high-pitched giggle quickly smothered. Shelley walked slowly to the door of the narrow room and peered inside, but it was empty except for an orphan mitten, a scarf or two, and a forgotten coat hanging in the shadows at the far end. The coat was a smooth camel hair; she recognized it as the property of Missy Ettinger, a freckled redhead who had joined their class this September when her family had moved to Green Hollow from Albany. Missy never let slip an opportunity to let the rest of the kids know the move from "the city" had been a step down for her, and among the girls she was unanimously despised. This antipathy did not extend, however, to her coat, which had come from an Albany department store and was considered the latest in elegant fashion. Shelley couldn't believe Missy had left without it. Yet it was the only one of its kind. Still unable to credit what she saw, she started toward the coat—and as she did so, the sound of her footsteps alerted the two people who had been sheltering in its folds: Missy herself, and Kip.

The sight of their faces popping out from beneath the coat was like a collision with an invisible wall. Shelley felt herself sway on her feet. There was a moment of utter stillness; then a giggle floated up into the air, and Missy put both hands over her mouth. Kip's face was red as a stoplight in the gloom. The three of them stood in motionless tableau for another heartbeat before Shelley turned and ran out.

A breathless Kip caught up with her on the stairs, his coat half on, one sleeve flapping. "Wait up, Shelley! For crying out loud! I said wait!"

Still numb from that invisible impact in the cloakroom, she heard the words but couldn't translate their meaning. Kip matched his pace to hers; the stairwell echoed hollowly with the sound of their steps. As they reached the ground floor, he grabbed her arm and brought her to a halt.

"Listen—" He seemed as stunned as she was by what had

happened. "She said she had a Christmas present for me," he blurted. "Then she kissed me."

Although some of the kids in our class had already begun to show an interest in such things as kissing, these matters were still incomprehensible to me and I had assumed that Kip's feelings paralleled my own. It would have been bad enough if I had caught him kissing someone I liked—say, Jennifer or Lisa. But Missy! It was a kind of double betrayal, the first time in our lives that our likes and dislikes had diverged. If he hadn't liked it, why had he lingered there in the cloakroom? And why, right now, wasn't he cursing and saying he hated Missy—that she made him sick—that her freckles were disgusting and her hair the ugliest color on earth? That he couldn't believe he had let her kiss him and couldn't wait to wash off the traces with soap, because Missy Ettinger undoubtedly had cooties? He was not saying these things because he did not feel them. I knew him better than anyone in the world, and it was painfully clear to me that during those moments in the shadowy cloakroom, with Missy's soft lips touching his and her little cold fingers playing with his shirt collar, I had simply ceased to exist.

Never before had I doubted my claim on Kip, any more than I had questioned my right to my own limbs, head or heart. He was my twin, half of a whole that had existed before either of us had breathed air—yet right then I had an inkling of a future toward which an irrevocable step had just been taken, in which forces I could not understand or control would conspire to separate us: a flashing glimpse of a time when others would usurp the intimacy I considered entirely my own province, and no one would stop them—least of all Kip himself. Beneath the numbness I was terrified.

Did the cold shadow of her thoughts fall across Kip's? They stood without moving at the bottom of the stairs while somewhere in the distance a noise grew steadily louder: the rhythmic squeaking of Mr. McNeal, the maintenance man, wheeling his cleaning trolley down a corridor. The shrill sound roused Kip at last; he shrugged the rest of the way into his coat and yanked his knit cap from the pocket, pulling it down over his ears. "Let's get out of here."

The silence on their short walk home was filled by the sound of their winter boots scuffing in perfect unison along the snowy sidewalk—a unison strangely unaltered in a world where everything else had abruptly changed. Kip did not speak, and Shelley could not. As their house came in sight he came to a stop in front of the Lockley Arms, scooping up a double handful of snow and rounding it between his mittens. A car went by, tire chains jingling. He let his snowball fly, yet even as it smacked against the back bumper, it was clear from his bewildered face that this act had failed to yield its usual satisfaction. Somehow things had gone wrong; he needed to set them right. His desperate gaze, scouring the snowy street for a solution, landed on the Lockley Arms. Abruptly he turned to Shelley. "Let's go see the swimming pool."

The words gradually penetrated her daze. Go see the swimming pool? A brazen daylight invasion of the Arms? It was crazy—and yet his proposal seemed to offer a frail, tempting bridge back to an existence unblemished by the scene in the cloakroom. *Let's go see the swimming pool.* A way to turn back time: an adventure in this forbidden place where they had shared others, before—before. Consequences crossed her mind but left no impression; against the devastating future she had dimly foreseen, what did it matter if she was a good girl? Kip was waiting for her response. She nodded, and together the two of them turned up the driveway.

The light was already beginning to fade from the gray winter sky. They walked side by side, footsteps crunching in the snow. The grounds were deserted and no acknowledgment of their presence came from the house on their left as they passed beneath the porte cochere and headed down through the parking lot toward the footbridge.

I want to get farther than Benjy did. Clearly this was still Kip's agenda. Memories of their previous visits quickened in Shelley's thoughts: the night last spring when they had entered the house, that dark quiver in the sky, as if the air itself had shuddered. And what about this past Halloween? An ancient forest, a band of merry men in green—a dream, changing to nightmare with the vision of Benjy Hendricks's scared face appearing out of the fog. Benjy was still avoiding them at school, and shortly before Thanksgiving his dog had died—failed kidneys due to old age, the vet had said, but remembering Caroline's contribution to the paper bag left on the front porch of the Arms, the twins had wondered.

The parking lot, shoveled clear, was deserted except for two cars. Along the gully at its foot, the pine trees sagged under a burden of snow, their drooping branches nearly concealing the entrance to the footbridge. The twins had to duck low to gain access. Kip led the way; Shelley followed. They had never gotten this far before, and their effortless advance possessed a dreamlike quality in which the scene in the cloakroom dwindled to nothingness. On the bridge a powdering of snow showed the marks of enormous footprints that could belong to no one but Royce; the sight gave Shelley jitters, but she kept them to herself.

On the other side of the footbridge, as Benjy had promised, they saw the carriage house, and opposite it the snowy hedge that hid the swimming pool. The gate to the pool stood ajar and they raced toward it, but the scene within was a disappointment: instead of the sparkling turquoise rectangle described by Benjy, what lay before them now was the pool drained and covered, surrounded by a few metal tables topped with snow. Shelley couldn't suppress a murmur of chagrin.

Then Kip pointed. "Look."

There it was, on the far side of the enclosure—the tall double gate Benjy had described. They hurried toward it, skirting the pool. As they drew nearer they could see the design: the pairs of circled letters, *L* and *A*. Beyond the gate was a white expanse of open meadow edged by snow-laden trees.

LA, LA.

I had imagined that gate so often that it was as if I had encountered it many times before, in many seasons. Now all its horizontals were delicately frosted with snow, even the foot of each L, the crossbar of each A— "I wonder what it means," I said as we reached it.

"What *what* means?"

"You know." I gestured. "La, la."

Kip snickered. "What are you, a halfwit? L,A. Lockley Arms."

It was so simple, so obvious, that I could only shrug my shoulders and feel stupid. Yet even after Kip had dispelled their mystery, they somehow remained the wordless syllables of a soundless song. In the stillness of that gathering winter dusk, I could almost hear the melody.

"Shelley." Kip's voice chased the silent music away before I could capture it. I turned to him, annoyed, but he didn't see; he was pointing into the enclosure beyond the gate, his profile to me, red-cheeked with cold under the dark blue wool of his cap. "Look. There's not a single footprint out there. Not even a squirrel's. Not even a bird's."

Where we stood, on the swimming pool side, they were all around us: the sketchy three-pronged prints of birds' feet, small paw prints of squirrels, larger ones that belonged to the cat, huge boot prints like the ones on the bridge, and of course our own. But what Kip said was true: the snow in the enclosure beyond the gate was utterly undisturbed. Just at that instant the setting sun broke through the clouds, spearing through the pines on the far side of the meadow to light the perfect expanse with a rosy glow.

Kip's mittened hand grabbed my arm. "Let's make snow angels in there." His face was alight with the sunset.

I pulled free. "You're crazy. This is far enough. We should get out of here before we get caught. Besides—"

"Besides what?" He rattled the gate, dislodging its trimming of snow. As the powdery whiteness drifted down on our heads, a chill went through me.

"Kip, stop it!" I cast an uneasy glance at the glistening meadow. Its perfection was like the melody floating unheard in air around us, beautiful but eerie, inhuman.

La, la . . . la, la . . . I could hear it clearly now—alluring but ominous, like the music in the poem Miss Friend had read us in class a few days before.

> *. . . that oft-times hath*
> *Charm'd magic casements, opening on the foam*
> *Of perilous seas, in faery lands forlorn . . .*

I shivered and tucked my chin deeper into my coat collar. Kip was laughing, drowning out the melody. "What are you scared of? Come on!"

"No," I said. "You do it if you want. I'll wait here."

He blew out his breath in exasperation; it hung visible in the cold air. "Okay, I will."

I watched him release the metal catch and push the gate open against the soft resistance of the snow. The sun, sinking fast, sent another pink flare through the pines across from where we stood, making us blink.

"Hurry up," I said. All at once trespassing had lost its charm. I was cold and hungry, it was almost suppertime, and in a minute we would have to leave the shelter of this adventure and return to our everyday lives. There was some reason I did not want to go back. Something had happened there, something bad, but the sunset light dazzled the inside of my head and I couldn't remember what it was. Kip was hesitating at the open gate. "Hurry *up,*" I said again.

He just stood there. I saw him bite his lip; a faint frown pinched his face. "Maybe . . . maybe I shouldn't spoil it."

As he reached out to close the gate, I remembered Missy Ettinger. The numbness that had gripped me in the cloakroom had dissipated and I could feel a smoldering lump in my chest where my heart should have been. I heard myself say, "I dare you," and as I spoke, the lump ignited. There was an intense flash of heat in my chest, like dry kindling bursting into flame. Beads of sweat popped out on my face, turning instantly to ice.

Kip stumbled forward as if I had pushed him. His foot seemed to hang an eternity in the air, and in that suspension of time I heard a bell ring somewhere. As the clear sound faded into the cold air, his boot sank deep into the snow inside the gate. He took two quick steps into the enclosure, pivoted and flung out his arms and fell backward into the snow. Behind the distant trees, the sunset winked out like an extinguished lamp.

The blaze inside me had burned out too. Hollow, weightless, exhausted, I stood waiting in the winter dusk for Kip to move his arms, to make the angel's wings, but he just lay there.

"Come on, Kip. For crying out loud!"

"Shelley." His voice was small, frightened. Desperate. "I can't move."

Chapter 5

And this is the moment in which—in the reconstructed version I later made for my parents and anyone else who asked, but ultimately for myself and my own conscience—I run to Kip and throw myself down in the snow beside him and hear the thin sound of my voice spiral up into the darkening air. "Help! Please! Somebody help us!"

What really happened was that I just stood staring at him, gripping the bars of the gate and feeling their heartless cold seep through my mittens into my fingers. I couldn't move. It was like the moment I had fallen in the driveway last spring, that endless moment lying paralyzed in the glare of light from the porte cochere—only now, instead of feeling Kip tugging on the back of my sweatshirt and hearing his voice urging me to *Come on, come on,* I was staring at his motionless shape embedded in the unblemished snow.

Shelley. I can't move. The words repeated themselves in my head, forming a counterpoint to the haunting melody of the gate. *La, la,* went the tune, *La, la*—and then a huge black glove laid itself on my shoulder, and its thick fingers grasped me very gently and drew me away from the gate.

I think my heart stopped as I looked up at Royce. I had never seen him up close before. In spite of the cold he wore no hat and I noticed he wasn't bald, as he looked from a distance, but had very fair hair cut close to his scalp. His eyes were pale green. He was wearing a thick parka, snow pants and boots, and to me he appeared roughly the size of King Kong.

Once he had moved me aside from the gate, he stepped through it and bent down to lift Kip in his arms. Kip made no protest. When Royce turned, holding him, I could see that his body was completely limp. That was the point at which I came out of whatever suspended state I was in, like a film that begins in flickers and flashes and then becomes a seamless flow of images. I found I could move again, and as Royce came through the gate with Kip in his arms, I caught hold of his parka. "Where are you taking him? He was just making a snow angel. He didn't mean to do anything wrong."

Dusk was thickening fast. Royce started back the way we had come, his strides so enormous that I had to run to keep up. His boots left chiseled prints in the snow and my own feet slipped and slithered beside them.

"Kip! Why don't you tell him? We weren't hurting anything—"

But Kip said nothing. I couldn't see his face, only a lifeless dangle of arms and legs over the rampart of Royce's arms. We reached the footbridge and I felt it tremble under Royce's weight as we crossed. As the Arms came in sight ahead, a few lit windows pricking its dark bulk in the twilight, I started to cry. The tears scalded my cold cheeks. I caught at Royce's coat again. "Please, mister. He didn't mean—we didn't—we weren't—"

The giant hesitated, glanced down and gave me a reproving little shake of his head, a mutely eloquent Stop-that-carrying-on look that made me swallow my sobs, wipe my nose on the frosty back of one mitten and follow in silence. I couldn't help thinking of Caroline the bulldog. If the mysterious denizens of the Arms had exacted so harsh a payment for her unwitting part in a Halloween prank, what hope was there for two flagrant trespassers? We went up through the parking lot, past the back steps that Kip and I had used for our illegal entry last spring, beneath the porte cochere, and—

And down the driveway to the street. When I realized that Royce was taking Kip home, home to our house, I started to cry again—not from fear this time but from sheer relief. And so I have only a blurred memory of Mother opening the front door to Royce's knock, hand flying to her mouth and her voice rising in dismay.

"Shelley—what happened? Oh my God! Kip!"

Chapter 6

If you think, as I did at the time, that a cup of cocoa and a hot bath were all Kip needed to revive him, then you are as wrong as I was. He had lost consciousness lying there in the snowfield behind the Lockley Arms, and it was more than two months before he opened his eyes again.

Doc Sheridan came right away, but he was plainly baffled by this sudden collapse. He examined Kip, frowning and shaking his head, and then said he needed to go to the hospital.

"But what *is* it? What's wrong with him?" Mother's voice was ragged. Dad and Marty hovered behind her, their faces tight.

Doc shook his head again. "I don't know, Elaine. He's in shock. Why, I can't say. We'll do some tests once we get him to Albany."

He's in shock. Why, I can't say. In the somber days after the ambulance had come and taken Kip off to the hospital in Albany, where the doctors professed themselves as stumped as

Doc had been, I floated in a kind of parallel limbo. Was he going to die? And if he did, would his momentum somehow drag me along, as it had on so many occasions in the past? During this first separation of our lives there were times when it seemed he was already dead, leaving my internal compass to spin aimlessly in the absence of its lodestone. Even my thoughts drifted in a vast silence broken only by the clear tone of a bell and a faint, frightened voice.

Shelley. I can't move.

And then—*La, la . . . La, la . . .* That unearthly melody with its nonsense syllables, like the teasing song of someone who knows a secret but has no intention of revealing it. The secret of a virgin snowfield, a coiling October fog, a sibilant murmur like waves breaking on a beach, a sudden blue-white dazzle in the night sky.

It was the Lockleys who paid for the ambulance, and for all the hospital costs our insurance didn't cover. My aunt let that slip to me a few years later, when their shocking fate had set the whole village abuzz and I repeated some tasteless joke about it that was making the rounds at school. We were setting the supper table together; Marty's eyes blazed suddenly in her mild face and she shook her handful of forks at me, like a vengeful goddess from some obscure domestic pantheon. "You watch your mouth, Shelley Davies! Those people were very good to this family. Very good."

Emma Lockley was among Kip's first visitors at home, all those wearisome weeks later when the mystified hospital staff at last pronounced him well enough to be discharged. She dropped by unannounced one afternoon: a queen in a crown of coiled golden braids touched with silver. Dad was out somewhere, at the E-Z Stop or the post office, and this visit from our distinguished neighbor sent Mother into a tizzy; I can remember her actually polishing the banister with the sleeve of her sweater as they climbed the stairs to Kip's room. Yet it was obvious even to me that Mrs. Lockley could not have been less concerned with the quality of Mother's housekeeping. Ushered into Kip's room, she sat cozily on the end of his bed.

"Hello, Kip. How are you feeling?"

Since his return to consciousness he had been withdrawn and taciturn, evincing not a flicker of interest in anything around him. Now, propped up in bed, his face white as the pillow behind it and blue shadows pooling beneath his eyes, he only looked at her dully, the way he looked at everyone these days. At last his lips formed a word that might have been *okay*.

"He's much better," Mother supplemented. "Just a little sleepy right now." She was wound tight as a spring, anxious lest our visitor take offense. I stood in the doorway watching.

"It's nice, isn't it," Mrs. Lockley was saying, "having a window right by your bed? It's quite warm out today. You can smell spring coming." It was nearly the end of March; there were rosy new buds on the bare branches of the trees outside his bedroom window, a bursting life where a week earlier all had been sterile and dead. Mother glanced guiltily at the closed window and bent to open it a few inches.

While her back was turned, I saw Mrs. Lockley take something from the pocket of her coat and slip it beneath Kip's mattress. I didn't see what it was. Looking up to find me watching her, she touched a finger to her smiling lips, then beckoned. Reluctantly I crossed the room, knowing Mother would have my head if my manners failed me now. What had Mrs. Lockley put under Kip's mattress? Her eyes, as I approached, riveted me with their intense violet color.

"And you are Shelley." The elegant English accent endowed my name with an unexpected glamor. I managed a mute nod. This close, her beauty was overpowering and I was suddenly abashed by the memory of Kip's and my crimes against her. Three times we had trespassed on her property, once even invaded her home and wandered shamelessly through its private rooms. She was holding out her hand and I took it. As her fingers clasped mine, our eyes met. In the depths of her clear gaze I seemed to glimpse a scene in miniature: a white winter twilight, two small figures standing at a gate.

I caught my breath. The next thing I knew I was standing in the snowy pool enclosure at the Arms, fingers tingling with cold inside my mittens and my breath making clouds in the winter air. Emma Lockley stood beside me, the hem of her black velvet coat brushing the snow. A richly embroidered shawl hid her bright hair. I gaped up at her, and wordlessly she pointed.

I looked. They stood a little distance away, by the gate to the meadow. I could hear their voices, arguing.

"Let's make snow angels in there."

"You're crazy. This is far enough. We should get out of here before we get caught. Besides—"

"Besides what?" He rattled the gate, dislodging a drift of snow.

"Kip, stop it!"

His laughter floated across the gathering dusk. "What are you scared of? Come on!"

"No." She sounded sulky. "You do it if you want. I'll wait here."

"Okay, I will."

I glanced uneasily at Emma Lockley. She seemed absorbed in the scene before us. With a sense of foreboding I watched Kip push the gate open. Instead of stepping through it, he stopped.

"Go on," the other me said. "Hurry up. I hope something awful happens to you. I hate you!"

Horrified, I grabbed Emma Lockley's sleeve. "That's not what happened," I whispered frantically. As she looked down at me, I felt the words die in my throat.

And then, between one heartbeat and the next, the scene had vanished. It was spring. Broad daylight. I was in Kip's room, standing beside his bed, my hand still in Mrs. Lockley's. What had happened? Some waking dream that was already fading from my mind, leaving behind a shudder of cold and gathering darkness, a heaviness upon my heart. I couldn't speak. She said nothing either, only gave my hand a gentle squeeze before releasing it.

She left shortly thereafter. While Mother saw her out, I remained behind in Kip's room. His eyes were closed. I reached under his mattress and felt around for the object I had seen Emma Lockley put there, found it and pulled it out—a little bag made of pale blue velvet, tied at the neck with silver thread. The contents felt crisp, like dried leaves, and gave off a sharp fragrance. I wondered if I should tell Mother or just throw it away. But in the end, remembering Emma Lockley's eyes, I did neither of these things. I replaced it beneath the mattress and said nothing.

Once Kip was clearly on the mend, all limitations on visitors were removed and there was a constant stream of them noisily clattering up the stairs, kids from the neighborhood and classmates from school. But they never stayed long, and when they came back downstairs they were subdued, disturbed by the listless boy in the bed who looked like their friend but didn't behave like him. Some, like Missy Ettinger, came only once. Others came several times before giving up; and a few, like Adam Leonard, lasted into early summer before fading away. But it was baseball season, and even Adam had better things to do than sit indoors with a boy who barely acknowledged his presence. After a while Kip's only regular visitor was Frog.

Frog was a year behind the twins at school, a bespectacled little boy with a big head who was some kind of math genius. His real name was Wheaton Glass, Jr., but because he had been born with webbed fingers, all the kids called him Frog. On the playground, when the boys were choosing up sides for a game, he would go berserk and start screaming if the numbers came out uneven. He took trigonometry with the high school students, and everyone knew he was a freak. But he came to see Kip almost every day.

Frog wasn't like the others. He didn't come expecting to be entertained by the old, brash, amusing Kip who tossed off jokes and schemes and ideas like a Fourth of July sparkler. No doubt he just liked being near this popular boy who had been inaccessible until now. With him he brought various treasures—a glossy stone bisected by a jagged white line, a pocket knife with an inlaid handle, a shiny new horseshoe nail, a Chinese coin with a hole in the center—exhibiting them as if for Kip's approval, leaving each one on the table beside the bed until his next visit, when he would replace it with another. Watching these objects come and go, at first Shelley thought they were gifts, and maybe Frog intended them as such—but Kip never showed the slightest interest in any of them, and one by one they were removed.

Ever since Emma Lockley's visit Shelley had found herself avoiding her brother's room, and as spring wore on she fled outside into the warming weather and the company of the neighborhood girls her age. By summer her friendship with Jennifer and Lisa had been cemented by a routine of long bike rides and equally long conversations in what they came to call their "clubhouse"—a shady private niche out behind Jenny's house, where the sheltering branches of a maple tree met the overhang of the garage roof. It was the perfect spot for three gawky eleven-year-olds, sunburned and mosquito-bitten, to trade gossip and ghost stories, gigglingly pool their scanty knowledge of the facts of life, and devise exotic futures for themselves. Yet for Shelley her twin's absence remained an aching void in which the others' voices seemed at times as distant and meaningless as the twittering of birds in the maple branches overhead.

In September Doc Sheridan pronounced Kip well enough to attend school, although he had missed so many classes that it was decided he would have to repeat the sixth grade. Shelley was humiliated for her twin but, typical of his behavior these days, he didn't seem to care. She grew accustomed to seeing him on the playground at recess, standing with his hands in his pockets and his head bowed, deep in conversation with Frog instead of playing ball with the other boys. For a time she thought they were snubbing him, until one day Adam accosted her in the hall between classes and asked her what was wrong with Kip.

"What do you mean, what's wrong with him? You know he's been sick."

"I don't mean that. I mean—" He gestured helplessly. Kids jostled them in passing, loud-voiced among the banging of locker doors. There was an ink stain on Adam's shirt pocket, a hurt look on his face. "He acts so different now. Like he doesn't even like me anymore."

Shelley shrugged and turned away. She didn't know how to tell him that his friend, and her twin, had vanished forever. Spring into summer into fall: the ache of her loss had changed with the turning seasons—green and growing at first, with a sour bite to it, then ripening into dark, bruised tenderness before it had withered, at last, to a husk. At home Kip was more an absence than a presence, so preoccupied by his own thoughts that he seemed to be looking through them all: Dad, Mother, Aunt Marty, Shelley herself. He lived there in the house with them, ate his meals at the table and slept in his own bed upstairs, but it was like harboring a phantom. The adults said he just needed time to recover fully. But they had not seen him lying in the snowfield behind the Lockley Arms.

Chapter 7

While Shelley might wonder what her brother saw in Frog, the friendship between the boys clearly pleased Mother, who was charmed by the idea of Frog (whom she insisted on calling "Wheaton") even if she didn't know quite what to make of the reality. These days he was a frequent guest at the Davies supper table, a waif with a scratchy voice and a head too big for his body, his conversations full of strange, erudite references. He was an only child, his father a rich banker who worked in Albany. Along with a ten-acre family estate just east of Green Hollow, the family owned a beach house on Nantucket where they regularly spent the month of August, and it was this connection with wealth and gracious living that delighted Mother. She must have had some instinct that this was an opportunity for Kip, a chance for him to break out of what she couldn't help seeing as a cycle of failure. But surely even her wildest dreams were outdone when Frog's father unexpectedly offered to send Kip, along with Frog, away to prep school the following fall.

The institution in question was the Clinton-Monroe Academy, a prestigious boys' school in western Massachusetts attended by Mr. Glass himself. Its reputation combined academic excellence and social status in a way that made people lift their eyebrows when they pronounced the name, putting an emphatic twist on the final syllable like the perfect knot in a black tie. Mr. Glass mentioned the idea one winter night when he came to pick up Frog after supper—just dropped his bombshell and drove off with a cheery wave, leaving a copy of the school catalog for Kip's stunned parents to examine. Later that night, Shelley overheard them arguing about it.

Mother wanted him to go and Dad didn't. Shelley wasn't eavesdropping exactly. She couldn't sleep, and they were talking when she went down for a glass of milk. As she reached the bottom of the stairs she could hear their tense voices in the kitchen.

"Don't you see?" Mother was saying. "This is a chance we can never give him. A chance to have it all—a really fine education, connections with the right kind of people. Real success. It's a godsend, a miracle."

And Dad: "I know, Elaine. I know it's a wonderful opportunity, but the timing is all wrong. He's been so sick. What he needs right now is a home and a family, not the environment of a competitive boys' school. Maybe in a couple of years—"

"A couple of years!" Her voice shook on the last word. "Graham, you can't negotiate something like this—it's the chance of a lifetime! In a couple of years, if Wheaton goes off to school and Kip stays here, the boys will hardly remember each other. Mr. Glass isn't going to put this offer on hold until we finally deign to accept it!"

"I just don't think Kip should be away from home right now. There's something about him—"

"He's *fine*. And it's not right now. It's not until *September*."

There was a brief silence during which Dad must have shaken his head, because Shelley heard Mother draw an audible breath.

"Elaine, please. Don't cry."

"How can you do this? How can you deny Kip this chance? Graham, are you—are you jealous? Jealous of Mr. Glass because he can afford to give our son all the advantages—"

She broke off and he said quietly, "All the advantages we can't afford to give him. Is that what you were going to say?"

A little wail announced Mother's tears. "Well, why don't you want him to go? I can tell you don't. You don't—not now, not even in a couple of years."

"You're right," he said. His voice was still quiet but Shelley could hear a tremor in it as he went on. "I don't want him to go. Not now, not in a couple of years. And it isn't because I'm jealous of Wheaton Glass—I wouldn't trade places with him for all the money in one of his banks. I want Kip to grow up with the kind of values he's learning here, in our home, in Green Hollow. I don't want him going off to a fancy prep school where he'll pick up a bunch of rich-boy prejudices. Where he'll start thinking that what's important in life is wearing a certain brand of shoes and belonging to the right club. I don't want him, or Shelley either, learning to use people, or confusing money with success. I want them to be happy with who they are, happy and at peace with themselves."

Shelley held her breath. When he had finished speaking the only sound was Mother's soft sobbing. On it went, muffled but unremitting, and she thought about what her science class had learned last week about water being able to carve a canyon through rock. As she crept back upstairs she could hear Dad saying, "Please, Elaine. Please don't cry."

Chapter 8

Kip was gone for three years. During that time the rest of the family scarcely saw him, except at Christmas. The Glasses took him over as completely as if they had purchased him—and as Shelley glanced through the Clinton-Monroe Academy Catalog and noted the staggering per annum fee for tuition, room and board, it struck her that maybe they had. During the summers he was enrolled, along with Frog, in Clinton-Monroe's special session of sports and seminars that lasted through the end of July; then the boys were whisked off to spend the short vacation weeks at the Glasses' summer house on Nantucket. During Kip's brief stints at home he behaved like a polite guest, keeping to himself when he wasn't offering to help with the household chores. His mother was thrilled with him: the perfect manners, the good grades, the clothes the Glasses had bought him, the aura of money and success that associating with rich people had given him; and Aunt Marty's attitude echoed hers. Dad seemed a little shy with him, and a little sad.

The most notable event of his absence, without question, was the accident resulting in the deaths of Everett and Emma Lockley. On the way home from a visit to friends in Vermont, their car plunged off a bridge into a river to be found the following day with their drowned bodies inside. For weeks afterward the villagers could talk of nothing but the tragedy. The Lockleys had been the pride of Green Hollow for as long as many residents could remember, and the deaths were so sudden, so shocking, that people wanted to blame them on something besides fate. For a time there were rumors of what Aunt Marty was fond of calling "foul play," but an investigation into the circumstances offered no basis for suspicion. A long drive in foggy weather, late at night—the consensus was that Everett, who had been at the wheel, must have dozed off. Yet Green Hollow had been robbed of its leading citizens, and Elaine Davies was not the only one to go around red-eyed for days afterward.

With the Arms in the spotlight of local attention following the Lockley tragedy, Shelley couldn't help recalling the childish obsession she and Kip had once harbored for the place. Now the memory embarrassed her. If he had changed, so had she: had become the good girl her mother had always wanted, decorous and obedient, attentive to appearances, a slave to her straight-A average in school. During Kip's visits home she kept her distance, as if his proximity might undermine her new virtue. Her fears proved groundless; this quiet, perfectly groomed prep-school boy in no way resembled the mischievous twin of her memories; nonetheless, when his visits were over and he returned to school, she was always secretly relieved.

The single flaw in her new identity was her friendship with Benjy Hendricks. She knew her mother disapproved of him, for reasons that were never made clear—but early on Saturday mornings they had begun to meet, not quite accidentally, at the far end of their block where a crumbling culvert was shaded by the weeping willows that gave the street its name. Concealed within a swaying green curtain of branches they sometimes talked, sometimes listened to the trickle of the brook below. Benjy's misfortunes—his lack of a father, his mother's hangovers—seemed to Shelley to balance the burden of her own. Not only had she been spurned by the good fortune that had favored Kip, but these days she harbored a puzzling, shameful secret: unlike Jenny and Lisa and the other girls her age at school, she had still not begun her monthly bleeding.

None of these matters, of course, could be discussed. But during the rambling talks she and Benjy shared beneath the willow tree, each instinctively recognized a fellow sufferer in the other. They talked about books they had read, their acquaintances in the neighborhood and at school—never about themselves. Sometimes they clambered down into the culvert's stone channel to launch makeshift boats downstream, and afterward, when he carelessly took her hand to help her up the steep bank, Shelley felt a secret thrill.

Kip, meanwhile, was crowning success with success. His second triumphant year at Clinton-Monroe had brought a pledge from Mr. Glass to finance his college education. News of this handsome offer caused varying reactions throughout Green Hollow, a flurry of envy, admiration and approval in which it was only Kate Conklin, owner and proprietor of Kate's Antiques & Collectibles on Main Street, who thought to comment on the contrast between Kip's existence and his twin sister's.

Shelley had been working part-time at the antique shop for nearly a year, and enjoying it. Kate was a dumpy, warmhearted woman in her forties, with frizzy copper hair and a big laugh, who decked herself out in beads, gauzy scarves, and long skirts that trailed the tops of her worn cowboy boots. Half her merchandise was valuable, the other half junk she had rescued because she felt sorry for it: there were broken dolls and ugly teapots, soap dishes with decals of Niagara Falls, a cuckoo clock that cuckooed thirty-two times every day at ten past four. She adored Shelley, and the news of Kip's latest good fortune made her purse her lips and do what, in her mock prissy moments, she called "saying a swear."

"Why, Kate!"

"Well, honest to God, Shelley!" Kate was arranging a display of old apothecary jars, and they clinked sharply behind her words as if for emphasis. "It's not fair. I mean, I'm happy for Kip. He's a good kid. But so are you! Why should he get it all on a silver platter while you get stuck working in a dusty old shop every day after school?"

"I like working here. It's fun."

"Not quite as much fun as spending your summer vacations on Nantucket Island," Kate said dryly. Her voice softened. "I'm glad you like working here. But that's not the point. It's just not fair."

Just not fair. For an instant the words triggered a screech of heartfelt agreement inside Shelley, who gave an uneasy shrug, horrified lest some trace of that ugly sound might have been audible. "I don't mind. Really. He's just been lucky."

Kate shook her head and straightened an errant jar. "Well, dear girl, you're more of a philosopher than I'll ever be. If I were you, I'd want to give him and his whole fairy godfamily a kick in the derriere!"

Chapter 9

But it was Kip who engineered his own kick in the derriere, and the inscrutable instrument of his downfall was a polar bear's tongue.

The first the family heard of it was a telephone call from the headmaster of Clinton-Monroe. He called Green Hollow High during third period and had Graham Davies pulled out of class, so there were rumors spreading like wildfire through the school even before Graham was off the phone. Kip was dead. Frog was dead and Mr. Glass had adopted Kip in his place. Mr. Glass was dead and had left his entire fortune to Kip and Frog, who had run off to Atlantic City in the company of two Playboy Bunnies. Jennifer raced up to Shelley in the hall between third and fourth periods. "Shelley! What's going on?"

"I don't know. I'm trying to find my dad."

He wasn't in his classroom, or the faculty lounge. Someone said he was still in the principal's office, where the call had come in, and Shelley headed there. Just as she reached the door, it opened and he came backing out, still talking to someone inside. "Well, I don't think it's the end of the world," she heard him say.

"End of the world? What is it? Dad? Did something happen to Kip?"

He turned and saw her. She noticed his lips were twitching the way they always did when he knew he shouldn't laugh. He put his arm around her. "He's fine, sweetie. Kip's fine. He's been expelled."

The following day Dad drove to Massachusetts to bring him home. He was in deep disgrace: the last boy to have been expelled from Clinton-Monroe had been caught capering naked on the lawn in front of the dining hall and subsequently removed to a mental hospital. In Kip's case the official reason, stated in a letter embossed with the Clinton-Monroe seal, was "vandalism of school property." What he had done was to steal the artificial pink tongue of a gigantic stuffed polar bear that stood on a pedestal in the reading room of the Clinton-Monroe library.

This enormous beast, rearing to an impressive height of nearly eight feet and slashing at the air with giant white forepaws the size of shovel blades, was the trophy of Alistair Clinton, school founder and big game hunter, who some time in the 1890s had killed it and brought the corpse back to Massachusetts to adorn a building full of books. According to Kip, the first time he saw the bear he was offended that so majestic a creature should be killed for sport. In the subdued light of the reading room its baleful glass eyes seemed to smolder with resentment, not only against its pointless death but against the ongoing indignity of its role as an enormous knickknack. And the worst of its humiliation was that pink plastic tongue.

Kip was sympathetic, but he was busy with his studies, with fencing and chess and lacrosse, and helping crew the Glasses' thirty-five-foot sailboat, the *Little Eva,* in the cold waters off Nantucket on vacations. During his first two years at Clinton-Monroe his pity for the polar bear's plight remained abstract. It was only in the spring of his third year, as tender April unfolded into balmy May, that he began to feel, as he described it to Shelley later, as if he had awakened from a long hibernation himself. To stretch and look around him, sniff the air and feel hungry and restless and ready for some indefinable change.

And to sense a certain kinship with the bear—the kinship of wild spirits bound and twisted to wrong purposes. The stronger this feeling became, the more the tongue irritated him. He came to the conclusion that something must be done to appease the suffering spirit of the bear. And that was to remove the tongue.

With Frog's help, a plan was conceived and flawlessly executed, but Kip had overlooked one possibility: that some innocent fellow student would be accused in his place. When this happened, he reluctantly confessed. In the uproar that followed, Frog's minor role got him put on probation, but that was really the only aspect of the whole affair that seemed to bother Kip at all.

Because he had miraculously regained the exuberant spirits I remembered from our childhood. I stood in the doorway of his room and watched him unpack, flinging shoes and ties and shirts out of his bag with the abandon of a puppy digging a hole in a flower bed. He looked up at me and grinned. He had grown—again—since Christmas, but a dark lock of hair overhanging one eyebrow gave him a startling resemblance to the little boy who had been my twin. "I think they should have let me keep the tongue," he said. "I mean, since they kicked me out because of it."

Mother could scarcely look at Kip. At every meal her pain and disappointment hung like a thundercloud over the table; several times she even burst into tears, while he dutifully hung his head and the rest of the family tried to keep eating. But to Shelley it was clear his mother's disappointment did not really touch him. "I'm sorry Mr. Glass is mad at me," he told her in private. "And I'm sorry I got Frog in trouble. But I'm glad I left that place. I didn't belong there."

It made her remember their parents' argument over accepting Mr. Glass's bounty, Dad saying he didn't want Kip to pick up a bunch of rich-boy prejudices. Had that happened? The past three years had unmistakably left their mark on him, a gloss of sophistication and confident charm he would never have gained in Green Hollow. As Kate Conklin, won over against her will when he stopped by the shop one afternoon, admitted grudgingly to Shelley, "That young man has got savoir faire." Yet beneath the polish lurked the essence of the curious, lively little boy who had masterminded their childhood adventures, and detecting that once-familiar glint of mischief in his eye, Shelley reminded herself to beware. After all, he had gotten himself expelled from school. Expelled! And the neighbors were undoubtedly talking.

On the twins' fifteenth birthday in early June, a smudged, hurried note arrived from Frog, resembling something smuggled out of a prison cell.

This place is necrotic in your absence. No evidence of brain activity, only the emission of noxious gasses. My parents are dragging me off to Switzerland for the summer. Switzerland! Inventors of the cuckoo clock! Why not France, Italy, even Spain? Au revoir, mon bon compère.

Hardly the sort of communication he would have gotten from anyone at Green Hollow High, where classes had just ended for the summer. The twins attended the graduation ceremony in the school auditorium and walked home afterward to sit on their front steps in the balmy June darkness, listening to the crickets. They didn't talk, but for the first time since Kip's return Shelley found herself beginning to relax in his presence. A car packed with rowdy graduates sped down Willow Street, horn blaring, and he turned his head to watch it. "I guess that's where I'll be going to school next year."

"It's not so bad."

"I never said it was. At least I won't have to wear a damn tie all the time." He made a strangling noise. "And I can still say the alphabet backward."

By common impulse we started to sing it, badly out of tune with each other and laughing at our own cacophony. Then we fell silent: someone was coming along the sidewalk. A voice said, "Shelley?"

"Benjy?"

His tall shadowy figure crossed the grass. He had been

among those graduating tonight, and for the past few weeks I had cherished the hope that he might ask me to the dance afterward, but he hadn't. We weren't as close as we once had been; weekend jobs had sabotaged our companionable Saturdays at the culvert. At school, away from our private place, our attempts at conversation were invariably awkward. Now he folded himself down on the porch steps beside me. "Hi, Kip."

"Congratulations." Kip offered his hand across my lap and Benjy shook it.

"Yeah, well. I made it through. That's a surprise, huh?"

"Aren't you going to the dance?" Kip was saying, and Benjy snorted.

"They wanted every senior to make a ten-dollar donation for decorations. Hell with that. I don't have money to throw away on flowers made out of snot rags."

I took a deep breath. He hadn't asked me to the dance because he wasn't going. It was as simple as that.

"You've got a job, don't you?" Kip was saying.

"Yeah—bag groceries at the E-Z Stop, get rich quick. But I think I've got something better lined up for this summer. Old Man Garrett wants somebody evenings, to drive the Mister Softee truck."

"I need to get a job," Kip said.

Benjy stretched long legs down the porch steps. "Why don't you apply at Janicot? They hire kids in their shipping room."

Kip shook his head. "I don't want to work in some dusty old warehouse packing books." He nodded across the street, toward the lit windows of the Lockley Arms. "I'd like to work there."

"You're nuts," Benjy said. "They don't hire kids. They've got their own private staff."

"But the place is under new management now, isn't it? Didn't something happen to the Lockleys?"

"I'll say it did. Their car went off a bridge into the Schoharie River. Both of them drowned."

"Oh yeah," Kip said. From the distance of Clinton-Monroe, the event that had rocked Green Hollow must have registered barely a flicker. "Who runs it now?"

"A relative of theirs," I said. "She's young." I recalled her arriving in the aftermath of the tragedy: a young woman named Snowden Mansell, slender, attractive, with tawny brown hair coiled in an elegant knot at the back of her head. She was not a great deal more visible than the Lockleys had been, and over the past couple of years I had been only obliquely aware of her comings and goings across the street.

Kip had turned to Benjy. "We went over there on our own, you know—Shelley and me. I lost my baseball cap over there."

"No shit!" I could feel Benjy's start of surprise. "Shelley, you never told me."

I shrugged. "It was a long time ago."

"Did you get in trouble?" Benjy was asking.

It was Kip who answered him. "Our parents never found out. The Lockleys never said anything."

"How far'd you get?" Benjy said.

Kip hesitated. In that brief pause I could hear, just as I had when we were small, the murmur of his thoughts among my own. *Should I tell him how we sneaked into the house? Will he think I'm a liar?* When he spoke aloud, it was studiedly casual. "Just to the parking lot. Then we ran into Royce. He chased us off."

Benjy nodded. "Yeah, that sounds familiar."

"He never caught you?"

"Nope. But I quit going anyway." He hesitated, then: "Had some real bad dreams about the place. Lost my taste for it."

"Bad dreams?" I said.

The piping of crickets seemed to grow louder. A loose board creaked as Benjy shifted position. "Guess I'd seen too many horror movies."

The three of us sat without speaking in the darkness. I glanced across the street at the Arms, remembering Benjy's scared face appearing out of a thinning fog, and some other things that couldn't possibly be real. A troupe of ragged men in green, a whispering rise and fall like breaking surf—only a child's imagination. Only that. Somewhere deeper in my memory a thin voice wailed *Shelley—I can't*—and I jumped as Kip's caustic voice beside me drowned it out.

"Horror movies? Well, you better watch out tonight. See? There's a full moon." He threw back his head and let out a wavering howl, and next door old Miss Motley's poodle Mitzi began a frenzied yapping. In spite of the warm June night a shiver ran across my skin. I elbowed Kip and he collapsed laughing, but Benjy didn't seem to notice. He was sitting rigid, his eyes fixed on the house across the street. The moonlight had caught a glisten of sweat on his upper lip, and I saw he wasn't smiling.

Chapter 10

It never occurred to Shelley that Kip was serious about wanting to work at the Lockley Arms. She was taken completely by surprise a few days later, when the twins arrived home around supper time—Kip had stopped by Kate's to walk with her—and Aunt Marty met them at the door with a funny look on her face.

"You had a phone call, Kip. Miss Mansell, at the Arms. You're to go over there tomorrow morning at ten."

Mother appeared behind her. "What on earth is this about, Kip? You're not in some kind of trouble again, are you?"

"Elaine—" came Dad's remonstrance from the living room where he sat reading the newspaper, and she turned back toward the kitchen with a sigh.

"I wrote and asked for a job," Kip told Shelley after supper, while they were doing the dishes, and shrugged at her astonished face. "Look, I've got to get a summer job somewhere. Especially now that I've ruined my chance for *real* success."

Mother's phrase. Although Dad had announced firmly that the Clinton-Monroe incident was finished, a closed chapter, Shelley suspected she was unable to keep from reproaching

Kip in private. It wasn't that she meant to torment him, but her sense of lost opportunity was too great to be contained. She wanted so much for Kip; and just as her dreams were coming true, with apparent nonchalance he had tossed them away. "They'll never hire you," Shelley told him. "Not in a million years."

But by noon the next day the job was his. It was Saturday and the whole family was home when he returned with the news, naming the handsome starting wage and describing his duties. He would assist Royce in the care of the pool and grounds, park the guests' cars and help serve in the dining room. He was to begin Monday. Dad seemed disgruntled by the prospect, but since it was a fait accompli there wasn't much he could do. Mother was delighted.

"I met Miss Mansell when she first took over the Arms. She's very nice, isn't she?"

Kip shrugged. "She's all right."

In Mother's eyes, the inn's present owner was bathed in the glory of its former ones. "Of course," she was saying, "anyone related to the Lockleys would have to be nice. What a tragedy that was!"

Kip loved working at the Arms. He loved operating the latest gadgets to maintain the perfect lawns and hedges, tending the shimmering turquoise rectangle of the swimming pool, donning a white shirt and black bow tie to serve the guests in the posh dining room—but most of all he loved driving some luxurious car the short distance from the porte cochere to a space in the back parking lot. Those few precious minutes behind the steering wheel of a Mercedes or a Jaguar, powerful engine purring at his command, filled his fifteen-year-old heart with joy.

It remained a matter of wonder to Shelley that her brother now possessed legitimate access to the place that had once been synonymous to them with the word *forbidden*. Adolescence had transformed her childhood fascination with the Arms into a prosaic respect for its reputation as an establishment of elegance and style; and now Kip had effortlessly become a part of this glamorous world. From him she gathered a fragmented picture of its life, like tantalizing flashes of light and color glimpsed through a keyhole.

Royce, it turned out, was both deaf and mute, although he managed to communicate by a system of nods and gestures, raised eyebrows and pursed lips. He used this method with everyone except the mistress of the house, with whom Kip had seen him employing some kind of manual sign language—his thick fingers flying while she watched intently, and then her quick hands shaping a reply. Royce, far from being the ogre of their childhood, proved himself a gentle, patient taskmaster who loved his work and clearly wanted Kip to love it too.

Jessica, the Arms' stout cook and housekeeper, had a sharp tongue with the staff and all hapless delivery people—but was meek as a lamb, Kip said, with Miss Mansell. Jessica's talents in the kitchen were fabled in Green Hollow (the dining room at the Arms was reserved exclusively for guests of the inn) and Kip could now attest to the truth of the legend, since on the nights he stayed to help Alicia serve in the dining room he was rewarded with supper afterward in the kitchen. With gusto he described these meals to his sister: poached salmon with asparagus, venison in burgundy sauce with sweet potatoes, Cornish hen stuffed with wild rice and truffles. Fresh-baked bread, crisp and lacy salads, ethereal sorbets—even with a stomach full of Aunt Marty's tuna casserole, Shelley could feel her mouth watering.

The staff was completed by Jessica's grown daughter Alicia, a goodnatured scatter-brain engaged to be married to a hardware store clerk in the nearby village of Woodston. The topic of her impending wedding dominated all conversation in the kitchen, while Kip gorged himself on gourmet leftovers and Rowan the cat perched on the counter nearby, blinking in disdain.

As for the guests, those exotic beings whose potential disapproval had cast such a shadow over the twins' childhood games, Kip's contact with them was minimal: a nod and a smile as he opened a car door or refilled a wineglass, a polite greeting if they passed him working in the flower beds or trimming a hedge. In the house he was restricted to the kitchen and dining room, with the upper floors off-limits. To him the guests were nameless and practically faceless—but their cars were not. Some cars returned again and again, and these he began to call "the regulars." Gray Mercedes, green DeSoto, black Hudson, black Jaguar, yellow Triumph, white Volkswagen: the owners of these particular cars visited the Arms frequently, and always at the same time.

It made Kip start to wonder.

Meanwhile Shelley was spending this summer, as she had last, working at Kate's. Her friends had jobs too—Lisa as a camp counselor in Maine, Jenny in the shipping room at Janicot Books. Benjy Hendricks was driving the Mister Softee truck, and despite Mother's tight-lipped disapproval Shelley got in the habit of joining him on his evening rounds as the white truck prowled the dusky streets, announcing its presence by an out-of-tune mechanical rendition of *"Que Será Será."*

I wasn't sure if I was Benjy's girlfriend or not. Although Mister Softee showed up in front of our house every evening after supper without fail, during our long drives together Benjy never attempted to so much as hold my hand. We rode through those warm twilights in a haze of unfulfilled possibility, the leafy summer streets unrolling before us like the indistinct landscape of a dream. In the companionable dark of the truck cab we remained mostly silent beneath the music's distorted warble.

I knew the adults in my family worried that our relationship might become serious. Although Mother—probably thanks to Dad's influence—never forbade me outright to spend time with Benjy, she made her opinion abundantly clear. He was not a young man who was going places. His dubious parentage prevented him, in her books, from being a nice person. And the notion of her daughter forming an attachment to someone who wasn't nice . . . Her anxiety on this point was undoubtedly the impetus for an awkward conversation initiated by Aunt Marty.

"You know, Shelley, a girl's good reputation is her most precious possession. She has to look out for herself. One impulse, one little mistake can ruin her whole life." She fidgeted, not looking at me, and added hopefully, "Do you know what I mean?"

"Yes, Marty. But you don't need to worry."

"Just remember that nice people . . . people who truly respect and care for you . . . won't ever ask you to do anything that's wrong. Anything you shouldn't."

Her squeamish avoidance of the singular male pronoun managed to suggest I was dealing with a crowd of importunate suitors instead of just Benjy, too shy even to touch me. But she needn't have worried: my upbringing had rendered me well aware that sex was a forbidden zone—something, like debt and public drunkenness, that started the neighbors' tongues wagging. And the irony of Marty's warning was increased by my secret knowledge that at fifteen, I still had not begun to menstruate and, it seemed to my bleak outlook, probably never would.

Kate was Shelley's mainstay during this part of the summer—Kate who put her easy companionship and fierce loyalty at her young employee's disposal without asking anything in return. Her response when she heard about Kip's job at the Arms? "Landed on his feet, didn't he? A yard boy. Goody for him." Out of tact, Shelley didn't reveal that Kip was making a weekly wage of more than twice what Kate was able to pay her.

The summer weekends brought a horde of antique-hunters to upper New York State and Kate's did a brisk business, often staying open late to accommodate them all. On one such evening at the end of July, Shelley was still busy behind the counter when Kip showed up, flushed and out of breath, to ask when she would be done.

"I don't know. Why?" It was past five, but the shop was still thronged.

"Because I need you. Since Alicia left I've been handling the dining room on my own, only there's a big banquet tonight. Jessica was going to help me, but this afternoon she slipped on the back steps and twisted her ankle. It's really swollen. She told me to ask you if you'd help."

"Jessica told you to ask me?"

His shoulders twitched. "Not Jessica. Miss Mansell."

Shelley hadn't thought Miss Mansell was aware of her existence, and this unexpected evidence to the contrary gave her a flustered but not unpleasant feeling. "I don't have anything to wear," she said. "And we're really busy here." The cash register jingled; Kate handed her an ivory-handled mirror to put in a bag.

"Shelley." Kip had lowered his voice out of some vague instinct for tact. "It could mean a job there, if they like you. I mean, Alicia's gone. It's really too much work for me by myself. And Jessica's ankle isn't going to get well overnight, is it?"

Shelley handed the bag to the waiting customer, who stepped away from the counter and was replaced by another. "Well?" Kip was saying, and she hissed, "I don't know!"

The cash register fell briefly silent as Kate glanced their way. "Is there a problem, kids?"

"They're short staffed at the Lockley Arms tonight," Shelley said. "They want me to help out."

"It's a big banquet," Kip supplemented. "They need her right away."

Kate rang up the purchase of an old saltshaker. "Oh, they do, do they? Well, it's up to you, dear girl. If you want to go, I can manage here."

"Really, Kate? Is it really okay?"

"Of course it is! Now would you get going?"

Kip hurried her down the sidewalk, babbling in her ear what was probably a summary of everything he had learned about waiting tables at the Arms. It could have been Homer recited in the original Greek for all Shelley knew. She was mulling over her vague recollection of the time they had walked boldly into the house—how many years ago?—and wandered through a series of beautiful rooms. Had it really happened? Oh, she knew they had gone to the Arms at night, and been chased away by Royce; she still had a scar on her knee from falling in the driveway. But the rest might have been a dream. She woke from her reverie to find Kip leading her straight to the Arms.

"Wait a second. I need to go home and change. I can't wear this." Shorts, sneakers, one of Dad's old shirts with its tails knotted at the waist, her hair tied back with a bandanna—Kate was not one to demand a dress code from her employees, and Shelley had attired herself for comfort.

Kip renewed his grip on her wrist. "Come on. They'll give you something to wear. That's what they did with me." When she continued to resist he said, "All the cars are there. You know. All the regulars."

At that she gave in and they went up the Arms driveway together, just as they had done on those other, clandestine occasions. Waning afternoon light slanted down through enormous trees to dapple the grass. The white house lay in soft green shadow punctuated by the pink geraniums in hanging pots along the porch. Voices and the quiet clink of glassware floated across the lawn; Shelley glanced up and saw two guests, a man and a woman, standing on the second-floor balcony. As the twins passed beneath the porte cochere Kip stopped to gesture at the gleaming vehicles that nearly filled the small parking lot.

"See? Green DeSoto. Yellow Triumph. Black Jag. Gray Mercedes. Black Hudson Hornet. White VW Beetle. They're all here."

He led her up the steps to the back door. They were steeper than she remembered; she could see how Jessica might have fallen. Then Kip was pushing the screen open, leading her into the kitchen where half a dozen pots bubbled and steamed on the enormous black stove, and every inch of table and counter space was covered with the makings of the banquet.

The room seemed full of people. Jessica tended the stove, her ankle swathed in a white bandage and a sheen of sweat on her ruddy face. Shelley recognized Royce's broad back at the sink where he stood scrubbing vegetables in a thunder of running water. And on her way into the dining room, catching the swinging door on her hip because her hands were full of feathery golden stalks of grain, was Miss Mansell, glancing back to say across the festive chaos as if they were old friends, "Shelley! You're here to save us. We'd have been ruined without you."

What do I remember about that night? A blur of bright colors, talk and laughter, the burnish of candlelight on rich textures and faces flushed with merriment and wine. Somewhere in the bustle before the guests sat down, Miss Mansell found me a white shirt, black trousers and a bow tie like Kip's, cloth-soled Chinese slippers for my feet, and sent me down to the laundry room in the cellar to dress. As if by magic, everything fit perfectly.

"You look elegant," she said when I reappeared. Her eyes, lively with gleams and shadows, surveyed me approvingly. I probably would have died for her then, but all that was required of me was to assist Kip in carrying trays from the kitchen into the dining room and giving a dish to each guest, serving from the left. When the plates were empty I had to take them away, this time from the right. Kip took charge of the wine. Between courses we sat at the kitchen table, watching Royce make cat's cradles out of string while we listened to the high-spirited hubbub from the dining room. In spite of the stage fright that froze my senses each time I passed through the swinging door, I had noted that there were ten guests, five men and five women, and that Miss Mansell had joined the banquet, wearing a velvety black dress cut very low. On a chain around her neck hung a little silver medallion no bigger than a dime, that now and again caught the light with a flash like some secret signal. The banquet was some sort of celebration, that much was obvious, but its cause remained a mystery to me.

Just after the dessert there came a moment when a hush fell over the dining room. We noticed it in the kitchen; Kip got up and crept over to the door, putting his eye to the crack while Jessica gave his back an exasperated look. In the silence I heard a quiet voice say something I couldn't catch, and then all the others took it up, louder, rising until it was almost a shout.

"To the Lady. The Lady!"

The musical touch of glass to glass gave way to another silence in which I imagined them drinking their wine. I glanced at Jessica but she avoided my eyes. The next moment, almost as if to preclude any questions, she had found half a dozen tasks that needed Kip's and my immediate attention.

Later, when the two of us were on our way home, I asked him what he had seen through the crack in the door. His voice was gruff as he answered. "They all stood up. Except her. The toast was to her."

This time I didn't have to ask whom he meant. "The Lady?" I said. "What does that mean?"

He shrugged.

Chapter 11

The offer of a job at the Arms arrived the following day, in the middle of Sunday breakfast. Marty answered the door and came back bearing a cream-colored envelope with Shelley's name on it. "Royce brought it. He makes me feel so *small*," she said as she handed it over. "And so *noisy*."

Kip launched into an exegesis of Royce's good qualities, but Shelley scarcely heard him. She was looking at the handwriting on the envelope, delicate and spare, tracing out the letters of her name: *Shelley Davies*. Beside her, Mother was leaning over eagerly to look, whispering, "Open it!" and Dad sent an irritated glance in her direction. The envelope wasn't sealed. Shelley took out the note.

Shelley, thanks for rescuing us last night. If you'd be interested in working here on a regular basis for the rest of the summer, we'd be delighted to have you. The hourly wage would be the same as Kip's, and your duties would include making up the guest rooms and helping out in the kitchen and dining room. I hope you'll join us. In any event, thanks again for last night.

Snowden Mansell

Mother finished reading first. Shelley heard an excited intake of breath as her hand was taken and squeezed. "Darling! This is wonderful!"

"But I'm already working for Kate." She stared at the signature on the note, torn between guilt and gratification. *It could mean a job there, if they like you,* Kip had said. They had liked her. Here was the proof.

"Oh—!" Mother waved a hand as if dispersing flies. "Stuck inside a dusty old junk shop, and she hardly pays you a cent. Just say you've had a better offer."

Kip was grinning. "What'd I tell you? When you're Jessica's size, a sprained ankle stays sprained for a lo-ong time. Pretty neat, huh, Shel? We'll both be working in the same place."

She waved the note under his nose. "Only *I* get to go upstairs, and *you* don't."

He snorted and Dad put in, "Hold on, honey. Didn't you just say you're already working for Kate? It's a perfectly good job. Why would you want to leave?"

The reproof dampened her exhilaration. He was right; how could she abandon Kate to go and work at the Arms? But Mother had already jumped in. "Graham, you didn't read Miss Mansell's note. They'll be paying her the same thing they're paying Kip. Why, she'd be a fool to turn it down!"

He was still looking steadily at Shelley. "Other factors can be more important than money, sweetheart. Doesn't Kate treat you well?"

"Yes," she mumbled.

"Graham, at Kate's she's nothing but a shop girl!"

Mother's sharp tone drew his gaze at last. "And at the Arms she'll be a chambermaid," he said evenly.

"She'll be a member of the staff of a very fine establishment. The people who stay at the Arms are certainly nicer than the ones who wander off the street into that junk shop of Kate's.

Honestly, Graham, I can't imagine why you wouldn't want your daughter to work in a place where she'll have a chance to be around nice people!"

During this speech her voice began to quiver. When she stopped speaking, there was a silence in which Shelley held her breath without daring to look at her father. At last she heard his sigh, and the creak of his chair as he sat back.

"At least give Kate some notice if you're going to quit, Shelley. Don't leave her in the lurch."

Quit Kate's? How could she? Yet the thought of refusing Miss Mansell's offer . . . Shelley gazed down at the remains of her Sunday morning pancakes, running her finger along the crisp edge of the note and pretending she was still trying to make up her mind. Behind the view she had adopted from her mother, of the Lockely Arms as a successful and elegant establishment, there lingered something of the forbidden citadel behind its high green wall. And behind that, so faint it was all but invisible, the image of a sprawling figure on a field of flawless white.

She glanced up at Kip. She had lost her twin that day in the snowfield behind the Arms, lost him as effectively as if he had died and been buried in the village cemetery at the south end of Green Hollow. Now, five long years later, he sat smiling at her across the breakfast table, vastly changed yet mysteriously the same. A shiver ran over her. Her gaze dropped once more to the note in her fingers.

I hope you'll join us. A summons to the very place where, years earlier, this enigmatic alchemy had been set in motion. How could she refuse?

Typical of Kate, she insisted Shelley begin work at the Arms immediately, rather than holding her to the two weeks' notice Dad had suggested. "Don't worry about it, dear girl! Cissy McIntyre's been nagging me for a job for months, and it'll be worth hiring her just to shut her up. Of course she's not you, but she'll be fine."

Benjy was not so understanding. When Shelley broke the news to him, mentioning that her duties in the dining room would frequently keep her at the Arms late at night, his response was a sneer. "What the hell do you want to work *there* for?"

His vehemence startled her. "Why wouldn't I? It's good money, a nice place—"

"Oh, sure. Bunch of snobs, think they're better than everybody else. Let me tell you something. They're not as nice as you think they are."

"They're nice to Kip," Shelley countered.

"Yeah, Mister Prep School." His tone said ordinary mortals didn't have a prayer, and she felt her confidence waver. Then she remembered Miss Mansell smiling at her. *You look elegant.* That gracious note. *Thanks for rescuing us last night.* "You're wrong, Benjy. They're not like that."

"Look, Shelley. I just don't want you to get hurt."

"Hurt? How could they possibly hurt me?"

He didn't respond, lapsing into a gloom that made their last night together on the Mister Softee circuit memorable only for its awkwardness. She couldn't fathom his attitude. Just because Royce had chased him off the property as a child, and he had had a few nightmares—! He would get over it; she was used to his moods. But from then on, even on the rare nights she got home early and sat waiting on the front porch steps, she heard the ice-cream truck's music only from a distance.

However, she was now a full-fledged member of the staff of the Lockley Arms—privy, like Kip, to the bustle that made up its daily life, and even arguably superior to him in her access to the upper regions of the house. The rooms they had explored so long ago, in what seemed a different lifetime, did not match her hazy memories—except for one, the tower room on the top floor, where she encountered the graceful white canopied bed that had floated through her dreams for years, its origin forgotten until now.

Jessica, puffing and groaning as she hauled her injured bulk up the stairs, instructed her new assistant in the art of making up the rooms. Beneath her critical gaze Shelley learned to reconstruct a rumpled bed, render a bathroom spotless, polish and dust and tidy a room to perfection. Downstairs in the kitchen she was put to work scrubbing, slicing, stirring, basting, all the hundred small tasks required to produce daily meals so appetizing that she was afraid her growling stomach would be audible to the guests who laughed and chatted in the dining room on the other side of the swinging door. Unlike Kip, who was completely at ease in these surroundings, she remained shy and a little overwhelmed. He had been conditioned by Clinton-Monroe and the Glasses, but the look and feel of luxury were new to her, and the thick towels, the fragrant soap, even Jessica's copper pots and pans seemed as beautiful in their own right as the brocaded chairs, the pale marble fireplaces and muted Chineses rugs. Beneath this seductive surface lay a murmuring stillness in which the ticking of the parlor clock was the loudest sound. Shadows flickered over the creamy walls like flights of golden birds, while at the far end of a dim corridor, a window framed a glowing rectangle of sunlit green.

Busy as Shelley's new duties kept her, she still had time to notice certain small details and events at odds with the daily routine of the Arms—an elusive subtext in which she seemed to discern a hint of the mysterious realm of her childhood. On certain nights, for instance, she and Kip were dismissed early, sent home without explanation as soon as they had cleared the tables in the dining room. There were certain of her questions that went unanswered, certain rooms that were off-limits, conversations that simply stopped when she appeared. Once, answering the telephone at the front desk without realizing Miss Mansell had already picked up the call in her office, she overheard a man's voice saying, "We found two more. I thought you should know."

"When?" Miss Mansell's tone, usually so pleasant, was curt.

"This morning."

Cautiously Shelley replaced the receiver in its cradle. The inscrutable exchange was, of course, none of her business, like so much else at the Arms. She had no wish to jeopardize her new job by being too nosy, and so she did her best to suppress her curiosity and behave as if she noticed nothing.

Kip, she discovered, had no such scruples. They were spending a lot of time together these days—going back and forth to work, sharing the dining room duties, eating supper afterward in the kitchen. On their afternoon break they were allowed to use the swimming pool, a privilege they refrained from mentioning at home out of the uneasy feeling that Mother would disapprove; instead they smuggled their swimsuits across the street in secret. Was it this tacit conspiracy, so reminiscent of their childhood, that finally convinced Shelley of her twin's return? It was a dream that had tormented her so often in his absence—the dream in which he was restored to her, unchanged—that she still distrusted the reality. But on those lazy late August afternoons, while they splashed in the pool and sunned themselves side by side on canvas lounge chairs, she began, guardedly, to let herself believe.

"Psst. Shel. Don't fall asleep." The words towed her upward through depths of drowsiness. She opened her eyes, blinked and squinted. The afternoon sun was behind Kip's head and she could see only a light-spangled blur above her. "Are you starting to wonder what's going on around here?" his voice said.

A cold drip of water ran down Shelley's spine as she sat up. "What do you mean?"

"I mean the regulars. Who are they? Why do they come here? Did you ever notice that whenever they're here, we always get sent home early?" A dramatic pause. Then: "What are they doing that they don't want us to see?"

Had she ever noticed? Of course she had. And, okay, wondered if maybe the presence of those particular guests—who never signed the register but were always together, always in sole possession of the inn for the night—was in some way connected with a certain locked door on the third floor. When she had asked Jessica about it, the housekeeper had handed her a sack of potatoes to peel. Within its dark alcove the door itself was scarcely visible, but whenever Shelley passed along the hallway its bright, oiled lock offered a tempting gleam. One day she had surreptitiously tried her passkey. It hadn't worked. Turning away she had found the cat, Rowan, watching her with eyes that glowed green in the shadows.

Kip's eyes, watching her now, had a similar glint. But she wasn't about to encourage him by telling him about the door, and he wasn't listening anyway. He was saying, "I wonder if it's got anything to do with the owls dying."

"With the what?"

"Owls. Royce and I have found half a dozen dead ones this summer."

Shelley stared at him. Into her mind popped the fragment of conversation she had overheard purely by accident. *We found two more. I thought you should know.* Two more what? Dead owls? A faint shudder seized her; adroitly she transformed it into a shrug. At fifteen she had perfected an air of barely concealed boredom that drove Mother and Aunt Marty crazy, and she took refuge in it now. "So?"

Kip regarded her wisely. "So, that's not normal. Before this summer, I've never seen a single one dead. Have you?"

"Maybe Rowan's killing them," she said. "Anyway, why would it have anything to do with the regulars?"

He leaned forward. Today they had the pool to themselves, but he lowered his voice all the same. "I see their car keys, remember? Most of them carry the same little doodad on their key chains. And guess what it is."

'What?" she said unwillingly.

"An owl." Solemn elation in his face: he loved a mystery.

"That's just coincidence." But goose bumps had hatched on her skin.

"Maybe, maybe not. But I'd like to know who they are. And why they come here."

Her gaze strayed past him to the far end of the pool enclosure. There was the tall double gate with its decorative letters *L* and *A*—standing, of course, for *Lockley Arms*; what else?—guarding an unmown expanse of green shimmering with gold and purple wildflowers. No one ever went into the meadow. No one ever passed through the gate. She shifted uneasily on the damp canvas of her chair. "Whatever it is, it's none of our business. Don't you go snooping around."

"None of our business! Remember when we were kids and we sneaked into the house—how we heard that ocean sound, and saw that flash of light? Remember the fog on Halloween?

We didn't just dream that stuff. It really happened. And it's still happening. Don't you want to know what's going on?"

For an instant Shelley was submerged in the sensation of being eight or nine, swept along by his irresistible momentum—but only for an instant. She was no longer the pawn she had been in childhood; their years apart had given her a measure of independence, and she clung to it now.

"You start sticking your nose where it doesn't belong, and sooner or later you're going to get caught, Kip." When he said nothing she pressed on. "Look, this is a good job, we're making good money here. Why risk getting fired? It's not worth it." It was startling how much her voice, making this sharp and sensible speech, sounded like Mother's. Good girl, her conscience said approvingly. But her heart was pounding.

We didn't just dream that stuff. It really happened. And it's still happening. Don't you want to know what's going on?

In her memory a cat's eye closed and opened in a slow jade wink.

Chapter 12

By that time August was nearly over. School hovered on the horizon—Kip would be a sophomore at Green Hollow High, Shelley a junior—and the twins found themselves reluctant to accept the fact that their association with the Arms was drawing to an end. Yet it was only a summer job. Jessica's ankle was nearly healed; she would soon be able to tackle the stairs again, and in the cool weather the grounds would no longer need the constant attention required during the summer months. The swimming pool would be drained and covered, the flower beds turned and the pots of geraniums brought inside as the place readied itself for the seasonal onslaught of foliage-viewers and skiers.

"But won't they still need us in the dining room?" Kip said. The two of them were holding a conference about this crisis. "And who's going to park the cars?"

"Whoever parked them before they hired you." Shelley was plunged in gloom by the prospect of forfeiting her status as a member of the exclusive world within the boundary of the hedge. However vigorously she might insist that the salary was what mattered to her, however hard she tried to be her mother's practical and sensible daughter, it wasn't the money she would miss. The hours she spent in the gracious white house enclosed by its green wall of leaves formed a heady antidote to the dullness of her ordinary existence. Deny it as she might to Kip and even at times to herself, she was irresistibly drawn by the suggestion of secrets underlying the household's orderly business. *The regulars. Why do they come here? What are they doing that they don't want us to see?* There was even a kind of dark thrill in the suggestion of a link between these mysterious guests and the gruesome business of the dying owls.

"Let's ask her to keep us on," Kip was saying. "On a part-time basis. After school, weekends. It's worth a try. The worst she can do is say no."

Shelley looked sideways at him. Why didn't he like Miss Mansell? He'd never actually said so—but from the morning of his job interview at the Arms, his attitude toward their employer had been a puzzle. He never said her name if he could help it: just "she" and "her," and if she came up in conversation he changed the subject. This apparent aversion bewildered Shelley, who for her own part was intensely curious about the young mistress of the Arms. She liked encountering Miss Mansell in the halls or on the stairs, receiving a smile and a glance from those unsettling gray eyes, so lively and at the same time so unfathomable. Who was she? A distant relative of the Lockleys, to whom they had left the Arms in their will: surely that explanation was sufficient. But there was the deference Royce and Jessica showed her, and the roomful of guests raising their glasses in salute. *To the Lady.*

The Lady. To Shelley, Miss Mansell's clipped speech, while not quite an English accent, hinted at a connection with that fabled island. An easy authority marked her manner, an air of being accustomed to giving orders and having them instantly obeyed, and Shelley pictured her in a velvet riding habit on the steps of some gaunt gray castle, giving last-minute instructions to the butler while a groom held her horse. *The Lady.* Was Miss Mansell an aristocrat living incognito in their midst, posing as a humble inkeeper for reasons that were no doubt sinister and/or romantic? "You do the talking," she told Kip. "You've been there longer than I have."

We chose the last morning of August to present ourselves at the door of her office, a spacious room opening off the antechamber that housed the registration desk. It was early, quiet except for the birds singing in the garden outside the open French doors. Seated at her desk with a pencil and an open ledger, Miss Mansell beckoned us inside. "What's up?"

Kip jammed his hands in his pockets and then, as if it was something he'd been told a hundred times not to do, took them out again and let them hang by his sides. I saw the fingers twitching a little. "We were just wondering. If you . . . if we . . . if maybe we could keep on working here once school starts. Sort of part-time. Evenings, weekends, something like that."

When he had finished Miss Mansell said nothing, only twisted the pencil in her fingers and looked at him while he fidgeted. Her hair was drawn back in its elegant, complex knot and she wore a loose blouse the color of lilac; I could see the silvery glint of the chain around her neck. Kip was red-faced and scowling, and I wondered what had happened to the savoir faire that had won Kate's admiration. If he had acted this way in his original interview it was a miracle he'd ever gotten the job. At last Miss Mansell said softly, "It wouldn't leave you much time for your friends."

He shrugged. "We'll manage."

"And your schoolwork?"

"What about it?"

I saw her blink. "You'd have to make sure you didn't neglect it."

"We won't."

She stood up and turned to look out at the garden behind her. Had his rudeness succeeded in annoying her at last? Beyond the French doors, leaves and sunlight shifted in a ceaseless play of gold and green. There was a clock somewhere behind us and I was preternaturally aware of its measured, hypnotic tick. I remembered a roomful of raised wineglasses: *To the Lady.* Whatever was happening here, Miss Mansell was at the center of it. I fixed my eyes on her back and held my breath while Kip stared down at the floor.

Finally she turned to face us. Even against the sun-dazzle from the garden I could see her frowning, and inside me rose the dismal certainty that she was going to say no. She was still fidgeting with the pencil; all at once it escaped and rolled across the desk, and as she leaned over to retrieve it the silver medallion slipped out of her blouse, twisting on its chain, glinting in the oblique light. For a fraction of a second it swung to face us and for the first time I saw the design engraved on it: a five-pointed star inside a circle. Beyond it I couldn't help seeing the shadowy cleft between her breasts within the loose neck of her blouse. Embarrassed, I averted my eyes—and a moment later heard her say, to my astonishment: "Well, if it's all right with your parents, we can certainly use you here."

It was all right with our parents, or at least with Mother. Dad raised a whole series of objections that she knocked down like ninepins, until eventually he must have seen it was no use fighting her. She talked a lot about the money, about our being able to put some away for college, even though it was obvious the money meant less to her than our connection with an establishment she regarded as the epitome of glamor and success. Once school began, our hours were cut back to evenings and weekends. On arriving at the Arms we were regularly quizzed, usually by Jessica but once in a while by Miss Mansell herself, as to whether we had completed our homework.

It infuriated Kip. "They act like we're in the third grade! Always nagging us!"

"They just don't want us flunking out of school. If we make all A's on our first report cards, they'll probably get off our backs."

He snorted. "I could make all A's even if I *never* did my homework."

The implied sneer at beloved old Green Hollow High might have stung if the whole business of school had not become slightly unreal to me. I went through the motions of studying, socializing, participating in the classes and activities, but the world seemed to snap into focus only at the moment I crossed the boundary of the Lockley Arms. I felt alive then, awake in a way that rendered the rest of my existence flat in comparison. Years later, at a performance of Gluck's *Orfeo,* my heart was wrenched by the first hesitant, wondering notes of Orpheus's entry into the realm of the blessed spirits, as the words of his aria—*Che puro ciel, che chiaro sol*—returned me for an instant to that place where everything seemed more vivid than life. Colors were brighter there, sounds and smells sharper, the sky indeed a more poignant blue beyond the fiery autumn trees.

All that fall the owls continued to die, their small feathered corpses appearing with increasing frequency, dotting the streets and yellowing lawns of the village like the fruit of some macabre harvest. Everyone wondered about the cause of the blight, and a man came from a state agency in Albany to investigate, but departed without offering an opinion. Shelley was glad she had glimpsed the pitiful little bundles only at a distance. In her memory a voice on the telephone murmured, *We found two more. I thought you should know.*

With the coming of cool weather Kip was put to work raking leaves and splitting wood for the fireplaces. There were savory stews and hearty soups on the menu now, corn fritters for breakfast instead of the summer's blueberry-buttermilk pancakes. Hot spiced cider was served in the parlor before dinner as hikers joined the antiquers—a younger, rowdier crowd who shouted their laughter and banged out bawdy songs on the upright piano in the parlor. The inn was busier, the dining room packed to capacity every night, and in the hectic atmosphere of the kitchen, as they dodged out of one another's way, their voices raised over the noise of clanging pans and running water, the staff of the Arms drew together into a close-knit, smoothly functioning unit.

Once dinner was over they could relax. The mistress of the house began to join her employees for their late-night suppers in the kitchen, and her presence transformed these meals into occasions of festivity. Shelley had never laughed so much in her life. Not only at the merciless raillery between Jessica and Kip, but at Snow's wry anecdotes about the trials of inkeeping, and even at Royce, who—pale eyes crinkling at the corners, his gestures so expressive that no one missed the words—pantomimed a tale of having surprised a guest in the act of eating the roses in the garden. In this intimate atmosphere it seemed natural for the twins to begin calling their employer by her given name. The hanging lamp with its copper shade illuminated only the surface of the round table and left the rest of the room in shadow, as if enclosing them all in a bright bubble of banter and laughter.

The awkwardness that had afflicted Kip in Snow's presence gradually dissipated over the course of those evenings until he became by far their brightest light—charming, confident, once more a model of savoir faire. Everything about him shone, from the casual elegance of his table manners to the burnish of lamplight on his dark hair. There were times when Shelley watched him in wonder, and times when she caught Snow watching him too. It almost looked as if, now that they had set aside their assigned roles as yard boy and employer, Snow was uncertain what to think of him. At moments she seemed slightly off balance, less sure of herself than usual, her confidence diminishing as his expanded. Shelley would see bemusement take over her face; the focus of those clear gray eyes would drift—and when he said something clever and amusing that made the others burst out laughing, Snow's smile would come a beat too late, as if her thoughts had been far away.

It would have been impossible to describe these evenings to

her friends, and Shelley didn't try. She suspected that to them she presented a picture of someone who had become a little too serious, a little too responsible for their taste, which quite naturally ran to football games, clothes, and boys. She couldn't pretend to share these interests, not even the last. Benjy was still cool to her (with Mister Softee in hibernation he was working full time at the E-Z Stop, where Charlie Dietz, the owner, had recently promoted him to cashier), and the boys at school struck her as boring and shallow. Besides, at the age of fifteen she had still not begun her menses, and this fact was always present, a grim inscrutable cloud at the back of her thoughts. What was wrong with her? The idea of discussing her deficiency with anyone was too humiliating even to contemplate, and so she kept it to herself.

Only at the Arms was she able to forget it completely, distracted by more compelling matters. She kept a covert but increasingly close watch on the "regulars"—the owners of the gray Mercedes, black Hudson Hornet, yellow Triumph, black Jaguar, dark green DeSoto Fire Dome, and white Volkswagen Beetle. It wasn't that these were the only people to visit the Lockley Arms more than once. But they came at least once a month, sometimes twice; they always came at the same time—and on those occasions there were never any other guests.

For these gatherings the tables were put together banquet-style, and Miss Mansell always joined the feast. Clearly these people were friends of hers, but why she should reserve the inn exclusively for them on certain nights—nights that followed no apparent pattern—remained a mystery. Was it some kind of club, its symbol the silver owl most of them sported on their key chains? Were its members concerned by the inexplicable plague that continued to afflict their mascot bird? But the snatches of conversation the twins overheard, on their way in and out of the dining room, never so much as hinted at the answers to these questions.

There were ten "regulars"—three couples and four single people. Kip's favorite among them was a tall, intense woman whose short hair clung to her skull in a flaming red cap. She wore a lot of jewelry, her throat and wrists sparkling with light and color in the candlelit dining room. Because she owned the black Jaguar V-12, the twins called her the Jaguar Lady. Shelley found herself partial to a handsome young man with black hair and a clipped mustache and beard, whom she dubbed the Prince. His loud, exultant laugh rang out again and again during those lively dinners, and hearing it she would imagine him with his head thrown back, lips showing red in his dark beard.

But by far the most exotic member of the company was a black man. Although he would have caused a sensation in Green Hollow, he usually arrived and departed after dark, his little Triumph slipping quickly in and out of the driveway, and it is unlikely anyone outside the boundaries of the Arms ever knew he was there. He was very handsome, even more so than the Prince, as Shelley came to see once she grew accustomed to his color. But the twins never mentioned his intriguing presence, or that of his friends, to their parents or anyone else: Snow had made it clear she required absolute discretion on the part of all employees, and any violation of this rule would mean a swift end to their association with the Lockley Arms.

So, except to each other, they kept their mouths shut—never volunteering information to their friends and family, deftly evading idle questions like the ones Kate asked when Shelley stopped by the antique shop for an occasional catch-up visit. "What kind of people stay there? All rolling in money, I bet. Big-city types? Anybody famous?"

To such queries Shelley gave only evasive, monosyllabic replies, and the subject was soon put aside as Kate dragged out her latest flea-market treasure to be admired.

Kip always let me know when the regulars had gathered. With a little jerk of his head toward the parking lot when he came into the kitchen to clean up and dress for dinner, he would indicate that the familiar cars were assembled, the yellow Triumph with its Massachusetts plates always arriving last. And instantly I would sense—or did I imagine it?—a spark in the air, a crackle like electricity moving through the house, connecting these mysterious guests one to another like the strands of an invisible web. In the dining room, Royce would have moved the tables together to form a single long one, and when I lit the candles along its snowy cloth their flames would stand higher than usual. Night would fall more quickly outside the windows, accentuating the warmth and color inside, and the evening would unfold in a dazzle of festivity that filled me, just catching its oblique reflection, with suppressed excitement. Outwardly I continued to insist to Kip that I wasn't interested in any secrets the Arms might harbor, that it wasn't worth risking my lucrative job to discover what they might be—but I doubt he was fooled by this pose of indifference. Surely he saw, long before I did, that we had already joined forces on what was to be the greatest of our adventures, and the last.

Chapter 13

And then—against Shelley's better judgment and in shameful contradiction of all her lofty statements to Kip about safeguarding their precious jobs—she snooped.

It wasn't a planned thing: just a chance presented and seized without thinking. Snooping was the last thing on her mind. On the contrary, she was hard at work, removing the winter bed linens from a cedar cabinet in the attic, loading them into a basket to be toted down to the cellar for laundering. As the cabinet emptied, she happened to notice a square, shadowy shape at the back of one high shelf.

A box. She had to stand on tiptoe to drag it toward her. As it came into the light she saw it was carved with an unusual pattern of interlocking fish and serpents, fuzzily visible beneath layer of dust. Not a large box, maybe ten inches by twelve, and eight deep. It was fastened with a metal clasp, but not locked.

From the effort it had taken to drag it forward, she could tell it wasn't empty.

Carefully she lifted it down from the shelf and set it on the floor.

"Kip. You're not going to believe what I found this morning."

The twins stood on the dark sidewalk while a shadowy procession of trick-or-treaters trooped past them. They had been told they would not be needed at the Arms this evening. Instead they were headed for a Halloween party at Jennifer's—but as they left the house, the sight of the Arms across the street had brought them to a halt. They knew the regulars were there tonight, and this knowledge seemed to lend the windows, lit behind drawn curtains, the same cryptic threat and promise as the wild, gusty night around them. Dead leaves swirled in an antic dance through the darkness; up and down the street the carved pumpkins on front porches looked sinister one moment, merry the next, as their candles alternately guttered and flared. A cold current of air found its way through the buttons of Shelley's coat. "What?" Kip was saying. "What'd you find?"

Hesitation was an afterthought, striking her only as she knelt on the floor in front of the box—a reluctant awareness that it was none of her business, that she really shouldn't look inside. But her hands were already undoing the catch and the lid came up eagerly, releasing a gentle, faded fragrance. Several objects—a wreath of withered flowers, a piece of rose quartz, a pair of tiny slippers fashioned of glinting brocade—lay on top of a picture in a tarnished frame. Shelley glanced at each before placing it on the floor beside the box. The framed picture turned out to be a photograph, but as she picked it up for a closer look, her attention was caught by something underneath it, flattened by its weight.

A White Sox baseball cap.

Was it—? Setting the picture aside, she touched the cap with unbelieving fingers. Felt the stiffness of the cheap cloth, looked inside to make sure. There it was, Mother's handwriting on the leather sweatband: the final proof. *Kipling Davies.*

So someone had found it after all. And said nothing, only kept it all these years, locked away like a treasure in a magic box. Someone—but who? Whose box was this? The wreath of flowers, the tiny slippers: a woman's keepsakes. Would the photograph provide an answer? She examined it. The three people pictured were young, far younger than she had ever seen them, but she recognized them all. There were the Lockleys, with their elegant patrician faces and pale eyes, and with them a younger and drastically slimmer Jessica. They were out in the herb garden, the two women seated side by side on the stone bench. Behind them stood Everett Lockley, one hand resting on Emma's shoulder, a faint smile on his lips. In Emma's lap was a tabby cat that looked exactly—*exactly*—like Rowan.

Of course it couldn't be. Emma Lockley could not be much past thirty in the picture, and the cat in her lap must be long dead. It was only some ancestor of Rowan's—and yet Shelley couldn't stop staring at the picture, and as she stared she went on absently rubbing the bill of Kip's baseball cap between her thumb and forefinger.

The twins stood beneath the shaking trees, oblivious of the passing trick-or-treaters, while Shelley talked. Not just about the box and its contents, but about the exchange she had overheard on the telephone, the locked door on the third floor, the interrupted conversations when she entered a room. It was a relief to confess it all, as if the last barrier between Kip and her had finally crumbled. As if they were truly twins once more. "How could that cat look so much like Rowan?" she finished breathlessly. "And how come they never said anything about finding your hat?" But Kip only met her questions with one of his own.

"Why'd they give us the night off tonight?"

What are they doing that they don't want us to see?

By the time they got to the Halloween party it was well underway. Jenny's parents had fled upstairs to their bedroom and shut their door against the insistent rock-and-roll music, and with their abdication things were loosening up. Some people were dancing, a few were horsing around an apple-bobbing tub in the kitchen, and several couples were necking side by side on the sofa in the darkened den. A steady stream of guests passed in and out through the sliding door to the back patio, where a pint of whiskey was being passed around. Faces were red, voices slurred and laughter loud. In the middle of the living room floor Jenny and her boyfriend shuffled together in a dreamy slow dance to the lively beat of "Monster Mash."

A crowd of sophomores fastened on Kip and bore him away, leaving Shelley to face Rick Hoffey, a senior with a square blond head who sat behind her in math class. He leaned close to her and she got a whiff of whiskey breath. "Hiya, Shelley. Wanna dance?"

"No thanks." She ducked past him and headed back to the kitchen, the only part of the house where there was any degree of light. In the refrigerator she found a Coke and poured it into a glass, then returned to the living room. Mark Townsend, captain of the basketball team, swayed up to her and produced a silver flask from his jacket pocket.

"Freshen your drink, lady?" He tipped the flask into her Coke, clinked it against the side of the glass and winked at her. "Cheers." He put the flask to his lips and upended it.

Shelley took a cautious sip of her doctored drink. It tasted all right. As time went on and she took more sips, the party began to seem like more fun. She danced with a couple of people, caught sight of Kip coming in from the patio with a flush on his cheeks, then lost him again. Eventually she wandered into the den.

It was dark in there, the only light the flickering television screen showing a vampire movie in honor of the holiday. No one was watching it. I stood woozily transfixed as Dracula, dressed in a flowing cape, crossed the rooftops to peer through a window at a girl in a negligee. She sat brushing her hair in front of a mirror, but of course she didn't see Dracula behind her because vampires don't cast reflections. He opened the window with his clawlike nails and stepped softly into the room. I felt my heartbeat quicken.

From the darkness at my back came a deep groan. Luckily I had already abandoned my drink somewhere, or I would certainly have dropped it then. I spun around, nearly losing my balance, and squinted into the TV-lit depths of the den to see not Dracula poised to spring, but a pair of bodies entangled on the sofa in the shadows behind me. I don't know who they boy was: all I saw of him was a set of bare buttocks above his lowered trousers. But the face visible over his shoulder was Lisa's. Her eyes met mine briefly in the poor light before she closed them again, putting her hands on the back of the boy's head in a curiously protective gesture. I stood stupefied a moment longer before stumbling out of the room and pulling the door shut behind me.

Shock had dissipated most of my alcohol haze, leaving vague nausea in its wake. Making my way through the slumped and staggering bodies in the living room, I reached the sliding door to the patio and there rested my forehead against the cold glass, concentrating on the bleak windblown beauty of the night outside. It was late, nearly midnight; the moon rode high in the sky. Across the yard, dead leaves blew wildly around the rickety wooden arbor leading to Mrs. Moss's beloved rose garden. As the din of the party swelled behind me I felt a suffocating pang of loss. Tonight was Halloween—of all nights the most entrancing to me, the very word once able to send shivers up my spine—yet as I grew older I could feel the mystery slipping away, dwindling year by year until at last it would become only the ghost of a memory, wailing silently in the dark. And standing there I thought I would give anything to rekindle the magic, if only I knew how. I watched the leaves lift in a whirling funnel.

Shhh—shhh— Like a stream of cold air penetrating the glass, a sudden chill tightened my skin. That eerie whispering—only dead leaves, of course, blowing across the flagstones of the patio, but it sounded unnervingly like someone trying to say my name. My breath had fogged the glass. I used the sleeve of my sweater to wipe it clear—

And saw a robed, hooded shape standing beneath the arbor across the yard.

One moment it was there, an apparition like a sinister monk out of a tale by Poe—the next, it had disappeared into the intricate pattern of shadows made by the withered vines on the arbor stirring in the wind. Shadows. That was all. Because why would someone stand outside Jenny's house on this cold night, watching the lit windows? Yet as I stood staring at the spot, the cold certainty grew inside me that I was being observed in turn. My heart began to pound. Only imagination—and then again, among the ragged shadows beneath the arbor, I caught the suggestion of an anonymous human shape dark as the starless night. Not moving. Just—watching.

Shhh—shhh—Shhhelley—

Only a fragile sheet of glass separated me from that whispered summons. A fit of trembling shook me from head to foot. Beneath the arbor, across a mere half dozen yards of lawn, the dancing shadows alternately concealed, revealed, concealed, revealed—

"Shelley?" Jenny's warm hand on my arm made me jump. "Come on, we're about to play the fortune-telling game. Golly, your skin's like ice!"

As she pulled me away from the sliding door I looked back across the moonlit yard, but there was no one visible beneath the arbor now—only the shadows of dead vines shaking in the chill October wind.

Chapter 14

Yet that eerie encounter was driven almost completely out of my thoughts by another one that followed close on its heels. And that was my encounter with Larry.

Larry wasn't a regular, just one of the dozens of skiers who came and went over the holiday season, leaving their beds in shambles and their wet towels on the bathroom floors. Blond and husky, red-faced except for a pale ring around his eyes from his skiing goggles, he had come with two friends, a man and a woman. Overhearing their conversation at breakfast on Saturday morning (they had arrived late the night before), I gathered he had invited a female companion who had canceled at the last minute. The others were trying to cheer him up. "Come on, Larry," I heard the woman say. "It's not like she hasn't pulled this stunt before. To hell with her. She's not worth feeling bad about."

Their day on the slopes must have wound up at a tavern, because when I saw them that night at dinner they were wreathed in a jovial alcoholic cloud. As I brought the food and wine they had ordered, Larry eyed his plate appreciatively. "Boy oh boy, I'm starving. That looks good, honey. And so do you." He winked at me, getting an uproarious laugh from his friends, and when I leaned forward to fill his wineglass, he put his hand on my behind.

It was there and gone so quickly I didn't have time to react, except with an internal spasm of revulsion that knotted my stomach and loosened my knees. By some miracle my hand stayed steady and I didn't spill the wine I was pouring—but I could feel my face burning, and a sickening weakness in all my limbs. The swinging door to the kitchen seemed a hundred miles away, its outline blurring through tears as I crossed the noisy dining room. I was dimly aware of Kip hurrying past me with a tray, of someone at Table Six asking for more bread—all of it overshadowed by that revolting touch. It had lasted only an instant, yet I could still feel it: a lewd, furtive exploration by a drunken stranger who did not even know my name. Furiously I blinked back my tears. It would be far more humiliating to admit to Kip or Jessica what had happened than to just grit my teeth and stay out of Larry's reach for the remainder of the meal.

When I entered the kitchen Jessica was busy at the stove; whatever my face may have showed just then, she wasn't looking. But Royce was. He sat at the table, an intricate cat's cradle suspended between his hands, and I saw the string drop into a limp tangle as he took in my expression. His pale brows rose in a question, which I ignored. I got a basket of bread for Table Six and went back into the fray. I suppose somewhere at the back of my mind was a childish fantasy of Royce storming into the dining room, yanking my tormentor out of his chair and hurling him through a window into the cold December night. But Royce did not appear, and the next time I returned to the kitchen he was nowhere to be seen. I didn't have time to think about it; most of the diners were ready for dessert, and Kip and I literally had our hands full.

Larry and his party were still working on their main course, and he signaled to me as I passed their table. My heart sank. I tried to stand out of reach, but a man was getting up from the next table, and as I moved out of his way I felt Larry's long arm clumsily encircle my hips and draw me close to his chair. "How 'bout I have you for dessert, sweetie pie?"

With his free hand he was finishing what was on his plate, shoveling in huge bites of rare beef as he leered up at me. Chortling to his companions: "Maybe it's a good thing ole Donna stood me up. Maybe I can make some time with our cute little waitress here." When I tried to twist free his arm tightened like a vise. "Wassamatter, honey? You shy?"

His fingers had begun to caress my thigh with a suggestive rhythm. To my horror I could not move or speak; I was gripped by a kind of dreamy revulsion, paralyzed as if by a poisonous bite or sting. I looked at the woman sitting with him, thinking that surely she would help me, tell him to stop, but she was as drunk and laughing as the men. I dragged my heavy eyes away from their faces, and that was when I saw Snow.

She was across the room, standing just inside the swinging door to the kitchen. She was staring straight at us—staring at Larry, I realized, her eyes so dark they looked black. As I watched, she lifted her left hand to her throat.

Beside me, Larry made a gagging, gurgling noise like a monster in a horror movie. His arm dropped off me and he grabbed his neck with both hands, his face turning purple and his eyes beginning to bulge. His woman friend shrieked, "Oh my God! He's choking! Somebody help him!"

Several people jumped up but no one seemed to know quite what to do. I stumbled back from the table in a daze, trying to catch sight of Snow through the commotion—unable at first, and then seeing her in the same spot, by the swinging door. As I watched, she let her hand drop from her throat, and exactly at that moment Larry made a violent retching noise and spat out a gigantic piece of beef onto the table.

In the aftermath of the excitement, as the dining room gradually returned to normal and Kip and I served dessert and coffee (Larry and his friends, sobered by the choking incident, had retired upstairs to their rooms), I went over in my mind what had happened. Larry had been so busy tormenting me that he had neglected to chew his meat properly, and a piece had gotten stuck in his throat. That was all. I could imagine a scenario in which Royce had reported the signs of my distress to Snow, who had come to the dining room to see what was wrong. Yet from there my imagination took a ridiculous, impossible leap. I kept seeing Snow raise her hand to her throat and hearing Larry make that grotesque choking sound. Seeing her drop her hand and watching him spew out the offending piece of meat. And remembering the way her eyes had looked as she stared at him. Black, without a spark of light.

I told myself that in the flurry and confusion I must have reversed the order in which I had actually seen events take place. Larry had choked and Snow's hand had gone to her throat in unconscious empathy, just as it must have dropped in relief as soon as he coughed up the meat that was strangling him. The look in her eyes had been not enmity but shock. Yet that was not how I remembered it. I daresay, given time, I would have managed to rewrite my version of the incident to fit reason and common sense. Things happening as they did, however, I never got the chance.

Kip and I left quite late that night. Royce did not reappear, nor did Snow. We helped Jessica wash up and were rewarded with a double helping of bread pudding, over which the three of us discussed the choking incident. I saw no reason to mention what Larry had done to me; the whole incident had been both frightening and disgusting and I just wanted to forget it.

We bundled ourselves into our coats for the short trip home, calling good night to Jessica as we trudged beneath the porte cochere. Except for the driveway, which Kip had shoveled clear that afternoon, everything was blanketed in snow, and as we drew level with the front of the house I stopped to admire the sight. The windows cast golden shadows on the white lawn; fantastic icicles fringed the gables and both porches, festooning the house with frozen lace. Above the roofline, cold blue stars pricked the dark sky. Kip kept walking.

"Kip, wait."

"Come on. I'm cold."

Something moved: a shadow in the overhang of the porch. A burly figure lurched down the front steps and across the snow-covered lawn in my direction, its breath steaming the air. "Hi there, sweetheart! Off work now, huh? Lemme show you how to party."

I took a step back, but Larry had already covered the distance between us, leaving a trail of smeared footprints in the snow. He stood swaying; I was afraid he was going to fall on me. "Kip," I said in a small voice.

Kip's footsteps made a crisp sound on the driveway as he turned and walked back. "She doesn't want you to show her anything." His tone of voice, superiority mixed with contempt, must have been something he had learned from the Glasses. "She doesn't want anything to do with you."

This ringing announcement, some degrees colder than the wintry air, managed to pierce Larry's drunken haze. He peered at Kip, a nasty look slowly overspreading his face. "Who the fuck're you?"

"I'm her brother," Kip said. He folded his arms and glared at Larry. I grabbed his sleeve. "Come on, let's go."

"Fuck that, baby," Larry said. "I been waitin' a long time out here in the cold for you." His hand closed on my arm just as Kip shoved him hard in the chest. Larry staggered back, taking me with him, and both of us nearly fell. He released me, swung at Kip and missed, and in horror I saw him cock back his arm for another try. He was drunk and clumsy but he was a man, a big one, and Kip was a boy. I tried to scream but the sound snagged in my lungs. And then, beyond their two mismatched figures, I saw someone standing on the porch, silhouetted against the open front door.

Snow. The sight of her gave me a flash of déjà vu, but this time she did not touch her throat. Both hands were in front of her, held slightly out from her body at the level of her waist, and this is what I saw.

Between her hands there was a pulsating ball of white light swimming with sparks of blue. As I watched she opened her hands and, with a crackling hiss, a dazzling stream of light shot out from her fingers toward Larry and Kip. I am only saying what I saw: a thick rope of light snaking through the air like water from a hose, its flickering radiance reflected by the snow beneath. It struck Larry, and for an instant his whole figure was outlined in electric blue. He reeled and tottered and fell on his back in the snow. I thought he was dead. Then he groaned, and a resounding belch floated up into the freezing air.

Kip and I stood looking at Snow. She looked back at us. Finally she wrapped both arms around herself, as if feeling the cold for the first time, and said mildly: "From now on, when this gentleman calls for a reservation, let's tell him we're full."

As if nothing more needed to be said, she turned back into the house, while Kip and I remained motionless in the cold night. For me the relief of seeing my tormentor laid low was mixed with a troubling, elusive sense of familiarity. A still figure lying in the snow . . . Kip touched my shoulder. "Come on, let's go home."

As we reached to foot of the driveway, we glanced back to see Royce heave Larry's inert bulk over his shoulder and carry him inside.

Chapter 15

Mother, Dad and Marty had already gone to bed. Upstairs, Kip beckoned Shelley into his room, closed the door and turned to face her, his eyes bright. "You saw that? You saw what she did?"

Shelley recalled a stream of light shooting through the air to envelop Larry's bulky shape in a bluish dazzle. She hadn't been able to speak since it happened; now her mouth felt numb and it was hard to form the words. "You mean . . . that light?"

Kip nodded and she whispered, "What was it?"

Instead of answering, he went to his dresser and rummaged briefly in a bottom drawer. When he turned, there was a book in his hands. "Do you know what a coven is?" he asked her.

"A what?"

"A coven." He held out the book; she peered at the title. *Witchcraft: A History & Guide.* Beneath the words was a picture—a symbol. With a shock Shelley recognized it.

A five-pointed star inside a circle.

A five-pointed star inside a circle. Little silver medallion twisting on its chain. *Witchcraft.* Her heart began a slow, hard beat of knowing even while her brain still resisted. Kip sat down on his bed and motioned impatiently and she took a seat beside him, watching him flip through the pages until he found what he wanted. "Here. Take a look at this."

Shelley edged closer, wrinkling her nose at the musty smell characteristic of old books. She didn't know what she expected. Certainly not what she saw—a drawing of a circle divided in half. The top portion was light, the bottom shaded. *The Wheel of the Year,* read the caption beneath. "It's a calendar," Kip was saying. "The dark half's winter, the light half's summer. And these"—his finger traced a series of lines radiating out from the circle's center—"are the dates of the traditional witches' Sabbats." As Shelley stared blankly at him he said, "That's when the regulars come."

She looked back at the drawing. Each spoke of the wheel was labeled. *Candlemas. Spring Equinox. Beltane. Summer Solstice. Lammas. Harvest Home. Samhain. Yule.* "Are you sure? Maybe it's . . . just a coincidence." A token protest, forced past her thumping heartbeat. *That's when the regulars come.* The design on the book's cover—the star inside the circle—dangling from a chain around Snow's neck. *Witchcraft.*

Kip was shaking his head. "It's no coincidence. I've been watching them since last summer, and everything fits, all of it. The same ten guests are there every time. Those ten guests, and no others." He closed the book abruptly. "And that's not all. Remember the first night you worked there, when they made that toast to Snow in the dining room—when they called her 'the Lady'? Shelley, the head of a witches' coven is traditionally called the Lady."

Shelley swallowed. Intriguing secrets were one thing—but a *witches' coven*? "Look," Kip was saying. "We're not talking about the kind of witch who wears a pointed hat and rides around on a broomstick. Witchcraft is an ancient pagan religion that got mostly stamped out in the Middle Ages by the Christian establishment. But it managed to stay alive by going underground, and now it's starting to come back. It's all about understanding the secrets of nature, celebrating the seasons—"

"And worshiping Satan," Shelley said.

"They *don't* worship Satan. That's just something the early Christian church made up to give them a bad name. Witches don't even have a devil. They don't believe in sin. It's okay to do anything you want, so long as it doesn't hurt anyone else. That's their law: *An' it harm none, do what thou wilt.*"

It was the first of the many times I was to hear that seductive and deceptively simple phrase, but I was too distracted just then to take it in. I stared at him suspiciously. "How come you know so much about all this?"

"It's in this book. Frog gave it to me. He's read a lot about witchcraft. He's interested in witches because they do magic. He has a real thing about magic."

"Magic?" I said.

"Focused energy. That's earth magic. We all have it inside us. But she knows how to use it. You saw what she did to Larry." Awe in his voice, and something else. Envy.

"He was bothering me before, in the dining room" I said. "Kip? You know—when he choked on his food? I think she made it happen."

"Good for her."

Alarm broke through my confusion and I clutched the sleeve of his sweater. "People can't do that stuff. It's not possible. *It couldn't have happened.*"

He pried the fabric from my grasp. "Well, it did. And people *can* do that stuff. Believe me, it was peanuts for her. She could have killed him. But she didn't, because it's against their code to do that. All she did was neutralize him, to keep him from hurting us."

I closed my eyes, picturing Snow on the porch, the ball of white light between her hands unfurling suddenly in a blinding stream. The image was too disturbing and I opened my eyes again. "Who *is* she?"

"I told you. She's a witch. What I think is that the Lockleys must have been the coven leaders, and when they died she became the new head of it. There are supposed to be thirteen in a coven, including the leader, but they only have eleven. That means they still haven't replaced the Lockleys."

"What abcut Royce and Jessica? Aren't they part of it?"

"I think they're sympathizers, or believers, but they don't belong to the coven. A coven's a pretty serious thing, like a priesthood."

I pointed at the circled star on the cover of the book. "And that? What is it?"

"A pentacle. The symbol of witchcraft."

"But what's it mean?"

Kip shrugged. "It's a symbol. It means a lot of things."

"It's on that medallion Snow wears," I said. "I saw it once."

He nodded. "She trusts us. I think, if we asked her the right way—Shelley, she might let us join."

"Join the *coven*?" I meant to laugh, but it came out sounding like some small animal's death shriek. "I don't want to join it!"

"Why not?" His eyes were bright. "I told you, they don't hurt anyone. Their magic is positive. It's good. Can't you feel it, whenever you're there?"

I started to shake my head. Then I thought of the radiant timelessness that lay, indeed like a spell, over that place in which I felt myself suspended like an embroidered figure in a bright and tranquil tapestry. Yet behind this picture was a darker one—of locked doors and dead owls, mysterious gatherings and a rope of blue-white light that could knock a grown man unconscious. A grown man, or . . . I thought of another, smaller shape lying motionless in a white field. I had wondered many times if Kip's recollection of that afternoon had been obliterated by his long period of unconsciousness. Now I said hesitantly, "Do you remember the day you got sick?"

Slowly his gaze found mine. "You mean when I tried to make that snow angel?"

"Then you do remember."

He nodded. "The Lockleys must have put a protection spell around the meadow to keep people out."

A protection spell. Maybe just an impulse at the back of your mind, taking root as you become aware of it—a sense that you shouldn't blunder into a place where you don't belong. A sudden reluctance to mar the perfection of a snowy field glowing in the last rays of the winter sun . . . and a brash little boy, determined as any other of his kind to leave his mark, had felt that natural impulse die away. Had been about to close the gate again, until—

A qualm went through me. He had changed his mind. He had been about to close the gate, and then—

(La, la . . .)

That moment had altered the course of his life, and mine.

I thought of the Lockleys. Their financial generosity during

Kip's illness, Emma Lockley's visit to our house. I remembered her violet eyes. The little bag she had tucked beneath his mattress, the finger she had touched to her lips, inviting me to share her secret . . . *A witches' coven.* All at once the lamp beside Kip's bed seemed small and dim, a feeble point of light in a night whose uncharted darkness shrouded not only the external world, but my inner one as well.

Chapter 16

Over the next few days it became clear that Kip was entirely serious about joining the coven. Shelley still found it difficult to swallow the idea that witches actually existed—and at the Lockley Arms, of all places! A respected, successful establishment, its mistress young and attractive . . . the notion was fantastic, absurd. Nor did the regulars fit her vague preconceptions of what a coven ought to be. Didn't a coven consist of ugly, warty old women on broomsticks? The regulars were sophisticated, witty, elegant—and half of them were men. Kip claimed that the term "witch" was correct for both sexes, that there was no such term as "warlock" in the practice of this pagan religion—but she still found herself squirming when he referred to the handsome, strapping Prince as a witch.

Undaunted, Kip reeled off facts to support his claim. There were the silver owls—a bird sacred to Hecate, Goddess of witches. The pentacle Snow wore around her neck. The bolt of white light she had hurled at Larry. He brought out the desk calendar on which he had been keeping track of the regulars' visits. Circled in red, the dates corresponded exactly to those of the traditional witches' Sabbats.

"There are four major ones—Lammas, Samhain (that's Halloween), Candlemas and Beltane—and four minor ones—the summer and winter solstices, the spring and fall equinoxes. Their year really begins with the winter solstice and ends at Halloween."

Shelley saw additional red circles sprinkling the months here and there. "What about these other dates?"

"Oh, those are the Esbats. Their monthly meetings. They hold those on the nights when there's a full moon."

Her nerves crimped. "And what happens then?"

"They raise a cone of power."

"What's that?"

"It's energy. A bigger, more powerful version of what we saw Snow do to that guy. Remember the flash we saw in the sky outside the window, that time we sneaked into the house? The whole group does it together."

"What for?" she said apprehensively, and he grinned. "Let's join and find out."

As winter ran its icy course he kept at her, bombarding her with information about what he had begun (pretentiously, she thought) to call "the Craft." Thus she learned that the word *witch* came from the ancient *witte,* meaning *wise*—that witches viewed existence as part of a continuing cycle of life, death, and rebirth—that there was no central authority, and each coven worshiped pretty much as it pleased, recognizing a few common principles.

"They see the forces of nature as symbolized by a Goddess and a God. Both the God and Goddess have changing aspects during the year—first she's a maiden, then a mother, and finally an old wise woman. He starts out as her son, then later on he becomes her lover. He dies each year in the fall, and she lives on and gives birth to him again at the winter solstice. It follows the cycle of the seasons. It goes all the way back to primitive times."

"Then why do people say they worship Satan?"

"Because one of the aspects of the God is Pan, the guardian of wild creatures. He has horns—that's how he got mixed up with Satan. Although it's possible Satan may have got his horns from the God of the witches, because the gods of one religion usually become the evil spirits of another. It's a propaganda thing."

A religion in which the Goddess was as important as the God, perhaps more so, was undeniably appealing. Protestant Christianity, even the perfunctory version doled out at the Green Hollow Congregational Church, had left Shelley a little resentful about Eve's supposed role in human troubles. What was wrong with being curious—with wanting knowledge? One of the aims of witchcraft, Kip said, was to seek wisdom. That sounded respectable enough. And he explained that if they were accepted as apprentices into the coven it would be only on a trial basis, to see if they suited one another.

Yet it was glaringly obvious to me that they would never let us join. Why should they? If they hadn't yet chosen replacements for the Lockleys, it must be because they were highly particular, searching for just the right people to complete their circle. Two local teenagers wouldn't stand a chance. Trying to imagine a scenario in which the pair of us presented ourselves as candidates, I found myself cringing with mortification.

Kip was more sanguine. "We wouldn't be working at the Arms at all if Snow didn't like us. But we are, and she does. And she trusts us. She knows we can keep our mouths shut. Besides—"

He stopped and I said, "Besides what?"

He looked at me solemnly. It was late at night and we were talking quietly in my room, the whole household asleep except for the two of us. "You have to promise not to laugh."

His face was so serious that I couldn't imagine what was coming next, but it seemed unlikely to make me laugh. "I promise."

"All right. I think . . . I think I've known her before."

"You mean Snow."

He nodded.

"What do you mean, before? Before what?"

He sighed. "Listen, Shelley. Those months I was sick—you know? There was a long time when I was just sort of drifting. I wasn't unconscious, exactly, but I wasn't awake. There was some weird stuff floating through my mind. Memories of places, things that had happened. And people. But they weren't *my* memories."

My skin started to crawl. I felt no inclination to laugh. "You were just dreaming," I said.

"Maybe. But even after I got out of the hospital I couldn't get that stuff out of my head. It was so much more real than anything that was going on around me. After I got to know Frog, I mentioned it to him and—well, you know how he is. He said, 'Oh, those are just your past lives. Your illness must have weakened your conscious mind and let the memories come through.' " He shrugged. "I've lost a lot of it in the past couple of years. But I remember a few things. I remember Snow."

"You mean, from another *life*?"

"You said you wouldn't laugh."

"I'm not laughing. I just think it's a lot more likely you were dreaming, or maybe delirious, and that's what you remember. A lot more likely than the chance"—the words were coming too fast and I had to stop for breath— "the chance of you remembering some past life where you and Snow just happened to know each other."

"I know it sounds crazy. And up until last summer, she was just one of those weird dreams. But when I met her, it was like I recognized her. It was like something made me apply for the job at the Arms. Like something was pushing us together."

It was so clear to me that he was making this up, inflating some kind of fever dream into this grandiose tale of reincarnation, that I began to get irritated. "You didn't even like her at first," I reminded him, and his face turned red.

"It wasn't that. It just felt wrong. The relationship we were in, with her as an adult and me as a kid. I hated calling her *Miss Mansell*. It's easier now. We're more like equals."

"Equals!" I said. "What were you in your past life?" And then, stunned by what I imagined I saw in his face: *"Lovers?"*

He lowered his eyes. "I'm not sure exactly. It's all pretty vague. I get the feeling we ended up as rivals, and she beat me out somehow. I know you don't believe me, Shelley. I don't blame you. But I think she'll let us into the coven. Because she owes it to me."

Chapter 17

Early March brought a heavy snowstorm followed by a sudden thaw. As the temperature rose into the fifties, various flowers appeared—crocuses and sprays of forsythia venturing into bloom even while patches of snow remained on the ground. Jessica called it false spring. Royce nodded and gave a thumbs-down sign. The Arms was practically empty that weekend, the skiers seeking winter elsewhere; instead of the usual comings and goings, the place lay wrapped in a humming serenity. And on Saturday morning, as the twins crossed Willow Street, Kip announced that it was time to talk to Snow about the coven.

"Are you crazy?" The mere thought made Shelly's insides knot. "Forget it. Count me out."

"Come on, you know you want to join."

"Maybe I do and maybe I don't. But they'll never take us, Kip. There's no point in even asking."

They started up the Arms driveway, seeing the front door of the house open and Snow lean out to let Rowan into the yard. The cat scampered away; Snow saw them and waved. All at once Kip cut across the lawn, leaving Shelley behind, his voice floating back to her. "Can we talk to you about something?"

Waiting in the doorway, Snow shaded her eyes against the morning sun. "Sure. Now?"

"Yes," Shelley heard him say. Then Snow was beckoning to her and she felt her legs carry her across the tawny winter grass. The impulse seemed to come from outside her, irresistible as an undertow that sweeps a swimmer beyond his depth. "Maybe we ought to go to your office," Kip was saying as she reached them, and Snow's eyebrows rose.

"Oh? Is this serious?"

"Yes. It is."

He led the way, I went next, and Snow brought up the rear, leaving her office door ajar. Her face showed nothing, but behind its careful neutrality I could sense amusement as she said, "How serious? Should I sit at my desk?"

Kip shook his head. She perched on the edge of her desk, laced her fingers together in her lap, and gave us an inquiring look. I glanced at Kip. I could see he was nervous, and this recurrence of his old awkwardness seemed to put Snow at ease. I kept my mouth firmly shut; this interview was his idea. As he took a deep breath, somewhere in the tender greening silence outside the house I heard a far-off peal of laughter. Only one of the few weekend guests, no doubt, enjoying a joke with another—still, it seemed like an advance judgment on what he was about to say. I squeezed my eyes shut. When I opened them nothing had changed: Kip was biting his lip and Snow was sitting on the edge of her desk with that same lack of expression.

"We know what's going on here," he said in a rush. "We know it's a coven."

"What?" A puzzled frown had appeared on her face, as if she thought she had misheard him. Whatever reaction we had been expecting, this wasn't it: Kip cast a flustered glance in my direction, but I only gave a little shrug that I prayed on some cowardly level might disassociate me from the whole business. He looked down at his fingers, intertwined like Snow's, then with great deliberation bent them back and cracked his knuckles.

"We know you're witches," he said, watching his hands. "You celebrate the Sabbats. Candlemas, Beltane, Lammas, Samhain. We know it's a coven, and *you*"—looking up suddenly—"are the Lady."

"And *you* have quite an imagination," she said. She was smiling now, but with one side of her mouth only, and I could feel an intent vigilance like a hunting cat's. "Where on earth did you get those words?"

"I've got a book. It tells the names and dates of all the Sabbats. And on those dates, there are certain guests here. The same guests each time. And only those guests.

"I see. And with the help of this book, you've decided that these particular guests are members of a witches' coven?" It sounded preposterous, put like that. When he nodded she laughed, as if she really found this interview amusing, but I noticed she hadn't denied anything he said. She resettled herself on the edge of the desk, to all appearances entirely relaxed, but I still had that sense of concealed wariness. "And do we fly around on our broomsticks turning curious little boys into toads?"

"Of course not," he said. "Witchcraft is a religion. You celebrate the seasonal festivals, you meet every month at the full moon, and you work magic. Not the little-boys-into-toads kind. Earth magic."

"And what do you know about earth magic?" Her voice had gone very quiet. She was still half smiling, but behind the smile was the taut menace of a cat poised to spring. I thought if he used one wrong word now, if he tried to pressure her at all, if he said anything about what we had seen her do to Larry—I didn't know what would happen, but it would be something awful. Kip must have felt it too, because I saw him swallow.

"Mainly just what I've read. But your coven only has eleven people, and it's supposed to have thirteen. Shelley and I want to join."

Behind us the office door closed suddenly, the smooth click of the latch clearly audible in the silence created by his words. I jumped and so did Kip. Snow had not moved, but I saw that she was no longer smiling. Her eyes had gone very dark. In that instant she looked as she had that night in the dining room when she had made Larry choke, and terror clutched me so tightly I could not breathe. There was not a shred of doubt in my mind that she had caused the door to close, or that she was capable of doing anything to us, anything she wished. Our fear must have been laughably obvious, because all at once her face relaxed and she folded her arms and smiled. It was exasperated, but it was a smile. "Honestly, you two. I have a lot to do this morning. Can't you tease me some other time?"

"She wasn't saying no," Kip insisted later. "She was telling us to wait. I didn't really think she'd let us in the first time we asked. She has to be sure we're serious. But she definitely wasn't saying no."

"The door," Shelley said. "Did she make it shut?"

"I think so. Don't you?"

She most definitely did. "But why?"

Kip smiled. "Maybe to give us a taste of what we're asking to get involved in."

Shelley was impressed by this apparent grasp of what had taken place during that unnerving interview. She was certain of only one thing: that Snow had been watching them, measuring them. "So what do we do now?"

"We do exactly what she told us to do. We wait."

And so they waited. On the surface it was as if the conversation had never taken place—or, as Snow pretended, as if the whole business had been a joke, tasteless but graciously forgiven. But now in the midst of the lighthearted banter over supper in the kitchen, the casual conversations in the hall, the discussions of household business, Shelley was revisited time and again by the nerve-racking sense that they were being constantly weighed in some private scale. The memory of that quietly closing door still gave her jitters. What were they getting themselves into? Maybe it would be better just to forget the whole thing.

Kip greeted this cowardly suggestion with a sneer. "You can if you want. But I'm not going to—not on your life."

Did she really want to forget it? Sometimes she thought so. *Witchcraft.* If Mother ever found out . . . Yet in spite of Shelley's misgivings, a series of circuitous, faltering steps conspired to lead her toward the subject rather than away. At the library, for instance: searching for a book for her history term paper, she somehow wandered into the occult section, where a small collection of books with odd titles shaded gradually into religion and philosophy. As she scanned them, one in particular—wedged between *Famous Haunted Houses of America* and *ESP & You*—caught her eye. *Malleus Maleficarum.* The Latin words meant nothing—Kip, not she, was the classical scholar. But the subtitle was in English.

The Hammer of the Witches.

Her breath caught in her throat. She moved closer. The book was old, its binding cracked and dull. With a furtive glance up and down the aisle, Shelley slid the shabby volume off the shelf and began to leaf through it with cold fingers.

Chapter headings jumped out at her. *Of the Ancient and Secret Knowledge of Herbs Healing and Hurtful. How Witches do Offer Babes and Children to Devils. Of the Dark and Horrid Harms with which Devils may Afflict Men. Of the Manner whereby Witches Transform Men into Beasts. How they Raise and Stir up Hailstorms and Tempests. How they do Magically Transport themselves from Place to Place.*

There was a shadowy engraving of a wild night landscape, trees bent double in a high wind and the dark air filled with whirling leaves. A breach in the ragged clouds showed a group of humped figures astride broomsticks, silhouetted against a full moon. *The Witches' Sabbat*, read the caption. *With willow whistles they summon the wind, and to their most unholy Sabbats they ride upon enchanted steeds.*

Broomsticks. Staring down at the picture, Shelley remembered Kip saying that witches didn't call it a broom. *They call it a besom. It's a fertility symbol.* Her blank look had made him blush. *You know. The joining of male and female. One end's bushy. Then there's the handle.* They had hastily dropped the subject—but now, as she bent closer to the page, the picture drew her irresistibly into its world. The bookshelves dissolved and she could hear the howling of the wind, the crack of whipping branches and the unearthly shrieking of the witches as they rode pell-mell through the storm. Suddenly it was easy to imagine the bucking motion of the broom beneath her, the cold wind snatching at her hair and the dark earth rolling by below.

Her breathing quickened. The dust drifting from the old pages tickled her nose, and she sneezed.

The sound shattered the hush of the stacks, dropping Shelley abruptly back to earth. Suddenly it seemed everyone in the library must know exactly what she was doing. Shoving the volume on witchcraft back in place, she fled in the opposite direction—but even safe among the history books, she was unable to escape the memory of that night scene with its stormy sky and humped, airborne shapes. Witches, sabbats and magic—the same words she had heard Kip use dozens of times in the past few weeks, appearing in an old book next to tales of summoning tempests and changing men into beasts. She knew he would scoff, say the accusations were only propaganda meant to discredit the Craft. True witches harmed no one and used their power only for good.

That was what Kip would say—but what made him such an authority? His knowledge wasn't firsthand. Was there any guarantee that the books he had read were more true, more accurate than the dusty old tome tucked away under Dewey Decimal 130? In his fascination with all things strange and magical, Kip saw only the bright side, a realm of dazzling delights. *They don't hurt anyone. Their magic is positive. It's good. Can't you feel it, whenever you're there?*

But what about Benjy's white, frightened face emerging from the fog on that long-ago Halloween? The death (merely coincidental?) of Caroline the bulldog? A small form spread-eagled in a forbidden snowfield? The black look in Snow's eyes as she stared at Larry and lifted one hand to her throat, and the impossible stream of blue-white light that had effortlessly struck him down? A phrase from the *Malleus Maleficarum* whispered in her head: *dark and horrid harms.* All at once the book seemed to form a narrow, obscure doorway connecting the cryptic present with a legendary and barbaric past, and the shadows spread across its threshold were dark indeed.

Chapter 18

The spring equinox came and went, and the twins went on waiting. They knew the next Sabbat was Beltane, also called May Eve. As the warming weather heralded its approach, Kip began to get antsy. “Maybe we should ask her again.”

“Don’t you think it’s her move now?” Shelley said, “I mean, she knows we’re interested. I don’t think we should push her.”

He shook his head violently, like a dog shaking water from its coat. “I don’t care whose move it is! I’m sick of waiting! I want to join now!”

“Well, she’s not going to let us in just because you throw a tantrum.”

His glance slid toward her. “Why don’t you ask her this time?”

“Me!”

“Come on, Shelley. I did all the talking last time. Maybe she’s waiting for *you* to say something.”

“I can’t. I just can’t.”

He finally managed to extract her reluctant consent. Although she doubted there was any truth to what he said—that Snow might be waiting to hear from them both—Shelley was aware that Kip had done all the work so far, taken all the risks while she had let herself be carried along. But wasn’t that how it had always been? She wasn’t cut out for the leader’s role. Now, whenever the three of them were alone together her heartbeat would accelerate, her mouth dry out and her palms turn slimy as she felt herself teetering on the brink of an abyss, knowing she had to jump and yet unable to do so. There weren’t many such opportunities and she fluffed a number of them. Kip was disgusted with her. She was disgusted with herself.

And then one night I just did it. It was after dinner. All the guests had finished eating; Snow was in the kitchen with Royce and Jessica. Kip and I were by ourselves in the dining room, stripping the soiled cloths from the tables, when he started nagging me in a whisper. "When are you going to ask her?"

"Well, not now."

"Why not?"

"Royce and Jessica are in there with her."

"We can ask her to come in here."

"No."

"Why not?"

"Because,"

"Because why?"

"Just because. Leave me alone."

"You're never going to."

"I am too."

"When?"

Our hissed exchange could not possibly have been audible in the kitchen, where dishes were clattering and water was running in the sink, but just then Snow pushed open the swinging door and glanced into the dining room. Our body language must have shouted conflict. She came into the room, catching the door as it swung shut behind her. "What's going on, you two?" Indicating the crumpled tablecloth I was clutching in front of me: "This looks like the beginning of a bullfight."

"It's not," Kip said. "It's not the beginning of anything." He gave me a disgusted look.

"Snow, remember what we asked you about, a few weeks ago?" I flung myself headlong into the abyss before I could lose my nerve. "Have—have you made up your mind?"

Did the whole room quake while I waited for her eyes to go black—for her to surround me with blue light or make the walls come crashing down? None of these things happened. Her eyes stayed the same except for two tiny vertical frown lines that appeared between her brows, and she seemed to be thinking about something else as she said, “Not yet, Shelley.” Then she went back into the kitchen.

For the rest of that evening Kip and I hardly dared look at each other, for fear the spark of our colliding glances would combust the air between us. *Not yet, Shelley.* No more evasions, no more pretending it was all a joke. Just—*not yet.* Supper went by in a blur. At last we were on our way home, the Lockley Arms behind us, and I saw our two shadows merge beneath the streetlamp as Kip seized me in a hug that nearly unhinged my neck. “Shelley! You did it!”

“Ow! You’re hurting me.”

He released me and caught hold of the lamppost, circling it in a blithe one-handed spin, his laughter floating up into the night air. “We’ll miss Beltane. But—Midsummer for sure!”

His ebullience was contagious and my spirits soared. I had done it; the suspense was over. Any doubts I might harbor about the wisdom of joining the coven were obscured just then by the glow of Kip’s approval. Laughing, we ran across our yard, so buoyed by excitement that we had reached the front porch before either of us noticed something lying on the top step.

I think we saw it at the same instant, but Kip identified it before I did. My mind, fumbling for a frame of reference, registered the dark mass only as a mound of earth inexplicably dumped on our front porch. Whoever had left it there had slung it carelessly from the shovel so that the dirt had spilled outward on one side to form a sweeping curve.

For a heartbeat or two, that was all it was—a puzzling mound of dirt. Then I heard Kip give a little grunt as if someone had punched him in the stomach, and some gear in my brain ratcheted and caught and I saw what it actually was. It wasn’t earth after all, but something that had once been alive.

It was a dead bird. An owl.

My skin had become a stiff, heavy garment weighing down my limbs. From very far away I heard my voice say “Is that—?”

Kip didn’t bother to answer. He was looking down at the dead owl, and after a minute I made myself look too. A limp heap of velvety gray-brown feathers, one speckled wing outspread in a beautiful, predatory curve. Now that I knew what it was, I could see the catlike eyes, wide open but milky and lifeless. The hooked beak was parted in a silent shriek, the feathered talons tightly clenched but empty of prey. I had seen the corpses before, of course—but always from a distance, never up close. They had never seemed quite real before. Not until now. It occurred to me that I was going to throw up. I turned my head stiffly toward the street, and the Lockley Arms filled my vision.

Do you know what a coven is?

I wonder if it's got anything to do with the owls dying.

I turned back to Kip, careful not to look at the dead bird. Aware of Dad and Mother and Marty asleep inside the darkened house, I kept my voice down. "I thought you said owls are sacred to witches."

"They are."

"Then why are all the owls in Green Hollow dying?"

He chewed his lip. "I don't know."

Last summer, before I had known about the coven, I had found a kind of grisly fascination in Kip's suggestion of a link between this sinister plague and the regulars at the Arms. The thrill had utterly vanished now, ousted by horror and revulsion. Maybe it was a disease, some natural phenomenon. But if it wasn't . . . recalling that this very evening I had reminded Snow of our request to join the coven, I felt my stomach twitch again. Kip said, "You're not chickening out, are you?"

Under the circumstances it seemed a poor choice of words. My eyes strayed to the corpse and ricocheted off. "It's not being chicken. There's something creepy going on, Kip. We shouldn't get mixed up in it."

Instead of answering he grimaced. "Let's get rid of this thing." Lifting the owl gingerly by one wing, he headed around the side of the house where the garbage cans were. I followed, staying close to him in the darkness but keeping my eyes averted as he removed the lid from one can and dropped the dead bird inside. Suddenly I heard him say, "What's *that*?"

The sharp query jolted me; my gaze skittered over the

driveway, the garage, the side of Miss Motley's house next door—all of it familiar by daylight but disguised now by a mosaic of moonlight and shadow. "What's *what*?"

He pointed tensely at the garage. "Over there. I saw something move."

"Probably a cat or something."

"No. It was big."

Big. A shudder crawled over me. As I stood staring into the impenetrable shadows around the garage, an image flashed through my head—Jenny's backyard last Halloween, the suggestion of a hooded figure lurking beneath the arbor. A spring breeze whispered suddenly in the surrounding leaves—*Shhhhhh*—and all at once I saw something move. A fluid shadow, sliding from one patch of darkness to another, flowing from the shelter of our garage to the dense leafy blackness behind Miss Motley's house.

Kip flung the garbage can lid at it, but nerves must have spoiled his aim. The lid struck the corner of the garage and bounced off, landing on the driveway with a deafening clatter of metal meeting concrete. We heard Mitzi start yapping inside Miss Motley's house; an upstairs light came on over there, and another behind us as a window was flung up over our heads and Dad called, "Who's out there? What's going on?"

Whatever had been there, it was gone. But Kip was right: it had been big. The size of a man. We stood wide-eyed, staring breathlessly into the shadows, hearing Dad say again, "Who's out there?"

Somehow Kip managed to say, "Just us, Dad."

"Graham?" Miss Motley's voice quavered out from next door. "What's happening out there?"

"Nothing, Lillian. Sorry to have disturbed you."

"Dad—"

"Come on inside, son." Dad's voice held a warning note: Miss Motley talked a blue streak, and if she got going it would be next to impossible to shut her up. "It's late. Time you two were in bed."

Chapter 19

Inside, Dad listened to their jittery tale with a wry look—a prowler? in Green Hollow?—and sent them off to bed. Shelley slept uncomfortably on the memory of the hooded figure in Jenny's yard. On the way to school in the morning she broached the subject of the previous night's scare, only to find that Kip had already drawn his own conclusion. "I bet it was just a hobo. He must have been sleeping in the garage, and we scared him off."

Scared—that skulking shadow with its swift, fluid retreat? She took a deep breath. "Listen, that's not the first time I've seen somebody hanging around. Remember Jenny's party last Halloween? There was somebody out in her backyard that night, watching the house. Somebody creepy."

"Creepy how?"

"Like—like—I don't know. An evil monk or something." If she mentioned Poe he would just laugh. "Wearing a long robe," she said. "With a hood."

"Shelley." His most patient tone. "That was just somebody in a Halloween costume."

This observation brought her up short, reminding her of the time he had demystified the letters on the gate to the meadow. *What are you, a halfwit? L,A. Lockley Arms.* Had she missed the obvious once again? *Somebody in a Halloween costume.* Now, as then, she had a defiant sense that the obvious explanation was not necessarily the true one—but Kip's skeptical face made it impossible to say so.

Nor did the appearance of the dead owl on their front porch cause any discernible dent in his desire to join the coven. But as April passed, then May—as June brought the twins' sixteenth birthday, Snow still said nothing, made no move, gave no indication that the subject of the coven had ever been raised at all. By now her noncommittal "Not yet" back in April had dwindled to a meaningless shadow that left Kip desperate. Alone with Shelley he talked of nothing else, going over and over the same ground like an animal pacing in a cage.

"What's she waiting for? Why doesn't she say something? Damn it! She has to let us in. She *has* to."

"She doesn't *have* to do anything," Shelley said, and then, quoting Aunt Marty: "Except die and pay taxes."

This flippancy earned her a scowl, which she met with a shrug. All in all, she was relieved by Snow's silence. She told herself she had never really believed they would be allowed into the coven. Too, that double encounter with the dead owl and the mysterious prowler had taught her that her appetite for excitement was smaller than she had imagined. When June began to run out with no further acknowledgment of their request—when Midsummer Eve finally arrived, when the long, hot day softened at last to summer dusk, when the parking lot filled with familiar cars and the candlelit dining room with familiar faces and still nothing was said—Shelley could not have truthfully claimed she was sorry.

"Jessica, what happened to the pie? Did you put it somewhere?"

Jessica's strawberry rhubarb pie was one of the fabled delicacies of the Arms, and she had made one to top off tonight's banquet. Earlier it had been cooling on the counter by the window, but now that the time had come to serve it, Shelley found the spot empty. Jessica came over to look, her broad forehead crinkling in puzzlement. "It was here a minute ago. Where—"

"It's right here," Kip said, coming in from the back porch and past them so swiftly that neither of them got a good look at the pie in his hands. "The pan was leaking and I had to clean it off. Bring the plates, will you, Shelley?"

It didn't occur to her to question his glib explanation: the pie was accounted for and the guests were waiting. Shelley took the stack of plates and followed him into the dining room. As she came through the swinging door, he had just set the pie down in front of Snow, who was sitting sideways in her chair, talking to the blond woman next to her.

Snow hadn't noticed the pie's arrival, but several of the others had. One by one, as they saw it, they fell silent. Kip backed away from the table, toward the windows. Shelley came to an apprehensive stop in front of the door, still clutching the plates. What was going on? By now the conversation had dropped to nothing. A palpable silence settled on the room, to be broken at last by Snow saying with studied calm, "Kip? Would you mind . . . explaining this?"

Shelley craned her neck to see what "this" was—and saw, to her incredulous horror, that the top of the pie had been decorated with a five-pointed star inside a circle. The design was inexpert but unmistakable. A pentacle, the symbol of witchcraft, had been rendered in what appeared to be vanilla frosting.

Kip shifted his feet. "It's just, you know . . . to wish you all a happy Midsummer Eve."

From the tremor in his voice I could tell the scene had played better in his imagination than it was doing in reality. The coven sat without speaking, although I saw some looks pass among them. I wanted to proclaim my innocence, blurt out that I had nothing to do with it, but I was afraid to open my mouth. I thought of the blue-white ball of light sizzling between Snow's hands, and remembered her saying *And do we fly around on our broomsticks turning curious little boys into toads?* Her real voice sounded in my ears, overlapping the one inside my head. "A . . . happy . . . Midsummer . . . Eve . . . ?"

"And to say we'd like to join the coven," Kip added, having evidently decided he might as well go for broke. I saw his eyes were squeezed shut. "If you'd consider trying us out."

The Jaguar Lady pressed one hand to her mouth, and beside her the Prince abruptly leaned back in his chair. The eldest member of the group, a bony old fellow with brambly eyebrows and a shock of white hair, cleared his throat. The woman beside him bowed her sleek head. Another woman leaned across the table and murmured something to the quiet pair opposite. The black man sat motionless, gazing at Kip. There was a slight snorting noise. Another. Suddenly they all started to laugh.

In the midst of the hilarity, as they leaned back in their chairs and let loose a storm of merriment that seemed to fill the whole house, I looked anxiously at Snow. She sat resting her head in her hand, shaking it now and then—whether in disapproval or disbelief I could not tell. When she lifted her face at last, she looked pale, but not angry. She held up a hand and the others quieted, shifting in their chairs to face her.

"I don't want to do this formally," she said. "This is the third time they've asked, and however . . . unusual . . . this last request may have been"—the Prince chuckled and then sobered as she went on—"it seems to me they're sincere. But for various reasons I feel I may not be the best judge. The rest of you must decide."

They all looked at us. Finally the old man with the eyebrows said, "Come and stand together, please."

This was the moment to state my disclaimer: to save myself by saying it was not my wish to join their coven, to participate in ancient ceremonies, or invoke unknown forces. To explain that this was Kip's brainstorm, not mine, and that I was merely being pulled in his wake, as I had been in childhood, like some helpless bit of flotsam bobbing behind a powerful motorboat. Instead I found myself walking over to stand beside him, feeling the pressure of eyes upon me. We stood side by side: a pair of teenagers identical from our flushed faces to our matching white shirts and black bow ties. I suppose, to the roomful of adults, there must have been something disarming in our patent nervousness. I was still in possession of the stack of dessert plates; the Jaguar Lady, who sat nearest, reached out and gently took them away from me. The little *clink* as she set them on the table was the only sound in the room.

"Why might you want to join us?" the old man with the eyebrows said suddenly. "Young man? Let's hear from you first."

Kip's gulp was audible, but he answered steadily enough. "A friend of mine lent me a book about the Craft. Everything I read seemed familiar somehow. Like—like something I'd done before."

"And what was this book?" This time it was one of the older women, her long dark hair liberally mixed with silver, who spoke.

"Uh, it's called *Witchcraft: A History & Guide* by Serena Wilson. I've also read *Magick in Theory and Practice* by Aleister Crowley."

Looks were exchanged and then the black man said, "So you want to become a follower of the Great Goddess." He had a beautiful voice, deep and calm. "Why?"

Kip took a breath and closed his eyes. There was complete silence in the room. When he spoke at last, his voice was just above a whisper. *"For behold, I have been with you from the beginning, and I am that which is attained at the end of desire."*

The silence remained unbroken when he had finished speaking. I sneaked a glance at him, scarcely recognizing my smart-alecky twin. The words, gibberish to me, obviously meant something to him. Slowly he opened his eyes and stared straight ahead of him at nothing.

"And you, young lady?" Eyebrows said. "What about you?"

While Kip was answering their questions I had been frantically trying to think of something to say when my turn came. Now my mind was a blank. I heard myself stammer, "I—well, I—" and then I remembered how, when Kip had been babbling his nonsense about knowing Snow in a previous life, he had mentioned some force pushing him to apply for a job at the Lockley Arms. As if it had been meant. "It's like something's drawing me here," I said. "Something that makes me feel alive." As soon as the words were out of my mouth, I realized with a jolt that they were true. It was not the success, not the glamour of the Lockley Arms that attracted me, but some tranquil radiance at its center. At that instant the accompanying glimpses of darkness and possible danger seemed to matter not one whit.

No one said anything for a long time. Then they all shifted in their chairs, and a kind of soundless sigh ran through the room.

Eyebrows cleared his throat again. "And so you think you want to join us. But do you understand what it means to become a witch? This is not a game, my young friends. The practice of our Craft offers as many risks and dangers as it does joys and rewards. The Goddess had a multitude of faces, and they are not all kind and beautiful. Your resolve may fail, and you may decide to deny her. But be forewarned: once you have known her, she will claim a part of you forever."

His words were a jarring reminder of all my apprehensions, but his eyes were kind. I couldn't think clearly; this whole bizarre interview was like something happening in a dream. When Kip gave a stiff nod, I imitated it.

Eyebrows glanced at the others. "Does anyone have anything to say to either of these two young people?" The faces around the table were solemn; no one spoke. After a pause he went on. "Then I'll agree to sponsor them for apprenticeship in the Green Hollow Coven. They've asked of their own free will to be taken into our circle. Does anyone wish to refuse them?"

Not a sound. Not a rustle. Eyebrows sat back and the woman with the sleek silver-dark hair, who I thought was his wife, leaned forward and began to speak. I had noticed her voice on previous occasions—deep for a woman's, reminding me of some rich fabric, velvet or brocade. "As apprentices, you'll join us in celebrating the festivals of the seasons. We will undertake to teach you the way of our Craft, and in return you will promise to keep the secrets of the circle, and to abide by our laws.

"Your apprenticeship will last a year and a day. At the end of this time, if all are willing, you'll be initiated into our circle as full members. If we have any doubts about you, or you about us, all obligation will be dissolved between us at that time, and we'll part in friendship. In that event, we'll ask only that you do not reveal what you've learned of us." She looked into Kip's eyes, then into mine. "Do you understand?"

We nodded.

"Are there any questions you'd like to ask?"

Questions? I had a number. Why were the owls dying? What was behind the locked door upstairs? The cat in that photograph of the Lockleys—was it Rowan? Why had they kept Kip's baseball cap? But I did not dare ask these things, and somehow, for the moment, the answers seemed unimportant. We shook our heads and she said, "Then tonight you will join us in celebrating our Midsummer rites."

They were all smiling now—all but Snow, who was leaning back in her chair, arms folded and eyes downcast, her whole posture passive. *For various reasons I feel I may not be the best judge.* What reasons? I stared at the crown of her smooth head as if I could fathom the meaning of those words.

Eyebrows was speaking again. "Actually, I have a question." Everyone turned to look at him and he smiled, a hundred wrinkles furrowing his angular face. "Are we ever going to eat that pie?"

Chapter 20

We were invited to join them in consuming the pie Kip had decorated. Those at our end of the table made conversation with us in a way no different from any other adults chatting with any other teenagers—asking us about school, our interests, our family and friends. When the coffee and pie were gone and the guests had begun to leave the table, Snow approached us.

"Go ahead and clear the table now. Then come to the meadow."

That was all. No congratulations, no words of welcome, and I could not read her eyes. *For various reasons I feel I may not be the best judge.* Was she annoyed by our—Kip's—effrontery?

As she moved away I looked after her, remembering how they had all fallen silent when she lifted her hand.

Downstairs in the laundry room we changed fumblingly, with unsteady hands, into our own clothes and returned to the kitchen to bid Jessica good night. She stopped her dishwashing to survey us with a half smile. "You two," she said. And shook her head.

Then come to the meadow. What would happen there, in that place where five years earlier Kip had paid such a high price for trespassing? We didn't know—but whatever it might be, our long wait was nearly over. Together we hurried across the dark parking lot. A full moon was rising over the tops of the pines that hid the gully and the whispering brook, but even by its light it was hard to locate the entrance to the footbridge and we hesitated, searching the feathery pine branches for the opening we knew was there.

And as we hesitated, they came from the shadows. Four faceless figures in hooded robes, moving so swiftly that they were upon us before we knew it. At the abrupt appearance of those dark shapes, identical to the one I had seen lurking behind Jenny's house, I let out a yelp. Two of them seized my arms; one whispered, "Hush," and I recognized the Jaguar Lady's perfume. As they hustled me beneath the low branches onto the bridge I twisted around, trying to see what was happening to Kip, but it was too dark and we were moving too fast. I smelled pine needles and heard my own footsteps on the boards of the bridge. My faceless captors moved in silence, keeping a firm grip on my arms. In a moment we had emerged onto the moonlit lawn between the carriage house and the swimming pool. But instead of turning in the direction of the meadow, they hurried me toward the carriage house, around the back where an open doorway made a dark rectangle in the moonlit expanse of white wall. One of my escorts turned back at the threshold. The other drew me inside.

It was dark. I could see nothing, only catch a trace of that familiar perfume. The Jaguar Lady. My heart was hammering. I reminded myself that this was the same woman who half an hour earlier had questioned me, with apparent friendly interest, about my plans for college—but another part of me shrieked that she was a stranger, that I knew nothing at all about her beyond the fact that she was a practicing witch. I thought of the chapter heading in the book I had found in the library. *How Witches do Offer Babes and Children to Devils.* I remembered the hooded shadow in Jenny's yard, that whisper like the sound of dead leaves—and when I felt her beside me in the darkness I gasped and shrank away.

"There's no need to be afraid," she said. "If you have any doubts, there's still time to change your mind."

Any doubts? They clamored inside my head, howling at me to run, escape, flee back across the street to my everyday life with its safe and narrow limits. Yet I knew I could never let Kip go ahead without me—and wherever he was at this instant, whatever he was doing, I knew he was not losing his nerve. I gritted my teeth. "I'm okay."

"Take a moment to think," said the soft voice beside me. "There's no harm in what we do. But we may violate some of the conventions you've been raised to believe in. And as Elymas told you, there are genuine risks involved, even for an apprentice. You should be very sure, before you join us, that this is truly what you want."

I gulped. "I am. I mean, it is."

"All right. Then take off your clothes."

"Take off . . . ?" My voice squeaked as I echoed her words. I had the sensation of sinking deeper into a nightmare. Where was Kip? Was something like this happening to him?

"Before entering the presence of the Goddess we perform a ritual of bathing to purify ourselves. Take off your clothes and go through the gate to the pool. Immerse yourself in the water. At the far end you'll find a robe waiting for you. Put it on and someone will come for you."

Her tone was so patient and reasonable that it seemed stupid to argue, but I couldn't help myself. "Take off my clothes and go all the way to the pool with nothing on?"

This time I heard a quiver of amusement in her voice. "No one's watching you, child. Just undress and go."

"*All* my clothes?"

"All of them."

The darkness was so dense that I felt no real shyness, only a shrinking vulnerability as I undressed and dropped my shorts, shirt, and underclothes on the floor beside my sandals. As an afterthought I unfastened the clasp that held my hair and added it to the pile. Then I stood still in the sheltering blackness, feeling disconnected from life on earth.

"Okay," I said at last. I could hear the quaver even in that short word.

"Go," said the gentle voice in the darkness.

The huge white moon lit the velvety lawn around the carriage house like a stage, or at least that was how it seemed as I slipped through the door and out into the night. The grass was warm, soft beneath my feet. At first I stood hunched over, paralyzed by my own nakedness, trying to cover myself with my hands. Then a faint breeze came and touched my skin all over, leaving a shiver of tentative pleasure in its wake. Slowly I straightened and let my hands fall to my sides. The summer night was a vast quivering bell of warm air; silvery light flooded earth and sky, rendering the surrounding leafy shadows black as ink. All around me, nameless stirrings and rustlings whispered to some unfamiliar self who now began to wake for the first time on this expanse of moonlit lawn. I felt the flesh of my nipples tighten, felt my loosened hair tickling my shoulder blades. Past the corner of the carriage house I could see the gate to the pool, set between moon-whitened stone pillars in the high hedge. It stood open and I ran toward it, feeling myself no more substantial than moonlight and shadow. My bare flesh seemed to blend seamlessly with the night air; it was as if, along with my clothing, I had completely shed my old existence.

As I stepped through the gate I caught my breath at the sight within: the bottom of the pool illuminated by glimmering lights that sent ripples and flakes of gold upward through the clear water. Someone was already swimming there, a dark head breaking the satiny surface. I drew back into the shadow of the hedge, my heart pounding, suddenly aware that I was standing stark naked in the middle of someone else's property with a dozen strangers about.

The swimmer stopped and shook water from his hair, and I realized it was Kip. I crept closer, staying in the shadows—waited until his back was turned and then flung myself breathlessly into the water. The dive took me into luminous depths, surrounding me with an explosion of phosphorescent bubbles. When I surfaced he was beside me, his head sleek as an otter's, wet chest and shoulders gleaming in the moonlight. "Ha! You finally got here. I thought you'd chickened out."

I shook back my water-heavy hair. "Did you have to . . . get here with no clothes on?"

He nodded. All at once I was acutely conscious of my own nakedness, and the wavering outline of his body in the water. We moved apart as if by the same impulse. "Now what?" Kip said.

"She told me there'd be a robe at the other end of the pool. She said to put it on and wait for someone to come."

"She?"

"Jaguar Lady. I recognized her perfume."

"Mine were men," Kip said. "I think one of them was the Prince. They said it's a purification ritual. In honor of the Goddess."

I nodded. "That's what she told me."

"Where you scared when they grabbed us?" he said.

"Were you?"

He grinned. "Terrified."

We both started to giggle. In the midst of our laughter came the faint, faraway sound of a bell, and I saw Kip's face sober, a mirror of my own. Without another word we swam to the far end, where we could see the robes, two dark bundles lying on the bricks that surrounded the pool. We climbed out of the water without looking at each other and put them on. They were made of some heavy, silky material that swirled around us when we moved. I tied mine shut with the cord provided and turned to face Kip; unsmilingly we moved toward the meadow gate.

LA, LA. Did I imagine the shadow of those letters on the silvery grass, as once I had imagined I could hear their silent song inside my head? Or were they real, both the shadow and the melody? The starred night spread its limitless canopy above our heads; all around us invisible leaves rustled in the darkness. Toward the center of the meadow, across the expanse of unmown grass, we could see a flickering light like leaping flames.

This time they let us see them coming, and it was even more unnerving than when they had taken us by surprise. Only two figures this time, approaching across the meadow, their hooded heads silhouetted against the glow of the fire behind them. Again dread clutched me; I suppressed the urge to grab Kip's hand for comfort, touching the cool metal of the gate instead. "They're not going to hurt us, are they?"

"I don't think so." He didn't sound as certain as I would have liked. "I think this is what they call 'the ordeal.' A symbolic annihilation that lets us be reborn as children of the Goddess."

"Annihilation?" I said.

But by then they had reached us.

They made no effort to conceal their identities: it was Eyebrows and the lady with the silver-dark hair. Although in the dining room they had seemed benign as fond grandparents, now their faces were stern as they opened the gate and motioned us silently into the meadow. There they proceeded to blindfold us. As the strip of cloth was tied behind my head an involuntary whimper escaped me; there was a reassuring murmur from Silverdark, but no words were spoken. Kip was bravely silent and I bit my lip, vowing to match his nerve.

And I needed that vow to carry me through. My blindness amplified all sounds: I could hear the piping of crickets, the stirring of the grass all around, a faint crackling that I guessed was the fire we had seen in the distance. Someone touched me, untying the cord around my waist. Nervously I clutched the edges of the robe together, but my wrists were grasped and gently guided behind me, where I could feel the cord being used to bind them. My elbows were bent until my bound wrists rested against the small of my back, the cord passed around my neck—and I felt, with mounting dismay, the ends being tied together. What was going on? Experimentally I relaxed my elbows—the cord tightened around my neck. Panic shot through me; then unseen hands were there, bending my elbows to relieve the pressure.

I took a grateful gulp of air. Before I could think further, a gentle pressure on my shoulder urged me forward. Blindly, tentatively, I set one foot in front of the other, feeling feathery grass tickle my legs as my robe fluttered open. At this point I had little concern for modesty; my thoughts were too busy chasing one another in a frightened circle. What was the purpose of the blindfold and the cord, and what would happen next? Kip had told me that each coven had its own initiation rituals. Would we be put through some shameful ordeal to insure our silence and our loyalty? I remembered only too clearly what the Jaguar Lady had said just now, in the darkness of the carriage house. *We may violate some of the conventions you've been raised to believe in . . . and there are genuine risks involved, even for an apprentice.* Just as clear in my mind was the apparent reluctance with which Snow had finally acknowledged our request to join the coven. *For various reasons I feel I may not be the best judge.* And in counterpoint to these echoes was the word Kip had used just now, as we waited at the gate.

Annihilation.

That blind journey seemed to take forever. Once I stumbled, jerking my arms in reflex, and the terrible cord locked tight around my throat—but my guide steadied me, relieving the pressure so I could breathe again. My knees shook as we walked on, accompanied by the whispering grass and singing crickets. No matter how I strained my ears, I could hear only these sounds. On and on we walked. Just as I had begun to resign myself to the idea that this journey would never end—and even to hope it would not, because of what might be waiting ahead—there came the unmistakable crackle of a briskly burning fire, and I was aware of a faint brightening beyond the blindfold.

We came to a stop. Standing there I sensed a gathering of people and felt the fire's heat—a horrifying reminder that my robe was hanging open in front. Unthinkingly I reached to close it; the cord squeezed my neck again and I gave a gasp that came as much from panic as from constricted breathing. Invisible hands covered mine and held them still. There was no sound but the snap of flames. At last a man's voice spoke. "Who comes to the gate?"

To my left I heard Eyebrows answer. "Two who would join our number."

"Name yourselves," the voice said.

I heard Kip say, "Kipling Davies" and felt the hands press mine. "Shelley Davies," I whispered. A bell rang, its clear tone vibrating along my nerves. The first voice spoke again.

"Enter our circle."

My blindfold was pulled off. I blinked and squinted at the blurred shapes surrounding the fire. Kip was beside me, Eyebrows behind him, and I glanced over my shoulder to meet Silverdark's gaze. She pushed me gently forward.

A circle had been mowed in the meadow's high grass, and around its edge stood robed and hooded figures, heads bowed so that their faces were invisible. At the center, beside the leaping fire, was a large flat rock on which I saw candles, a silver goblet, a couple of small bowls and a wicked-looking knife with a black handle. Beside the rock was an iron cauldron exactly like the one witches are supposed to use. Moon, fire, knife, cauldron—and most of all, the sight of those anonymous black-robed figures rendered my knees so shaky they threatened to buckle beneath me. What had we gotten ourselves into? Beside me Kip too seemed unsteady on his feet; his shoulder kept bumping mine.

One of the robed figures stepped forward and I recognized Snow, her eyes a silvery gleam within the shadow of her hood. For what seemed like a long time she regarded us in silence before she spoke. "You have entered a place of power, where birth and death, joy and sorrow, dark and light meet and make one. In this circle we are between the worlds and outside time. Do you come of your own free will?"

The sound of her voice was reassuring—the same voice that joked with us in the kitchen late at night, answered the telephone and issued instructions about running the house. Well, almost the same, but not quite. Gone was a certain detachment, an undercurrent of amusement—as if now, for the first time, she spoke to us straight from her heart. *You have entered a place of power, where dark and light meet and make one.*

Do you come of your own free will?

I gulped and nodded and saw, out of the corner of my eye, Kip doing likewise.

"Unbind them."

It was the black man, resembling a beautiful dark angel in his robe, who freed us. I took a deep breath of relief as the cord slipped from my neck. He handed the cords—they showed red in the firelight—to Snow, then lit two small white candles and gave one to Kip and one to me. Snow was speaking again.

"Of your own free will, do you undertake to apprentice yourselves to our Craft for the interval of a year and a day?"

Clutching the flickering candles in our hands, we nodded again.

"Kneel down."

We knelt and raised our faces to her.

"The candles you hold are the symbol of your past life. Extinguish them now."

Kip blew his candle out. The alacrity of his response took me aback and I hesitated a moment before imitating him, aware of a faint vertigo as I watched the smoke curl off the wick. I heard Snow say, "Do you swear to hold all coven workings sacred, and never reveal them to any outsider?"

We nodded and she said gently, "You must speak."

I forced the word past the dryness in my throat and heard it come out together with Kip's. "Yes."

"Do you swear never to reveal the name of any coven member to anyone outside this gathering?"

"Yes."

"Do you swear to honor the Triple Goddess of birth, death and renewal, and the God who is child, lover and sacrifice?"

"Yes."

"Do you swear to obey the law of our Craft, never using what you learn from us to cause harm to another?"

"Yes."

She hesitated, as if the next words were irrevocable. At last she said, "Then light your soul candles now from our fire, as a symbol of your new lives freely chosen and begun on this night."

Your soul candles. A chill gripped me. What were we doing? Embarking on some unimaginable journey out of the Brothers Grimm, offering ourselves to an ancient, secret faith of mystery and magic. I thought, with something akin to desperation, of school—Benjy—Marty with her hair in curlers—but these images were fuzzy and far away. Kip and I held our small white candles to the fire. Their wicks flared and caught. As a few drops of wax fell hissing into the blaze, I saw with a shock that they were the bright red of freshly shed blood. *Tssss—tssss*—I flinched as the flames lapped them up, and from a great distance heard Snow say, "You may stand."

I stumbled to my feet, my heart racing, only vaguely aware of her opening my robe, tracing a sign between my breasts and another on my belly. The first felt like a pentagram, the second a triangle. The liquid she used, some fragrant oil, stung for an instant and then dried in the fire's heat. Snow closed the robe, retied the cord around my waist and leaned forward, her nearness bringing a startling wave of heat as her lips grazed mine. I lowered my eyes to my candle, sheltering its dancing petal of light with one cupped hand while she repeated the ritual with Kip. When it was done she stepped back.

"May the spirit that brought you to us stay with you from this moment onward, to light the rest of your days. Now come and greet your new brothers and sisters of the Craft."

Of the Midsummer rites that followed, I can recall only a jumble of fragments in no coherent order. I know there was food and drink, spiced wine and small cakes tasting elusively of honey. I remember woven garlands of roses cast into the fire, and the Goddess and God invoked with ceremonial phrases followed by a measured chant that hovered at the edge of song until the voices became a stranded net that captured and stilled my conscious mind. I remember a burning sensation centering around the spot on my abdomen where Snow had traced the triangle, and a fey light in her eyes like a reflection of the glimmering moon overhead. And I remember music, two of the coveners playing a flute and tambourine as we took turns leaping over the bonfire, at last joining hands in a winding spiral dance beneath the moon, a joyous confluence of music and dizzy motion that swept away all reality but its own. Somewhere at the back of my mind I guessed that anyone watching from a distance would squint and blink and finally shake his head, convinced of seeing nothing more than a golden swarm of fireflies in the tall grass, hearing only the piping of crickets in the vast moonlit summer night. For were we not between the worlds?

I remember Snow at last raising the black-handled knife to salute the moon above, then the earth at her feet. Her gaze traveled around the circle in silence, meeting each of ours in turn before she spoke the phrases that—at that first hearing and ever after—prickled my spine with their simple beauty.

"The circle is open, but unbroken. May the peace of the Goddess remain in our hearts. Merry meet, and merry part, and merry meet again. Blessed be all who gather in Her name."

And our murmured voiced answering together, "Blessed be!"

It seemed to me we had been transported far from the world we knew, for an interval of days, perhaps years. When Kip and I got home and crept up the stairs, I saw with amazement that the clock on the landing showed only a little after one. In the darkened hallway outside our rooms the two of us exchanged goofy, exhausted grins before parting.

But for me there was one more surprise that night, a special gift from the Goddess. Undressing for bed, I discovered blood: my menses had begun.

Let the magician, before beginning his work, endeavor to map out his own being.

——Aleister Crowley, *Magick in Theory & Practice*

Chapter 1

Waking early on Midsummer Day, Shelley could recall no dreams, only dazzling images from the ceremony that this morning seemed the most exotic of dreams. Firelight, chanting voices . . . in the summer sunshine spilling across her bed, she found herself trembling. No dream. It had happened: she was an apprenticed witch. And in proof there was the blessing of the Goddess—the aching flow of blood that made her at last a woman, no longer a child. Hugging her knees, she happened to glance at the clock beside her bed. Ten past seven! She jumped out of bed as if stung. Apprenticed witch or not, she was due at the Arms at half past.

Kip was waiting for her on the front porch, hair gleaming wet from his shower—another reminder of last night, finding him in the pool. Had they really run naked across the dark lawn, swum together under the moon-swept sky? She remembered the refraction of his body in the lit water. Had he been looking at her as well? If it had been a dream, they had shared it in the way they sometimes had as children, and she saw his face redden as they looked quickly at each other and then away.

Once they had parted company at the back steps of the Arms her self-consciousness subsided. Jessica treated her exactly as usual and she slipped into the familiar routine of serving breakfast to the guests, trying to ignore the discomfort of her menstrual cramps. Only Eyebrows, Silverdark, and the Prince were present in the dining room (it was a Wednesday morning, and the others had already left) and they greeted her warmly, like old friends. Had she really stood virtually naked in front of them last night? The rite seemed to have transpired in some no-man's-land between dream and reality; silently she repeated the phrase to herself: *Between the worlds.*

By the time breakfast was done and she had started on the dishes, the pain in her abdomen had grown intense. She had retreated to the kitchen table to rest her face in her hands and try to catch her breath between assaults, when a touch on her shoulder made her look up to find Snow beside her. "Oh! I—"

"Are you sick?"

"Just cramps."

"Well, let's see what we can do."

I watched as she set the kettle on the stove and chose two small glass canisters from a cupboard. With no outsiders present at the inn she had dressed for comfort, in jeans and an old shirt with the sleeves rolled up—yet I couldn't forget how she had looked last night, in the witches' circle. *The Lady.* Now the meaning of that title was clear. When the water began to boil she filled a cup and added some of the contents from each jar, crumbling them between her fingers. A spicy fragrance rose from the cup as she set it down in front of me. "Careful. It's hot."

She sat with me while I sipped the tea. Little by little the painful spasms diminished, replaced by a suffusing warmth. We didn't talk, but as I sat watching the steam from the hot liquid dissipate in the air, all at once it came clear to me that it was Snow who was responsible for this double-edged gift, this blood flow with its promise and pain—that with last night's tracing of the sign of the Goddess on my skin, she had been the one to negotiate my long overdue release from childhood. I looked up at her. Scarcely realizing I was speaking aloud I whispered, "Thank you."

Her eyes, pools of silver light, held mine. Could she read my thoughts? When she spoke at last her face was grave. "There's something I want you to understand, Shelley. What happens in the circle is both valid and real. But it's not the same as everyday life."

"I . . . kind of feel like it was a dream."

"In a way it was. A dream is real, and in it you exist as yourself, but not the same self who sits here now. The circle has its own reality, just as this"—she gestured at the kitchen around us—"does. The two may shadow one another. But they're not the same."

She seemed to be making a disclaimer, to be telling me last night's ceremony had played no real part in triggering my body's inevitable change. But at the same time, in spite of her serious expression, I thought I could glimpse a smile dancing far back in her eyes—a spark that hinted otherwise. As I puzzled over this contradiction she touched my wrist lightly. "Finish your tea."

Shelley's education as a witch began that same afternoon, when she was released from her duties into the custody of Silverdark. She had to remind herself that she knew another name for this woman now: her witch name, shared only with a privileged few. So she was Grimalkin as the two of them crossed the shady footbridge together—a leggy teenager in shorts and an elegant older woman in a silk dress. On the bridge they stopped to watch schools of minnows trail their shadows over the brook's pebbly bottom.

"Nature shows us the face of the Goddess," Grimalkin said. "Ever changing, always the same. The moon waxes and wanes and waxes again, the earth moves through its seasons, and we believe that our lives follow this same pattern of life, death and renewal. The ancient Greeks had a beautiful name for it: 'the eternal return.' "

"What about heaven and hell?" Until this summer, when Kip had rebelled and Dad had backed him up, regular attendance at the Green Hollow Congregational Church had been part of Mother's regimen of proper behavior for her offspring. Although the bland sermons had left little impression on Shelley, a few fragments of doctrine had stuck. But Grimalkin was shaking her head.

"Witches don't believe in life after death. We believe in life after birth. Life is a great gift, to be celebrated and enjoyed. Why else would the world be so beautiful?"

There on the footbridge with the scent of pines in the air and the dappled water murmuring below, birds singing and the lawn making an emerald shimmer beyond the trees, these reassuring words made all Shelley's earlier misgivings seem groundless. When Grimalkin took her arm and continued across the bridge, she went willingly.

By day the scene bore little resemblance to the moonlit landscape through which she had run naked the night before. Grimalkin led her to a gnarled oak near the carriage house and sat her down in its shade. "I want you to close your eyes and keep them closed until I come for you. That's all. But there are two things you must avoid. Don't fall asleep, and don't let yourself daydream. Just keep your eyes closed, sit still, and listen."

Shelley's pulse began to race as she shut her eyes tightly, anticipating some test of courage or character along the lines of last night's ordeal with the blindfold. Without Kip she wasn't sure she could carry it off. She wondered where he was—if he was going through the same process under different supervision. The muscles around her eyes were aching and she relaxed them with an effort, sensing as she did so that Grimalkin had gone and she was alone.

Don't fall asleep, and don't let yourself daydream. No danger of the first. Her nerves hummed like taut wires as she sat beneath the tree—but as the moments passed and nothing happened, it became difficult not to lose herself in her thoughts. Her mind spawned a burst of images from last night, accompanied by a ferment of speculation on what this latest exercise might mean. Hooded figures and dancing flames, the signs of witchcraft traced upon her skin—were they watching now, those who remained from last night, waiting to see if Grimalkin's instructions would be obeyed? How long would they leave her here? As she shifted restlessly, Grimalkin's voice sounded inside her head. *Just keep your eyes closed, sit still, and listen.*

Listen to what? On an afternoon so peaceful, what was there to hear? And then gradually, beneath the quiet, she began to notice a subtle interweaving of sounds. Birdsong. Rustle of wind in the leaves over her head. Buzz of a passing bumblebee, approaching and then receding. A dog barking in the distance.

Beyond the tall hedge on the other side of the carriage house, a murmur of distant voices, as people unloaded a delivery truck behind the E-Z Stop. What would Benjy Hendricks say if he could see her sitting under a tree with her eyes squeezed shut, like a child playing hide-and-seek? His voice sounded in her head: *I just don't want you to get hurt.*

A door slammed somewhere far away. The wind fluttered the leaves above her. She could hear the lazy flow of water in the brook, a musical murmur that just tickled the boundaries of hearing, blending with the others.

La, la . . . la, la . . . a fragment of melody like a tantalizing summons to a secret place. Momentarily it slipped away, dissolving into meaningless stirrings and rustlings, the random rhythms of a summer afternoon, only to return like the effortless flowing of the breeze across the grass. She knew that song. As a child she had been aware of it drifting through her head, haunting her. Soundless and wordless, enigmatic, unearthly, yet hinting at an inward, secret joy; a promise beyond the touch of time or human woe. The song of the gate to the meadow, where last night she and Kip had been apprenticed to a witches' coven.

La, la . . . la, la . . . Was that the secret? Was that you wanted to tell me all along? Kip's sarcastic voice answered her. *What are you, a half-wit? L, A. Lockley Arms.* But regardless of what he said, wasn't it more than that?

He pushes the gate open. A rose-colored ray bursts through the pines on the far side, temporarily blinding us, and in that instant the eldritch melody fills my head.

La, la . . . la, la . . .

I blink. As my vision clears I see Kip still standing at the gate. The soundless melody grows louder, sounding its silvery, unmistakable warning, and I say: I d— I d—

I don't think you ought to.

But ignoring my good advice he stumbles forward into the snowy meadow, flings his arms out and falls backward. I wait for him to move his arms, to make the angel's wings, but he just lies there.

La, la . . . la, la . . .

Behind the inhuman little song his frightened voice is scarcely audible.

Shelley. I can't move.

La, la . . .

Shelley—

"Shelley."

At the touch on her shoulder, she started violently and opened her eyes—blinked at Grimalkin sitting on the grass beside her, and the summer afternoon around them. Was it real, or just a flimsy curtain hastily lowered over the immediacy of that winter twilight? She shivered as Grimalkin touched her shoulder once more. "Are you all right?"

Shelley made herself nod. She had let her mind wander, that was all. In spite of Grimalkin's instructions she had been dreaming, creating foolish fantasies. The older woman rose from the grass and motioned for her to follow, and Shelley automatically matched her pace as they walked over the bridge. Midway across, Grimalkin said, "Did the Goddess speak to you?"

"No." And then, because it sounded so blunt and final, she added hesitantly, "Or if she did . . . I didn't understand."

Grimalkin glanced at her with a half smile. "That comes later. What's important now is learning to listen."

As they reached the end of the footbridge and ducked beneath the pine branches, Shelley saw Kip and Eyebrows—or Elymas, as they were now supposed to call him—emerge from the shadow of the porte cochere. On her brother's face was the same bemused expression she guessed must be on her own.

There were more lessons that weekend, beginning with the names of the other coven members. The owners of the green DeSoto were Tamarack, stout and bald with a toothbrush mustache, and Senta, his petite, cheerful wife. The Prince was Archer. The quiet dark-haired brother and sister were Indigo and Reed; the blond woman who always arrived with them in their Hudson Hornet was Silkmoth. But the most prominent names were those of Everett and Emma Lockley, recurring in every lesson, spoken with a boundless love and respect that made Kip and Shelley begin to wish they had known them.

"This was Emma's athame. I once saw her use it to capture a storm that would have downed trees and power lines all over the county. It still holds a measure of her power. We're very fortunate to possess it."

"Everett always said, 'Magic is anything we don't understand. To the human race, at this point in our development, most of the cosmos is magic.' "

Andreas, the black man, gave the twins a guided tour of the herb garden, introducing them to the various plants and briefly describing the traditional medicines and charms of the Craft. As he talked, Shelley noticed something stuck in the ground nearby—a metal marker shaped like a skull. "What's *that*?"

Andreas looked where she was pointing. "The skull? Oh, that marks the poisonous corner of the garden."

"Poisonous?" Kip gazed at the plants with new interest.

"Yes. This one's belladonna; over there we have hemlock, thorn apple, hensbane, mandrake." Andreas smiled at their wide-eyed faces. "No, we don't go around poisoning people. These plants can be used in harmless medicinal doses, and on occasion we can make use of them in our rituals. Belladonna, hensbane, and mandrake, for instance—together, those three make up the ointment that enables witches to fly."

Looking quickly at him Shelley caught his lips twitching. He was only teasing—wasn't he? Flying ointments, magic potions—anything seemed possible in this sunny herb garden. Separated from the flower garden by a low stone wall, it formed an enchanting world unto itself, a sleepy domain of droning bees and warm whispering breezes where, in obedience to the broken nub of the old stone sundial, time seemed to stand still.

Yet we learned neither spells nor incantations. Instead there were mental exercises intended, Elymas told us, to develop and focus the intuition and imagination. I did my best to follow his instructions, but no matter how hard I tried to focus my thoughts they simply went their own way, running in all directions like children on a playground, while my body contributed an array of distracting itches and fidgets. Nor did I meet with better success when Gwynneth, formerly known as the Jaguar Lady, introduced us to the art of visualization.

"Imagine eating an apple? But why?"

She smiled at my obvious puzzlement. "Because you're learning to create reality, and it's easier to begin by re-creating some familiar experience in detail. As your imagination becomes more disciplined, you'll be able to visualize things that have no actual existence in the physical world—and eventually, by the power of mind and will, to bring them into being."

"Magic," Kip said.

"Exactly. Magic is a process of using the inner world to shape the outer one. You must know what you want, know you can get it, and focus on it completely. Your desire becomes real by force of will. When a coven performs a magical working, all its members combine to form a single will."

I tried to stifle a protest and failed. "But how can something imaginary become real?"

The red-haired witch raised her eyebrows. "Are you so sure you know what *real* is? In the world of physical senses, of objects and categories, everything is set apart from everything else. But there's another face of reality in which nothing is separate. The magician becomes a bridge between the two."

Her words did little to clear up my confusion or reassure me. Ashamed of my doubts, I plunged headlong into the exercises, but it was like throwing myself against a stone wall, and Kip's apparently effortless progress only compounded my frustration. Back in the days when we had been in the same class at school, I had always been the more diligent student, the one striving to please the teacher while he took the role of class cutup—and since then, the lost year of his illness had given me at least the nominal edge of being a grade ahead of him. Now that we were again on equal footing, it was humiliating to find myself so plainly outdone.

But even Kip had his setbacks. In his eagerness to begin working magic, he wanted to rush through what he considered the tiresome preliminaries; the year and a day of our apprenticeship stretched like an eternity before him. Half a dozen times I heard Elymas patiently remind him that there were no shortcuts to a genuine understanding of the Craft.

"Step by step, Kip. Magic isn't a game. It's a study of the inner nature of things, a subtle and complex discipline. If you want to practice it safely, you must go slowly; otherwise you may find yourself out of your depth."

"But in the book I've got at home, some of the spells are so easy! I could do one right now!"

"I don't doubt it. But those spells are what we call glamours, tricks that do no more than temporarily beguile the senses. Before you're ready to practice genuine magic, you must understand the responsibility involved. A true witch never uses magic to interfere with another's free will, or without a clear and needful purpose." Elymas's white brows formed a troubled angle as he toyed absentmindedly with the silver owl on his watch chain. "It's natural to want to test your skill. But remember: although magic is neutral in itself, in the hands of inexperience or ill will it can destroy. And in evoking it you must always pay for what you get: that is what we call the Threefold Law. *What you send, good or bane, returns threefold.* So take it slowly."

I was trying my best, but my visualized apples remained flat and flavorless. Gwynneth showed no more concern over my lack of success than Elymas had. "It doesn't matter, Shelley. It'll come."

"When? When I'm thirty? Forty? Ninety?"

She bent her elegant close-cropped head—I suspected to hide a smile, because when she looked up there was still a trace of it on her lips. "When you're ready for it."

"I'm ready *now*."

"Being ready isn't something you decide on. It happens. In its own time."

They all talked like that occasionally, in riddling phrases I would have despised if they had been spoken without the ring of meaning that set them apart from similar but somehow empty words uttered by my parents and teachers. I trusted Gwynneth and knew she was dealing with me in good faith.

But I harbored a secret fear that she and the others had far overestimated my abilities, and that unlike Kip I was doomed to disappoint them all.

"Shelley, what's the matter?"

Summer was at its height, and Snow and I were sitting together on the stone bench in the garden, where the late afternoon light was pure gold and the air sweet with roses and honeysuckle. I was biting my lip, wondering why she had summoned me from the kitchen, where I had been helping Jessica polish the silver. Ever since that first night in the witches' circle I had been a little shy in Snow's presence—a little awed by the idea of her as the heiress of a long line of wisewomen, shadowy voices bequeathing to her the ancient, hoarded secrets of moon and tide, star and season, herb and stone. But just now she was looking more exasperated than mysterious, so I said, "Nothing."

"Okay. I want you to watch, and do as I do."

She began to rub the palms of her hands together. Slowly at first, then faster. The motion hypnotized me; I sat gawking until I saw her nodding at me to imitate her. *Do as I do.* Hurriedly I complied, rubbing one hand against the other, aware of heat building between my palms (still smelling faintly of silver polish) as I increased their friction. Faster . . . faster . . . A muscle between my shoulder blades started to burn. I wanted to stop, but Snow's eyes, holding mine, would not permit me. *Do as I do . . .*

All at once she stopped and held out her hands in front of her, palm to palm, not quite touching. Reproducing the movement, I couldn't stifle my surprise. "Oh!" Between my hands was a tingling like an electric current, but more intense—as if some prickly, unseen entity were squirming in my grasp. Unnerved, I shook my hands violently and wiped them on my thighs. The tingling died away. I noticed one corner of Snow's mouth drawn up in that familiar half smile. "What *was* that?" I blurted.

"Your life force. What the Chinese call *chi*."

"Is that the same as earth magic?"

Her smile deepened, grew symmetrical. "You sound like

Kip. But you can call it that, so long as you realize there's nothing supernatural implied in the term. This so-called 'earth magic' is a study of the secrets of nature, and works only in accordance with her laws—but you can accomplish quite a lot with it, once you've learned to use certain abilities you were born with."

Certain abilities. An image slipped across my mind: my drunken tormentor Larry outlined in bluish light. In this golden summer garden it seemed very far away. "Use them for what?"

"For whatever you like so long as you cause no harm. There's no need to float passively through life, Shelley. There are always circumstances over which we have no control, but in many cases you can shape them as you wish, to enrich your life and the lives of those around you. The Hebrew Kabbalists, who were very wise in the ways of magic, believed that after death each one of us must answer to God for every unhappy moment we bring upon ourselves in life, and for each opportunity for happiness we let pass by. Now—enough talking. I want you to try it again."

I made a face. "It's creepy, Snow."

"Creepy in what way?"

"Like sticking your tongue on a nine-volt battery." The buzzing between my palms had been less painful, but similar in intensity. And it had been increasing. Seeing her eyebrows go up, I realized how stupid my remark had sounded. "Some boys in my science class last year were doing it," I muttered. "They dared me."

She laughed. "And you couldn't resist."

"Well, I—" I could feel hot color rising in my face.

"Oh, I know." She turned serious again. "But in a way you're right: there's power dormant in the unconscious. It's just a matter of learning to tap it. Now go ahead."

I placed my palms together. An overwhelming reluctance spread through me: I didn't want to experience that unsettling sensation again. I looked appealingly at Snow and she met my gaze.

"We have a saying in the Craft, Shelley. *Where there's fear, there's power.* Try to push past the fear."

"Did Kip do this already?" I said.

The words burst out on their own; I hadn't even known I was going to ask such a question. From her face I saw at once that it was a mistake. Her eyes darkened. "What difference does that make? You need to find your own direction, not copy everything Kip does. Don't count on him always to be there to lead the way."

The words stung, as if she had suddenly slapped my face, and I felt myself recoil. *Don't count on him always to be there.* What did she mean? The flat emptiness of my existence during my years apart from Kip—the memory was like an awful nightmare I had all but forgotten till now. *Don't count on him always to be there.* How could Snow say such a cruel thing? So matter-of-factly, as if it wasn't at all unthinkable that Kip and I might be separated again—as if, in her opinion, it was inevitable. In that moment all my worshipful feelings went for naught; I almost hated her.

"Remember," she was saying, "you have the power to form your own life. Use it to act, not react. It's always easier to let someone else set the standard, but you need to take responsibility for who you are. *Do what thou wilt* doesn't mean so much 'Do as you please' as it does 'Be true to yourself.' In order to do that, you must get to know yourself—not just the parts you feel comfortable with, but your whole self. Do you understand what I'm saying?"

I nodded mechanically—but in truth I scarcely heard her, my thoughts still ringing with those hateful words.

Don't count on him always to be there.

Chapter 2

As the summer passed, the Davies twins became accustomed to inhabiting two different worlds. Outside the hedge that surrounded the Lockley Arms they were a pair of ordinary teenagers, working hard at their summer jobs. Inside, they continued their training as apprentices in a witches' coven. Their delicious sense of belonging to a secret world was only slightly marred by the discovery that certain aspects of it remained undisclosed. Kip's questions about Green Hollow's devastated owl population, or the locked room on the third floor, were deflected with a gentle "Try to be patient. In time you'll be told whatever you wish to know." No one ever said in so many words that apprentices must prove themselves before they could be entirely trusted—but even Kip could grant the need for caution in a tradition haunted by memories of the era Tamarack called "the Burning Times."

"Witchcraft may no longer be against the law," he told them, "but plenty of prejudice still exists against us. Don't be tempted to tell your friends about the coven. You'll find they won't understand."

Shelley was soon to discover for herself the wisdom of this advice. As she and Kip left the Arms one night they could hear mechanical music announcing the presence of the Mister Softee truck, which Benjy Hendricks was driving for the second summer in a row—and when they reached the foot of the driveway there it was, parked a few doors down, surrounded by a crowd of children clamoring for Fudgsicles, Creamsicles, Rocket Ships and Eskimo Pies. Shelley was heading toward it when Kip's voice stopped her. "We just *had* dessert."

His scornful tone said Mister Softee's wares couldn't hope to compare with Jessica's perfect banana crumble. And he was right, of course. But she missed Benjy, who had waved to her several times in passing, and this year's tune was "Let Me Call You Sweetheart." "I'm just going to say hello."

Her footsteps caught the cadence of the lilting music as she went toward the truck. Benjy, framed by the serving window, greeted her across the cluster of eager heads. "Hey, Shelley. How's it going?"

"Okay. You?"

"Can't complain." He scowled down at an upstretched hand. "You're a nickel short, Alex."

"C'mon Benjy, cantcha float me?"

"Who am I, Rockefeller?"

But Shelley saw him hand over an Eskimo Pie. She waited while several more transactions were completed and the last young customers had drifted away to devour their frozen treats in silence. Benjy slouched across the sill. "What can I get you?"

"Oh, nothing. I'm broke anyway. I just came to say hi."

"On the house."

"Oh no, Benjy, I—"

"Come on, let me treat you. What'll it be?"

It seemed rude to refuse his offer. "Ice cream sandwich?"

"Excellent choice, Modom." He produced one with a flourish. "That's how you have to talk, isn't it? At that stuck-up place where you work?"

Shelley stiffened. "It's not stuck-up. It's really nice."

He shrugged and gestured at the ice cream in her hand. "Aren't you going to eat it?" And when she had peeled back the wrapper and taken a bite: "Want to sit in the truck a minute?"

She hesitated, then climbed into the cab. Benjy shut off the engine and the music died with a wail, leaving the crickets in sole possession of the summer night. They sat without talking while Shelley consumed the fast-melting sandwich and licked the last bits of sticky chocolate wafer from her fingers. "Thanks," she said at last. "I'll pay you back."

"Forget it, why should you? None of the other kids ever do."

"Oh, is that what I am? One of the kids?"

"I'm sorry, Shelley," he said quickly. "I—no, you're not a kid. I—I was noticing you've really changed a lot in the last year or so. Really grown up."

This acknowledgment was mollifying. But she was aware of how great a role the Lockley Arms had played in any transformation she might have experienced, and his snide remark about the place being "stuck-up" still rankled. She knew she couldn't tell him about the coven, but she couldn't resist trying to communicate something of what it meant to her. "You meet a lot of interesting people at the Arms," she said. "You know, sophisticated. You get to hear a lot of different ideas about things, instead of the same old outlook. It really makes you question stuff you always took for granted."

"Yeah?" His tone was flat. This wasn't working out the way Shelley had planned. She tried again. "Come on, Benjy. Maybe I'm not explaining it very well. What I mean is, they think for themselves. You ought to appreciate that."

"Me?"

"I remember you wouldn't spend money on those stupid paper flowers for the dance," she said. "That was a decision to go against the crowd."

He snorted. "That was a decision not to spend money I didn't have. Listen, Shelley. I'm not interesting or sophisticated, and I'm not rich enough to afford a different outlook. I'm just a jerk who peddles ice cream to kids at night while other guys are snuggled up with their girls. So don't try to compare me to your fancy new friends."

The last phrase sizzled with hostility. Shelley stared at his shadowy averted profile, then at the tight grip of his hands on the steering wheel. "My mistake," she whispered. In that instant she hated him for so vehemently rejecting what she had been trying to share, and herself for minding. She opened the door and started to get out. At the last moment she remembered her manners and said haughtily, "Thanks for the ice cream."

He lunged across the seat and caught her arm in a grip that made her gasp. His face was so close that she thought he was going to kiss her, but he didn't. In the darkness his breathing was harshly audible. "Hey. Anytime."

Your fancy new friends. Benjy's bitter phrase continued to rankle at the back of my thoughts even while I was compelled to admit it contained a measure of truth. This new, hidden part of Kip's and my existence rendered the remainder so dull in comparison that we begrudged every minute spent outside the enchanted boundary of the hedge. As July ended and the Sabbat of Lammas approached, our anticipation mounted to a fever pitch. We knew Lammas marked the end of the growing season. But otherwise we had little notion what to expect, and it was with some trepidation that I asked Kip if he thought magic would be a part of the ritual. He shook his head.

"My book says the Sabbats are for celebration, not business. They only do magic at the Esbats, the full-moon meetings. And we can't go to those for a long time yet—not until we're initiated."

Yet for me there was plenty of magic that Lammas night. The casting of the witches' circle is a ritual of ageless beauty, capable of touching the heart and spirit even when every word and gesture have become familiar, and that night awakened some dormant part of my psyche that, true to Elymas's warning, I have never since been entirely able to deny. From the first clear chime of the bell across the moonlit meadow, the ceremony held me in thrall.

The central fire was kindled, and the circle traced around it with dagger, salt and oil. Candles were lit at the four compass points to welcome the spirits of air, fire, water and earth. I watched Snow move to the center of the circle and raise the black-handled athame to the moon overhead.

"Honor to you, Great Mother, Lady of Many Names. We ask your blessing upon our circle." As her words rose into the night air, the uplifted blade caught a sudden gleam of light from the white orb above, as if in acknowledgment.

"Merry meet," the phrase went round as we took our places, "Merry meet." The stone altar was piled high with marigolds and sheaves of grain. From the circle of hooded figures standing with bowed heads, an anonymous voice spoke.

"This is the festival of first harvest, the time to reap what we have sown. A time to celebrate, and a time to mourn. For the sun has passed its zenith, and now the waning days lead down to darkness, where all who travel on the Wheel are bound."

As a flute began to play an eerie minor melody, I was seized by a sense of having been snatched from my own era, catapulted far back into some misty time of plagues and gibbets and wild wolves, when outlaws roamed the greenwood and small bands of Goddess worshipers gathered beneath a younger moon. Goosebumps tightened my skin. The firelit figures defining the circle's perimeter seemed to shift and blur, transformed into the substance of myth. Did one of those hoods conceal Pan's curling horns, or Jack-of-the-Green with his beard of living leaves—or even the heartless moonlit gaze of Blodeuwedd, the ancient mother owl? I shivered inside my robe. Accompanied by the plaintive flute, a man began to sing.

I am the stag of seven tines.
Over the flooded world
I am borne by the wind.
I descend in tears like dew, I lie glittering.
I fly aloft like a griffon to my nest on the cliff,
I bloom among the loveliest flowers.
I am the oak and the lightning that blasts it.

When his voice had fallen silent the flute continued on, following its own meandering course. August Eve: summer's end. The lonely windblown notes and faint crackling of the fire cast a brooding spell over the gathering; we all stood staring into the flames, feeling the presage of autumn creep into our bones.

Gradually the music slipped into a merrier key, a livelier pace. A tambourine joined in and hands on either side seized mine, but as we began to move around the circle I couldn't shake the sense that time had slipped some gear and shunted us far back into history. Did it matter? The wild music and coiling motion of the dance fuddled my brain; amid the blur of laughing faces and leaping flames. I floated in a dream. All at once a shout awakened me and I saw that someone else had joined the dance—a life-size figure fashioned from corn husks, with a crude painted face. As our spiral unwound into a circle the coveners passed him around, tossing him back and forth, everyone shouting out loud as he was thrown high in the air. The woven shucks of his arms and legs flapped comically and in the firelight his face wore a simpleminded smile, but I knew who he was: the God of the harvest, the God of sacrifice.

Around the dancing circle he went. I flinched away the first time he came in my direction, and someone else reached out to catch him; but the next time he struck me squarely in the chest and I seized him by reflex, amazed at how flimsy he was, how light. As I tossed him high, the ringing shout that rose above the music filled me with a burst of delight. The spiral closed in once more, winding more and more tightly until breathless firelit faces shut out the darkness and we had to try not to stumble over each other's lively feet—then all at once we were unwinding again, the circle opening out into the night.

It happened without warning: one moment the God was among us, a carefree dancer—the next, someone had flung him into the fire. Voices cried out, my own among them, as the flames blazed up fiercely, transforming his smiling face to a charred husk. I was still standing dumbfounded when Snow stepped forward. Except for the gloating crackle of the fire, there was perfect silence in the circle until she spoke.

"From a tiny seed, the grain grows to ripeness in time. Now the price is paid, the harvest taken, yet from this sacrifice shall spring new life. Know it is thus with all children of the Great Mother. Let the old wane, that the young may wax anew. Ever turns the Wheel."

"Ever onward," came the murmur of response around me. "Ever onward," the words repeated over and over, "Ever onward," becoming a chant that set us all again in motion, the dance facing us first in, toward the fire, then out toward the night—a turning wheel irresistibly rolling from light to darkness and back to light. Dark to light, faster and faster, until the opposites became one. When we stopped at last and released one another's hands, I saw the fire send a funnel of bright whirling sparks upward into the night sky.

Chapter 3

Much as the twins would have preferred to concentrate entirely on their fascinating new existence, the outside world had its own demands. September brought school, and school brought problems. "Wait a minute, Shelley, will you?" When English class was over, Dad called her back on her way out the door. He was frowning. "What's this I hear from Sarah Dince about you wanting to quit the *Quill & Scroll*?"

Miss Dince was the faculty adviser for the school literary magazine. Over the past three years a number of Shelley's poems and stories had appeared in its pages, and the previous spring—fulfilling a dream she had harbored in secret since freshman year—she had been appointed the editor. But things had changed since then. Compared to her recent experiences with the coven, the *Quill & Scroll* seemed childish and shallow and she wanted nothing further to do with it. And so today she had sought out Miss Dince and resigned her position, using her after-school job as an excuse.

Taken aback, Miss Dince had pointed out how impressive the editorship would look on her college applications, how valuable an experience it was, and so on—arguments that failed to sway Shelley in her determination to abandon a pursuit she now deemed valueless. She stifled a sigh. Was Dad going to put her through the same routine?

"I won't have time, Dad. My job—"

"Honey, working over the summer was one thing. But if this job is going to interfere with school—"

"*Quill & Scroll* isn't school. It's extracurricular."

"I know what it is, I was the faculty adviser for eight years. I just want you to think about what I'm saying. Both you and Kip spend way too much time over at the Arms."

I just want you to think about what I'm saying. Shelley made a murmur of acquiescence. She respected Dad's opinion, after all; and that respect had recently been bolstered by a secret pride at how adroitly he could capture the attention of her restless classmates and herself at the end of these very long, very warm school days. It was too bad he was so opposed to the idea of Kip and her working at the Arms, but privately she was counting on him to let the matter drop. Didn't Dad always let her have her way? She didn't give it another thought—at least not until the next morning at breakfast when he brought it up again, this time with more force. "The two of you spend more time working than you do studying. And that's not right."

The twins exchanged a panicky glance. Dad was rarely adamant, but when he was . . . Were they about to be deprived of their reason for spending time at the Arms? "We always make straight A's on our report cards," Kip said.

"I know you do. But there's more to school than good grades. There are friends, activities—"

Marty, who took Dad's every cause immediately to heart, was nodding agreement. "At Clinton-Monroe you played all kinds of sports, Kip. Since you got back, you haven't tried out for a single team."

He sent her a withering look. "I was on the lacrosse team and the fencing team at C.M.A. They don't have those sports at Green Hollow High."

Dad blinked but let this contemptuous remark pass. "Another thing, Shelley. You accepted the editorship of the magazine. You have a responsibility to the other people on the staff."

"All right! I'll *do* the stupid magazine!"

There was a silence, and then Mother said sweetly, reasonably, "It seems a shame to browbeat Shelley into doing something she doesn't want to, when another student would be thrilled to take over the editorship. And really, Graham, I think we should be thankful the children are so willing to work after school. After all, if they want to go to a good college, they're going to have to pay their own way. *We* certainly can't afford to send them."

A few minutes later the twins had gratefully escaped from the breakfast table and headed off to school.

"That was close." Shelley was trying to suppress the image of Dad's defeated face, and the irony of Mother making it possible for them to continue their apprenticeship to the coven undisturbed. "What if he'd made us quit? All because of that stupid magazine!"

Kip kicked an acorn along the sidewalk. "Well, you did say you'd do it."

"I know I did, but that was before . . . anyway, like Mother said, it's not like they can't get somebody else! Whose side are you on, anyway?"

He gave her an oblique glance. "Yours, of course. But I've heard Snow say basically the same thing Dad was saying, about not neglecting our outside lives. If she knew about *Quill & Scroll* she'd probably make you do it."

"Well, she won't know. Unless you tell her." By now he was a few steps ahead and she couldn't see his face. "Kip?" she said in sudden consternation. "Don't you dare tell her!"

He laughed and kicked the acorn again. "She can't really *make* you, you know. Or maybe she could, I don't know. But she wouldn't. Because that would be interfering with your free will."

"I'm not worried she'll put a spell on me, for crying out loud," Shelley said crossly. "I just don't want any more lectures."

The smile had faded from his face. "She's worried about us," he said. "She's not sure she should have let us join."

"What?"

"Remember that night—how she stood back and let the others decide? She wasn't sure. She wanted us, but there was something holding her back." *For various reasons I feel I may not be the best judge.* The memory of Snow's words aroused the same anxiety Shelley had felt on that first hearing. A horrifying doubt seized her. She knew how badly she was doing at the exercises, how miserable her progress had been so far. Was the coven sorry they had let her in? What if they were keeping her only out of pity, or because they wanted Kip? He had stopped on the corner of Main Street to wait for the light and she caught up with him, fighting to swallow the lump that had formed in her throat. "Why wouldn't she be sure?"

A big truck came barreling down Willow and stopped beside them with a plaintive wail of brakes. From his high cab the driver glanced down incuriously, stubbled jaws working a wad of gum—seeing them, no doubt, as a couple of ordinary teenagers discussing football and friends. Kip said, "I think she's worried something will go wrong. Because it went wrong between us before."

"Before?" Shelley said.

The light changed to green. The truck heaved a gusty sigh; the engine coughed and roared as it rolled through the intersection. Kip gave his sister a quick glance as they started across the street. "I told you, Shelley. I've known her before."

What were you in your past life? Lovers?

"Oh yeah," she said flatly. Of course she didn't believe him. His previous-life story was nothing but bombastic make-believe, the invention of a little boy with a big imagination. But following him across Main Street, she felt her heart close like a fist.

Chapter 4

How many times during those first few months did Shelley swing back and forth between anxiety that she might not meet the coven's standards and the equally worrisome fear that she might? If Kip was frustrated by the length of their apprenticeship, to her it was a comfort that the moment of decision lay so far in the future. Only at the beginning of October, when disaster struck, did she begin to understand that, in every sense that mattered, the fateful moment had already come and gone.

"No supper tonight, something's come up. You'd best get home now. It's late."

The twins looked at each other, then back at Jessica. They had finished a busy night in the dining room to find her alone in the kitchen, no sign of Snow or Royce. *Something's come up.* The housekeeper's set face discouraged questions; they changed their clothes and left the house, shrugging into their coats against the early October chill. As they went down the driveway, hungry and curious, Kip broke the silence. "What's that supposed to mean—something's come up? What kind of thing?"

The answer proved to be a mere dozen yards away, just beyond the hedge. Reaching the foot of the driveway they saw a flurry of activity halfway down the block: floodlights had turned the dark street artificially bright, and a gigantic news camera bobbed above the heads of a crowd. As Shelley started toward the spectacle, Kip caught her arm. "Look! Isn't that Andreas's Triumph?"

She turned, but there was only a red flash of taillights disappearing past the hedge. "I didn't see. Come on, let's find out what's going on."

They hurried down the street. A crowd had gathered on the sidewalk in front of the Leonards' house, watching a puffy young man in a rumpled jacket who was talking earnestly into the camera.

"—And here with me now is County Sheriff Joe Bisset. Sheriff, we've been told that so far there are no clues as to the missing boy's whereabouts."

Sheriff Bisset, who sometimes moonlighted as a clown at children's birthday parties, blinked as the microphone was thrust in his face. "Well, that's true. His mother sent him off to the E-Z Stop just after supper—for a box of brownie mix, I think she said, but he never showed up. He was on his bike, and there's really only one route he would have taken, right down Willow here and left on Main, but nobody along the way recalls seeing him. We've got search parties out, going house to house. We haven't turned up anything yet. But if he's anywhere in the area, we'll find him."

"Oh," Shelley heard Marty's voice say behind her, and her aunt's thin fingers seized her own. "Elaine! The children are over here." Mother appeared out of the crowd of Willow Street residents and the four of them huddled together, listening to the plump reporter who again had the white glare of floodlights all to himself.

"Eleven-year-old Alex Leonard was wearing jeans and a green T-shirt printed with the word 'Slim' when he left home on his bicycle more than four hours ago, on an errand that should have taken fifteen minutes at the most. He has not been seen since, and we can only hope his apparent disappearance will soon be explained harmlessly away. As yet, the Leonard family has not been available for comment. But our hopes and prayers are with them tonight as they wait for news of their son. In Green Hollow, this is George Horn for Channel Six News, Albany." He lowered the microphone and spoke across the onlookers' strained silence. "Okay, Bruno, that's it. Let's go."

Once the news truck had driven away the crowd began to disperse, a hushed murmur of voices drifting into the night. "Where's Dad?" Shelley asked, and Mother answered, "He volunteered for one of the search teams. He may not be back till late."

"Poor little Alex!" Marty burst out suddenly. "Oh, I hope he's all right!"

As they joined the other families heading home down the sidewalk, Kip held Shelley back to mutter in her ear, "They're going to do something. The coven. About finding him."

"Huh?" Still stunned by the news, she scarcely heard him.

"Didn't you see Andreas's car? That's why he's here."

Glancing down the street at the white tower rising beyond the hedge, she felt hope flare. "You think they'll use magic to find him?"

"Not *they,* Shelley. *We.* We're part of the coven now. They have to let us help."

"We're only apprentices."

"So what? Together we make thirteen. They need us."

This assumption struck her as brash. "If they do, they know where to find us." And then, because his determined expression didn't change. "Kip. You don't even know for sure if that's what they're doing."

By the time Dad got home, gray-faced with fatigue, it was past midnight. The rest of the family gathered in the upstairs hallway in their pajamas to hear his report.

"Nothing. Not a trace of him. No one saw anything."

"But—but—" Marty's protest trailed off into silence. Standing in their midst, Dad seemed to doze off for a moment, then jerk awake. "There's no sign of his bike either, and Joe thinks there's a chance he might have run away from home. We'll search again in the morning."

Once the adults had gone to bed, Shelley peeked across the hall to see light beneath Kip's door. He opened at once to her soft knock. "What are you doing still up?" she whispered.

"Shut up and come inside."

Once he had closed the door, she became aware of being clad only in her nightgown, Kip in a T-shirt and pajama bottoms. They had conferred thus a million times as children, but they were older now, and ever since the night they had swum naked in the pool . . . she pushed the thought away. Now the important thing was that she didn't want to be alone. She couldn't stop remembering that sinister hooded figure in Jenny's yard, the fluid shadow moving between their own garage and Miss Motley's house . . . and now Alex had disappeared—Alex, who lived right here on Willow Street, who had tagged annoyingly after them when they were all younger, whose big brother Adam had played ball with Kip. Run away from home? That didn't sound like Alex, who loved sweets and would have been greedily anticipating the brownies his mother was planning to make. No, he hadn't run away.

She shivered. Kip had gone to the window to stare out across the street, toward the Arms. All at once his slumped shoulders tensed; he leaned forward to peer down at the dark street below. "Black Jag! It's Gwynneth! They *are* going to do something. And they're going to do it without us."

Shelley reached the window in time to see the sleek black car, ephemeral as shadow, turn into the Arms driveway and glide out of sight beneath the porte cochere. Kip was scowling. "Remember what Gwynneth said about a coven working as a single will," she reminded him. "We're not ready for that yet."

"I am," he said through his teeth.

All the past weeks of watching him sail through the lessons and exercises, while she floundered in his wake, boiled up inside her and she said shortly, "Well, maybe they don't think so."

His eyes ignited. For an instant Shelley thought she had infuriated him; then she realized she was witnessing the birth of one of his crazy schemes. He wheeled away from the window and started for the door. "Kip, what—"

"I'm going over there."

"And do what?" She grabbed his arm. "If they wanted us, Snow would have said something." When he didn't answer she added, "She'll just send you home."

"Not if she doesn't know I'm there."

"What are you talking about?"

"I just want to see what they're doing. Maybe I can help them without their knowing it."

She had a vision of him skulking in the dark meadow outside the boundary of the circle, witnessing whatever unknown ritual was taking place. *I just want to see what they're doing.* A circle of figures in hooded robes, no different from the one she had seen skulking in Jenny's yard. Somebody in a Halloween costume . . . or a witch in traditional garb? A phrase whispered in her head—*offer babes and children to devils*—and foreboding prickled her skin. Whatever was going on across the street, Kip mustn't go barging into it. "You're crazy," she said. "I won't let you do it."

Disdain flickered across his face. "You can't stop me."

"Want to bet?" Shelley's heart was pounding. "I can scream," she said. "And when Dad and Mother and Marty come running in here, you can explain what I'm screaming about."

His eyes narrowed. "You wouldn't do it."

"Try me."

"Shelley, dammit—" He jerked his arm free from her grasp and backed two steps toward the door, eyeing her warily. She took a deep breath and opened her mouth.

I was bluffing, of course, but I must have convinced Kip, because he lunged forward as if to put his hand over my mouth. As I flinched away, the backs of my knees came in contact with the bed behind me, and I lost my balance and fell across it. His momentum landed him squarely on top of me. The impact knocked my breath away. Black spots danced before my eyes; for an agonizing interval I struggled to draw air into my outraged lungs. Finally I managed a strangled gasp, and then another, so absorbed in this essential process that I was only vaguely aware of Kip still lying on me. And then, as breath returned, my awareness shifted suddenly to his face above mine.

In the gold-flecked hazel eyes, a look of dreamy shock had replaced the single-minded purpose of a moment ago. All at once I was burningly conscious of the flimsy layers of fabric separating us. Of his weight and his warmth and one point in particular, where something was prodding the inside of my thigh. I suppose I knew what it was—and knowing, I should have shoved him off me instead of doing what I did.

I closed my eyes.

I could feel my heart, a deliberate beat that made shimmering patterns on the inside of my eyelids. I could hear Kip's breathing, perfectly synchronized with those patterns. Each of these rhythms—heartbeat, patterned light, breath—seemed to merge with the others, causing time to part and flow around us without touching. The two of us floated, unfettered by past or future, as once we had done in the womb, in a suspended present in which I could not tell where his flesh ended and mine began.

And then the bed jounced as he pushed himself abruptly off

me and sat up. A second later, I heard his odd, breathless voice. "I guess you're right. Anyhow, it's late. We should get some sleep."

Chapter 5

Shelley slept badly. Her pillow was a sack of rocks, the bedclothes a suffocating tangle. Alex's disappearance, the hovering image of that hooded shape—these things would have kept her awake in any case, but they were very nearly eclipsed by the shock of what had happened in Kip's room. Although *nothing,* she protested silently to herself again and again, *nothing* had actually happened. Yet the memory kept returning unbidden: the warm weight of his body pressing against hers, the dazed look on his face. Was he lying awake across the hall, thinking about it too—or was he standing at his window in the dark, staring across the street at the moonlit facade of the Arms?

The next morning was a Saturday. When she got downstairs at seven, Kip had already gone to work. "He said he had a lot to do, and he wanted to get started early." Marty, her bangs still in their morning curlers, brought Shelley a bowl of cereal and sat with her at the kitchen table while she ate. "The search parties went out again early this morning, and on the radio they gave a phone number for people to call if they have any information. So far there's been no news. It doesn't seem possible, does it? Things like that just don't happen in Green Hollow."

Remembering a small feathered corpse lying on the porch steps, Shelley winced and got up to put her empty bowl in the sink. *Thing like that just don't happen in Green Hollow.* Didn't they? There was no reason to connect Alex's disappearance with the unexplained blight that had annihilated the village's owl population over the past year. No reason. Just a vague, formless dread . . .

In spite of the warm weather she could smell autumn in the air as she hurried across the street to work. What was Kip up to? The front yard of the Arms boasted a scattering of yellow leaves and fresh windfalls beneath the apple trees, but no sign of her twin. Nor, she noted with surprise as she passed beneath the porte cochere and came in sight of the parking lot, was there the expected collection of coveners' cars—not even Gwynneth's Jaguar, although she could swear she had watched it turn up the driveway late last night. Wait—wasn't that a gray Mercedes, sandwiched between the truck Royce used for errands and a Pontiac sedan that must belong to a guest? A closer inspection revealed the Vermont plates. Yes, Elymas and Grimalkin were here. But what about Gwynneth and Andreas? And the others?

It was seven-thirty and she was overdue in the kitchen to begin serving breakfast; for now, her questions would have to wait. Or would they? Returning to the kitchen after serving the guests with omelettes and croissants, fruit and coffee, she tentatively sounded Jessica for information. "I thought I saw Elymas's car in the parking lot." Neither he nor Grimalkin had appeared in the dining room, and she wondered if their presence was supposed to be a secret.

Jessica, removing a tray from the oven, answered without looking at her. "Could be sleeping in. They got here late."

"And Gwynneth? I thought I saw her car last night."

This time Jessica glanced up, an appraising look that made Shelley squirm. Deep, unfamiliar grooves dragged the housekeeper's mouth down at the corners. "She left already. Most all of them did. They got busy schedules, things to do. No time to stand around and gossip."

This last comment was a pointed one. Shelley took a freshly brewed pot of coffee and slunk in silence back to the dining room, but as she filled the cups of two smiling old ladies in spectacles and cardigan sweaters, her thoughts were churning. The coven had gathered last night, and for what other purpose than to discover Alex's whereabouts? But why had their two new apprentices been excluded?

There was no clear answer to this question, and no sign of Kip until breakfast was over and the guests had left the dining room. Then, heading for the kitchen with a laden tray of dirty dishes, Shelley heard his sulky voice on the other side of the swinging door. "What do you mean, she's still sleeping? What's the matter with her? She doesn't usually sleep this late."

And Jessica's tart reply: "I guess she can sleep as late as she likes without *your* permission. She was up half the night. Not that it's any of your business."

"Up doing what?" he was saying as Shelley came in.

"I told you." Jessica turned her back on him. "None of your business."

Rowan, perched on the counter, flicked his ears back and yawned in Kip's scowling face. Shelley took her tray over to the sink. In the brief instant Jessica glanced her way, she could have sworn the housekeeper's eyes were full of tears. Behind her, the door to the dining room swung open and Snow's voice said, "If there's any coffee left, we would love some."

Turning, Shelley caught her breath at Snow's haggard face. Fatigue had drained her skin of color; the shadows beneath her eyes were like charcoal smudges on parchment. She smiled, but it was only a perfunctory tightening of her lips, lapsing the next instant as if she couldn't sustain the effort. Jessica jerked her head at the twins and they followed Snow back into the dining room, Shelley with the coffeepot and Kip trailing behind with a stack of cups.

Elymas and Grimalkin were sitting at a table by the window. In the wash of morning light they too were visibly spent. They murmured a greeting and then were silent, watching dully as Kip set cups in front of them and Shelley poured the coffee. "Thanks," Snow said when they were done. It was clearly a dismissal, and Shelley started back toward the kitchen. Then she heard Kip speak.

"You know, I thought we were supposed to be part of"—his

voice dropped from its normal pitch to a fierce whisper— "part of *things*. Shelley and me."

Shelley, making an indecisive halt halfway across the room, saw the three adults look first at one another and then at Kip. He stood beside the table in a truculent posture, arms folded across his chest. "And?" Snow said at last.

"And last night you had a meeting without us!"

Snow sighed. It was as if every ounce of her vitality had been sapped and only sheer force of will kept her functioning. Elymas's shoulders had an unaccustomed weary sag that made him look, for the first time since Shelley had known him, like an old man. Grimalkin seemed drawn into herself, almost shriveled.

"It was about Alex, wasn't it?" Kip was saying. "You were trying to find him. Maybe we could have helped! Isn't thirteen better than eleven?"

Shelley's throat had gone dry. Afraid this exchange might be overheard, she glanced quickly into the entrance hall, but it was empty. Neither Elymas nor Grimalkin said anything. Snow drank some coffee and set the cup down. She looked past Kip to where Shelley stood, then back up into the boy's face. "I'm sorry we had to leave you out. But it was for your safety."

This answer plainly irked him; his next question was brusque. "Did you find Alex?"

Snow swallowed. To Shelley it was clear she was trying to be patient with him even though she was visibly exhausted and disheartened. This time her voice shook a little as she said, "I'm afraid Alex is dead."

Dead. The word landed with a dull impact like a dropped stone. Again Shelley remembered the dead owl on the porch, its soft plumage the same brown as Alex's hair. *Dead.* Kip's mouth was hanging open. When he spoke again, the surliness had vanished and his voice was hushed. "Are you sure?" And then when no one answered and the silence was more convincing than words would have been: "What happened?"

Shelley saw a quick glance flash between the three at the table, but Elymas's answer was only an echo of other, earlier evasions. "We have to ask you to trust us, Kip. Not to ask too many questions for the time being. When we can tell you more, we will."

Later, Shelley went looking for her twin and found him cleaning the pool, using a net with a long handle to fish out the drowned leaves. She wanted to discuss the devastating news about Alex, but instead she found herself remembering last night, and what had happened in his room. A qualm went through her and she said angrily, accusingly, "You're making a mess of that."

Kip looked startled. The rescued leaves, it was true, were scattered untidily across the bricks around the pool, but he would sweep them up when he was done. He shrugged, resuming the sweep of his net through the water as a breeze brought down another brittle shower from the trees. Shelley retreated to one of the canvas chairs and sat down, bewildered by the unreasoning but powerful urge to quarrel with him about something. Anything.

"Shelley." He had stopped sweeping and was looking at her.

"What?" she snapped.

"It wasn't an accident. Somebody killed him."

The hushed words abruptly deflated her anger; she felt horror take its place. "Wh-why would somebody kill Alex?"

"I don't know. But somebody's been hanging around our street. Remember the night we found the owl on the porch? There was somebody by the garage—"

A whisper of leaves, a sliding shadow in the darkness. "I thought you said it was a hobo!"

"Well, maybe it wasn't."

A squeak of metal interrupted them: Grimalkin was opening the gate, waving as she crossed the grass. She looked greatly recovered; she must have slept since they had seen her at breakfast. "We have to be off now, so I wanted to say goodbye. And to say how sorry I am about what's happened. You knew the boy?"

They both nodded; a lump came to Shelley's throat. Alex, who would have just learned to sing the alphabet backward, who was always short a nickel or a dime for ice cream . . . She swallowed. "Grimalkin? Are you sure he's—?"

Lines creased the older woman's face; she nodded slowly. "I'm afraid so."

"Have you told the police yet?" Kip said.

"No, and we won't. The boy's parents need time to come to terms with what's happened. They wouldn't believe it, coming from us; they would want more proof than we can give. And we don't want to become overtly involved."

"But you're already involved. You had that special meeting—"

Grimalkin lifted her hands tiredly and let them fall to her sides. "Of course we wanted to do what we could. But we were too late to save the boy, and at this point any public involvement on our part would serve no purpose. We have to protect ourselves. Don't you see, any crime involving children poses a serious threat to the coven. If our existence should become known . . ." She sighed. "There's so much ignorance, so much prejudice and fear surrounding witchcraft. Many people still believe the old stories that we sacrifice live children or babies in our rites."

How Witches do Offer Babes and Children to—Shelley's heart began to race as she thought of that hooded shape watching Jenny's house. "But that's not true . . . I mean . . . is it?"

"What matters in this case," Grimalkin said softly, "is not what's true, Shelley, but what people believe. And even though witches are no longer burned at the stake, there are other kinds of persecution."

Burned at the stake? Shelley gulped, remembering Tamarack's graphic descriptions of what accused witches had endured in medieval times. Stripped and shaved, suspended off the ground by their thumbs, their skin pierced with sharp implements, their bones crushed. *Many people still believe we sacrifice live children* . . . She couldn't help noting Grimalkin had failed to deny the accusation outright. Suddenly she was weak all over, grateful she was sitting down. What had Kip gotten them into? Why had she listened to him instead of to her own doubts about joining the coven—why had she followed his daredevil lead? Dare*devil.* The witches had taught her that the devil played no part in their practices—but the average person, including her own family and friends, simply took it for granted that witchcraft was rooted in evil and nourished by blood. That ominous hooded silhouette flickered once more at the back of her thoughts and she pushed it away. *Things like that just don't happen in Green Hollow.* Didn't they? Suddenly what had seemed a random series of deaths—the Lockleys, the owls, now a child—struck Shelley as not random at all, but part of a larger pattern: a shadowy, cryptic web whose strands converged unmistakably at a single point.

The Lockley Arms.

Chapter 6

MISSING CHILD ALERT

Below the stark words was a photograph of Alex wearing a baseball cap. On his shoulder rested a disembodied hand—belonging, as it happened, to his brother Adam who had been cropped out of the picture, but adding an eerie touch nonetheless. *Missing since October 3rd,* ran the text. *Last seen riding his bicycle in the area of Willow and Main streets around 7* P.M. *Wearing jeans, a green T-shirt with the word "Slim" in white letters on the front. If you have seen this boy, please contact state police at the number below.*

The posters were everywhere in Green Hollow these days: at the Texaco station, the laundry and the E-Z Stop, in shop windows, on church bulletin boards, in the hallways at school, and on every lamppost along streets bright with autumn trees. Nearly every evening there was some mention of the disappearance on the TV news from Albany, accompanied by a brief clip of Alex's parents with their bruised, suffering faces and brave words—"We haven't given up hope. We know our boy will be found."

As the days passed, the village waited anxiously for this good news. No one dared suggest any other outcome; as Marty said, things like that didn't happen here. But the streets were deserted after dark except for police patrol cars, and when the twins left the Arms at night, Royce escorted them home.

Aware that the coven's safety depended on their discretion, they said nothing about what they knew, but it was a heavy burden to know Alex's fate while the rest of the village remained ignorant. At times the unwelcome knowledge felt to Shelley like a silent scream in a nightmare. *We haven't given up hope. We know our boy will be found.* How could people not guess the truth? Although the coveners remained uncommunicative on the subject, a conversation with Elymas confirmed Kip's conjecture that Alex had been murdered.

"But there's got to be something you can do!"

"We've cast a binding spell to try and prevent further killings. It may or may not be effective, but for now it's our only option."

"Can't you put a curse on whoever did it?"

Elymas shook his head, his expression grim. "Remember your lessons, Kip. Magic is a double-edged weapon that affects the maker of the spell as well as the object. *Whatever you send, returns threefold.* And a curse is no exception."

Further killings: the words chilled Shelley to the bone. Was the binding spell all that protected them from a nameless, faceless murderer? Who was he, and why did he go clad in a witch's hooded robe? Anxiety made it difficult for her to concentrate on her exercises, but she kept plodding away, achieving little or nothing while Kip left her further and further behind. It was impossible not to resent his easy progress. Why did everything have to come so quickly to him? It wasn't fair—just as it wasn't fair that he had been clumsy and stupid enough to fall on top of her in his room. The incident still lingered silently between them, creating a tension that refused to go away.

* * *

Meanwhile, the local concern over the missing boy did nothing to hurt business at the Arms. The weekends continued to bring a flood of tourists eager to see the spectacular mountain foliage, and the staff were run nearly off their feet. By the third such marathon Jessica was exhausted. On Sunday evening, when the crowd had thinned, Snow gave Royce and her the night off and took over the kitchen herself.

The twins were set to work on a dish that could technically, Shelley supposed, be called a lamb stew—if so pedestrian a name could do justice to a concoction so delicate and savory. Along with the tender cubes of lamb there were parsnips in it, carrots and raisins and yellow onions, red wine and honey, all simmering together in a cauldron-like pot on the stove.

"And a little of this, and some of this, and . . . oh, definitely this—" Snow's fingers hovered over the glass jars of herbs in the cupboard, selecting some and passing them to Shelley, who added them to the bubbling stew while Kip stirred. Enticing aromas invaded the air, heightening the gleam of the copper pans on the walls and burnishing the brass push-plate on the swinging door. Outside, against a slate-colored sky, the trees surrendered the last light from their high branches, but as dusk gathered outside the windows the kitchen grew brighter and cozier until everything beyond its walls, even the shock of Alex's death, began to retreat into the distance—and Shelley, watching her brother's face through the delectable steam rising from the pot, thought hazily that maybe he wasn't as annoying as she had thought him in recent weeks. The twins were famished long before the guests started to come down to the dining room, but when Kip raised the stirring spoon to his lips to filch a taste, Snow seized his wrist. "Keep out of there!"

"But I'm starving!"

"We'll eat later."

At the time, the prohibition seemed no more than a cook's standard defense of her pot—but as the evening went on, as the twins served the guests with crusty loaves of fresh bread, salad, bottles of robust red wine and steaming, fragrant bowls of stew, Shelley began to notice a gradual change in the atmosphere of the dining room. Among the dozen or so guests, from the shy young twosome in the corner to the talkative quartet by the window, a pervasive air of intimacy had set in. Normally Shelley was too concerned with the proper performance of her duties to pay much attention to the diners beyond their requests for food or drink, a clean napkin or another fork. But on this night as she passed in and out of the dining room it was impossible not to notice the way people had begun to lean together across the tables, to join hands and turn their chairs in a way that enhanced their privacy. Even the candles burned with a softer, more romantic glow. By the time the main course was done, at every table there were soft murmurings, glances that lingered, small shifts of movement bringing the diners into ever closer proximity.

"Would you like coffee? Dessert?" Her offers fell on deaf ears. Across the room Kip was signaling her; they headed for the kitchen and let the door swing shut behind them to find Snow rummaging in the refrigerator.

"What do you two want for supper? There's bread and cheese, and some smoked ham."

"Is there any stew left?"

"Not a morsel."

Kip wandered over to the stove and peered into the depths of the pot. "Damn. They ate it all."

"Nobody wanted dessert," Shelley said. "Or coffee either."

"No, I don't suppose they did."

Something in Snow's tone made Shelley peek into the dining room. She couldn't suppress a surprised exclamation at what she saw. "They're all gone!"

Kip came hurrying over to look. The dining room was deserted. Empty chairs stood askew, pushed back from tables where candles burned low. Napkins had been tossed down; an abandoned scarf formed a bright question mark on the floor. It was as if an entire roomful of people had disappeared as unexpectedly as poor Alex. From somewhere upstairs came a faint shriek dissolving into laughter, and suddenly Shelley understood. She turned and leveled a finger at Snow. "*You* did it!"

Snow only raised her eyebrows.

"You did! The stew—you put some kind of love potion in it! Didn't you?"

Snow had started to slice the cheese and ham. Without looking up from her task she said, "Don't we want our guests to enjoy their stay?"

Shelley caught her breath. No circle had been cast, no magic words pronounced, and yet . . . She thought of the rising curve of romance she had noticed during the meal, the guests growing more intimate with each bite of that delicious lamb stew. "It was the stew," she said in wonder. Kip started to snicker and Snow glanced up, mischief in her eyes.

The three of us burst out laughing. It seemed wrong somehow, when Alex was dead—but the laughter was irresistible, a buoyant wave that caught and lifted us until we floated weightlessly on its crest. The paroxysms robbed us of breath and strength, reducing us to helpless giddiness. Snow collapsed in a chair; Kip and I clutched the counter for support. The colors of brick and glinting copper shimmered around us as Rowan appeared, purring thunderously, and made the rounds from Snow to Kip to me and back again—Snow, Kip, myself, rubbing himself against our shins as if binding us together with some invisible skein.

The laughter ebbed finally of its own accord. Snow's hair had started to slip out of its elegant knot; now she removed the pins and let it spill free. With it loose, hanging halfway down her back, she looked no older than we were. She shook back its shining fall. "All right. Who wants supper?"

We were all ravenous, and there wasn't much in the way of conversation as we sat around the table devouring bread and cheese and smoked ham, with a bowl of Jessica's cranberry compote on the side. Kip smiled at me and I smiled back. The irritation and resentment that had plagued me in his presence in recent weeks had dissolved with the laughter, and I felt drowsy and relaxed beneath the circle of light that lay over the table. Rowan perched on the counter nearby, surveying us with his blinking green gaze.

Except for the occasional smooth slide of china over wood

as someone pulled a platter closer for another helping, there was silence. Silence in the kitchen, and in the darkened house above—a silence whose secrets I could all at once vaguely discern, as if my vision were inevitably adapting from the bright uncomplicated daylight of my childhood to a stage of life in which all colors were darker, richer, filled with subtle tints and oblique shadows invisible to me until now. *Don't we want our guests to enjoy their stay?* I raised my eyes to the dim ceiling overhead, listening to the fraught silence, and lowered them to find Snow watching me with a faint, complicit smile.

Silence. Until, his mouth half full, Kip broke it. "But is it really okay to do something like that? Aren't you using magic to control them?"

Snow blinked. The cat leaped lightly off the counter and strolled across the table to rub his head against her cheek. She lifted one hand to caress him, her long shining hair mingling with his fur. The sight made me imagine some medieval painting—the beautiful young witch and her familiar. Two pairs of eyes, one jade and one silver, rested on Kip with the same unfathomable gleam. "To control is to break. The secret is to bend, to shape *without* breaking. Do you understand?"

He nodded and broke into a smile; her answer seemed to satisfy him. But at the back of my mind there was a whisper that said, softly but distinctly, *Whatever you send, returns threefold.* I couldn't help thinking back to the way the three of us had laughed together with such abandon; and I wondered if we had not been bewitched a little too, by that magical stew whose aroma still lingered in the kitchen air.

Chapter 7

Late in October, Alex's bicycle was found buried beneath a pile of dead leaves in the park. Although the media jumped on this discovery as "an important clue in the disappearance of a Green Hollow boy," it soon became apparent that it was nothing of the kind. Muddy and beginning to rust, the bicycle yielded no hint of either Alex's whereabouts or his fate. Nonetheless the news caused a buzz throughout the village, and once again the disappearance became the sole topic of conversation. Everywhere people were saying, "Do you think he was kidnapped?" and Kip and I tried not to look at each other.

Knowing my twin, I suppose I should have been able to guess what he was planning. After all, Samhain was coming—Samhain, the witches' name for Halloween. A night of power, Gwynneth told us, when the veil separating the seen and unseen worlds is at its thinnest, when for a few short hours the dead mingle with the living. A sacred night outside the framework of linear time, a vantage point from which the future becomes visible.

"You stare into a piece of dark glass," Kip told me later, when we were alone. "After a while you start seeing visions. It's called *scrying*."

"Visions?" I put on a skeptical face. "Visions of what?"

"Anything. The past. The future. Other realities."

"Come off it, Kip."

"I'm serious. It works by depriving you of sensory input. Once your mind gets bored enough, it shifts into a different mode. An *extra*sensory one." He grabbed my wrist so suddenly that I jumped. "Shelley. What if we could scry *him*?"

"Him?"

"You know. *Him.* The guy who killed Alex."

All at once the pit of my stomach was cold. I pulled free. "The others must have tried it already. If they couldn't do it, we can't."

He turned away with a shrug, but his thought reached me as clearly as if he had spoken. *I'm going to try.*

For me, the mere prospect of reclaiming the magical Halloweens of my childhood offered more than enough excitement. Kip's illness had marked the end of my trick-or-treating days; since then I had stayed home on Halloween to hand out candy and join Dad in watching the horror movie marathon on TV. Last year there had been Jenny's dismal party. But this year . . . this year I would once again celebrate my favorite holiday as it deserved.

There was no banquet that night, when the coven came together at the Arms to celebrate this greatest of all the Craft's festivals. Instead we all fasted—in preparation, Elymas explained, for the visions we might experience within the circle. The moon had risen orange in the dark October sky by the time we silently crossed the carriage house lawn toward the pool. Silently, that it, except for me. The crisp air made my teeth chatter and my empty stomach kept up a rumbling accompaniment. The robed figure just ahead of me glanced back; within its dark cowl I caught the glimmer of Gwynneth's sympathetic smile.

Halloween. All Hallow's Eve. A night of cats and candles, pumpkins and apples—of mystery and disguise, when spirits prowl the streets and skeletons dance in graveyards, their bones rattling merrily. And a night of witches: everyone knows that. Ugly old crones with scraggly hair and warty chins, screeching and riding their broomsticks across the wild, windblown sky, grotesque silhouettes dark against the moon. The pool had been blessedly heated for our ritual bath, but as I climbed out and hastily redonned my robe I was already shivering again, remembering the engraving in the *Malleus Maleficarum. With willow whistles they summon the wind, and to their most unholy Sabbats they ride upon enchanted steeds.* By now I knew these images were derived from none other than the Goddess herself in the guise of Cerridwen the Hag, the ancient wisewoman to whose vast cauldron all souls return to await rebirth.

There were two circles that night, as there always are when true witches celebrate Halloween: one circle for the living and one for the dead. In the first the customary fire is kindled. The second, adjoining it, lies in darkness. We gathered without speaking around the fire, and looking around the circle I could not suppress a qualm at the sight of those hooded figures. *Many people still believe the old stories that we sacrifice live children or babies in our rites.* That wasn't true; the coven had done its best to save Alex. But from whom? Edging a little closer to the bright, weaving flames, I returned Andreas's smile. On this of all nights, it was a comfort to be able to recognize familiar faces—to remind myself that these people were my friends.

Beside the stone altar I noticed a jumble of sticks and straw that resolved itself, as I looked more closely, into a pile of handmade besoms. *Broomsticks.* A sensation of liquid cold formed at the top of my spine and trickled slowly downward. I glanced up at the moon, huge in the night sky, and it held my gaze as Snow broke the silence of the circle.

"We gather at the crack of time. On this night the veil is thin between the worlds. The dead walk, and to the living is revealed the Mystery: that every ending is but a new beginning. Here in this time out of time, we stand able to look both forward and back. Let us welcome to our circle those we have loved in the past, that we may celebrate with them once more. And on this night open your inner eye, that you may pierce the veil that hides the future." She paused. The whisper of the fire stirred the stillness. When she spoke again, her tone had changed from solemn to exultant. "Tonight we fly between the worlds. Make ready for the journey!"

The nature of those preparations took me completely by surprise. A container of some greasy substance was circulated among us, and without ceremony people opened their robes and began to smear its contents onto one another's bodies.

There was a little laughter, like a shower of sparks from the humming current of anticipation in the circle. Gywnneth appeared beside me and reached inside my robe; I flinched as her quick hands applied the oily paste to my skin. To distract myself I glanced up again at the enormous moon that loomed almost close enough to touch.

Tonight we fly between worlds. The ointment began to sting; I let out a gasp as its biting heat penetrated my skin and sank into the muscle beneath, rousing the urge to jump, run, turn cartwheels. *Fly.* I gave an involuntary hop. Gwynneth looked up at me with a smile and closed my robe, knotting the cord firmly around my waist. "Come," she whispered. The circle was reforming, and we hurried to take our places.

With willow whistles they summon the wind. And all at once I heard them—the whistles shrilling, summoning us to take up our besoms and dance. Higher and higher they wailed, filling the night with their unearthly noise, and as they wailed the wind suddenly rose, snatching at our robes and whipping the flames into fantastic shapes until sparks were flying everywhere, the black air alight with glowing flecks. Behind the shriek of the whistles and the cold rushing of the wind rose a sly rattle like rollicking bones, and our living limbs quickly caught their rhythm. What greater delight than to be a witch on Halloween, dancing on the edge of a dark wheel that spun on the blazing axis of the fire? At the edge of the meadow the shadowy pines whipped and tossed as if dancing with us. The wind was at our backs, pushing us roughly along as it tugged at the besoms in our hands.

Faster and faster we danced. No matter that I grew lightheaded and out of breath; my enchanted limbs kept moving. The ground became a springboard that sent me higher into the air with every step. I had a hazy, faraway memory of the sunny herb garden, Andreas's voice saying faintly, *Belladonna, henbane, and mandrake, for instance—together, those three make up the ointment that enables witches to fly . . .* The memory slipped away. Between steps I was suspended for long intervals, floating like a leaf on the chill October wind, while the shadowshapes of my companions cavorted around the fire and the bones and whistles made wild music beneath the moon.

The moon. Once more my eyes were drawn upward. Now its smoky disk filled half the sky. As I gazed transfixed, a strong gust of wind suddenly swept me high into the air, and this time I did not come down. There was a vivid, horrifying impression of the earth falling away beneath me, the dark meadow spiraling into nothing as I soared upward. Cold air rushed at me, ballooning my hood and rippling my robe, lifting the hair from my scalp and blowing an involuntary shriek back down my throat.

Impossible—it couldn't be happening—but it was. The moon was in front of me and I hurtled toward it at breakneck speed, clutching for dear life to something I realized belatedly was the handle of the besom I rode, bucking and plunging beneath me like an unruly horse. *To their most unholy Sabbats they ride upon enchanted steeds* . . . Wild laughter burst from my throat. Against the dazzling moon ahead, dark specks darted and swooped; faint shouts and cries reached my ears across the buffeting wind. My head was spinning and I was careful not to look down. Could this be happening? Were we really flying through the air—flying gloriously high on our besoms above the unsuspecting village, where carved pumpkin grins lit the dark streets and young trick-or-treaters smelled magic in the wind? Flying . . . riding the air and the moon's floodtide . . . Dizzy terror cursed through me, a terror laced with awe, glee, breathless exhilaration—and beneath all else, the shameless pleasure of straddling that rocking broomstick. I threw back my head and screamed for the fierce and impossible joy of it. No need to be quiet, to be careful, to worry about what the neighbors might think. I was free, flying between the worlds.

Straight toward the moon I flew. Its luminous face, mottled with shadow, filled my vision as I drew closer. Thought loosened its grip and drifted away; all sound ceased and I seemed to rush forward in a vacuum, with only the pressure of silent wind on my face. The last traces of night sky disappeared, blotted out by that enormous, shimmering circle of light; all physical sensation had vanished except for a throbbing pulse in my fingers where they clutched the besom's handle. This close, even the shadows were transformed to light. Afraid, I shut my eyes—then, even more afraid, opened them again to find myself blinded by radiance. And into that radiance I flew.

Beyond, it was dark once more. I blinked, bewildered to find myself on solid ground. Blinked again to find a dim scene slowly forming around me: hooded shapes, the red embers of a dying fire. A cauldron stood beside a stone set with unlit candles. As if we had never left the meadow. Yet I knew what this place was—a shadow cast between the worlds, an oblique reflection of the real circle we had left behind. The air seemed smoky; shapes were indistinct.

An arch of leafless branches and withered cornstalks marked the entrance to the circle of the dead. Grimacing pumpkins stood sentinel on either side, joined by a solitary robed figure, face hidden by the folds of its hood.

"You know me as the Horned One, the Traveler on the Wheel. On this night I guard the gate between life and death, through which all who live must pass one day. Yet tonight the old year is finished, the new is yet to come. The gate stands open between the worlds and the dead have returned. Who wishes to join them in fellowship?"

Murmurs rose around me in response. "I do . . . I do . . ."

"I do," I whispered.

The hooded figure lifted a flickering candle. "Then take light, for in the circle of the dead you shall find none."

Following the others, I took an unlit candle from the altar and touched it to his. One by one, carrying our small brave lights, we passed into the dark circle. As I ducked beneath the woven arch something brushed my head—only a dry corn husk, but it felt like the caress of a ghostly hand. A shudder convulsed me, then faded to intermittent trembling.

The gate stands open between the worlds, and the dead walk. I joined the circle of kneeling figures. Darkness pressed close, eager to devour our tiny candle flames. I tried to shelter mine with a shaking hand; it seemed on the verge of going out. A voice spoke softly.

"We are gathered in the circle of the dead. For these few

moments, let us pause and think of loved ones who have passed on. Let us light this place with our memories, as one day we shall want others to do on our behalf. And as these lights burn, so may the light of remembrance burn for those we have loved—for what we shared with them, and what we were to one another."

We placed our candles in a circle on the ground. I sat staring at mine—and miraculously, as I watched, its feeble flame began to burn higher, brighter, until it was dancing merrily on its wick. Through the fog in my head I tried to think about dead loved ones. My thoughts shied away from Alex, so I concentrated on Grandma Davies, Dad's mother. My memories of her were so faint (she had died when Kip and I were four) that my candle should have been the merest flicker—but still it brightened, golden with a deep violet center, and I kept my eyes fastened upon it.

No one spoke. There was a faint whispering that might have been the cornstalks rustling in the wind—yet the wind had died away. As the moments passed I began to feel an eerie certainty that there were more of us than there had been a few minutes before. As if our company were gradually increasing. Had others begun to join us in the darkness? Without daring to raise my eyes, I seemed to sense other presences coming quietly to kneel among us. A swirl of invisible robes, a rustle that sounded like dry husks but might have been a whispered greeting—

I held my breath and steeled myself to lift my gaze. My skin prickled as I saw that the air had thickened to a flux in which hovered a multitude of hazy shapes, forming and dissipating from one instant to the next. Did I discern ghostly faces, insubstantial hands—or were the wisps of fog playing tricks on my befuddled brain? Across the circle there was a green gleam of eyes. Rowan? What was *he* doing here? He blinked at me lazily—and all at once, at the edge of my vision, I could make out throngs of shadowy figures mingling with the twelve I knew.

Who were they, these others joining us by candlelight, drawn to our circle of tiny flames? Were the Lockleys among us now, celebrating the Samhain festival with their old friends? *Let us welcome to our circle those we have loved in the past, that we may celebrate with them once more . . .* Terror and wonder unfolded inside me—the sensation a thousand times more heady than the special Halloween enchantment I had found so intoxicating in the past, and suddenly I understood that all those childhood Halloweens, no matter how magical, how mysterious, had been mere travesties of this night's true power.

And then I saw Rowan arch his back and hiss softly, and followed his glowing gaze to see a dark shape beyond the periphery of the circle, scarcely visible against the darkness. Hooded and robed, a skewed shadow of those within the circle. Restlessly it moved back and forth as if eager to join us, probing for some point of entry. A chill crept across my skin. Did the others know it was there? A touch on my arm made me jump—but it was only one of the coveners passing me a cup of spiced cider. I took a dazed sip and handed it on, and when I looked again the prowling shape had vanished.

The cup had made its way around the circle. The last covener poured the remainder on the ground. "Farewell, dear friends. Know we will not forget you. The circle remains unbroken, now and always. Merry meet, and merry part, and merry meet again."

Did phantom whispers return the familiar words? The mist was already dissipating, a few wisps lingering as if reluctant to depart. As I rose to my feet, my head swam and my knees nearly gave way; I wondered woozily what had been in that cider. But the others were heading back through the gate and I hurried forward, stumbling in my eagerness not to be the last.

Once we had passed through, the gate was dismantled and thrown on the central fire, which had nearly gone out. The dry stalks and branches blazed up brightly to illuminate a dark figure waiting in the shadows beside the cauldron. A shock jolted me—but it was only Grimalkin, her face painted chalky white, the eye sockets blackened and lips crosshatched to mimic a skull.

"Behold the Hag, the Reaper in whose cold breath is the

coming of winter." Her voice was like the dry-husk voices of the dead. "No charm, no spell can avert this season. For death is the shadow cast by growth and beauty, a shadow ever deepening as they play themselves out. To Cerridwen all souls must one day return. Within her cauldron, time's circle is complete. Past, present, future: on this night, seek in these waters what you will."

A low chant began, a whispering tide of breath gradually shaping itself into long drawn vowels that mingled in the night air. As the whisper became a croon, the sounds multiplied inside my head, meeting one another and bouncing off to form reverberations that blurred my thoughts. I found myself echoing the chant—found unknown syllables welling up inside me to exit through lips that moved without my conscious volition. Random chills ran through me, small turbulences that rose and died away of their own accord. An eerie, warbling wail burst suddenly from the droning matrix of the chant to etch itself on my brain as a jagged white peak of sound. As it sank away, a flurry of other savage noises erupted, moans and howls and cries—an interval of sheer, shrieking pandemonium falling away gradually to a murmur once more.

On the opposite side of the circle, a tall figure rose. In the firelight I caught the glint of red hair at the edge of the hood: Gwynneth. She moved toward the cauldron to rest one hand on the iron vessel's lip, gazing into it while the rest of us continued to chant. I watched her surreptitiously. What did she see? Moon and stars reflected in the water's dark mirror—or something else entirely? In my mind a faint voice said *The future . . . the past . . . other realities . . .* I tried to swallow, but my throat was like sandpaper. As I remembered the other things I had experienced this night, suddenly anything seemed possible.

At last Gwynneth straightened and went back to her place. Her head was bowed; I couldn't see her expression. Others followed one by one. Kip was the fourth; I knew him at once, even in the anonymous hooded robe. As he leaned over the cauldron, gripping the rim with both hands, I knew what he was hoping to see: the identity of Alex's murderer. His hood hid his face, but his shoulders were knotted and his knuckles white as he stood staring into the cauldron's depths.

The past. . . Was he seeing it now, watching images form on the water's surface—seeing Alex riding his bike down the dark street that evening a month ago? Seeing someone hail him, step into his path? Seeing a face, one he could identify? *The future*. . . Was he seeing newspaper headlines, flashing cameras, a cringing man hustled away by police? Himself hailed as a hero? *Within the cauldron, time's circle is complete.* I could no longer hear myself chanting, even though my lips still moved. All at once I knew Kip was going to do it. He was going to solve the mystery, do what the adults in the coven had been unable to accomplish. He had mastered the exercises so quickly, so easily, as if it were second nature to him, as if he had done it before.

I told you I've known her before.

I stared at his bent head, my heart hot and swollen in my chest. He was going to do it. It wasn't fair. And then I saw him shrug and shake his head, and felt my chanting falter. As he turned away from the cauldron, the firelight crossed his face and I caught its sulky look. He had failed! Not that I was glad. I just thought maybe he had reached too far this time—maybe he wasn't as adept as he had thought. That was all. I wasn't glad.

Others followed him to the cauldron, one by one. Finally there was only the fire with its restless flames. A hand touched mine and I found Snow beside me, indicating the cauldron.

"Me?" The whispered word blended inaudibly with the chanting, but she nodded.

"Oh, no. No, I can't."

"Yes, you can."

I shook my head and she gave me a push. Not a hard one, but somehow I was on my feet, stumbling into the center of the circle. My head was swimming, and beneath the dizziness I felt hot and embarrassed and afraid. I had no desire to be center stage, or to see the future. If Kip had failed, what chance did I have? The cauldron was in front of me and my eyes shied away from it, up to the Halloween moon overhead. Another wave of dizziness seized me. I swayed on my feet, reached out—

And grasped the cauldron's rim. *On this night open your inner eye, that you may pierce the veil that hides the future.* My heart was pounding and I could scarcely breathe. Slowly I lowered my eyes. The darkness within the cauldron gave me a thrill of fear, but I made myself keep looking. I could hear the soft chanting around me, and see the bright blur of the fire to one side. Then the inky blackness began to draw me down.

Down. Something moved in the cauldron's depths, triggering an answering tremor in my gut. I shut my eyes quickly, but it didn't help: against the inside of my lids I could still see that dark swirling motion of the water struggling to form some shape. Cold began to tick along my veins, freezing the blood inch by inch. When I tried to draw breath I couldn't; my lungs had congealed into blocks of ice. I heard myself make a whimpering sound, felt the rough iron rim under my hands and thrust myself back from it.

And then Snow was there, close behind me, her arms supporting mine, warm hands covering my icy ones. Her urgent voice spoke in my ear. "Remember, Shelley. Where there's fear, there's power. Don't run away from it. I'm right here with you." Heat from her body flowed into mine, melting the frozen carapace that locked my breathing. I took a gulp of air that stabbed painfully into my lungs. Tears spilled from my eyes and scalded my cold cheeks. Snow's hands tightened on mine.

Where there's fear, there's power. I forced myself to look. To watch the images taking shape in the cauldron's depths—forming and changing from one instant to the next, flowing one into another and another without pause, so quickly that at first I could not follow them. And then I began to recognize faces—but so altered I scarcely knew them.

Benjy, his eyes closed and a barred pattern of light and shadow across his features.

Snow, with the athame clenched in her hand and a look of cold fury on her face.

Kip, in tears.

These all went by in a tumbling blur, until at last the water's surface settled—

And I saw Kate. But not the Kate I knew, with a grin lighting her broad face beneath its riot of coppery hair, or poised with hands on her hips and the toe of one cowboy boot tapping, about to "say a swear." This was Kate haggard and changed, her face so sunken that the bone was visible beneath the flesh, her hair thin and lusterless, and a beaten, cringing look haunting her mouth and eyes.

"No," I whispered, and as I spoke the vision seemed to turn sadly, hopelessly in my direction, meeting my gaze across the yawning gulf that separated us. I cried out and twisted away, fighting wildly against some force that seemed to restrain me—then came to myself all at once, on my knees beside the cauldron, in the circle, the moon bright overhead and the coven gathered around me.

I burst into tears; hands touched me reassuringly. I caught sight of Kip's awed face among the others. Two of the women helped me gently to my feet. "Where's Snow?" I quavered, and heard them say, "She's right here."

They moved aside and there she was, her hood pushed back, holding one hand to her mouth. When she took it away I saw her lower lip was bleeding. "Snow! What happened?"

She gave a rueful smile. Blood trickled from the cut and she dabbed at it absentmindedly. "It's not serious. You're stronger than I thought. I couldn't hold you."

"I—did that?"

She took my hands. "You were frightened."

As her eyes searched mine the horrifying vision came close again. "Kate," I whispered. "Kate Conklin, who runs the antique shop. I used to work for her. She—she's a wonderful person. But she was sick—dying." Tears rose again, choking me. "Is it really going to happen?"

Around us the hooded figures of the coveners were motionless as standing stones in the moonlight. In all the enormous night, I could hear only the faint crackling of the fire.

"Scrying is an art, Shelley, not a science," Snow said at last. "In the visions time isn't linear, the way we normally experience it. What you saw may not happen for many years. But remember the words of the Hag: everyone dies. Without death there can be no change, no rebirth. No life." She spoke gently; but to me the words were bleak and comfortless, the blood on her face a reminder of human fragility and pain, and I turned away from her and wept.

Chapter 8

But it was not Kate who became ill that winter. It was my father.

Long after Halloween was over, the shock of the scrying cauldron stayed with me. At night I had bad dreams; by day the red and white stripes of Kate's shop awning made me flinch. I kept to myself, scuttling head down through the halls at schools, avoiding anyone who knew me well enough to ask what was wrong. When Kip tried to pump me for details, I snapped at him that it was none of his business. Snow added nothing to what she had said that night in the circle, but occasionally I caught her watching me.

As in the past whenever I felt battered and unappreciated, I found myself troping toward Benjy. Our quarrel of last summer seemed minor in the light of everything that had happened since, and on my way to work after school I began dropping by the E-Z Stop to chat. Our conversations were brief and disjointed, interrupted by his duties behind the counter, but he seemed glad of my company. On his breaks we retreated to the relative intimacy of the Mister Softee truck parked out back, where it was easier to talk. These sessions—though certainly not profound, and further handicapped by the necessity of avoiding the touchy subject of Lockley Arms—were balm to my bruised spirit. Benjy didn't care if I could visualize an apple or not. He liked me just the way I was.

As winter set in, we could see our breath inside the truck. My fingers and toes grew numb; the tender skin of Benjy's nose and ears turned bright red, yet neither of us suggested abandoning our privacy for the warmth of the store. One afternoon he tried to give me his scarf.

"No, Benjy, you'll freeze. I'm okay. Really." The winter wind had been rising steadily all day, and the old truck creaked and rattled around us, porous as a sieve. As I smiled at him the image from the scrying cauldron slipped across the back of my thoughts, as it was wont to do at unexpected moments. *Benjy, his eyes closed and a barred pattern of light and shadow across his features . . .*

"Look," I heard him say, "you're shivering. Just take the scarf, huh?"

"I don't need it. Here." On impulse I slid across the seat to snuggle against him. "Isn't this better?"

For a few heartbeats he sat immobile, then put his arm around me at last. "Yeah." But he seemed uncomfortable. Didn't he want to kiss me? Suddenly I wanted him to. I wanted to feel what I had felt that night in Kip's room when he had fallen on top of me—only for Benjy this time, as if I could use the new experience to bury the old. But he was so stiff, so shy . . . I turned my face toward him, closed my eyes and waited hopefully—but I was still waiting when a hollow crash outside the truck made my lids fly open and the two of us jump apart. It turned out to be only the wind, toppling one of the garbage containers behind the store to fill the parking lot with a melee of tumbling cartons and flying sheets of newspaper.

"Jeez." Benjy was staring assiduously out the window, pretending a deep interest in the gigantic hedge that marked the boundary of the Arms, now swaying like field grass against a sky the color of a fresh bruise. "Look at the sky. It's going to be some storm."

And it was. The snow arrived early that evening, borne on howling winds. It was only a few days before Christmas; bundled figures shouted holiday greetings as they struggled home through the blinding billows, and the jingling of tire chains from passing cars sounded festive as sleigh bells. But as night drew in and the storm's severity increased, no one ventured out who didn't have to. The streets, already deep in drifts, were silent except for the whistling wind, deserted except for the occasional tense driver creeping along, windshield wipers working furiously against the dense white shroud. Over at the Texaco station on Main Street, Willie Dixon planted a yardstick in the snow and read its depth as eight inches at half-past seven. By nine, it was at sixteen.

The Lockley Arms was nearly empty that evening, the route from the Thruway impassable to all but the most foolhardy travelers, and the Davies twins had plenty of leisure to notice that the weather was causing their employer a certain amount of concern. How many times did Shelley watch her twitch a curtain aside to glance out at the shrieking blizzard and then turn sharply away, those two tiny frown lines visible between her brows? Kip reported seeing her in consultation with Royce, their hands shaping a wordless exchange that brought a look of uneasiness to the pale giant's face. Jessica muttered to herself as she cooked, evidently offended that the delicious aromas emanating from her kitchen had failed to hurry the storm on its way.

Rowan perched on the window seat in the parlor, staring out at the white chaos, motionless except for his twitching tail.

By late evening the streets and sidewalks of Green Hollow were impassable, but it hardly mattered; no one was going anywhere. All over the village people huddled around television sets and radios, listening for news of the weather, learning that most of the Northeast was experiencing cloudy skies, with a few scattered flurries and temperatures in the thirties. Only in a small area of upstate New York was there a persistent patch of bad weather that refused either to dissipate or move on. TV weathermen, wielding pointers and charts, used words like "low pressure" and "unusual storm pattern" while the wind wailed with a desolate voice and the snow, heedless of terminology, continued to whirl down from the heavy sky.

During the night, high winds and accumulated ice toppled

trees and brought down power lines, and on the morning of the winter solstice, shortest day of the year—and longest night—the residents of Green Hollow woke to cold and lightless homes. Outside the blizzard still raged. Flying snow filled the air; wind rattled windowpanes and crept through unsuspected crevices in every house, moaning and screaming like something demented until it was impossible not to suspect it of being alive and consciously malign. Inside their cold dwellings people glanced uneasily over their shoulders as they rummaged for flashlights and candles. Those with working fireplaces put them to use; others, like the Davies household in which the fireplace was purely decorative, peered dubiously up their chimneys. The twins headed for the Arms, where every hearth was ablaze and Jessica was handily cooking biscuits and beef stew over the fire in the parlor.

Willie Dixon looked in vain for his yardstick; it was completely buried. His shortwave radio reported that a state of emergency had been declared for the entire county. The severity of the storm prevented crews from repairing the power lines, but government snowplows were attempting to open Route 23 between Green Hollow and the Thruway, and by afternoon a procession of rescue vehicles struggled through the blizzard with blankets and sandwiches. The occasional determined traveler made it through as well. In twos and threes, the coveners arrived at the Arms for the Sabbat celebration—Andreas last, his tiny car dwarfed by the snowbanks piled on either side of the driveway by Kip and Royce, who had begun shoveling that afternoon. By that time it was full dark, and for nearly twenty-four hours there had been no sign of slackening in the storm's fury.

And it was present at the Sabbat feast like an unwelcome guest—bringing a forced note to the usual banter, putting a strain on the smiling faces around the table. At times the banks of candles in the dining room dipped and guttered all together, allowing the shadows to edge closer to the table before another burst of laughter drove them back. Shelley's eyes sought Kip's. On such a night it was impossible for the Sabbat to be held in the meadow. It would have to take place somewhere else—and where could that be, if not the locked room on the third floor?

The locked room. Tonight, at long last, would they discover what lay behind that mysterious door? Across the banquet table their eyes held, then broke apart as the wind outside let out another savage howl.

When dinner was over Snow rose from the table and led the way upstairs. Beneath thick carpeting, the steps creaked softly as thirteen people mounted them without a word. Some of the coveners turned down the second-floor hall while others continued up the next flight. Snow beckoned to Kip and Shelley and handed each a key and a small paper packet.

"You'll use these rooms tonight, to bathe and change into your robes. Add these herbs to your ritual bath. Be ready in half an hour."

The fragrant candlelit bathroom was so pleasant that Shelley lingered too long in the tub; there was scarcely time to shrug into her robe and knot the cord around her waist before a tap came on the door. She found the dark hallway crowded with hooded figures. One nudged her—Kip, and she nudged him back as the procession moved toward the stairs.

A single candle burned at the far end of the third-floor hall. The locked room. Its door stood open at last, but still nothing was visible of the chamber beyond, only a kind of shimmer. Shelley watched people entering ahead of her: one by one, they stepped up to the shimmer and disappeared, as if this doorway led to some other dimension, a place *literally* between worlds. She didn't know she had stopped moving until she felt Kip shove her and saw that a gap had opened ahead of her in the line. She stumbled and recovered herself on the threshold. The shimmering light was just ahead. Extending a questing hand, she touched fabric. A curtain. She pushed it aside, as the others had done before her, and stepped forward.

Into total darkness.

I suppose it was some kind of backhanded justice that after all our curiosity about what lay beyond the locked door, there was nothing to see. Nothing. Only a blackness in which disembodied hands grasped mine and passed me on to others until I reached the place where I belonged. Once I was standing still, the silence was as total as the darkness.

"This is the winter solstice, the longest night of the year." The hollow whisper seemed to emanate simultaneously from all directions, spiking my whole body with a chill. *"Darkness triumphs. The earth lies cold and barren, and hope is at its ebb."*

The silence returned. My eyes had begun to play tricks on me, filling the surrounding darkness with pale flecks like flying snow. Flying snow? When I blinked, the illusion grew stronger—the walls becoming transparent, revealing the blinding fury of the blizzard outside—and then suddenly the storm was all around us. As I stared, transfixed, across the chaos I seemed to discern the vague outline of a huge, hooded figure with arms spread wide—summoning the wind and snow, hurling them viciously at the village. A frigid wind blasted through the room, whipping our robes wildly around us and freezing our bare flesh on contact. Was it only illusion? I fought the urge to run for shelter, struggling to hold my place in the circle as I shivered and gasped for breath, dazedly aware of the hollow voice speaking above the wind.

"Even now, within the womb of the Mother, center and circumference of all that exists, the cycle renews itself. From death into life. From darkness into light. Tonight we turn the Wheel to bring the sun."

Icy hands on either side found mine. Slowly, leaning into that merciless wind, we began to circle the room. Clockwise. Deosil. The direction of increase.

The shrieking wind was bitterly cold. But the motion carried me along, and the pressure of hands on mine. Round and round, gradually gaining speed, we whirled through the cold and boundless night. Now and again I thought I saw colored sparks riding the wind currents; one by one they brightened and faded and died away to nothing—yet there was one spark that remained, that never disappeared. Just a flicker at first, there in the midst of our circling figures, slowly growing brighter.

A candle's flame. As it burned higher the wind began to

drop, diminishing until at last the snow fell softly. Still we circled. The snowfall began to decrease. Little by little the winter night receded, fading until the room was once more walled in darkness, lit only by that single candle. Around its tiny light, center and axis of an infinite spiral, we went on circling. Turning the Wheel. When at last the motion slowed and stopped, when we released one another's hands and sank to the floor, I found myself panting and bathed in sweat as if I had run a race. A race against the dark.

"Like this small light," Snow's voice said, "the sun returns to us each year from the darkness, to grow again into strength. Thus is the God reborn, the promise renewed. For death holds within it the seed of life, and—"

A soft double tap at the door interrupted her.

And that was when I saw how truly practical witches are: how actually, as well as philosophically, down to earth. No one fussed over the interruption of the rite; there wasn't time. Snow and Archer exchanged a look and he went swiftly to the door, pulling his hood back as he went, while the others moved in to conceal the altar. Automatically I moved with them, lurid fantasies of discovery running rampant through my head. We were naked under our robes. Locked in a darkened room. Who would believe—

Archer was at the door only a moment. He beckoned to Snow; they conferred briefly before she turned back into the room.

"Shelley? Kip?"

My blood ran cold. Numbly I went forward, seeing Kip do the same. Snow reached out and took our hands. "You must dress quickly. Your father's been taken ill. Your aunt is waiting downstairs."

Shelley's hands were shaking too badly to function and the coven women took charge of her, putting her into her clothes as if she were a small child. Even in her dazed state she was comforted by their presence, although for some reason she couldn't seem to grasp what had happened. Dad taken ill. Marty downstairs. Her mind kept bouncing back and forth between those two facts, unable to go beyond them. Dad was never sick, not so much as a cough or a cold. And it was impossible for Marty to be downstairs. She was part of the other world, the one outside the boundaries of the Arms. How could she be downstairs? And how could Dad be ill?

As the women bundled Shelley out of her borrowed room into the hall, she saw Snow come flying down the stairs from the third floor, a fluttering candle in one hand. She was fully dressed, her hair bound once again in its customary knot. A door opened down the hall and two shadowy figures appeared: Kip, with Archer behind him. Just at that instant there was a commotion down below.

"What's taking them so long? What on earth is going on up there?" Marty's voice, strident and nearly hysterical, and then Jessica's: "Now, Miss Davies—"

"I want to see those children this instant! Do you hear me? I don't care what kind of a meeting they're in! Their father may be dying!"

"Marty!" Shelley shouted, and ran for the head of the stairs. Her aunt was down at the foot, wild-eyed in the beam of Royce's flashlight. Kip was right on Shelley's heels. Seeing them, Marty tried to maneuver around Royce as he stood blocking the way.

"Children! Your father collapsed shoveling snow—Doc says it's his heart. An ambulance is coming to take him to Albany. Your mother will ride with him. We'll follow in the car."

At the sight of the twins Royce had moved aside. Marty rushed past him, almost colliding with them on the stairs. Then Snow was there, saying, "Do you want someone to drive you, Miss Davies? I'd be glad to."

In the light of Snow's candle they watched Marty struggle for good manners. She was clearly outraged by the inexplicable delay in their appearance, and Snow was the obvious person to blame. Yet it was a generous offer and a sensible one, and like everyone else in Green Hollow, Marty was more than a little impressed by Snowden Mansell. The twins saw her take a deep breath. "Thank you, you're very kind. But we can manage on our own. And we must hurry."

Shelley felt Snow's hand grip and squeeze her shoulder hard. Then, along with Kip and Marty, she was hurrying out of the house into the freezing night.

Chapter 9

The blizzard had stopped, but Shelley scarcely noticed, distracted by the sight of the ambulance parked across the street. Beyond its flashing red light she saw the front door of her house open and two white-clad figures emerge with a stretcher. The motionless shape bundled upon it looked too small to be Dad, yet she caught a glimpse of his pinched, colorless face as the stretcher slid into the back of the ambulance. Mother came tottering down the front walk, Doc Sheridan by her side. She looked at them with glazed eyes. "He'll be all right." Her voice was pitched too high. "He'll be fine. Marty, be careful on the way to Albany. The roads are very slippery."

Doc Sheridan climbed stiffly into the back of the ambulance and she followed him. The doors slammed. The two attendants jumped into the front seat and the siren began to wail as the white vehicle pulled away. Shelley stood staring after it, not feeling the cold but seeing her breath make frosty clouds in the stunningly clear air.

Icy as it was, Route 23 was the best road to the Thruway and we took it. The drive seemed endless. The bleak winter-locked landscape crawled past on either side, Kip and I holding our breaths whenever the car lurched on the treacherous road surface.

As soon as we were well underway Marty blurted out the details of Dad's collapse. "Once it stopped snowing, he said he wanted to get the front walk cleared, you know, before it started up again. I told him, Kip—I said you'd do it when you got home, but he said you'd probably be worn out from doing the Arms. He said he'd save you the trouble. And I guess it was just too much. After about fifteen minutes I looked out to see how he was doing, if he wanted some hot chocolate or something, and he was just lying there on his back in the snow." She drew an uneven breath. "Doc was wonderful. He came right away. He called the ambulance and gave your mother something to calm her down." Darting a look across at me in the passenger seat beside her: "Elaine's really devoted to him, you know. She was beside herself."

"Was he unconscious?" I said.

"Not when we found him. His eyes were open and he was looking up at the sky. He said, 'Look at the stars, Elaine. Aren't they magnificent?' " Her voice cracked; she hunched closer to the wheel, squinting at the slippery road ahead. After a pause she said, "After we got him inside he seemed to let go. He just . . . drifted away."

Once we reached the Thruway we made better time. Considerably less snow had fallen here, and the plows had recently been past. We rode in silence, Kip and I staring out our respective windows. Another forty minutes and we were in Albany, seeing only a scattering of snow on the ground as we followed the nearly deserted streets to the hospital.

I had been here before, years ago, to visit Kip. But those visits had been planned, and in daylight, and now I had no sense of recognition as the building came in sight. Inside, Marty made her way up to the desk and spoke to someone in charge while Kip and I waited just inside the entrance. Suddenly the door behind us flew open and a woman rushed in carrying a small child, its head swathed in a towel. We jumped out of her way; across the room a pair of double doors swung wide to let her in. Through the opening we caught an instant's glimpse of bustling green-clad figures and a wildly gesticulating man in a dark overcoat, and then the doors closed.

Marty came over to us. "He's been admitted, but we can't see him yet. Doc will be down to talk to us in a little while. We just have to wait." Her years of experience as Doc's receptionist had given her an air of medical know-how that, however unfounded, was somehow reassuring. We sat down, joining the half-dozen strangers who sat staring at the swinging doors leading into the treatment area. One or two people paced back and forth in front of the elevator. Outside there was the occasional wail of a siren.

As long as I live, I shall never forget that waiting room. Its walls, tan to a height of about four feet and white above, are branded forever on my memory, including a long wavering rusty stain just inside the door, beginning in the white and descending down into the tan, that must have been blood. I stared at those walls and that stain, willing the sight of them to fill my entire consciousness, leaving no room for thought. One by one the other people left and were replaced, all of us waiting.

At last the elevator doors opened and Doc Sheridan emerged. Marty rushed over to him; he patted her shoulder, peering over the tops of his glasses at Kip and me as we approached. "We've got him pretty comfortable, I think. I'm going to let you see him for a minute or two. Come along."

On the way up in the elevator he confirmed his initial diagnosis. A heart attack. "Happens, you know. Fellow leads a bookish type of life, a sedentary existence, then goes out one cold night and starts shoveling snow—it's a shock to his heart. But Graham's not an old man. Prognosis is pretty good."

Somewhere in the upper reaches of the hospital, the elevator doors opened to let us off. Doc led us down a dim corridor smelling of disinfectant and lined with doors. We passed a clock and I saw that it was after midnight. As we walked, Kip's cold fingers caught mine and squeezed them hard.

Inside Dad's room a faint light burned. Mother sat in a chair beside the bed, glancing up when we came in but making no other acknowledgment of our presence. As my eyes went to the bed, a hot lump filled my throat. Dad was in an oxygen tent. Behind the clear plastic curtain his face was white and drawn as I had seen it on the stretcher, but his eyes were open and he was trying to smile at us.

There wasn't much to say, nor time to say it. A squeeze of the hand, a few mumbled phrases from each of us and then his eyes closed again. I'm not sure how we got out of the room, but all at once we were standing in the hall and Doc was telling us there was nothing more we could do tonight.

"But we can't just turn around and go home," Marty quavered. "I mean . . . we can see him again in the morning, can't we?"

The doctor rubbed a tired hand over his face, dislodging his glasses so they dangled from one ear. He fumbled them back into place. "Why don't you camp out in the patients' lounge? Bed down on the couches, try to get a little sleep. Probably not a good idea to drive back in this weather anyway."

And so we ended up in the lounge, a drafty, dreary room at the far end of the hall. There were several couches upholstered in orange vinyl, a television and a table strewn with dog-eared magazines. We were all exhausted; no one felt like talking. Kip stuck his nose in a copy of *Time*. I went to the window and stared out at the icy streets. A moment later Marty touched my shoulder. "Shelley, can I talk to you a minute?"

I followed her down the hall. There was an alcove with a water fountain and a couple of vending machines; she beckoned me into it and turned to face me. Although I had seen her shed no tears tonight, she must have found a private moment to cry, because her eyes were puffy and rimmed with red. When she spoke her voice was shaking. "I want to know exactly what's going on over at the Lockley Arms."

Once, when I was eight and trying to duplicate some stunt of Kip's, I had fallen off my bike and had the wind knocked out of me. I had that same sensation now. I heard a gasping, unfamiliar voice say, "What?"

Her red-rimmed eyes stared into mine. "You heard me. When I went over there, Jessica Childress said you and Kip were in a meeting. And that gigantic *man* wouldn't let me go upstairs. Now, I want to know just what kind of a meeting it was."

I tried to swallow and couldn't. The past couple of hours had obliterated all thought of the ritual, but now it came rushing back. Shadowy hooded figures circling a darkened room, a single candle flickering in their midst. *Tonight we turn the Wheel to bring the sun.* "It was just a—a staff meeting," I said.

"Then why weren't Jessica and that *man* there? They're part of the staff."

"It was just for dining room staff."

"Dining room staff? You mean you and Kip? What on earth do you need a meeting for?"

My thoughts had stalled, but fortunately my tongue had not. "In case we have any questions . . . any problems . . ."

"The two of you meet with Miss Mansell?"

I nodded dumbly.

"And she keeps you until eleven o'clock at night for this?"

"Not usually," I said. "Tonight . . . there was a problem with one of the guests."

Marty blinked. "What kind of problem?"

Invention deserted me. What kind of problems did guests usually cause? Sometimes they spilled things. Occasionally someone asked for some exotic dish to be prepared on the spot. Once a man had passed out and his face had landed in his plate. The idea of having a meeting to address such trivia was absurd. And then an unpleasant memory came to my rescue and I said, "He was getting . . . handsy."

"Handsy—with you?" Marty's expression went from suspicion to horror, then softened to concern. "Oh, *Shelley*."

"It's okay. Miss Mansell says she won't let him stay there again."

"Oh, you poor baby—"

"It's all right, Marty. Really."

"But why did it take them so long to fetch you? And why wouldn't that *man* let me go upstairs?"

I swallowed. "He gets confused sometimes." Silently I begged Royce's forgiveness for this slander. "I guess he just didn't understand."

In the end I think it was Marty's perfect willingness to accept Royce as some sort of semi-idiot that got me off the hook. She went in search of a bathroom while I made my way back to the lounge, where one lamp was lit and Kip was sprawled on the sofa facing the window, asleep with his head lolling back. I sat down beside him and tried to recall my conversation with Marty. Had I said anything I shouldn't have—given anything away? I was too tired to think. Across my brain flitted the image of her face, the eyes outlined in red. Then Dad's, trying to smile behind the plastic oxygen tent . . . Mother's, glassy-eyed . . . Doc Sheridan, his glasses dangling from one ear . . .

Outside the window it had started to snow. As I sat watching, the thick white flakes seemed to descend dreamily over my thoughts as well, burying them in drifts that grew deeper and deeper until I sank into a kind of trance. I still had some sense of my surroundings, of Kip moving restlessly beside me, muttering to himself, of a radiator hissing in a corner and a siren somewhere in the distance—but I was separated from them by the endless silent falling of the snow. It was soft, that snow, soft as a pillow, and I was so tired . . .

Sssss . . . Only the hiss of the radiator, releasing steam. Outside the wind rose, as if in answer, and somewhere in my brain an alarm bell went off. I tried to clear my head of the snowdrifts, but in spite of their softness they were surprisingly heavy. Beside me Kip suddenly groaned and shuddered, and I knew I had to clear my head, to try and think—but the more I fought the smothering drifts, the heavier they became.

Sssss . . . There it was again, rubbing my nerves raw. All at once my head was clear. Through the window, beyond the barrage of tiny frozen particles whirling out of the night, I could see the silhouettes of darkened buildings where a few lights burned. Superimposed on that dim cityscape was a reflection of the lamplit lounge, myself on the sofa, Kip slumped beside me. And over everything, outside and in—that billowing, lacy veil of snow. Only a snowstorm, perfectly normal for this season, this region—so why did I feel such foreboding? I stared at the obscure skyline beyond the glass, paralyzed by the nameless dread pressing against my heart. And as I stared, between one moment and the next, it was there. A huge, hooded shape.

Dark as the night sky, it seemed to form itself imperceptibly from the space between the buildings—an illusion, surely; and yet once I had seen it, I couldn't *not* see it—that same, terrifyingly familiar shape I had glimpsed earlier during the ritual, arms outstretched to unleash the elements. I sat staring at it, my heart squirming like some soft, helpless creature trapped inside my rigid body. It wasn't really there. It couldn't be. It was imagination, illusion, a trick of my exhausted brain. But the whispering, moaning wind sounded just like a raving voice, and the snow whipped through the air like the folds of a vast, icy cloak.

Why didn't Kip wake up? Why didn't Marty come back? All at once I saw the huge shape spread its arms wide—and the windowpane exploded inward with a splintering *crack* that sent glass flying everywhere, the fragments hanging suspended in a glittering cloud for an instant before they fell. The noise, or my gasping shriek, woke Kip at last: I saw his eyes open, wide and shocked, just as the storm burst through the gaping window frame.

Swirling sheets of snow enveloped us; biting wind stung our faces and hands and snatched at our clothing as if trying to tear it off. The savagery of the attack stunned me; I couldn't move, but Kip yanked me off the sofa and together we stumbled for the door. We had nearly reached it when the wind slammed it shut with a deafening bang and a flock of birds attacked us—or not birds, I realized fuzzily—magazines, their pages flapping wildly as they sailed around our heads. Just as we managed to beat them off, the lamp rocked wildly on its base and fell over, plunging the room into darkness.

The night sky outside the window rushed in as we clung together, hearing the wind's howl turn to a whining glee. It pelted us with snow, clawed our hair and fumbled roughly at our clothes with icy, invisible hands, moaning and mumbling in some grotesque parody of passion. Breathlessly we struggled toward the door, but it shoved us back, sending us careening around the room like drunks, driving us against the walls and furniture with punishing force. There was snow down my neck, in my nose and mouth and eyes. Through frozen lashes I could see Kip's mouth moving in his contorted face—but whatever he was shouting was lost in the pandemonium around us.

A violent gust sent us stumbling across the floor to collide with the gaping window frame and we hung gasping across the sill, heads reeling at the sight dimly visible through the blinding billows—a dizzy vista of whitened sidewalks and wet streets above which we swayed precariously, buffeted and mauled by turbid white wind that seemed bent on snatching the very breath from our lungs. Crashes and thuds came from the room behind us. Something struck my head a glancing blow; I ducked aside and saw the lamp shade go flying past, tumbling end over end into the wild winter night, beginning a long, sickening plunge down through the air toward the earth below. In horror I lifted my eyes to the huge figure hovering against the sky. If we lost our grip, would we fall, like the lamp shade—or would we be swept across the screaming air into the folds of that vast, cold robe? The prospect was too horrible to imagine; I turned to Kip in desperation. He shouted again, and this time I understood the words.

"—coven—call them—help—!"

I managed to nod. Desperately we clung to the icy sill, holding each other's gaze, joining our thoughts in a frantic cry for help. It was a hopeless impulse—and then suddenly, beneath the roaring wind, we seemed to hear the sound of distant voices. No more than a hum at first, reaching us from far away. Were we imagining it? But it continued—never faltering, steadily growing louder until we could distinguish a chanting rhythm of unseen voices, rising and falling in patterns like the shining mesh of an intricate net.

A net of voices, weaving a magical snare for the storm.

The tempest mounted to a snarling frenzy. My hands were torn from the sill; I felt my feet leave the ground and waited in terror to be propelled through the open window, to begin the hideous descent—or worse, some unholy journey across the seething air—only to hear the voices rise to meet the wind, the two forces meshing in taut crescendo inside my head. For a timeless interval the sound held me suspended; then I felt myself hit the floor and stumble backward as the wind abruptly released its grip. The voices rang triumphant against the darkness. For an instant the sound was clearly visible: a net of radiant strands at whose center one dazzling white spark flickered and flashed as if alive.

And then a hand shook my shoulder and my eyelids fluttered open, and I found myself staring at the zipper tab of Marty's parka, flickering and flashing as it reflected light from the lamp nearby.

I was slouched on the sofa, Kip asleep beside me. No trace of our horrifying ordeal remained—no hint of the havoc wrought by the wind and snow. My ears and fingers still stung with cold, but the window was intact, the room in perfect order: magazines on the table, lamp upright and shining brightly, every piece of furniture in its place. These facts, slowly forcing themselves into my brain, seemed too miraculous to be believed. Those shining voices . . . I found myself listening for their lingering echo, but the lounge was silent except for the hissing of the radiator in one corner.

Sssss . . . The sound sent a frisson along my nerves and my eyes flew again to the window—but there were only buildings silhouetted against the darkness beyond the pane: constructions of concrete, metal and glass forming a geometric pattern against the night sky. Of the huge hooded figure, of the devastating storm we had experienced—not the slightest sign. Marty was looking at me and I opened my mouth, but nothing came out. Beside me Kip's face was contorted by a scowl, his hands in fists. When I touched his arm he didn't wake, but his face relaxed and I saw his fingers slowly unclench.

"You were making some funny noises," Marty whispered. "Were you having a bad dream?"

Chapter 10

With Dad in the hospital, Christmas came and went almost unnoticed. Mother had friends in Albany who offered to put her up, thus sparing her the tiring daily trip back and forth. At first Marty made the trek every day, accompanied by the twins; then, once Dad was pronounced out of danger, every other day. Between visits she returned to work and the twins escaped across the street to the Arms. There things were predictably busy during the holiday season, but Snow seemed reluctant to let them help out.

"Your school's still on vacation. Don't you want to spend some time with your friends?"

"We're not in the mood."

"It's like they're afraid to have too good a time around us."

"We'd rather stay busy."

Snow received this fusillade of excuses with a faint smile. "All right, fine." And then, as they started hastily out of the office before she could change her mind: "One more thing—"

They turned back to find her no longer smiling. She hesitated, then: "I think you know the man who killed Alex is still at large."

There was a silence in which the ticking clock seemed to grow louder. Shelley swallowed. That hooded shadow, summoning the wind and snow . . . that net of shining voices . . . She and Kip hadn't talked about the dream, if that was what it had been, but the memory flooded her with dread. She heard Kip say, "But the binding spell—"

"Will help protect you here in the village, but not elsewhere. And you're safe when you're with Royce. When you're not, you need to be on your guard."

Kip opened his mouth and then shut it again at the sight of her closed face, as if remembering what Elymas had said the morning after Alex's disappearance. *When we can tell you more, we will.* When he had gone Shelley lingered behind, running one finger along the edge of the door frame. Snow was watching her, the silvery eyes unreadable, and she stammered a little as she broached the topic on her mind.

"D-do you think the coven could do a healing spell for my father? Doc thinks he's not getting better the way he should."

Snow sighed. "Ordinarily we'd be happy to, Shelley, but at

the moment I'm afraid our hands are full. A healing spell's a good idea, though. You can perform it yourself."

"Me?"

"Yes, you."

Shelley was taken aback. "But I don't know any spells!"

"I'll teach you what to do."

Later that day Snow summoned her back to the office, where an assemblage of objects lay spread on her desk. A folded piece of cream-colored cloth, a blue candle, a small glass jar filled with what looked like dried herbs . . . Shelley approached the desk and touched the candle with a tentative finger, hearing Snow say, "Can you sew?"

"Can I—?"

"Sew. You know. Use a needle and thread?"

Confused, Shelley nodded. "A little." Marty had taught her to sew on a button and baste a hem. But what did sewing have to do with magic? Snow shook out the cloth to reveal a generous square.

"This is unbleached muslin. You'll use it to make an image of your father."

"An—image?"

"It doesn't have to be perfect, just a symbolic representation. You'll draw it, cut and sew it, stuff it with these healing herbs—angelica, lily of the valley, marigold, heartsease—and then add something personal to your father. A few hairs, for instance, if you can find some."

Shelley dragged her eyes away from the square of cloth to Snow's face. "You mean . . . like a voodoo doll?"

Watching her now with arms folded, Snow nearly smiled. "We call it a poppet. The poppet will represent your father and help you focus on the idea of his recovery."

"Why do I have to put his hair inside it?"

"Because this kind of spell requires a physical link between the poppet and the person it represents. But the physical link is just an aid. The real connection must be made mentally, by the worker of the spell."

The worker of the spell. It took a moment for Shelley to recognize herself in that phrase, and then her heart plummeted.

Hadn't she failed dismally at the simplest visualizations, even the eating of an imaginary apple? If Dad had to depend on her, he would never recover. "Can Kip help me?"

Snow's pale gaze held hers. "Shelley, this was your idea. Don't run away from it. Remember: where there's fear—"

Where there's fear, there's power. How many times had Snow tried to overcome her reluctance with that phrase? "Okay." She took a deep breath and stiffened her spine. "Tell me what I have to do."

When she left the Arms that night, she carried her magical supplies tucked deep in one pocket of her winter coat. A light snow had begun to fall during dinner. Royce accompanied the twins down the whitened driveway and waited while they crossed the street and went up the front walk to their house. At the foot of the porch steps they turned to wave and saw his bulky silhouette lift a hand in answer before trudging back up the driveway toward the Arms. Suddenly Kip kicked the fresh snow at his feet, sending a white shower through the air. The savage movement startled Shelley, whose thoughts were on her impending task.

"Kip! What's the matter with you?"

"It's our fault."

"What is?"

"What happened to Dad."

"Are you nuts? How could it be our fault?"

He was quiet, brushing the snow off his gloves. Then he said, "Maybe we shouldn't have gotten mixed up in this."

Shelley stared at him. Snowflakes descended out of the night sky, turning luminous as they entered the compass of the porch light, covering his hair with a filigree of white as she watched. "Mixed up in what? The coven? It was your idea to join!"

"I know." His lips were trembling—from cold, she thought, until she saw the unshed tears in his eyes. "But something bad's going on. First Alex—now Dad—"

"Kip, Dad had a heart attack shoveling snow! It's got nothing to do with what happened to Alex!"

"Are you sure? If we hadn't had that storm, he wouldn't have had to shovel snow."

Her hot reply died unspoken as the words sank in. *If we hadn't had that storm* . . . That huge hooded shadow, wielding the elements in its hands. As if he knew her thoughts, Kip said, "It wasn't a dream. Not completely, anyway. He's real. He's the one who killed Alex. And he's the one who made the storm."

You saw somebody in a Halloween costume. Did he even remember his own scoffing words? The prospect of being able to say I told you so offered little comfort now, and instead she said, "Who *is* he?"

"Shelley. What kind of person can call a storm?"

"A witch," she whispered, and when he nodded: "But how—how could a witch kill a child? The Rede—"

"My guess is he's a renegade," Kip said. "Probably operating on his own. He'd need to kill, in order to raise power." He hesitated. "He knows about our coven, otherwise he wouldn't be targeting Green Hollow. What if . . . Shelley, did you ever think maybe the Lockleys' deaths weren't an accident?"

"What?"

"Maybe he killed them. Maybe that was the beginning. Now there's some kind of struggle going on between him and the coven. And because of us—because of us, Dad got stuck in the middle. So in a way, it *is* our fault."

Shelley stared at him through the falling snow, his words reverberating in her head until fury exploded suddenly inside her and she grabbed his coat and shook him. "Shut up! Shut up! How can you say something like that? After you dragged me into this—after everything that's happened!"

He gaped at her. She was reminded of the time his baseball had rolled across the street—how he had stood there with the same dumbfounded look on his face, deserted by his boundless ingenuity. She had been forced to pick up the pieces, cross the street and get the ball. And now—how dare he start indulging in remorse, when the whole thing was his doing? He had plunged into it headfirst, enticed by the thrill and the mystery, seeing only what he wanted to see, ignoring the possible dangers and drawbacks. He had disparaged her doubts: now he was wallowing in his own. "It doesn't matter whose fault it is!" she said. "Do you hear me? It's too late! Whatever's going on, we're already part of it, and you can't change that now."

•

Upstairs in her room she set to work with unsteady hands—smoothing the muslin flat on her desk, penciling upon it the outline of a simple human figure. Snow had said it didn't have to be perfect. And that was a good thing, because no matter how she sketched and erased and tried again, the emerging shape persisted in resembling a gingerbread man a good deal more than it did her father. At last she gave up trying to improve it. Doubling the cloth, she cut out the figure and carefully sewed the two pieces together, leaving an opening into which she stuffed the fragrant herbs and added three hairs she had found on one of her father's jackets. A stitch or two, and the poppet was sealed shut.

She sat back to examine it with a critical eye and felt her feeble hopes shrivel to nothing. It looked pitiful: a white, misshapen thing, faceless and crude. How could she improve it? Snow had told her to mark it with any symbols that would help her identify it with the idea of her father's healing. It was his heart that was the problem. Should she give the poppet a heart? With a red ballpoint she drew a lopsided Valentine heart on the poppet's chest, then surveyed it once more. If anything, it looked worse now—especially the blank, featureless head. It needed a face. She chose a black ballpoint and bent over the tiny stuffed figure, scowling in concentration.

And the Goddess must have guided her hand. The pen made a few quick marks—only a few, and stopped. But examining her work Shelley saw she had somehow reproduced, with a caricaturist's economical mastery, Dad's tired smile and the rueful quirk of his brows.

Because of us, Dad got stuck in the middle. So in a way, it's our fault.

She winced. Whether or not there was any truth to Kip's theory about a renegade witch scheming against the coven, she knew one thing was true. Dad had never wanted them to be part of the Arms. How many times had he tried to get them to quit, only to be fobbed off or browbeaten into letting them keep their jobs? Tears welled up in her eyes and she wiped them impatiently on the back of one hand. A witch, even a clumsy apprentice witch, had no business sniveling while preparing a spell—and maybe she could undo, by magical means, whatever fault had been committed.

Clearing off the rickety little table she used as a nightstand, she moved it to the center of the room. Upon it she placed the blue candle, along with three things she had brought upstairs from the kitchen: a glass of water, a box of matches, and a saucer of salt. Her stomach was twitchy as she repeated Snow's instructions to herself, making sure to follow them exactly. The actions she was now performing were those of a solitary witch casting her circle, and Snow had warned her not to make a mistake. *The circle is essential, Shelley. It forms a protective boundary for the self in a situation where you must let conventional boundaries go. And once you begin to raise power, the circle will contain it until you're ready to release it to its purpose.*

She switched off the lamp on her desk, leaving the room to the shadowy illumination of the waxing half-moon. The snow had stopped; the world outside her window was white and still. Placing the poppet on her makeshift altar, she lit the candle, sprinkled three generous pinches of salt in the water and took the glass in her hands, hesitating a moment, reviewing what she was supposed to do.

Begin in the north. Walk clockwise in a circle, sprinkling the water a few drops at a time. Increase your pace gradually. As you feel energy building inside you, release it along the boundary of the circle. You may feel resistance in the air, a sensation like walking through water.

Slowly she began to pace out the circle in her darkened room. Clockwise, round and round. After half a dozen circuits she still felt nothing—no energy building inside her, no resistance in the air, nothing but a kind of burning self-consciousness even though she was all alone in the room. What was she doing? Parading around her bedroom in the dark, sprinkling salt water on the floor around a table laden with an odd assortment of objects, among them a doll intended to represent her father. She thought of Marty confronting her at the hospital. *I want to know exactly what's going on over at the Lockley Arms.* What would her aunt say if she could see what was going on right now, under the same roof where she was probably sitting up late, reading one of her detective novels in bed? It was one thing for Snow to talk about focus and healing energy, entirely another for an inept apprentice to achieve those slippery skills that had eluded her from the start. All at once she felt helpless, abandoned—pushed from the nest long before she had the remotest notion of how to fly. Self-pity flooded her, sluicing away all resolve, and her pace faltered and stopped. She couldn't do this. What had happened to Dad might well be their fault—hers and Kip's—but she was powerless to fix it. What had ever made her think otherwise?

The next morning it was snowing again, a soft sprinkling of white flakes on top of last night's few inches. The sight only compounded my depression over my dismal failure with the spell. At the Arms I served breakfast to the half dozen guests present, then busied myself in the kitchen, dreading the prospect of seeing Snow. When she appeared and beckoned me into the back hallway, I joined her reluctantly.

"How'd it go?"

I looked down at the floor. "It didn't."

"What happened?"

"Nothing."

"Well, how far did you get?" Her tone was patient.

"I couldn't even cast a circle," I mumbled. "It just wouldn't work."

"How long did you try?"

"I don't know. But it wasn't working."

Glancing up, I saw her lips compress briefly. "It's true magic doesn't always work, Shelley, even for an experienced practitioner. A focused will is like a blade that needs constant sharpening in order to keep its edge. But in this case, I think you just gave up too soon."

The reproof stung. It was as if she wanted something from

me, as if she were pushing me toward something, I had no clear idea what. Again I had the sense of being expected to do more than I was able, long before I was ready. She seemed to care nothing for my struggles so far—for the desperate efforts it had cost me to make what precious little progress I had. A sense of injustice filled me, and I lost my temper. "Why should I have to do it all by myself? Why can't you help me?"

Her voice was soft. "I will, if it turns out to be necessary. But you can't always count on outside help. Sooner or later you need to find your own power."

"But what if it doesn't work?" My voice cracked and I lowered it with an effort, mindful of the guests in the house. "What if I make a mess of it, and he dies?"

"He's not going to die, and you won't make a mess of it. Don't give up just because it isn't easy. Why should it be?"

"It's easy for Kip!" I said.

Her level look warned me I had said the wrong thing, and I shut up. There was a short silence. Then she said, "We aren't talking about Kip. We're talking about you." When I tried to answer, she held up her hand. "No. Just listen. Do you think I don't know how hard you've worked these past few months? I've been watching you, I know what you're been going through—but it's time you understood that the barrier you've been struggling against is yourself. Haven't I told you a hundred times that where there's fear, there's power? Look into a lit candle, and inside the bright flame you will see a dark one. Each of us has a shadow self hidden away, made up of everything we fear about who we are, what we're capable of—but denying that self doesn't make it disappear."

While she was speaking I started to shake. I had a dim, terrible sense that what she was saying would change everything and make all our lives forever fatally different. Without understanding why, I was afraid. In the kitchen a few feet away, Jessica had turned on the radio and a female vocal group crooned the words, "Pop-sicles, i-cicles" in vapid harmony. They sounded like voices from another world. I must have looked as stricken as I felt, because Snow's face softened at last. She reached out and her fingers brushed my cheek.

"Shelley. The power within you is a gift from the Goddess. But only by knowing yourself can you make it your own."

That conversation drifted in and out of my head for the rest of the day as I made beds, cleaned bathrooms, emptied wastebaskets, dusted lamps and polished doorknobs and swept the floors until the house was spotless. Snow's words had bewildered and upset me. *Where there's fear, there's power.* I had plenty of fear. Was she saying I had power in equal measure? The idea was inconceivable. Last night's failed spell was only the latest in a long list of frustrations in which the skills we were supposed to master still hovered beyond my reach. The suspicion was always gnawing away, somewhere at the back of my mind, that Kip had been my passport into the coven—that they would never have accepted me on my own. Now Snow seemed to be saying something quite different. *The power within you is a gift from the Goddess.* How could she be so certain? Maybe I was hollow inside, a substanceless shell. Maybe my fear hid only emptiness.

Tentatively I set down my dustpan and leaned my broom against the wall. Alone in the guest room I was supposed to be cleaning, I began to rub my hands together until I felt them grow warm and then hot, until my arms and shoulders ached with the effort.

More . . . a little more . . . keep going . . . I stopped abruptly and held my palms apart, alarmed by the tingling, buzzing sensation between them—a force so palpable I could mold it into an actual shape if I so desired. But I didn't desire. I thought of a rope of blue-white light snaking through the air, casting its flickering shadow on the snowy ground beneath, and the memory made me flinch. I shook my hands until they flapped on my wrists, then rubbed them on my thighs until the tingling was gone.

Chapter 11

The evening bulletin from the hospital was the same: no change in Dad's condition. After supper I went upstairs and shut myself in my room. I had no desire to try the healing spell again, but I was haunted by Kip's outburst last night. Had we really endangered Dad by our association with the coven? If there was even the slightest chance I could help him recover, wasn't I bound to do so? I protested to myself that I had already tried and failed.

Don't give up just because it isn't easy. Why should it be?

It's easy for Kip.

If I balked, would Snow decide to let Kip do the spell—even though, as she had pointed out, it was my idea? The thought made me spring off my bed and go to the dresser where I had hidden my magical materials. Without giving myself time to think, I set up my makeshift altar. I turned out the lamp, lit the candle and stirred three pinches of salt into the water. And then once more I began to pace out my circle. Clockwise, beginning in the north.

Where there's fear, there's power. As yet I felt no fear, only a return of the hot self-consciousness that had assaulted me the night before, the same sense of attempting a task for which I was hopelessly unqualified. Again and again I dipped my fingers into the water and let the drops fall to the floor. Nothing was happening, nothing at all. But my feet kept moving anyway, circling the room as mechanically as if I were on a treadmill. One step and another, and another, and then another. There were intervals when I counted, and others when I lost count. My fingertips began to pucker from their contact with the salt water, yet the glass still seemed full. How many drops before something happened, or until the glass was as empty as I felt myself to be? My own doubt was a soft but impenetrable wall against which I had to push with every step.

It's easy for Kip. The thought was a goad. I had to do this: had to even the score, prove myself as good as he was, show them all I wasn't the helpless incompetent they thought. Desperately I plowed forward against the dark. Keep moving. Don't stop. Don't give up.

Don't give up just because it isn't easy. Why should it be?

The power within you is a gift from the Goddess.

A gift from the Goddess . . .

The Goddess . . .

All at once the barrier gave way. My feet stopped moving and I stood still. A profound silence had fallen over the house; behind the silence was a faint humming like a vast, spinning wheel—growing and growing until it filled my ears, until I could feel myself whirling swiftly around the rim of the wheel, so swiftly that the motion itself became stillness. My skin rose to gooseflesh. I tried to remind myself that I was in my own bedroom, in my own house, in the village where I had been born.

With a spell to perform. A little unsteady on my feet, I went to the altar. The candle was burning brightly, and beneath the surface of the wax I saw flecks of gold that had been invisible before, flashing and twinkling like distant stars. *Look into a lit candle, and inside the bright flame you will see a dark one.* There it was—the dark flame at the center. *Everything we fear about who we are.* I forced my eyes away from it and picked up the poppet; in the candle's glow its expression resembled my father's more than ever. Time to begin. Carefully I sprinkled the little figure with salt water, and there in the bright darkness I heard myself speak as if listening to a stranger: a young, shaking voice saying the words Snow had taught me yesterday afternoon.

"Blessed be, thou creature made by art.
By art made, by art changed.

No longer cloth, but flesh and blood.
I name thee Graham.
Thou art he, between the worlds, in all the worlds.
Blessed be."

I stared at the doll in my hands, trying to charge it with healing energy. Gathering all my concentration, I tried to see my father strong and well. Tried to hear his voice, imagine the sound of his laugh. *By art made, by art changed.* A cloth doll with a whimsical expression and a red cartoon heart like Raggedy Ann's outlined on its breast. I could feel the weave of the fabric between my hands, the grainy texture of the herbs inside. Healing herbs and three strands of Dad's own hair. *No longer cloth, but flesh and blood.* I bit my lip, closed my eyes and clasped the poppet tightly, forcing myself to take deep breaths as I tried to put into practice all that Gwynneth had taught us. *Magic is a process of using the inner world to shape the outer one. You must know what you want, know you can get it, and focus on it completely. Your desire becomes real by force of will.*

My father, Graham Davies, well and strong. Lifting me up, a small child, to touch the star on top of the Christmas tree. Riding Kip on his shoulders. Playing catch with the two of us in the backyard, reading to us after supper at night. Teaching me how to swing a baseball bat, tie a shoelace, drive a car. Standing in front of my English class, reciting a poem while we all listened spellbound. But all these images were flat, the awkward constructions of an unskilled amateur, and I felt despair open like a pit beneath me. I couldn't do this. It was too hard.

It's easy for Kip.

And if I failed, Kip would do it. Kip would get all the glory, all the attention, all the praise, just as he always had. It wasn't fair. I bit my lip and tried harder. Reminded myself of the time Dad had accidentally put maple syrup in his coffee instead of cream. How, in spite of his refusal to attend church, he liked to sing "Amazing Grace" in the shower. How he used to sit out on the porch after supper in the summers and recite his favorite poems out loud, until Mother made him stop because she was afraid of what the neighbors might think. How, in one of those poems, there was a line about plucking the silver apples of the moon.

My hands began to tingle. Faintly at first, then vigorously, as if I were grasping some fast-vibrating object. Afraid to look, I squeezed my eyes more tightly shut and concentrated on making the pictures in my mind. I made our old car pull up in front of the house, made the door open and Dad emerge, color in his cheeks. Made us all gather around the dinner table, laughing and talking, easy and happy together as we had never truly been. Made Dad's arms come around me and the softness of his worn corduroy jacket rub against my cheek. Made his lips twitch the way they did when he wanted to laugh but knew he shouldn't. Faster and faster the images came, shifting like the patterns in a kaleidoscope, and within that radiant profusion I seemed to see my father's face change and grow younger—to see live green leaves sprout from his hair and the gentle light in his eyes brighten to a wild, exuberant gleam.

My own eyes involuntarily flew open, and panic jolted through me as I saw my hands engulfed in blue-white light, glowing eerily in the darkened room. I knew that light. I had seen it before, in far more spectacular form, shooting through the air in a flickering stream to send a grown man sprawling to the ground. I thought of Snow's eyes, like tunnels of darkness as she stared at Larry across the dining room and lifted one hand to her throat. *It's natural to fear that self, and what it's capable of.* Now I had summoned that power—a capricious, mysterious force I had neither the ability to control nor the skill to direct. *Although magic is neutral in itself, in the hands of inexperience or ill will it can destroy.* Helplessly I stared at the poppet between my hands, watching as the light around it burned brighter and brighter until at last the little figure was nothing but a small dark blot at the center of a field of dazzling white

(I hate you)

(Shelley I can't move)

suddenly obliterated by a blinding burst in which past, present and future seemed to fuse. My eyes clamped violently shut against that devastating flash. For some interval, I don't know how long, I was suspended in a void that might have been sleep.

When I opened my eyes again, the room was dark. The candle guttered in its saucer, a wick floating in a pool of wax. What had I been doing? Casting a healing spell for Dad—but just as things seemed to be going well, I had somehow fallen asleep. How could it have happened? Confused, I examined the poppet: it appeared unchanged. I had failed again—failed Dad when he needed me to succeed. But as I blew out the candle's feeble flame, there was an instant when I seemed to see a strange, exuberant face wreathed in green leaves, glimmering like a ghost against the darkness in the room.

Chapter 12

"Well?" Snow said.

I shifted my feet. "I tried. I really did. But from what my mother said on the phone this morning, he's no better."

Perched on one corner of her desk, she smiled a little. "Give it a chance. A spell needs time to work, just like a seed that's planted. Tell me what happened."

I gulped, ashamed of the truth. "I . . . I can't really remember."

"That's not uncommon at first. But you did as I told you."

"Yes." As I stared out the French doors at the wintry garden, the image of that strange leaf-haired face came back to me and haltingly I tried to describe it, bogging down at last into an inarticulate mumble. "It was like . . . he wasn't Dad anymore."

"But Shelley, that's wonderful!" She came close and took my shoulders. When she turned me around to face her, I saw she was smiling.

"It is?"

Shaking me gently: "Didn't you recognize him?"

"Who?"

"Pan. The Horned God. The Green Man. He has as many different names as the Goddess, but they all mean the same thing. Life. Energy. Change. Your spell called him on your father's behalf, and he answered you." As I stared doubtfully at her she said, "All you have to do now is continue what you've begun. Every night, spend a few minutes holding the poppet in your hands, seeing your father healthy and strong."

"But when you get a chance, can the coven do a spell for him too? In case mine doesn't work?"

"Yours will work."

I looked away. I knew I hadn't told her everything. But how could I, when I had unforgivably disgraced myself by dozing off? Guilt and shame boiled up inside me. "Just in case, Snow. Please?"

Could she hear my desperation? "As soon as we possibly can, Shelley. But I really don't think we'll need to."

There were still a few days of Christmas vacation remaining when Kip received a piece of unexpected and not entirely welcome news: Frog was in town. This was a departure from the Glasses' custom, which was to spend the winter holidays at a ski resort in Colorado. But it seemed Mrs. Glass had broken a leg on the slopes and, more or less immobilized, had opted for the comforts of home. As soon as the family arrived in Green Hollow, Frog excitedly contacted his old friend and suggested a rendezvous at the Pig & Whistle.

Close as they once had been, Kip was lukewarm about the proposed encounter. His oath of secrecy to the coven meant he would have to conceal the very part of his life that meant most to him. Acutely aware of how much his life and Frog's had diverged, he begged Shelley to come along and she readily consented—grateful, these days, for any distraction from her worries.

When they arrived at the Pig, it was packed with hungry teenage customers who kept the waitresses darting busily back and forth through the crowd. Frog sat in a booth by himself, isolated in the midst of the hubbub, and they threaded their way toward him across the noisy room.

"Hey, man! Long time!" Kip clapped him on the shoulder. "You remember Shelley, right?"

"Sure I do." His voice was high for a boy's. "Hi, Shelley."

"Hi." Remembering him as a dead ringer for Mr. Peabody's Pet Boy Sherman, she had to hide her surprise at the sight of this pleasant-looking bespectacled youth with his good haircut and expensive clothes. The three of them settled into the booth. Maggie, one of the waitresses, swooped down on them. "What'll it be, kids?"

They ordered Cokes and an order of fries to share. Kip sent Shelley a mute appeal. She cleared her throat. "How's your mother?"

Frog ducked his head sideways without looking at her. "Oh, she's okay. She says her leg doesn't hurt anymore, but her toes itch and she can't reach them to scratch."

"How long before she can get the cast off?"

"Five weeks at least." He smiled nervously and for a split second he was almost handsome. His skin was clear, the eyes behind the thick lenses were dark blue—and as he managed to meet her eyes at last, Shelley was astonished to see a beautiful flamingo pink slowly stain his cheeks. She kicked Kip under the table to let him know it was his turn to say something, and he rallied.

"So how's good old C.M.A. these days?" Without waiting for Frog's answer he turned to Shelley. "You think that stands for Clinton-Monroe Academy, but really—"

"Really it's Criminal Mind Academy," Frog broke in.

The laughter was forced. Maggie brought their order. Kip seized his Coke and took a long drink; Shelley stifled a sigh and addressed Frog again. "You just have one more year after this, right? Aren't you a junior?"

He nodded. "Yeah. I might graduate next January, though. I've finished the whole math curriculum, and I'm taking advanced Latin and Greek this year."

"Is Bugsy still teaching Latin?" Kip said.

Frog snorted. "Who else? He's the only one old enough to

have known Julius Caesar personally." The two of them snickered while Shelley nibbled a french fry. The references to Greek and Latin were a reminder of the esoteric rich-boy's world Kip had briefly inhabited and then so casually tossed away. "Remember Mercer?" Frog was saying. "That guy with the big ears?"

Was the conversation finally off the ground? Shelley turned and scanned the restaurant, letting their words sink into the surrounding babble as she searched for rescue. And she was in luck: Lisa and her boyfriend, Tom, were waving from a booth across the room. She mumbled excuses to Kip and Frog, who were talking freely at last. As far as she could tell they didn't even hear her. She slid out of the booth and made her way through the jumble of tables to join Lisa and Tom with a sigh of relief. "Who's that with Kip?" Lisa wanted to know.

"Remember Frog?"

Lisa peered across the room. "Frog? He's improved, huh?" She nudged Tom with her elbow. "Don't you think?"

Tom favored Frog with a bored glance. "He looks like a geek."

"What's he doing here?" Lisa said. "Isn't he supposed to be off on some fancy vacation?"

"His mother broke her leg skiing, so they came home. Kip hasn't seen Frog in more than a year. He made me come along because he didn't know what to say to him."

"Well," Lisa said, "they look like they're doing all right now."

Following her gaze Shelley saw what she meant: the two dark heads bent together in intense conversation across the table in the booth.

It was more than an hour later when we finally left the Pig and headed for the Arms. Kip went straight to the carriage house to look for Royce while I climbed the back steps. Entering the kitchen I could smell the spiced wine Jessica was mulling for the skiers who had mobbed the inn that weekend, and as I borrowed the spoon for a taste she said, "Snow was looking for you."

"Looking for me?" Apprehension turned the wine sour on

my tongue. Just then steps came down the back hall, and I looked up to see Snow smiling in the doorway.

"Your aunt called. Your father passed his tests today with flying colors. They want to keep him a few more days to make certain. But if nothing changes, he'll be coming home on Monday."

Monday—! I heard the spoon clatter to the floor before I was even aware my fingers had lost their grip. Then I found myself in her arms, laughing and crying, and she was hugging me and whispering, "What did I tell you?"

Confused, I drew away from her. "Jessica! Did you hear that? My father's coming home!"

"That's wonderful, sweetie." I was enfolded in another embrace, this one voluminous and slightly floury. "I'm so glad!"

"We have to tell Kip!" I could hear how shrill my voice sounded, but the others didn't seem to notice. Jessica peered out a steamy window.

"There they are now, him and Royce, coming across the parking lot." She tapped on the pane and made hurry-up gestures. Peering past her I saw the two thickly clad figures break into a run, arms windmilling and streamers of breath trailing behind them. Jessica opened the back door as Kip came bounding up the steps. "What? What's the matter?"

"Come inside!" she snapped at him. "You'll freeze us all to death!"

He lurched into the room, Royce behind him. "Marty called," I said. "Dad's coming home Monday."

Kip stared at me. For an instant his face was a perfect blank, and then it cracked in a wild grin. He let out a whoop and grabbed Royce's gloved hands to execute a brief jig. "Really? Monday?" Releasing Royce, he came at me with arms outstretched and I ducked away. "Don't touch me! You're all frosty."

"I think this calls for a celebration," Snow was saying. "Is that wine ready?"

It was, and Jessica poured us each a mugful. We stood around the kitchen sipping the delicious potion, Royce watching our faces with a smile on his lips. Relief made me giddy; I had taken only a sip or two of the wine but I felt slightly drunk. Dad was coming home Monday. My spell had worked. *My* spell—yet even now I noticed all eyes were on Kip, who was repeating an exchange he had overheard at the hospital between a seasoned nurse and a young doctor. "So he says, 'What do you think *M.D.* stands for, Nurse?' and she says, 'In your case? *M*aternal *D*eprivation!' "

Everyone laughed, even Kip at his own story, shaking back his tousled hair. How quickly he had shed his worries, all his fears about endangering Dad—how blithely he had left the solution up to me. It had been my spell that had saved the day, and yet everyone was looking at him. "You're lucky Mother's in Albany," I said. "Once she sees what a mess your hair is, she'll make you get it cut."

The snappish, fretful words rang in the brief silence that followed. Kip passed a self-conscious hand over his hair, the thick waves glinting in the lamplight as they fell away from his touch. So soft it would feel, sliding between my fingers. I turned away, regretting my ugly outburst, hearing Jessica say, "Mercy! Quarter past five already? They'll be coming in from the slopes soon; we'll need to serve this wine. And I've got to get dinner started."

She began bustling around the room, the rest of us trying to move out of her way. In the commotion, finding myself close to Snow, I mumbled, "Thank you."

She smiled into my eyes. "I didn't do it, Shelley. You did."

"No, but—" I meant to simply raise my mug to her, a kind of wordless salute, but my light-headedness combined with the nearly full vessel to slop the wine over the edge in a generous spill. Snow saw it coming and jumped back out of the way—but Kip was right behind her and she bumped into him, momentarily losing her balance. His arms came round her in reflex. As they swayed awkwardly in that impromptu embrace, I saw his lips part and his cheeks go from their normal color to a fiery red. But that was not all I saw. He was only an inch or so taller than Snow; their faces were almost level. So there was no way I could miss the same flustered look, the same sudden telltale color on hers.

And then the moment was past, as quickly as it had come. She righted herself; he dropped his arms. She moved away from him, took a dish towel from the counter and knelt to wipe up the spill. I looked around the room. Jessica, wielding pots and pans in a frenzy, had barely noticed the incident itself, let alone its nuances. But Royce had; I saw his eyes flick from Kip to Snow, then meet mine and glance off as he bent to tighten his bootlace.

Kip had busied himself with using his sweater sleeve to polish the brass push-plate on the swinging door. The back of his neck was crimson and although he was trying his best to stand in a way that concealed it, there was a noticeable bulge in his pants. I glanced from him to Snow. As she straightened from wiping the floor I could see the color beginning to fade from her face, leaving a bright streak across her cheekbones. She waved the wine-stained towel under my nose. "Nice try. You almost got me."

She sounded out of breath, as if she had been running. She didn't look Kip's way, and he didn't turn, but I could feel their awareness of one another like a taut, trembling cord stretching between them. *What were you in your past life? Lovers?*

"I'm sorry," I said, and she gave a gasping little laugh completely unlike her usual one. "No harm done."

But there was.

Chapter 13

As promised, Dad came home from the hospital the following Monday, looking somehow younger, less tired than the twins remembered ever seeing him. As he folded the two of them into a hug they could feel a new strength in his embrace—

and when Shelley looked into his face, an impish, leaf-haired visage seemed to superimpose itself momentarily on his beloved features. She blinked and the shadowy face was gone; she might have imagined it. She rubbed her cheek against the shoulder of his soft corduroy jacket. "Welcome home, Dad."

Yet his recovery only left space for other worries. Was there any substance to Kip's notion that the coven's mysterious enemy had somehow caused his heart attack? Who was this elusive, malign presence who could command the elements and shape their dreams at will, and what was his connection with the coven? *My guess is he's a renegade. There's some kind of struggle going on. And because of us, Dad got stuck in the middle.*

And then came Kip's announcement that Frog had decided to throw a party. Mr. Glass had left town on business and Mrs. Glass, concerned only with her itching toes, had given her consent and put the servants in charge of the details. A party? Recalling Frog's dismal shyness at the Pig, Shelley couldn't imagine this had been his idea; more likely Kip had talked him into it—yet how could there be any real merrymaking while Alex's killer was still out there? Snow's somber warning about being on their guard was fresh in her thoughts. But when she voiced her concern to Kip, he dismissed it with a shrug. "Of course it's safe. Everybody'll be going together in cars. And school starts on Monday. We deserve to have a little fun."

Most of the village seemed to share his view. In the three months since Alex had disappeared, the general panic had receded and most people were eager to believe the tragedy had been an isolated incident. Word-of-mouth invitations to the party met with a good response.

"I hope you know what you're doing," Shelley told Kip, and he answered with a little smile too redolent of mischief not to arouse her suspicions. He was up to something, no doubt about that.

But she was unprepared for the sight that met her eyes on the night of the party, as she entered the palatial game room located in one wing of the Glasses' mansion on the outskirts of the village. The festivities were in boisterous progress, a hubbub of voices competing with the rock-and-roll music blaring from huge speakers in the corners of the room, and several dozen guests were already present. Nothing strange about that. The strange thing was that they were neatly divided into two groups. All the boys were over by the game tables, talking and laughing loudly, and games of Ping-Pong and billiards were in full swing.

All the girls were on the sofa with Frog.

It was a long sofa, amply stuffed, and Frog was embedded in the deep cushions in the middle. To the left and right of him were girls. Hanging over the back of the sofa behind his head—girls. Curled up at his feet and perched on the plump upholstered arms—

Girls.

They were teasing and joking with him, playing with his hair, fooling with his glasses, trying to hold his hands and laughingly fondling the necktie he had put on for the party because at Clinton-Monroe the boys wore ties everywhere but to bed. If he had been some famous movie star, they could not have been showering more attention on him. Shelley stared, then turned to Kip in astonishment. "Would you look at that?" He didn't answer, but she saw that same little smile on his face.

"What's with the harem?" Lisa, with whom the twins had ridden over in Tom's car, was tugging at Shelley's sleeve. "Come on, let's go see what the attraction is. Maybe he's giving away free hundred-dollar bills."

What was the attraction, indeed? There were mutterings from the game tables where the boys had congregated, but they seemed more amazed than annoyed. Bonnie Merriwether was stroking Frog's hair; Liz Stalcup was whispering in his ear. He was grinning wildly, his face the beautiful shade of pink Shelley had noted at the Pig & Whistle. Surely it was only a matter of time before his glasses would begin to fog over. Lisa was heading for the sofa and Shelley started to follow, but was stopped by a hand on her arm—Kip, beckoning her into a corner. By now she was more than ready for an explanation of that little smile. "Okay. What's going on?"

His eyes had their gold gleam. "Guess."

"I can't guess. Just tell me."

He indicated the scene on the sofa with a jerk of his head. "I did that."

"You?"

Putting his lips to her ear: "I cast a spell for him."

"You *what*?"

"Shh! I found it in the back of my book—how to make a love charm and charge it with magic."

Shelley pulled away and looked at him. He grinned as he glanced over at the sofa again. "Shelley, it's *working*."

Of that, there was little doubt. A flicker of unease passed through her as she looked from Kip's elated face to the unlikely scene on the sofa. This had to be his own brainstorm, not something the coven had sanctioned. "Does he know you did it?" she whispered.

"Sure. He's got the charm in his pocket right now. And he was there when I cast the spell."

"Kip! You didn't tell him about the coven?"

"Of course not. I let him think this is something I've been doing on my own. We used to talk about magic all the time at school." They were watching Frog as they talked, and now they saw Sarah McGill succeed in loosening his tie. He made a feeble protest; there was a giggling, squirming struggle as several girls joined forces to remove the tie. Frog disappeared momentarily to resurface with his glasses askew and his face redder than ever. A female arm waved the tie aloft as a trophy.

"I hope you didn't overdo it," Shelley said, and Kip laughed. "Are you kidding? The guy's in pig heaven."

Her insider's knowledge seemed to render Shelley immune to the spell. She loitered at the fringes of the party, keeping an eye on the door for Benjy. He had exhibited little enthusiasm when she had told him about the party, but she had a feeling he might show up. As time passed and he didn't appear, she started a game of Ping-Pong with Kip. At last she saw Benjy come slouching in, clearly ill at ease in the posh surroundings. Kip sent a fast shot her way; she let it go by and put down her paddle.

"Hey, where're you going? You're winning!"

"I don't want to play anymore. Benjy's here."

Kip came around the table frowning. "Listen, Shel, there are plenty of nice guys here tonight. Why waste your time on Benjy?"

"What?"

"Well, I hate to say it, but he's kind of a loser."

A loser? Mother's disapproval was easy to dismiss, but her twin's casual contempt stung. What right had he to criticize her friendship with Benjy, when he himself had a ridiculous crush on Snow? She gave him a cool look and left him standing by the table.

Benjy's sullen face brightened as he caught sight of her. "Hey, there you are. Look at this place. This room's bigger than my whole house."

"Mine too." Feeling Kip's eyes on her back, Shelley was suddenly self-conscious. "Uh, you want something to eat? There's lots of stuff over there."

She turned toward the refreshment table, but Benjy caught her arm. "Wait, Shelley, I don't want anything. This party looks like a dud. Let's you and me go for a ride."

"A ride?"

"I've got the truck."

"Well, I—" A commotion at her back distracted her: somebody had turned up the music and the other boys were raiding Frog's pool of admirers for partners. Seeing Tom drag Lisa by main force away from the sofa and onto the dance floor, Shelley was abruptly reminded of Kip's spell. "I'd better not, Benjy. I—I think I need to stay here."

"What for?"

"Well—" She stopped. Impossible to explain what Kip had done, or why she felt obliged to stay and keep an eye on things. "Don't you want to dance or anything?"

He shook his head in obvious distaste, and Shelley was suddenly afraid he would leave. She bit her lip and glanced behind her again. Everyone was dancing now, Bonnie with Frog. Suddenly Marian broke away from Glen Westerly to cut in. As she seized Frog's hands in hers, Liz, Kathy, and Lisa could be seen abandoning their own partners to move in Frog's direction.

Shelley turned back to find Benjy looking restless. "Listen," she said. "Let's find someplace quiet, okay? Where we can talk."

He shrugged, then gave a reluctant nod, and they struck off down a corridor, trying to leave the noise of the party behind. Shelley was relieved not to witness the scene on the dance floor; she could always check back in a little while to make sure matters hadn't gotten completely out of hand. This spell—why had Kip done it? Was it because, in spite of Elymas's warnings, he couldn't wait to put his new skills to work—or because he had overheard Snow giving her the credit for Dad's recovery? Was this his attempt to even the score? Couldn't he even allow her one small triumph of her own?

She and Benjy wandered through the house, peeking into rooms as they passed. In one, an elderly lady—the housekeeper, who was supposed to be acting as chaperone?—snored in an easy chair, her mouth open. Another held nothing but a glossy grand piano and an enormous harp. All radiated a cold perfection that, unlike the comfortable elegance at the Arms, seemed to discourage intrusion. Passing a bathroom, Shelley stopped. "Wait for me, Benjy. I'll be out in a minute."

Even the bathroom was intimidating—exquisitely gold and white, with matching hand towels and tiny cakes of soap shaped like seashells, too perfect to use. Her face looked alien in the mirror with its gold filigree frame, but she took a moment to meet her own eyes resolutely. She was determined that Benjy was going to kiss her tonight, and she was going to enjoy it. More than that: she was going to feel a passion that would burn away the memory of what had happened in Kip's room last October.

I must have taken too long in the bathroom; when I emerged Benjy was nowhere in sight. I went down the hall and into a room that seemed less forbidding than the others—a sunroom with wicker furniture and lots of potted plants. Beyond a wall of glass doors, a fairyland of snowy lawns was visible. I stood looking at the view without really seeing it, thinking of the scene in the game room. *I cast a spell for him.* As I pictured

Frog red-faced, awash in girls, a sound from the doorway made me turn. Expecting Benjy, I was surprised to see Frog himself standing there.

"Oh—hi, Shelley." He glanced furtively down the hallway behind him, then offered me a shamefaced smile. "I'm hiding."

"I don't blame you."

He crossed the room to join me by the glass doors. "Did Kip tell you what he did?"

I nodded. There was an awkward pause. I cleared my throat. "Looks like it's working."

He gulped. "Yeah."

We looked at each other and started to laugh, our breath misting the glass and obscuring the moonlit vista outside. Frog dug into his pants pocket, took something out—a little cloth bag, I saw, tied at the neck with thread—and showed it to me. From it emanated a dreamy summer fragrance reminiscent of the herb garden at the Arms. "Amazing, huh?" he said.

"Uh-huh."

The glass had cleared; moonlight glittered on the snow outside. A lock of hair had fallen over Frog's forehead, and all at once he looked handsome in the slightly disheveled way I associated with the French movie stars who sometimes adorned the magazine covers at the E-Z Stop. As the charm's fragrance wafted over me again, I found myself wondering what it would be like to kiss him. Did all boys kiss the same? I saw him swallow, his Adam's apple moving up and down, and this palpable nervousness filled me with unexpected tenderness. Shyly his hands touched my shoulders.

"Hey!" Kip's voice made us both jump. Even from the doorway his presence filled the room, sending the magical moonlit shadows scurrying into the corners. In three strides he had crossed the floor and reached between us, putting one hand on Frog's chest as if to restrain him. "What the hell do you think you're doing?"

Frog blinked. The hand on his chest evidently rendered him speechless, and his silence seemed to infuriate Kip. "Hey, I asked you a question! Are you nuts? She's my *sister,* jerk! Keep your hands off her!" He ended this speech with a shove that sent Frog stumbling back.

"Kip, stop it!" I said.

"Dammit, Shelley, you ought to know better. It's just that damn spell!"

Another protest was on my tongue, but it remained unsaid. It struck me that he was right. Certainly Frog, cringing from Kip's wrath, cut a far less desirable figure now than he had a few moments ago. How could I have ever compared him to a French movie star, or considered the idea of kissing him? Any such desire had vanished now, as completely as if it had never existed. He had taken off his glasses and was polishing the lenses on the tail of his shirt, making a nervous sniffing noise as he did so. Kip stood glaring, his hands in fists, and I held my breath and prayed Frog wouldn't give him an excuse to start swinging.

Frog put his glasses back on. "Sorry." The muttered word was scarcely audible. He didn't look at us. Kip didn't answer and neither did I, because I could think of nothing to say. Head down, Frog left the room, shoving the charm back in his pocket as he went. When he had vanished I took a cautious breath of relief. "You didn't have to be so mean to him."

"Mean! I let him off easy." Kip's teeth were clenched as he spoke. "I do the asshole a favor, and look what I get in return! He—"

We heard voices in the hall: Benjy's, then a mumble that must have been Frog. A moment later Benjy's tall figure appeared in the doorway of the sunroom, peering hesitantly into the shadows where Kip and I stood. "Shelley? You in here?"

"I'm here, Benjy."

He fumbled inside the doorway and an overhead light came on, making us all blink. I hadn't realized Kip and I were standing so close together until I saw the odd look on Benjy's face. "What's going on?" he said.

"Nothing."

"Nothing? What're you doing in the dark?"

I shrugged. "We were just looking at the snow."

"Is that so? Well, the two of you sure look cozy. Don't let me butt in."

The host of shadowy improprieties implicit in his sneer created a moment's shocked silence. Then Kip said, "Why don't you shut up?"

"You wanna make me?"

Were they going to fight? Frog had posed no threat to Kip; Benjy was a different story. He was taller, even if Kip was more solidly built. As they stood bristling at each other like a pair of angry dogs, the illogic of the situation suddenly struck me and I seemed to hear Elymas's voice saying, *What you send, returns threefold.* Uneasiness spread through me; I touched Kip's sleeve. "Listen, let's all just go back to the party. Okay?"

After a moment he shrugged and nodded. I took a deep breath of relief. But Benjy was still scowling at us—and realizing my hand was still on Kip's arm, I quickly took it away.

Over the next few weeks the repercussions of Kip's magical working continued to expand outward, reaching as far as the stuffy halls of Clinton-Monroe before rebounding, with increased force, back to Green Hollow. After the unpleasantness at the party, however, communications had lapsed between Kip and Frog; thus the twins had no inkling, until one nasty, sleety evening in mid-January, that the chain of events set in motion by the spell was continuing to unfold.

"Shelley, when you're finished down here, come straight up to the third floor."

Snow had stopped her in the back hall with these startling instructions just as she was heading down the cellar stairs to change into her serving clothes for dinner—simply made the curt announcement and then vanished. And now, as Shelley rushed to satisfy the hungry guests who had sought shelter at the Arms from the ugly weather—as her hands smoothly set down plates, uncorked bottles of wine, and replaced guttering candles—one question reverberated in her wind.

Had Alex's killer struck again? It seemed horrifyingly possible, yet she could hear no reference to such a catastrophe in the conversation among the guests. In the busy, noisy dining room it was impossible to catch Kip's eye. Had he been given any more information than she had? She could discern no difference in his customary performance—as usual, he was the debonair waiter, handsome in his spotless white shirt (hers already had a splash of gravy on one sleeve) and black tie, delivering some witticism that set his whole table laughing as he filled their wineglasses from a candlelight-burnished bottle.

Her suspicions grew when several of the coven members showed up for dinner: Grimalkin and Elymas taking a quiet corner table, Gwynneth arriving in time to join them for coffee. A little later the front door opened to admit a group of people in wet winter coats—Archer and Andreas accompanied by Tamarack and Senta, the four of them heading straight upstairs without stopping. A current of icy air followed in their wake, spreading through the dining room—a reminder that no matter how convivial things were in here, the night outside was raw.

When you're finished down here, come straight up to the third floor. Shelley bit her lip. Surely only a dire emergency could justify a gathering of the coven on such a nasty night. A dire emergency. What else could it be? The door opened again to admit Silkmoth, Reed and Indigo, along with another blast of icy wind. She watched them hurry upstairs. The dining room was beginning to empty and she found herself eyeing the remaining guests nervously. Always before, when the coven had met, only its members had been present at the inn—but tonight the place was packed with strangers and the risk of detection seemed magnified a thousandfold. All her nightmare fantasies about being exposed as a witch, accused of worshiping the devil, came rushing back in force; as she refilled the cups of a well-dressed couple in their sixties, the handle of the coffeepot nearly escaped her sweaty grip. What expression would replace those affable smiles, if only they knew?

At last the dining room was empty. When Shelley brought the final precariously loaded tray into the kitchen, Gwynneth was waiting. "Go on up, Shelley. Tonight we'll be doing things a little differently, because of the other people in the house." Her wry smile acknowledged the need for caution. Shelley set her tray down by the sink. She felt guilty about leaving Jessica to clean up the kitchen by herself, but the housekeeper waved her off. "You go ahead. They're waiting for you."

"What about Kip?"

Jessica's eyes flickered. "He's gone up already."

Royce was guarding the third floor, his bulk effectively blocking the head of the stairs. He moved aside to let Shelley pass, waggling his fingers in response to her smile. A wedge of light split the darkness of the corridor as a door opened nearby. "Shelley? In here."

Except for Snow the coven women were all there, changing into their robes without speaking. Shelley shed her clothes and put her robe on, shy in this communal situation and too apprehensive by now to ask the questions that clamored in her head. When they were all ready, Grimalkin opened the door and they filed quickly into the hall. In the darkness Shelley could scarcely see the hooded silhouettes in front of her, although Royce's reassuring outline was visible against the light from the stairwell. And then they were crossing the threshold of the ritual room and she heard the door click softly shut behind them, then another click as someone turned the bolt.

The men were already present, and the women formed the other half of the circle. Half a dozen white candles on the altar illuminated the room. By their wavering light Shelley noted the other objects present: a small cauldron, a pitcher of water, and a tall red candle, unlit. She looked for Kip and found him between Reed and Andreas. When would the purpose of this grim gathering be announced? With every passing second her nerves wound themselves more tightly. A cup of salt water was passed around the circle in symbolic purification, and when her turn came to take a sip, the bitter taste seemed the very flavor of anxiety.

Once the cup had made its full circuit, Snow set it aside and made an uncharacteristically abrupt motion with her hands. "Let's sit down."

In silence they sat crosslegged on the floor. Shelley's palms were slippery; the bitter taste of the water lingered stubbornly in her mouth. She lowered her eyes to her lap and waited.

"I want to thank you all for coming tonight," Snow said. "I

know the weather is terrible, and you have better things to do. But I called this meeting because certain events have come to my attention." She paused for a moment before going on. "Events caused by the irresponsible working of magic."

The hush that followed her words made the previous silence seem light and airy. Heart thudding against her ribs, Shelley slowly raised her heavy eyes. Snow was looking now at one person in the circle, and everyone in the room followed her gaze.

Kip.

All Shelley's vital processes—heartbeat, breath, even the flowing of her blood—seemed to pause for an incalculable space while she watched her twin return Snow's cold stare. Finally he looked down into his lap. When Snow spoke again, her voice was neutral. "Kip has something to tell us."

For what seemed like a long time, he didn't speak. Then he said sulkily, "It wasn't supposed to happen the way it did."

Silence again in the circle. Then Elymas cleared his throat and said, "Why don't you tell us what happened?"

"It was just . . ." Kip's voice died away; he had to start over. "I tried to do a friend a favor. And it worked a little too well."

"Meaning?" Grimalkin said.

He chewed his bottom lip. "I worked a love spell for him. And now the girls won't let him alone."

A ripple of reaction ran around the circle, relief and even amusement lighting bleak faces. Snow's remained tight-lipped and pale; she waited for the others to settle down before she started to speak. "This is the situation as far as I know it. Kip's friend is the only son, very shy, of a wealthy family here in the village. He attends an all-male prep school. Over the Christmas vacation he gave a party at which a number of local girls were manipulated, by means of magic, into thinking they had fallen in love with him.

"After he went back to school, the girls continued to keep in touch. This afternoon one of them took a bus to Massachusetts and was caught by the campus police trying to sneak onto the school grounds for a rendezvous with the boy. She told one of the officers that since this happens to be a leap year, she was planning to surprise him with an early marriage proposal."

It was as clear from Snow's summary as from the expression on her face that she found nothing the least bit funny but about these events; her usual air of detached amusement had deserted her. But Shelley saw some of the others struggling to look serious. Although no one laughed, the air of tension in the circle had drained away. Gwynneth said, "Kip, this spell you worked. Describe it exactly, please."

He shrugged. "I found it in a book. You make a charm and charge it with the power of the four elements. That's all. But the girls were all over him." His eyes flicked toward his sister and then away. Shelley could feel the blood rushing to her face, but no one was paying attention to her. "Does your friend still have the charm?" Senta was asking.

"I guess so." Kip hesitated, then glanced at Snow. "I brought the picture you asked for."

She nodded without looking at him. He produced it from a pocket of his robe and it was passed around the circle for inspection: a crumpled color photograph of Frog standing on a beach. Elymas said, "Was your friend present at the working?"

Kip's gulp was audible. "Yes. But I didn't tell him anything about the coven. I let him think I've been doing this all on my own." He paused and then added, "I'm telling the truth, I swear."

No one spoke and then Grimalkin said mildly, "We believe you. But this spell must be broken. And that is why we are all here tonight."

Kip's face reddened and I felt my own blush renew itself, this time on his account. His actions had caused untold inconvenience to these busy, harried adults, interrupting their routines and dragging them from their homes to make a long journey through bad weather, all in order to undo the mischief he had so lightheartedly embarked upon. Yet if I knew my brother, the flush on his cheeks came as much from defiant pride as from embarrassment. I knew how he had yearned to try out his magical skills, how frustrated he was by his apprentice status, and how it must have irked him to hear Snow credit me with Dad's recovery. Now his spell on Frog's behalf had been proved an unqualified success—so much so that it required a gathering of the entire coven to set it aside.

Snow took the red candle from the altar and started to light it. But the flame trembled in her fingers, and the candle slipped from her grasp and fell to the floor, rolling a little way before Grimalkin retrieved it. The older woman put a hand on the younger's shoulder, murmuring something in her ear. I saw Snow's lips tighten, but she shrugged and turned away and Grimalkin took her place.

Astonished as I was to see Snow relinquish her role as high priestess, there was no chance to wonder about it then. Grimalkin was lighting the red candle, anchoring it in its own drippings at the bottom of the empty cauldron, where it protruded a few inches above the rim. When Reed and Tamarack had filled the cauldron with water from the pitcher on the altar, she motioned the rest of us to stand.

"Tonight we pace the circle widdershins, the direction of decrease. For this same reason we meet on a night with a waning moon. We are working not to bind a spell, but to dissolve one. So let the power we raise together be the power of extinction."

She closed her eyes and I saw the others do the same. The audible rhythm of their breathing gradually excluded all other sound. I squeezed my eyes shut and tried to join in, but I couldn't concentrate. Through slitted lids I stole a peek at the yellow flame burning just above the lip of the cauldron. Grimalkin's husky voice spoke above the sound of our breathing.

"Picture in your mind the face of the boy on whose behalf this spell was cast. A spell to attract others to him. The power of the spell lies in this bright flame, burning hot as physical desire. As the candle burns, that power grows."

While she was speaking I saw the flame reach higher into the air. Within its quivering brightness I seemed to glimpse Frog's face as it had looked while we stood in the darkened sunroom. I saw the lock of hair falling over one eyebrow and the nervous movement of his Adam's apple, and felt the spell of standing close to him surrounded by the scents of summer, while the world outside was covered in snow.

We started to move. Counterclockwise. Widdershins, the direction of decrease. Pacing the boundary of the circle slowly at first, then faster, putting one foot in front of the other, one and then the other, over and over until the motion took us and we no longer had a choice. Round and round, like the backward spinning of an ancient wheel, unraveling that which had been too carelessly spun. Like a film run in reverse: boiling lava sucked down into a volcano, waterfalls reeled up onto high cliffs, lightning withdrawn into the sky.

Unraveling. Unraveling. Would the village of Green Hollow be dismantled—would houses unbuild themselves, virgin forest be restored, a leafy silence cover the place where we had been? These thoughts skimmed the surface of my mind and vanished. Backward . . . backward . . . until motion shifted seamlessly into stillness around the turning axis at the center. We were still; only the candle flame moved, spinning like a top. A humming sound, a great vibrating silence, rose in the air. The candle burned down to the level of the water and began to flicker. One last time it flared up, then sputtered and abruptly went out. A thin wisp of smoke spiraled upward.

We came to a sudden standstill—it came as a shock to me that we had been moving all this time—and Grimalkin said softly, "Like smoke let the power of this spell be dispersed. May no trace of it remain. We ask the Goddess's indulgence for the worker of the spell, knowing he meant no harm, and her blessing on the boy for whom it was cast. May this occasion remind us that love is not a trick, not a glamour cast by artifice. When body and spirit are one, erotic love becomes a sacred discipline, a pathway to the mystery. To such, there are no shortcuts."

She smiled, lifting the hands of Elymas and Gwynneth on either side of her and then releasing them.

After we had changed back into our clothes, I went downstairs to see if there was anything to be done in the kitchen, but Jessica had left the place immaculate. Kip was nowhere in sight. I was standing there in the dimly lit kitchen, wondering if he had gone home without me, when I heard steps crossing the dining room. The swinging door opened and Elymas peered in. "Ah, Shelley! Are you standing guard? I was going to raid the refrigerator." He was in his pajamas and bathrobe; unlike the others, he and Grimalkin had decided to stay the night.

"I think there's some chocolate cake left," I said.

He found it and cut a generous slab. "Some for you?"

"No thanks."

He poured a glass of milk and sat down at the table with his feast. "Well, will you keep an old man company?"

I took a chair willingly. I loved Elymas: his endless patience, his enthusiasm for everything he taught us—and of course his eyebrows. They twitched now as he surveyed my face. "What's bothering you, my dear?"

"Is Kip in a lot of trouble?" I blurted. "Is he going to be kicked out of the coven?"

"Of course not." Elymas swallowed a mouthful of cake. "Wherever did you get that idea?"

"It's just . . . Snow seems so mad at him."

He sighed. "She has a lot on her mind these days. At a time when the coven needs to focus its energies elsewhere, it's hard for her not to resent any distraction."

I thought back to her response to my request that the coven perform the healing spell for Dad. *At the moment our hands are full.* "You mean the man who killed Alex, don't you? You're trying to keep him from hurting anyone else."

His face was bleak. "We're doing what we can. And assistance is on the way."

I thought of Kip saying, *He's a renegade. There's some kind of struggle going on between them.* If I asked Elymas, would he tell me what was going on? But my mouth wouldn't form the words; instead I reverted to our earlier topic. "But Kip didn't really harm those girls, did he? It's not like he was controlling them. Wasn't he just . . . shaping them?"

Elymas put down his fork. "What do you mean?"

"Well, that's what Snow said, the time she made a magic stew for the guests."

"A magic stew?"

"There was some kind of love potion in it. Once they ate it, they got so romantic they couldn't even wait around for dessert. But she said it wasn't the same as controlling them. She said the secret is to shape, to bend without breaking."

He sat silent, staring at nothing, leaving the remainder of his cake untouched. After a minute I said, "Elymas?"

He didn't look at me. He closed his eyes and began to massage his beaky nose with one hand, as if he had a headache. Seen like that, he looked frail and old. Finally he said, "Magic has a way of following its own course, Shelley, often regardless of the practitioner's intent. That's one of the reasons we make a point of employing it only when necessary. But 'necessary' is a relative term, and it's always easier to judge someone else's behavior than our own. Do you understand what I'm saying?"

Did I? To me it sounded as if Snow's magic stew had been no different than Kip's runaway love spell—but if that was the case, what right had she to be so angry at him? My confusion must have been obvious. Elymas's pale blue eyes met mine. "Beware of thinking Snowden is perfect, Shelley. If you idealize her you are hurting, not helping her. Never forget that the high priestess or priest is as human as the rest of us, and as capable of mistakes." A shadow flickered in his gaze. "She has great power, a gift from the Goddess. But there's always danger in such power. It's difficult to use with restraint, all the more so because she's so young. To some extent, even the most practiced magician is merely the servant of a force we only partly understand. There are so many traps, so many snares . . . If Emma had lived out her natural span, Snowden would have had more time to learn to master her gift."

I stared at him. In my unqualified admiration for Snow, it had never crossed my mind to think of her as someone who still had some growing up to do. She always seemed so wise, so authoritative, so perfectly in control. Now Elymas's words suddenly showed her in a different light. I found my voice. "But if she . . . why wasn't someone older chosen as the Lady? Why not Senta, or Grimalkin?"

"It was obvious from the day Snowden joined us that she was the Goddess's choice. She came to us very young, even younger than you and Kip. But we could all see it." His eyes rested on my face. "Now I see it in you as well."

"In *me*?" I said, stunned.

"Yes." He smiled faintly and patted my hand. "And now it's very late, my dear, and tomorrow is a school day. Shouldn't you be getting home?"

Chapter 14

January waned, but the tension at the Arms did not. Although the love spell cast on Frog's behalf had been dissolved and the matter was theoretically closed, Snow remained cool and distant to Kip. His response was to sulk. Royce, Jessica and Shelley tried to ignore the cloud hanging over the household—but the pretense was a strain, and for Shelley there was the added burden of her late-night conversation with Elymas, with its oblique warnings and promises.

A few days before the Candlemas Sabbat, a certain guest arrived early in the afternoon. Shelley heard him in the entrance hall, talking to Snow with an English accent, but when she went to investigate there was only the tail of an overcoat rounding a corner of the stairs. Checking the register, she found his scrawled entry halfway down the page: *J. Blackbridge. Taunton, Somerset, England.* The address intrigued her. She had inherited her mother's passion for any and everything associated with England, and from her indiscriminate reading she had concocted a pastiche of kings and queens, castles and knights, foxes and hounds, tea and scones, the Tower of London and Toad Hall, cricket and Covent Garden, Eton and Empire—an entire romantic world contained in the word *England*.

So J. Blackbridge was assured of her interest in advance. As the guests began to gather in the dining room she picked him out at once. Not young, but not old either. Cropped white hair, brooding eyes beneath thick black brows, a stocky torso that, even seated and motionless, seemed to radiate energy. Although his pale, manicured hands lay perfectly still on the white tablecloth before him, Shelley had an odd, fleeting impression that their stillness was unnatural, as if they were being forcibly subdued. Altogether an interesting guest: unobtrusively she pointed him out to Kip. Inky eyes fixed on space, he sat at a corner table by himself.

But not for long. His dinner companion arrived almost at once, and he rose politely to greet her—Snow, dressed as elegantly as for any Sabbat feast, giving Shelley a smile as she filled their water glasses, but otherwise bestowing all her attention on the visitor. During the meal they conversed in murmurs, leaning across the table with their heads so close together that their curious young waitress was able to catch none of it, not so much as a single word. Back in the kitchen she tried pumping Jessica about J. Blackbridge until the housekeeper said sharply that he was a guest and entitled to his privacy like any other. But Kip was quick to announce his opinion that the Englishman was a witch. "He's here on business. To help catch the guy who killed Alex."

Jessica snorted. "Since you know so much about *business,* why can't you learn to mind your own?"

But once dinner was over they were summoned to Snow's office, where they found her with the mysterious English visitor. As they entered the room she smiled at them.

"Here they are—our two apprentices, Shelley and Kipling Davies. Shelley, Kip, I'd like you to meet Jonathan Blackbridge, high priest of the Silver Web Coven in England."

High priest of the Silver Web Coven in England. The phrase fluttered Shelley's nerves. So Kip was right: this was the promised assistance—a witch come all the way from England to snare Alex's murderer. The somber eyes examined them deliberately before Jonathan Blackbridge said in his elegant accent, "Someone in your family is an admirer of English literature."

Shelley waited for Kip to do the talking. When he remained silent she said, "Our father's an English teacher."

The visitor fixed his eyes on hers and said softly, *"That orbéd maiden, with white fire laden—"*

He broke off. The black eyes bored into hers. As a strange numbness spread through her limbs, Shelley remembered her earlier impression of his hands as creatures subdued against their will. She heard herself whisper, *"Whom mortals call the moon."*

Jonathan Blackbridge smiled. "A very beautiful salute to the Goddess, don't you think? I'm pleased to find you conversant with the works of your namesake, young woman." Shelley could feel herself blushing. Kip, beside her, gave an audible snort and Jonathan Blackbridge glanced at him. He was still smiling, but his lips were thinner now. "And you, young man? If I were to give you a random quotation from the works of Kipling, do you think you could complete it?"

"No." The curt syllable flattened the air in the room. As Kip and Jonathan Blackbridge stared at each other in a silence that started to become awkward, Shelley was swamped by bewilderment. Had she missed something? What had caused this antipathy between her brother and the visitor? Snow broke the silence smoothly. "Everett and Emma were both trained by Jonathan's coven. He knew them very well. He'll be joining us for the Candlemas Sabbat."

Shelley made a sound she hoped conveyed enthusiasm—more than she actually felt, to counteract Kip's glowering presence at her side. What was the matter with him? Snow and the visitor had noticed it too; she saw them exchange the complicit smile adults use when children are being tiresome. "Why don't you two go have your supper?" Snow said. "You must be starving. We'll see you tomorrow."

Back in the kitchen they finished their supper in record time, without conversation, and took leave of Jessica. The silence continued unbroken as Royce walked them home. Once they were alone, Shelley could finally say what she was thinking.

"Kip, what's the matter with you? You were really rude to him!"

He turned toward her with a savage movement, mimicking Jonathan's accent. *"Someone in your family is an admirer of English literature."* And in his own voice, heavily laced with scorn: "Give that man a cigar."

"He was just making conversation."

"And the two of you spouting poetry at each other! For crying out loud, Shelley! How corny can you get?"

He yanked open the front door while she started to splutter an inarticulate defense. She couldn't understand his reaction to the visitor, who was after all a distinguished member of the Craft. The remark about their names might have been patronizing, but not offensive. She cast back for other reasons, rerunning the whole encounter in her head. They had walked into the room to find Snow and Jonathan sitting with their chairs drawn close together. Snow had looked beautiful. "You're just mad because Snow got all dressed up for him," she said, and saw him, halfway through the door, flinch as if each word were a flung stone.

Of course I knew Kip "liked" Snow, as we said in the parlance of the day. His fantasy about having once been her lover, even if it was supposed to have happened in some other existence, was perfectly transparent. But I had clung to the idea that it was just a boy's crush on an older woman—until recently, when I could no longer ignore the fact that the attraction between them was mutual, excluding me. And that was why I had gone privately to Snow (had you guessed?) and told her about the unauthorized love spell Kip had cast for Frog.

It didn't work out the way I planned. I hadn't meant to get Kip in so much trouble, and certainly I never dreamed the whole coven would become involved. All I wanted was to create a small rift between him and Snow—a disruption, something that would jolt them out of their acute awareness of each other. I'd told myself I was tattling for Kip's own good, ensuring that he learn a lesson about the proper use of magic. I'd envisioned a scene in which Snow reprimanded him, in which they were both reminded of their respective ages and positions and the distance between them. That was all. Something to clear the air—a breathing space.

But the business of manipulating human behavior is a perilous one, even without the use of magic, and my clumsy attempt to do so may have exacerbated the very situation I wished to relieve. For Snow herself may not have realized, until I came to her with my tale, how deeply she took Kip's actions to heart.

The Candlemas Sabbat was held outside in the freezing February air. Nonetheless there was no shivering among the line of black-robed figures crossing the snowy meadow beneath the crescent moon—far from it. The coven went barefoot through the snow, naked beneath their robes and glad of it, protected from the cold by the mixture of stimulating herbs added to their ritual baths. Yet for one member of the procession, the warmth of her skin only accentuated the sensation of cold misgiving inside her. Eyes fixed on the frosty hem of the robe ahead of her, Shelley couldn't keep her thoughts from the matter that had occupied them all afternoon.

(She hadn't been eavesdropping, only been doing her job. Some of the coven had arrived early and closeted themselves in Snow's office, and Jessica had sent her to find out if they wanted something to eat. When her knock had met with no response, hadn't it only made sense to open the door and look inside?)

The ritual bell jarred her to attention: they had reached the center of the meadow, and it was time to form the circle. The cauldron overflowed with dead pine branches whose sharp fragrance drifted in the brittle February air, and now Snow used her candle to set them alight. As they flared up, crackling and sparking, she blew out the candle and spoke.

"Tonight we gather to banish the spirit of the old year. Before the new flame can be kindled, the last traces of the old fire must be cleared away. The hopes and fears of the past year grew from a tiny spark, blossomed into fullness and died in time. Soon only their embers will remain, waiting to be pushed into the shadows. Thus let us free our minds of the past."

(Snow's office had been empty. Beyond the French doors, the wintry white garden shone in the afternoon sun. One of the doors had stood open a crack, letting in a current of icy air and the sound of a voice.

"—certainly understand your reluctance. But extreme situations call for extreme measures."

A British accent, crisp as the February air. Shelley had halted halfway across the room. There they were, outside in the garden: Jonathan and the others, standing by the snow-topped stone bench with their coat collars turned up against the cold. In the glittering white landscape their darkly clad figures were somber except for Grimalkin, bright as a cardinal in her long red coat. Shelley drew back quickly. Had they seen her? Unlikely. The room lay in shadow; anyone looking toward the house would catch only a reflection of the winter garden in the glass doors. She knew what she should do. Leave the room now, forget what she had heard. Some part of her fully intended to do so. But her feet did not move, and Senta's voice reached her. "I won't be party to a cursing. The time may come, but not yet. There must be some other way."

A cursing. The word rang in Shelley's ears—sinister, medieval, giving off a harsh, hollow tone like an ancient rusted bell, abruptly cut off as Jonathan spoke again.

"Why not offer him something you know he wants?" When the others remained silent, he said, "Come now, you all know what I mean. I'm speaking of your two young apprentices."

There was a pause in which no one moved or spoke, and then they all started talking at once. Shelley could hear the protests and refusals—could see Tamarack stabbing the air with a gloved forefinger to punctuate his remarks—but her skin suddenly felt too tight, as if it had shrunk on her bones.)

As the present obtruded once more, her gaze skittered around the circle. The scene around the fiery cauldron seemed shadowed by a past too dark to decipher. *Something you know he wants.* Terrifying as it was, the proposal had frightened her less than the pause that followed it: that brief, endless interval in which the coven had apparently considered Jonathan's words before rejecting them. And it was the pause rather than the protest that remained with her now—that beat of silence compounded over and over until it became an immense void in which her questions reverberated shrilly. Who were these people? Could she honestly say she knew them? She didn't even know their real names, much less what they did for a living, where they made their homes . . . only that they were engaged in a struggle with some formidable enemy. Were she and Kip intended for some role in the struggle? Was this the reason for their easy entry into the coven?

"With salt do I banish all that has gone before in the quarter of the East."

Shelley jumped, startled by the familiar voice beside her. Grimalkin was sprinkling salt on the ground, blowing a plume of frosty breath across it. "By the element of air do I rededicate it to the Mother, and in her name declare it sacred."

East, south, west, north: air, fire, water, earth. Shelley forced herself to follow the ritual as each quarter of the circle was purified and rededicated in the name of its sovereign element. Last was Tamarack, his stout figure easily recognizable in the anonymous robe as he knelt stiffly to trace a pentagram in the snow. "With salt do I banish all that has gone before in the quarter of the North. By the element of earth do I rededicate it to the Mother, and in her name declare it sacred."

As he rose to his feet, the bell rang once again. The fire in the cauldron had burned out, and now Snow tipped the iron vessel to spill the glowing embers onto the frozen ground.

"The past is done. Let us put it behind us now, and light the flame of the new year."

Shelley glanced furtively from the unlit candles on the altar to the last coals of the old fire, rapidly dying in the snow. Where would this new flame come from? As she watched, the last red spark faded to lifeless black and the coven stood in darkness beneath the moon. Jonathan Blackbridge stepped forward, hood thrown back on his shoulders and the moonlight shining on his white hair. From the altar he took the athame,

Snow the goblet of wine. They raised the knife and cup in a salute to the thin sliver of moon, then turned to face each other.

The frozen meadow was utterly still. High overhead the stars glittered like tiny ice crystals, while within the circle the air seemed to quiver with the concentration of the high priest and priestess. She extended the cup in her outstretched hands. He raised the knife above his head and slowly lowered it into the water. The faint moonlight lit the coiling cloud of breath between them as again he raised the knife high, again sank the blade into the cup.

Time stopped. The circle of hooded figures beneath the dark sky had existed forever. A third time the blade was raised. Lowered. All at once Snow caught her breath sharply, her gasp clearly audible in the taut silence.

As Jonathan Blackbridge withdrew the athame from the cup, the others saw pale flame flickering along its blade. Fire, born of water. An exhalation of delight ran round the circle as the high priest raised the knife. The brave flame danced wildly from its tip, its colors caressing their upturned faces.

"May the shadows in our lives be banished by this new light. As the sun drives back the cold and dark of winter, so let this light inspire us, in the year to come, to replace folly with wisdom, uncertainty with knowing. Blessed be all children of the Goddess."

A murmur answered him: "Blessed be."

With the athame he lit the other candles on the altar and gave one to each covener until the circle was ringed with tiny flames. Everyone was smiling; there was a sense of buoyancy and hope. The goblet of heated wine was passed around, and when each had taken a sip, Snow began to speak.

"On this night, an ancient tale tells us, the wandering souls of the dead are at the mercy of Gwyn ap Nudd, the Pale One. With his pack of white, red-eared hounds, he harries lost spirits away to the underworld. Tonight, in the spirit of that old legend, let us drive away all fears and worries, the last lingering traces of the old year." She set her candle down and the others followed her example. The circle of flames made golden, flickering pools of light on the snow; above them the coveners' faces were expectant as they stood silent, unmoving.

Waiting.

Waiting . . . for what? A phrase whispered in my head—*offer him something you know he wants*—and my insides shrank to a cold knot. The meadow lay white and still, the sky black overhead except for the thin shaving of moon, a brittle sparkle of infinitely distant stars. It seemed we were the only living souls abroad.

It came from far away at first, a sound ethereal as moonlight: the long silvery call of a hunting horn echoing across the snow-covered meadow. A shiver ran across my hot skin. *Gwyn ap Nudd, the Pale One, with his pack of white, red-eared hounds.* The horn sounded again, louder, and this time I imagined I could hear behind it a faint, frenzied baying. It couldn't be—and then, as the sound came a third time, someone in the circle gave a shout and we all began to run.

Across the meadow's white expanse toward the gate, floundering up to our knees in the crusty snow, plunging and nearly falling, our arms flailing for balance—we ran. I knew Gwyn ap Nudd and his hounds were only an old legend, but I was filled with cloudy fears urging me to flee, an irresistible impulse that came from my body, not my mind. The fierce, insistent call of the horn filled my head, threaded with the eager belling of the hounds. *Hounds?* I didn't dare look back. I could imagine the pack only too clearly—sleek white bodies nearly invisible against the snow, ears and eyes glowing redly like the coals of the old year's fire. Their baying grew louder. I tried to force more speed from my legs, but the deep snow made me slow and clumsy. Around me I caught glimpses of the others struggling through the drifts.

All at once a vast pursuing shadow fell across the moonlit snow around us. Horned—huge—silent—on it came, a man's shape with the head of a stag, its antlers trembling with unearthly light. Terror knifed through me; I pushed my straining muscles for more speed, but it was hopeless—I could never outrun that monstrous shadow. The horn sounded again, so near the blast seemed to pierce my heart—and as it died away I could hear the dogs at my heels, a ragged, eager panting.

They passed right through me. For an instant I ran surrounded by swift shadows, their jaws agape with unearthly howls. An answering shriek burst from my throat; suddenly I was cold all over, the warming power of the herbs obliterated in an instant. *Cold.* I was naked beneath my flimsy robe, knee-deep in snow, slashed by the icy winds of a February night. And then the pack was past, fleeing over the meadow in front of us, melting into the moonlight to leave no trace behind, no paw prints in the snow. The horned shadow paled and vanished. Yet we continued to run—pursuing now, no longer pursued, the meadow echoing with exuberant shouts. And now I ran on air, as if I had miraculously escaped a fate so dire I need never fear anything again. For those few moments, all my worries were put to rout—not just the ominous fragment I had overhead this afternoon, but all the tension and confusion of the past four months—Alex, the scrying cauldron, Dad and my spell, Kip—all blown to shreds by the freezing February wind.

Shelley had no real memory of getting from the meadow to the house, only a blurred impression of stumbling up the back steps to the kitchen and being welcomed into the kitchen by the half-dozen coven members who had preceded her. Someone handed her a cup of hot chocolate and she tried to thaw her nose in its steam.

The rest arrived right on her heels. They all crowded together in the warm kitchen, laughing and talking, panting from the cold chase. Kip appeared at her side. "What's in that cup? I'm frozen."

He reached for her hot chocolate. As she surrendered it a voice sounded in her ear: "May I join you?" The same silky British accent she had heard in the garden this afternoon, making unspeakable suggestions. She kept her face blank as she turned to face Jonathan Blackbridge. He was smiling at her. "I'd like to hear your opinion of the ritual."

"Oh, it was . . . uh . . . great."

The black eyes held hers. Could he read there the knowledge

of what she had overheard? When he took his gaze away it was like being released from a strong grip. He turned to Kip. "You might be interested, young man, to learn that the joining of the knife and the cup is known as the Great Rite, symbolizing the union of the God and Goddess. It's a form of hierogamy, the sacred marriage that appears in many ancient religions. Of course, in ancient times the ritual union was more than symbolic."

Was there a taunt in his words? Shelley saw him glance across the room and her eyes involuntarily followed his. It was Snow he was looking at—Snow, who stood talking to Gwynneth and Andreas, oblivious of his scrutiny. As he gazed at her, his thick fingers absently caressed the delicate white curve of the cup in his hand. "It's a pity, really," he murmured, "that the rituals have become so watered down over the centuries. One can't help fearing we've lost something essential in the name of civilized behavior."

He looked at Kip again and smiled. His hand was still stroking the cup, and the suggestive motion made Shelley remember Snow's gasp at the moment the athame had caught fire. *In ancient times the ritual union was more than symbolic.* She saw a faint flush creep into Kip's face; he was remembering it too. Then he shrugged. "Yeah, the old ways were a lot better. Didn't the ritual used to end with everybody tearing the priest-king to pieces and drinking his blood?"

The effectiveness of this thrust was in its nonchalance. Jonathan's expression did not change; even the shape of his smile remained, but above it Shelley saw him blink. At the same moment there was a sudden small *pop*—and looking down, she saw that the cup had cracked in his hand.

He didn't speak, nor did they. In the silence that formed and grew, Shelley could hear snatches of the conversations going on around them—Silkmoth and Indigo talking about music, Senta saying something about Venezuela. At last Kip said, "Looks like you might've cut yourself," and Jonathan set the pieces of broken cup on the counter, glancing casually at his fingers.

"Nothing serious." He nodded blandly at them and moved away.

They watched him go. Shelley found she had to swallow more than once before she could say, "Is that true—what you said about the old ways?"

"You bet." A muscle was twitching in Kip's cheek; his burning gaze was riveted on Jonathan, who was now talking to Tamarack. "The priest-king stands for the God. The way things are done these days, his death's only symbolic. But at Eleusis he was actually murdered at the end of every year, in a ritual sacrifice."

Ritual sacrifice. A cold current rippled her nerves, repelling the room's bright warmth, transforming friendly and familiar faces into members of an ancient tradition steeped in secrecy, rife with occult matters of which the modern world was perilously ignorant.

Offer him something you know he wants. Your two young apprentices.

Chapter 15

"Oh my God, Shelley—did you hear?" Lisa's eyes were brimming with tears. "Another kid's disappeared." The final school bell rang shrilly, but the stunned students scarcely registered it as the horrifying news spread up and down the hallways. *Another kid's disappeared.*

For everyone but the Leonard family, the impact of Alex's disappearance had inevitably dulled with the passing of time. The ubiquitous posters bearing his picture, tattered and faded by the winter weather, had become a familiar part of the landscape, and the pre-Christmas blizzard with its power failure and property damage now took precedence over his unknown fate in most conversations. But now—Shelly stared dumbfounded, hearing Senta say, *I won't be party to a cursing. There must be some other way.* And Jonathan: *Why not offer him something you know he wants? Your two young apprentices.*

"His name's Daniel Chaffin, and he's only five years old," Sarah McGill volunteered. "They said on the radio he went outside to build a snowman. His mother was watching him through the front window. The phone rang and she went to answer it. When she got back, he was gone. There were just some footprints in the snow, leading down to the street and stopping there."

Shelley's stomach was churning; she could feel sweat breaking out on her cold skin. The phrase *ritual sacrifice* whispered in her head. A child. Five years old. *How Witches do Offer Babes and Children*—As she became aware of a sneaking, squirming gratitude that she and Kip had somehow been reprieved, horror at her own selfishness nearly eclipsed her pity for the victim. Overwhelmed, she fled to the nearby girls' bathroom and lost her lunch.

It was nearly half an hour before she felt steady enough to walk the few blocks to the Arms. She and Kip always made the trip together after school, but she guessed he had been unable to find her and had gone on ahead. She hurried there now, bursting into the kitchen to find him with Jessica and Gwynneth, who had remained behind after the Sabbat. Gwynneth was arranging fresh flowers in a vase, talking as she worked, and he was listening with a scowl on his face.

"—dissolved the binding spell two days ago," she was saying. "Jonathan thought that if he could tempt the killer into action, he could overpower him. But he failed. Things got out of hand, and now he and Snow are trying to salvage them."

"How?" Shelley whispered, and Gwynneth twitched a jonquil into place and glanced up. Her bleak expression was far from reassuring. "They're upstairs preparing a spell for the release of the child who was taken."

A spell. Shelley's knees went weak with shamed relief. Of course they would try to save the child by magic, the way they had tried with Alex. They had been too late to save Alex, but maybe this time . . . "Why aren't you helping them?" she heard Kip say.

"Because the kind of spell they're using works best with only two."

"Only two? What—"

This time Gwynneth didn't look up. "Together those two can raise a lot of power, Kip. You may not like Jonathan, and in this situation he may have made a serious error in judgment. But he's an adept, a witch with many years of knowledge and experience. With Snowden's help, there's a good chance he'll prevail."

Shelley swallowed hard. Snow and Jonathan, up in the ritual room on the third floor, embarking together on some unimaginable rescue effort between the worlds . . . *The kind of spell they're using works best with only two.* The words triggered a flashing image of the Sabbat circle—two robed figures standing face to face, the space between them fraught with tension.

During dinner she was too busy to pay attention to Kip. He must have performed his duties adequately; at least there were no dropped trays, no disgruntled diners hailing her with requests for items he had forgotten. But afterward, at the kitchen table with the rest of them, he sat slumped over his plate, twiddling his fork but eating nothing. Conversation was sparse in any case—everyone's thoughts were on the crisis at hand—and his distraction might have passed unnoticed if Gwynneth hadn't had to ask him twice if he wanted dessert.

"Huh? Oh. No thanks." He got up abruptly from the table, knocking over his chair in the process, and stood staring down at it as if he had no idea how it had come to be in that position. Royce picked it up and righted it. Kip's eyes roamed blankly around the room, like someone who has blundered in, disoriented, from a blinding storm. Everyone looked at him and Shelley heard herself say, "Are they finished yet? How long does it take?"

Gwynneth answered her. "No, they're not finished. And it will take as long as it takes."

At breakfast the next morning Kip was still dazed and hollow-eyed, and Shelley guessed he had stayed up all night, or most of it. When Mother fussed at him he said he'd been studying for a history test. The conversation quickly returned to the topic of yesterday's kidnapping, which was undoubtedly being discussed around every breakfast table in the county.

"This—this *monster* has to be stopped!" Mother's voice was shrill. "Why don't the police do something? I thought the FBI was going to get involved! But they've never found poor Alex, dead *or* alive, and now this one—so young—"

At school too there was talk of nothing else. They learned that the little boy's mother was a housewife, that his father was an accountant, that the FBI was definitely on the case. Every class was derailed from its lesson into discussions of the kidnapping that ranged from animated to near hysterical. If Kip actually had a history test, which Shelley doubted, it was probably canceled. No one seemed able to think or talk of anything but the two kidnappings; in the light of what had happened, the mystery of Alex's disappearance was suddenly, chillingly solved. The Lockleys, the owls, the children—how could these things have taken place in Green Hollow, the place where nothing bad ever happened? As her classmates talked, Shelley kept thinking of the room on the third floor at the Arms, of Gwynneth saying quietly, *Those two can raise a lot of power.*

She arrived at the Arms that afternoon to find Snow in the kitchen, sitting at the table with a cup of tea. By now she should have known what to expect, but she was shocked by this translucent ghost with the waxen white face and empty eyes, so insubstantial a breath might dissipate her altogether. Shelley knew that every magical working must exact a price. Had this one cost too much? Carefully she pulled out a chair and sat down. "Are you okay?"

Snow gave her a flickering smile. "I'm fine."

"Fine? You look—"

"It'll pass, Shelley."

"Did it work? The spell?"

As Snow reached for her tea Shelley could see her hands shaking. Slowly she lifted the cup and sipped; even the act of swallowing seemed to take enormous effort. Finally: "I hope so."

At that point Jessica came bustling in with half a dozen tasks to keep Shelley busy till it was time to change for dinner. Kip was nowhere in sight. As she climbed the cellar stairs, he came dashing down them, out of breath but offering no explanation for his lateness.

There were about ten guests in the house that night, enough to keep the twins busy in the dining room. Neither Snow nor Jonathan appeared for the meal. As Shelley was bringing coffee for the last few diners, she glanced across the entrance hall and saw Jonathan sitting by the fireplace in the parlor, a glass of wine in one hand. His face had a sunken look, as if a portion of the flesh had melted away beneath his sallow skin. Silently Shelley nudged Kip and nodded toward the seated figure, receiving only a fraction of a shrug in response.

She carried her tray of dirty dishes into the kitchen and set it on the counter by the sink. Here the atmosphere was more congenial: Snow sat at the table with Royce, watching him construct his cat's cradles, while Gwynneth helped Jessica with the dishes. There was a fair amount of noise in the room—water running in the sink, Jessica and Gwynneth talking above the clatter of dishes—but as Shelley stopped to admire Royce's latest creation, the other sounds dropped into the background and all at once she could hear what was being said on Jessica's radio, playing quietly in its spot on the counter.

"—interrupt our broadcast to bring you this special bulletin. Five-year-old Daniel Chaffin, who disappeared yesterday around noon from his home in Green Hollow, has been found. He was discovered—"

The only sound she could make was somewhere between a gasp and a shriek. Everyone looked at her. She pointed speechlessly at the radio and Gwynneth dived for it, turning up the volume at the same moment that Jessica shut off the water. The announcer's voice blared suddenly through the room.

"—youngster has been examined by medical personnel and appears entirely unharmed. His miraculous release is a sad reminder of the unknown fate of young Alex Leonard, who disappeared last fall under similar circumstances. However, police stated that Daniel was able to supply them with certain clues that may prove useful in bringing the kidnapper to justice.

"Repeating that bulletin once again: Daniel Chaffin, the five-year-old boy who was apparently kidnapped yesterday from Green Hollow, was found just an hour ago wandering along the edge of Route 23 about six miles from his home. He is unharmed, and police say he has given them certain details that should assist in their investigation—"

Abruptly Snow stood up and took a few blind, stumbling steps away from the table. Shelley saw the cat's cradle collapse into a tangle of string as Royce's eyes followed her questioningly, but it was Jessica who undertook to mime the announcement for him as the radio returned to its regular broadcast. Gwynneth had intercepted Snow and now held her in a fierce embrace, murmuring to her beneath the music. Their two heads, flame red and pale brown, were close together. Snow's shoulders were convulsed; with a jolt Shelley realized she was crying. Her sleeves had fallen back to reveal a startling mosaic of purplish bruises on both wrists. Gwynneth looked up just then and caught Shelley staring.

"We need to let Jonathan know, Shelley. Can you find him and ask him to come in here?"

He was in the parlor, she remembered, trying not to think about the bruises—because the news, slowly sinking in, could not have been better. The child released, unharmed . . . the spell had worked! As she passed through the dining room she saw the guests had finished and gone, leaving their empty coffee cups. Where had Kip disappeared to? Once she had delivered her message to Jonathan, she went in search of her twin.

It was unlikely he would have changed his clothes and gone home, yet he had been acting so odd lately . . . She ran down the cellar stairs to check. His clothes were still where he had left them, thrown helter-skelter in his earlier hurry to change. Where could he be? Returning to the first floor, she could hear voices in the kitchen, and the fact of the child's safe return hit her once again. They had done it, Snow and Jonathan. Their spell had worked. A miraculous release, the newscaster had called it, yet the miracle had been purchased in the harsh coin of magic, the devastating fatigue on the practitioners' faces, Snow's sudden burst of weeping—and those ugly, unexplained marks on her wrists. Queasiness came over Shelley as she stood at the top of the cellar stairs listening to the murmur of voices from the kitchen. She wanted to rejoice, to experience relief and pride and awe, but the memory of those bruises was like a weight on her heart—and there was something else too, something that nagged at her as she stood there. Kip—that was it. Where was he?

She resumed her search. One guest browsed the bookshelves in the parlor; two others were watching television in the common room on the second floor. Otherwise all doors were shut, all corridors and stairways empty. Slowly Shelley started to climb the stairs to the third floor—but she was only halfway up when the sight of the dark hallway above gave her a bad feeling. She turned quickly and went down.

"Shelley, what's the matter?"

It was Gwynneth who noticed me standing in the kitchen doorway. At her words the others turned to look.

"I can't find Kip."

"Can't find him?" Snow had recovered a measure of poise. "Where'd you look?"

"J-just about everywhere."

"Perhaps he went home," Jonathan said.

"You looked upstairs?" Gwynneth was saying, and then, when I didn't answer at once: "Shelley?"

"Not on the third floor," I whispered, and saw a look pass among them all. Snow, Gwynneth and Jonathan started for the stairs. I trailed after them, no longer able to suppress the formless dread rising inside me. They climbed too quickly for me to keep up, and I had just reached the second floor landing when I saw light blossom in the hallway above, and their three figures come to an abrupt stop. Forcing my flagging legs up the last flight of stairs, I looked past them down the corridor and felt my heart drop heavily, like a hanged man cut loose from his rope.

The door of the ritual room was ajar.

Chapter 16

Kip was inside. The first thing I saw was the cloth sole of one of his Chinese slippers, the ones we wore to serve dinner, visible in the faint spill of light as Snow pulled back the curtain that concealed the inner doorway. The light came from a candle guttering in a dish near the center of the room. Moving closer, I could see Kip sprawled facedown on the floor. A square shape near one of his hands caught my eye. At first it was only that: a square shape. And then I recognized it.

It was a black box—noticed in Jonathan Blackbridge's room two days ago, by me, and duly described to Kip. By me. It had been closed then. Now it was open, revealing a glimmer of curved glass inside. As I stared at it I could hear myself saying, *It's got some kind of symbol inlaid in silver on the lid,* and Kip's eager reply: *There's a scrying glass in that box, Shelley. There's got to be!* And then Jonathan picked up the box and closed it with a snap, and the sound jolted me out of the past, back to the unthinkable present.

Snow and Gwynneth were on their knees on either side of Kip. Between them they turned him over carefully. His eyes were closed and I saw Snow lift one of the lids, then search for the pulse in his throat. She and Gwynneth looked at each other. In the poor light I couldn't read that look. I heard myself blurt, "What's wrong with him? What happened?" All I could think of was that time in the snowfield six years earlier, when he had violated the Lockleys' protection spell and it had nearly killed him. What had he done now? Taken Jonathan's box, somehow gained entry to the ritual room—

"I would say your brother decided to try his own solution to our crisis," Jonathan said. He was standing beside me, holding the box against his chest as if he thought I might try to snatch it away. "And it didn't work out the way he planned." His murmur conveyed more wonder than condemnation. "The arrogant little fool. What can he have been thinking? He didn't even cast a circle."

He might have said more, but I didn't hear it; I was listening to Snow and Gwynneth, who were having an argument. Snow was saying, "I have to go after him," and Gwynneth was saying, "You can't. You're exhausted."

"I have to," Snow said sharply.

"Snowden, no. Neither you nor Jonathan has the strength at this point. It's too dangerous, and I'm not going to let you do it."

It startled me to hear Gwynneth speak so sternly to Snow. To realize that, of the two, she was the elder by a good ten years—that she must already have been a seasoned witch by the time Snow had joined the coven. Snow bit her lip and looked down. I saw her touch Kip's head, her hand moving blindly over his hair. "Somebody has to go after him," she whispered.

"I will," Gwynneth said. She glanced up. Even in the poor light I could see her gaze settle on me. "And Shelley will help me."

I gulped. "Go after him? What do you mean? He . . . he's right here."

Instead of answering, she held out her hand to me. I moved closer and took it reluctantly, noticing how the bright stones in her rings caught the candlelight. Gently she pulled me down beside Kip. I stared at the pale, still face, the closed eyes beneath their straight dark brows. Was this how I would look if I were dead? I heard Snow say, "It's too risky. She's not ready. And if he already has Kip—" and Gwynneth said firmly, "She'll be all right. You and Jonathan have weakened him; that'll work in our favor. You've done your share. Now go and rest."

Weakened *who*? Jonathan came forward, helped Snow very gently to her feet and led her toward the door. I scarcely saw them go. Gwynneth was speaking in my ear. "It looks as if Kip was trying to learn the kidnapper's identity by a magical process called 'overlooking.' How he knew about Jonathan's scrying glass—how he got into this room—well, it doesn't matter now. But he went about it all wrong, Shelley. He didn't cast a circle for his own protection, and he didn't work with a partner who could ground him. Now he's lost."

"Lost?" I said. "Lost where?"

Her shoulders lifted slightly. "The scrying glass leads between the worlds."

Gooseflesh spread across my skin as I stared at her, unable to speak. *Between the words.* A place without dimensions. A seamless, shimmering web where opposites became one. A dream, or the true face of reality. The place where witches cast their circle—yet possessed of its own perils. I remembered what Snow had told me about the circle forming a protective boundary during magical workings. Yet Kip hadn't cast a circle, and now he was adrift without that boundary, between the worlds. At the mercy of . . . what? A dark hooded shape flickered behind my eyes and guilt stabbed me. This was my fault. I had told him about the box, knowing perfectly well what it was—knowing it would intrigue him. Had I also known he wouldn't be able to resist the chance to try and outdo Jonathan?

Now I sat numbly as Gwynneth cast a circle. A small one, just big enough to contain herself, Kip and me. She used no athame, no salt or water, only her hands and a few murmured phrases; nonetheless I was aware of the charged boundary forming around us like a wall, invisible but solid as rock. The rest of the room receded in a blur. Gwynneth turned to me. "Time to put your visualization practice to work, Shelley. Don't be surprised by what you may see. Remember that the mind's instinct is to reshape everything it encounters into images it can understand. Are you afraid?"

"Yes," I whispered, and she gave a little nod.

"Good. Where there's fear, there's power. Now, breathe with me."

She knelt on Kip's opposite side and we joined hands across his body.

If in the past I had found it hard to empty my mind, to let the rhythm of my own breathing supersede thought, those difficulties were forgotten now. With that first long inhalation I felt myself sinking, slowly at first and then faster, plummeting downward and inward at a speed that gave me no time to be afraid. Each breath, drawn and released, took me deeper on the journey to some inner place where all awareness of my surroundings faded and disappeared. Last to go was the dwindling sensation of Gwynneth's hands clasping mine. Only her eyes remained, glowing before me in the dark like Rowan's, full of golden sparks that began, as I watched, to escape into the air around us. They were everywhere, those sparks—darting back and forth, rising and falling, glowing and fading. Gradually I realized they were the flying sparks of a bonfire.

It was night, and I was in the depths of a great forest, far wilder and more primitive than the forest I remembered from Kip's and my sojourn in the fog, that Halloween night now so long ago. The bonfire blazed in a little clearing surrounded by enormous trees overrun with vines. The tops of those trees were invisible in the blackness above, and the firelight stroked their trunks with patterned shadows that were never still.

Kip was lying beside me. I reached out to touch him, jerking my hand away in horror when I realized that what I had taken for my brother was only his clothing, empty garments mimicking his shape. I turned to Gwynneth for reassurance and got another shock. In place of the tall red-haired woman I knew, a tawny jaguar crouched beside the fire.

Don't be surprised by what you may see. Remember that the mind's instinct is to reshape everything it encounters into images it can understand. I repeated Gwynneth's words over and over to myself while my heartbeat stuttered in my temples and the clear amber eyes of the jaguar returned my stare. Irregular black spots patterned her golden fur; her muzzle was pure white except where each long firelit whisker was rooted in a precise dot of black. She seemed a miracle of exotic color and design, too perfect to be real—yet there was no doubt she *was* real; I could see the gleam of moisture on her pebbled nose, the small shiftings of her eyes as she watched me. In the black depths of each pupil a tiny bonfire burned, and beside each bonfire was a huddled shape I recognized as my own. At last the jaguar rose and stretched with sinewy grace, her forepaws scant inches from Kip's clothes. Then she padded toward the trees.

Panic flashed through me. However overwhelming her presence might be, without it I would be alone in this unknown forest—all by myself, with no other company than this pile of empty garments that resembled the melted witch in *The Wizard of Oz*. The jaguar had reached the edge of the trees. I stumbled to my feet—but as I started after her, she turned and looked at me. Her lips drew back to reveal gleaming teeth and a menacing growl rumbled in her throat.

I froze. The growl subsided to a soft mutter. This was what she wanted, then: for me to stay here, by myself, while she went into the forest. Was she going in search of Kip? Was it truly Gwynneth in that fearsome animal shape? It seemed impossible, and yet . . . She was still waiting, staring at me over one spotted shoulder, her eyes eerily luminous in the dark underbrush. I began to understand there was something she wanted from me, something more than simply remaining behind. I gazed into her eyes. Something . . . but what? Stay by the fire, and . . . what?

The flames crackled, sending sparks upward into the dark air as somewhere in the fire's depths a log collapsed.

A log . . . fuel. A fire needs fuel. I glanced around and saw a broken branch lying on the ground—picked it up and tossed it on the fire. When I looked again, the jaguar had vanished.

How long did I keep vigil in that unknown place, tending the fire and waiting for her return? The heat of the flames warmed my face and hands while the chill night pressed against my back. All around me in the dark forest there were mutterings and soft moans that might have been the wind, except that I could discern no movement in the cold air. What was out there, prowling back and forth, peering through the thick forest growth at this lit clearing where I sat alone, waiting and keeping the flames high? Twice I heard thrashing noises nearby in the darkness and jumped to my feet, certain it was Gwynneth returning—but each time the noises passed by, fading gradually into the distance and making me fervently thankful they had come no closer. And then came a sound that jerked me to my feet. Kip's voice. "Shelley—?"

My heart leaped. I ran to the edge of the clearing and strained my eyes against the dense darkness. "Kip?"

"Yes. I'm here."

"Where? I can't see you!"

His voice sounded fainter, as if he were moving away. "Here . . ."

"Can you see my fire?"

"Yes . . ."

"Well, come on then!"

"Why can't you come to me?"

"To you?" I gazed into the impenetrable blackness before me. He sounded so far away. "Gwynneth said—Gwynneth wants me to tend the fire."

"Gwynneth's there with you?"

"Not now," I said.

"Good. Because three's a crowd."

"What?" I said.

"You heard me." All at once he sounded much closer. "Who needs Gwynneth? Who needs anybody else? Just you and me . . . isn't that enough?"

A shudder like some huge invisible animal seized and shook me in its teeth. "Shelley?" Kip was saying. "Isn't that right?"

"Yes," I whispered.

"Then come on."

"You mean . . . out there?"

"Why not? It's dark. Private. No one can bother us. We'll be all by ourselves." His voice held a silky, insinuating note I had never heard in it before. *Just you and me. Isn't that enough?* I thought of Benjy saying, *The two of you sure look cozy,* and cast a quick look over my shoulder at the fire. Already the flames were beginning to die down; it needed my constant attention. If I let it go out, how would Gwynneth find her way back?

"Forget about Gwynneth. She's not your twin." His voice was just above a whisper now, tickling my ear as if he were standing right beside me. "We'll be together, Shelley. Here in the dark. Don't you want that? I do."

My skin went hot and then cold. "But where are you?" I said. "Why can't I see you?"

"The fire's too bright, that's all. I'm right here. Just give me your hand."

Leave the clearing and step into that fathomless black wilderness? The thought was terrifying—yet regardless of what Gwynneth had said, Kip had come to no harm. He was out there, wanting me to join him, his voice promising things I did not dare think about. "Give me your hand," he said again.

Poised at the clearing's edge, I stretched a tentative hand into the blackness beyond and felt it go instantly numb, as if it had ceased to exist. I recoiled with a gasp.

"What's the matter?" he said. "Shelley! Come on!"

I stood trying to chafe sensation back into my numb fingers. "But the fire," I said. "Gwynneth—"

"Fuck Gwynneth, fuck her bloody and tear open her throat and feast on her flesh!" said Kip's voice. "I'm your twin! If you love me, forget Gwynneth and come on!"

I stood stunned, my head spinning. It was Kip's voice, but Kip could never have said those words—and then in the darkness there was a rasping snarl, and a sudden strangled scream in a terrible voice that wasn't Kip's at all.

And then nothing. Nothing but a bitter, breathy sound that might have been chuckling or sobbing, or something in between: I could not have put a name to it, but it made my blood run cold. For as long as that eerie hybrid noise came seeping out of the dark I stood listening, frozen by fear. When it died away at last, I forced my stiff limbs into motion and returned to the dying fire to pile on more fuel. In a few minutes I had the blaze high again, but it would not warm me. I sat and hugged my knees, staring into the flames to keep from looking at Kip's abandoned clothing. A ferment of questions boiled in my head. *Where am I? Who was I talking to? What's happened to Kip? If Gwynneth doesn't come back—what will I do?*

I gathered every stick and fragment of wood from the edge of the clearing, building the fire to a roaring blaze, a homing beacon for Gwynneth in her search. And as I fed the fire I chanted, "*Find him, find him,*" in a hoarse whisper that helped curb my fear. The twisting orange flames kept me busy, devouring the offerings I brought them and greedily demanding more, embracing the larger pieces with a sensuous hunger. Sparks floated and drifted across the darkness. At last I looked across the leaping flames to see her there. The jaguar, standing at the clearing's edge.

She held something in her jaws, the way a cat carries a kitten. For an instant I thought it *was* a kitten, and then I saw it was a fawn—or a bear cub, or a lamb, or a human infant—and then I realized it was none of those things, or maybe all of them: an opalescent dazzle that changed its form from moment to moment, struggling to find its shape.

The jaguar crossed the clearing and deposited her burden on the pile of clothing near my feet, lifting her head to look at me. Gazing into those bottomless amber eyes, I felt myself fall into them.

Chapter 17

Of the remainder of that evening Shelley could recall very little. Somehow she and Gwynneth must have returned from their quest, bringing Kip with them, but the details were lost to her. All she could remember, from the moment she looked into the eyes of the jaguar until some time later when Royce guided Kip and her home across Willow Street, was a hazy image of Snow bending over her, and her murmured words: "Well done, Shelley. Gwynneth says you were very brave." At that moment she was still dressed in her serving clothes, and if she pressed her nose to her sleeve she was certain she could smell woodsmoke—but she and Kip changed before they left the Arms that night, and so the proof of what she had experienced, if it had ever existed at all, went straight into the wash. By the time she crawled into her own bed, she was too tired to care whether any of it had really happened or not.

Kip was safe. That was all that mattered. He was back from wherever he had been; he could walk and talk, even if the former did resemble a sleepwalker's daze and the latter was slurred and hesitant, as if he had drunk too much of Jessica's spiced wine. He seemed scarcely aware of what had happened, and Shelley, for one, was not in a state to enlighten him.

She woke the next morning aching in every muscle. Thinking required enormous effort, like a painful shifting of lead weights from one part of her brain to another. When she finally dragged herself downstairs to the breakfast table, she saw the same fatigue on Kip's face. The rest of the family, brimming with excitement over the astounding release of Daniel Chaffin the evening before, never noticed.

"They broke right into the middle of *I Love Lucy,*" Mother was saying. "I couldn't imagine what was going on! But when they said the little boy had been found, well—"

Kip's head, bowed over his cereal bowl, wavered slowly upright and Shelley saw his mouth open in stupid surprise. He didn't know! Of course not—by the time the news had been announced, he had already embarked on his own private enterprise, and in the following uproar no one had thought to tell him. But his ignorance, if he revealed it now, was going to look very strange. She kicked him under the table. He winced and looked at her reproachfully, but said nothing.

"They said on the radio this morning the police are looking for a man in a white truck," Marty was saying. "That's what the little boy told them. The kidnapper drove a white truck, and he was tall and wore a dark coat. But why did he let this one go? I guess there's no doubt it's the same man who—"

Who killed Alex. No one said the words, but they hung in the air above the table until Dad got up abruptly and took his dishes to the sink.

* * *

Now that her brother was safe and sound, Shelley's complicated tangle of emotions had dwindled to two—awe at his colossal nerve, and curiosity. As they left the house and started off to school on wobbly legs, the latter gradually won out. "Kip. What on earth were you trying to do?"

He darted a glance at her and shrugged. "I just wanted to help save that kid."

"But how'd you get hold of the box? And how'd you get into the ritual room?"

A faint smile replaced his defensive look. "I knew the box was in Jonathan's room. His door wasn't even locked! The ritual room—that took a little planning. I knew Royce must have a key, and he always hangs his key ring on a nail on the back porch when he comes inside, because Jessica says the clinking drives her crazy. I snagged it yesterday, just before dinner. Ran upstairs, found the key, unlocked the room, ran down, put the keys back."

Now she remembered him coming late and out of breath to change into his serving clothes. He had waited till dinner was over, then taken the box into the ritual room. And then? A dreamlike fragment—leaping flames, a pair of amber eyes—grazed the border of her thoughts and was gone. "You're in so much trouble," she said.

She thought she saw his lips quiver; then he scowled. "I wouldn't have done it if they'd let me help them. But they'd rather do a *special* kind of spell, just for two!"

"You're only an apprentice! They didn't need your help." And then, when he didn't answer: "Do you remember . . . what it was like?"

His shoulders twitched. "I couldn't last night. Now it's starting . . . starting to come back." His face had suddenly lost all its color, and in spite of the icy February air she could see sweat beading his upper lip. "It was dark," he whispered. "Just . . . *dark.* And there was somebody going through my mind—opening it up, touching everything in it, taking anything he wanted, anything he could use. Memories, thoughts, feelings . . . private stuff. Stuff I never even . . ."

He broke off. Shelley stared at him, remembering his voice saying, *We'll be together. Here in the dark.* The same dark where greedy unknown hands had ransacked his most intimate thoughts. For what? *Anything he could use.* That gibbering sob-laughter from the depths of the forest—She thought of Gwynneth saying to Snow, *You and Jonathan have weakened him,* and wondered what would have happened to Kip, and to her, if they had not.

After school she waited for Kip outside on the steps as usual, but he failed to show up. Had he already gone to the Arms to face up to his punishment? Last night Snow had seemed more upset than angry, but it was impossible to forget how strongly she had reacted to the Frog incident—and that, in comparison to this, had been nothing but a harmless prank. Shelley ran the few short blocks, stopping at the foot of the driveway to catch her breath and gather her thoughts. What was the hurry? Whatever was going to happen, it would happen in private; her presence was neither wanted nor required. Yet a sense of impending doom drew her, moth to flame.

The kitchen was empty, only a simmering pot on the stove indicating that Jessica was not far away. Shelley left her books on the table and went softly down the back hall toward Snow's office. Now she could hear Jessica in the parlor, fussing at Royce about a window that wouldn't stay up. Across the anteroom behind the registration desk, Snow's office door stood ajar, no sound from within. Was it over already?

Then I heard Kip say, "I'm sorry, okay? I don't know what else you want from me. It was stupid, I know that. But it turned out all right. And the kid's safe, thanks to you and Mister High Priest."

Even from where I stood I could hear the false bravado in his tone. I should have turned around and left, but instead I tiptoed across the anteroom and slipped behind the door to listen. Snow hadn't answered. The door wasn't open wide enough to provide a respectable crack between it and the frame, and I could see nothing. But I could imagine her looking at him—the level, wordless look that could reduce me to jelly in a matter of seconds. Finally he mumbled something and she said, "What?"

"I said—you did sex magic with him, didn't you? That was how you raised the power."

His voice was shaking. If he had sounded a fraction less young and miserable, I suppose that question would have finished him. As it was, I think my heart stopped for the duration of the pause that followed, renewing its beat only when she said coldly but with perfect calm, "I can't imagine why you would think that is any of your business. In any case what we're discussing here is your behavior, not mine."

I heard him release a long quivering breath. "I was just trying to help. I don't see what you're so mad about."

"Because it was irresponsible." Her voice had gone several degrees colder. "By your actions you put yourself in unspeakable danger. And not only yourself. Gwynneth, who had to go after you. And Shelley, who helped her."

"Look—" He sounded aggrieved. "Look, I just figured you could use all the help you could get! You keep it all a big secret, you won't tell us anything, but I know what's going on. I know this guy is—"

She cut him off. "You may think whatever you like. But what you must learn is that magic is not a game. It's a deadly serious art that involves real dangers and temptations far darker than anything your adolescent imagination can devise. Until you learn that, you cannot expect to be trusted with serious and delicate matters. And if you continue to endanger others by your stupidity, I won't have you in this coven."

There was a breathless, excruciating pause. Then he said, "Are you throwing me out?"

She exhaled sharply, the explosive sound clearly audible from where I stood. There was another long pause. When she spoke again, her tone of voice was completely different. No longer furious—pleading. And she said something very odd. She said, "I don't want us to hurt each other this time."

I think I stopped breathing then. I heard him say, "Do you remember . . . the other time? Do you? Because for me . . . it's like a dream or something. It's like I can feel it drifting around at the back of my mind, but as soon as I try to focus on it . . . it just slips away."

She said quietly, "We aren't meant to remember."

"But do you?"

"Not really. I just know that whoever we were, and whatever happened, you always leaped before you looked, just the way you're doing now. And it ended in a lot of pain for us both. *That* I remember. And I won't go through it again."

Another of those blank intervals. I couldn't picture what might be happening inside the room. Even more disturbing than the bizarre dialogue was the intimate tone that made it sound as if they had known each other . . . a lifetime. When Kip spoke again I heard his voice crack. "I can't—I can't *remember,*" he said. "What did I do? I didn't mean to hurt anyone. Especially . . . especially not you."

"Maybe that's why we're getting another chance," she said. "And why I'm asking you, this time, to think about responsibility."

I heard him take a gasping breath. Even then, it was a moment or two before I realized he was crying. I couldn't remember Kip ever crying, and it must have taken him as much by surprise as it did me. All at once the door was flung wide with such force that it would have hit me if I hadn't jumped back. Kip burst into the anteroom, tears streaming down his face. I stood frozen in horror at being caught eavesdropping, but he ran right past me without stopping, out into the hall, and a few moments later I heard the back door bang shut. He had never even seen me.

I should have crept quietly away then, done my best to forget what I had so imperfectly witnessed. But I told myself there had to be some alternate explanation for their words—some simple, obvious meaning I had missed somehow—and it only made sense to find out what it was. Then I could stop wondering, stop fretting over something that was, after all, impossible. I forced myself to count to sixty twice, listening to the silence inside the office. Then I made some noise, as if I were just entering the anteroom, and peeked around the edge of the door frame.

Snow sat behind her desk, elbows propped on its surface and face buried in her hands. When I tapped gently on the door frame she didn't move. "Snow?" I whispered. But she was too far inside herself to either hear or answer. I stood there for a few more moments, and then I went away.

Chapter 18

Jonathan Blackbridge left a few days later. Outside in the parking lot, while Royce loaded his bags into the car, he encountered Kip for the first time since the incident with the scrying glass. They eyed each other, then Jonathan offered his hand and Kip shook it in a perfunctory way. The English witch smiled faintly.

> " *'There is none like to me!' says the cub*
> *in the pride of his earliest kill.*
> *But the jungle is large and the cub he is small.*
> *Let him think and be still.*

"That, young man, is Kipling. You would do well to familiarize yourself with those particular lines."

This parting shot was wasted on Kip. Since the session in Snow's office he had been dazed and silent, performing his duties like an automaton. At supper in the kitchen he was as silent as Royce. There were times when Shelley saw his face suddenly begin to sweat and his eyes rigidly focus on nothing, and then she knew he was reliving his experience with the scrying glass. She offered him what comfort she could—taking his icy, unresponsive hand and sometimes receiving, in return, a wan fragment of a smile.

Snow's threat to expel him from the coven must also have been weighing on his mind. Although she had taken no action on it, she had withdrawn to a businesslike distance from which her interaction with the staff was minimal. Shelley found herself missing the old intimacy—but at the same time, watching Snow and watching Kip, noting how their paths never intersected, she could not deny a certain sneaking relief.

Meanwhile the general rejoicing over little Daniel Chaffin's release had shifted to a push for the capture of his abductor. The nightly news gave extensive coverage to police efforts, and TV viewers heard again and again the only known facts about the kidnapper. He was tall. He wore a dark coat or cloak, and drove a white truck. The dearth of information was filled by endless speculation about his possible motive for releasing his second victim unharmed. Had he undergone a change of heart? Had some chance circumstance made him lose his nerve? However it had happened, it was a miracle. A miracle. A miracle. Each time Shelley heard the word, the image of Snow's haggard face and bruised wrists flashed through her mind.

The mood in Green Hollow was grim. This second kidnapping, miraculously as it had ended, had presented the villagers with sobering proof that there was a dangerous criminal in their midst. Playgrounds were deserted, shops closed early, the streets were empty after dark; and guests at the Lockley Arms, knowing nothing of the circumstances, made jokes about little towns that rolled up their sidewalks at dusk.

Yet there were some villagers who, for reasons of their own, still ventured out after nightfall. Getting ready for bed late one night, Shelley heard a noise at her window—a *click* like some small object striking the glass. She looked out, saw no one . . . then a dark shape in the shadows beneath the trees. A dark shape. Her heart seemed to stop beating in the instant before the figure stepped forward into the spill of light from her window.

Benjy. Her knees sagged with relief; she had to grab the sill for support. He was motioning for her to open the window, and fumblingly she obeyed.

"Hey!" His whisper sounded loud in the February night stillness. "C'mon down."

Why not? It was Benjy—her own backyard—and she was curious. What was he doing here? She crept downstairs, put her jacket on over her nightgown and slipped out the kitchen door to find him waiting on the back step, hands in his pockets and a cloud of breath in front of his face. "Nice night, huh? Colder'n a penguin's behind."

Shelley was too edgy to feel the cold. "What are you doing here, Benjy?"

He shrugged. "Just wondered if maybe you'd like to go for a ride." Ever since the fiasco at Frog's party he'd been cool to her. Was this an offer of truce? "It's the middle of the night," she said.

"It is?" He shoved back the sleeve of his jacket and squinted at his watch. "Shit, I'm sorry. I didn't realize—"

"Never mind. I'm glad you came by."

And she was. The kiss that was supposed to have happened at the party still hovered between them, an unfulfilled promise. And there was nothing to stop him now, was there? They were alone. No one to watch, no one to interfere. As she moved closer to him, he noticed her open jacket. "Hey, aren't you cold?" And then: "Jesus, Shelley. You're in your . . ." Speech deserted him; he fumbled with the zipper and drew it up to her chin, his knuckles grazing her breast in passing, sending a tingling sensation through her. "You're gonna freeze," Benjy muttered.

"I'm okay." Her nerves were vibrating from that accidental, intimate touch; she let out a breathless laugh. Benjy jammed his hands back into his pockets. An awkward silence descended, broken only by the rattle of icy branches in a wind that molded Shelley's nightgown to her legs. All at once the backyard, crisscrossed with black shadows, seemed unfamiliar and almost menacing. "You shouldn't be out by yourself," she said at last. "Not with the kidnapper hanging around."

"Huh! I'm too old to interest that creep. He only picks on the little ones."

"Do you know him—the one who got away?"

"Sure I know him. I know all the brats in Green Hollow. Unless there's one that doesn't like ice cream."

The conversation subsided; the wind rose again. Impatience flooded Shelley as she watched Benjy hunch his shoulders inside his denim jacket. They'd be out here all night if she left it up to him. She gathered her nerve and whispered, "Don't you want to kiss me, Benjy?"

She saw him blink, then swallow. "Yeah. Yeah, I do." His hands came out of his pockets. Gently he touched her face, his half-frozen fingers so tentative that, closing her eyes, she could imagine snowflakes lighting on her skin. They moved closer together; she could hear his uneven breathing. At last his cold lips met hers. She put her arms around him beneath his jacket, and when she felt how he was trembling she let her mouth open under his.

She was doing it. She was kissing Benjy—one of those forbidden French kisses she and her friends had discussed as children—but the sensation, though disconcertingly intimate, was disappointing. Wasn't she supposed to be excited? Benjy was; that was obvious, but she felt nothing. She pressed closer to him, searching for the promised thrill.

We'll be together, Shelley. Here in the dark. Don't you want that? I do.

As the words floated through her head, all at once it became Kip she was kissing—Kip whose tongue was in her mouth, making her legs go suddenly, deliciously weak, Kip whose eager hands unzipped her jacket and reached inside to touch her, setting off a series of exquisite tremors all through her body. Shocked, she pulled away—and it was Benjy again, dazed and panting, apparently unaware of what had happened. He caught her fingers in his. "Come on."

Shelley clung to his hand; that brief but terrifying transformation had left her head spinning and her heart in her throat. "Where?"

"Just for a little ride, huh? At least we'll be out of the wind."

Still shaken by what had happened, she tried to think. It was Benjy she had been kissing, Benjy whose touch had aroused her at last. If they sat in the truck and tried it again, wouldn't his embraces wipe out the memory of that other, imaginary one? Badly as she wanted this result, she felt its temptation subside at the thought of what would happen if her parents found out. She drew her jacket close around her and shook her head. "I can't, Benjy."

"Sure you can." He tugged at her hand, pulling her off the back step.

"No, listen, I—" Her halfhearted protest collapsed suddenly into a frightened gasp. "Look out!"

The man came out of nowhere. One instant there was no one; the next, a bulky shape appeared behind Benjy, its arms reaching out. As he swore and ducked to the side, all at once Shelley recognized his assailant.

She clapped a hand over her mouth to stifle her yelp. It was Royce. He made no further move, and in the moonlight she could see worry on his face as he held up his gloved hands and frantically wiggled the fingers. By now she knew him well enough to translate the gesture. Wait, he was saying. Hold on a minute. I can explain.

But Benjy was already stumbling at him, arms windmilling wildly. Royce backed up, his hands placating, and Shelley lunged forward and seized the back of Benjy's jacket. "Benjy! It's only Royce!"

"Only Royce!" He stopped, panting. "Shit! Didn't he chase me enough when I was a kid? Why the hell's he after me now?"

"Shh!" She was afraid he would wake her family. "He's not trying to hurt you. He's just looking out for me." She turned to Royce. "Isn't that right?"

Royce nodded vigorously, reaching out to give Benjy's shoulder a tentative pat.

"See?"

"Yeah, great." Benjy straightened his jacket, regarding the big man suspiciously. He was nearly Royce's height by now, but probably less than half his weight. "He can understand what you say?"

"Of course he can."

"So tell him it's okay, and let's go."

Royce shook his head.

"He can read your lips," Shelley said.

"You mean he's saying you can't go with me? Well, read this, jerk!" He faced Royce, suddenly furious. "We're not on your precious property now, so butt out! Get it? Come on, Shelley."

He reached for her hand again, but Royce touched her shoulder and made a series of rapid gestures whose meaning she could follow well enough. He couldn't let her go. It was late at night. It wasn't safe. She knew that. He was sorry. One gloved fist touched his heart with a twisting motion. Sorry.

"He's not going to let me, Benjy."

"Dammit, Shelley—" His rage was on the brink of becoming tears. She saw him look at Royce and gauge his chances in a physical confrontation: nil. For a moment longer the three of them stood there in the cold night—Shelley shivering in her jacket and nightgown, Royce with his fist frozen in position above his heart, Benjy simmering with frustration. All at once he flung up his arms and strode away, throwing his parting words back over one shoulder.

"You want to let those fucking people run your life, fine! Just leave me out of it from now on!"

Chapter 19

As the winter gave way to spring, fear gradually eased its grip on the village. Although the man the media had christened "the Green Hollow Kidnapper" had not been captured, neither had he struck again. There was a sense that all the precautions and curtailments were effective, a hope that he might be caught any day—and a secret, selfish wish that if he was not, then at least he might move on.

But who was he? What was his connection with the coven? the twins' questions went unasked. Around the coven members these days was the familiar, unbreachable wall adults raised whenever there was an issue they didn't wish to discuss. *When we can tell you more, we will.* Clearly that time had not come. As the Spring Equinox Sabbat came and went, as the weather grew increasingly pleasant, there were still no explanations from the coven—only abrupt arrivals and departures, conferences in Snow's office from which the participants emerged with grim faces, plainly preoccupied with matters to which the coven's apprentices were not privy. On certain nights, as she crossed the street with Royce and Kip, Shelley thought she glimpsed a motionless shape within the dense shadow of the hedge. But she might have been imagining it.

The end of April brought the Beltane Sabbat—the halfway point on the witches' calendar, when the Wheel rolls from darkness into light, celebrating the fertility manifest everywhere in the blossoming, buzzing, burgeoning springtime world. Bright in the night sky, the waxing moon turned the meadow to silver as the coven gathered around an altar heaped high with flowering hawthorn. They had fasted that evening, but Shelley was no longer aware of her empty belly—only of the night and the moon, the crackling fire and the flowers' heady sweetness. A goblet of wine went round the circle and she drank deep, feeling it go immediately to her head.

The drum began.

Softly, like a great heart beating—the heartbeat of the living earth, quickening in anticipation, gradually growing louder and more insistent until those in the circle could feel it resonating inside them, every pulse attuned to its beat. Elsewhere in the village people might have pricked their ears, sensing some faint vibration of the air, like thunder from another world, before they shrugged and dismissed it as imagination. But for those around the fire, the drumbeat's urgent rhythm had become all that existed.

baBOOM baBOOM baBOOM baBOOM

Soft spring air, the scent of flowers, moonlit darkness, a lingering taste of wine on the tongue. As the drum beats on, the moonlight is transformed to heady fragrance, the air to wine, the wine to moonlight. Sound and darkness are inseparably joined.

baBOOM baBOOM

And the body irresistibly answers that restless, relentless beat. Nerves quiver; blood hurries through the chambers of the heart; lips part and eyes dilate. Breath quickens. Flesh kindles.

baBOOM.

The beat stopped. The cessation of sound was like the earth dropping away beneath my feet; I had an instant's sensation of falling, plummeting through dizzy space, before I recaptured my bearings—surprised to discover that my own heartbeat, which had seemed so inextricably bound to the drum, had continued on in that breathless, electric silence. No one moved. The hush encompassed the entire meadow, until at last a single cricket began to pipe. A summer sound. From the other side of the circle, a robed figure stepped forward and spoke. Head still spinning with the wine and the beating drum, I did not recognize the voice—only that it was a woman's.

"On this May Eve we gather to enact the most hallowed of our rites. As our Lady takes the part of the Goddess, so tonight the God will choose one of you to represent him. Listen within yourself for his summons, that you may know it truly; for a bane falls upon any member of the circle who falsely claims this sacred charge."

When she stepped back there was silence except for the soft chorus of crickets all around. Three other figures moved forward; one stood motionless while her hood was drawn back to reveal her face. It was Snow. The others placed a wreath of flowers on her head. Again a woman's voice spoke. "Tonight is a night of joy, for now we bring the summer in. The God has reached the fullness of his strength; the maiden Goddess awaits her young lover. By their joining the age-old cycle of life shall be fulfilled. Let the greenwood ring! Let the dance begin!"

She moved to lead the dance and the rest of us followed as the drum started up once more. Behind it rose the chanting, soft at first, rising as the coven joined hands and moved deosil around the circle.

> *boomBOOMboomBOOMBOOMboomboomBOOM boomBOOMBOOMboom*
> *Sumer is icumen in, lludè sing cuccu!*
> *Groweth sed and bloweth med, and springth the grenwude nu!*

Snow stood motionless by the fire, her chin lifted and eyes closed. Once I thought I saw a fit of trembling run over her from head to foot. I was light-headed from the sound of the drum, the dancing and chanting, the leaping fire and the sight of her solitary figure against it, now lit, now shadowed, like some shape in a dream. Fragments whirled through my mind, throwing off sparks: the word *grenwude, greenwood* like the shimmering echo of a familiar impish face wreathed in leaves. I could no longer feel my legs moving; the interwoven rhythms of voice and drum turned the circle, carrying me effortlessly along. How long were we in motion? All at once everything stopped—drum, voices, movement—and I became aware of a second figure within the circle.

A male voice rang out. "Welcome the young king of the greenwood! For he offers his strength to the Goddess, that the Wheel may turn without ceasing."

Voices rose in answer and I found mine among them. "Ever turns the Wheel!"

Two coveners lit brands from the fire and lifted them high to illuminate the scene. The king's attendants led him up to Snow and stripped off his robe, and in the blaze of the torches I could see his eyes glittering between half-closed lids that made him seem entranced. A sheen of sweat had turned his skin to molten gold, highlighting the lithe muscles in his chest and arms. His hair clung to his wet temples in thick, curling locks. He resembled some exquisite classical statute of a young faun—or, to be more accurate, a young satyr, sculpted in bold detail down to the eager shaft jutting from his groin.

It was Kip. In the time it took for recognition to register in my dazed brain, the two figures on either side of him had placed a garland of leaves upon his head and pressed him to his knees in front of Snow. They removed her robe. Her hair, unbound beneath its garland of flowers, half veiled her breasts; firelight flickered across her naked body and filled her pale eyes as she stood looking down at the leaf-haired, kneeling figure before her—and in that instant I saw them not as people I knew, but as Goddess and God, embodied in our midst.

The maiden Goddess awaits her young lover. I caught my breath; every hair on my body stood on end. Slowly she knelt to face him and they clasped hands. I saw them in profile against the firelight, their heads crowned in living greenery. Then she lay back and drew him down on top of her.

Everyone shouted, a burst of exultant sound rising like a fountain into the night sky. The torchbearers plunged their crackling brands into the cauldron, drowning them in a hissing cloud of smoke and steam, bright flames quenched by the cool waters within. Darkness rushed back; the whirling circle formed again to the sound of the drum, joined now by wild flute and tambourine, and I was drawn irresistibly into the motion, unable to watch what was happening in the center by the fire's leaping flames. Of course I knew. But the fasting and the ritual bath, the wine and the drumming had altered my perceptions to such an extent that I couldn't think—couldn't make the necessary mental connection between one moment and the next. For that interval I simply became the dance, the music, the chanting, the ancient ritual spinning itself into a web of moving light and shadow beneath the moon.

It was the music that signaled, at last, a change in the pace of the rite. First the drum dropped out, then the frenzied tambourine, and the dancing gradually slowed and came to a halt. Finally only the flute remained, playing a yearning solo in the moonlight. I looked around and saw couples stealing away into the lush grass of the meadow—Andreas and Grimalkin with their arms around each other, Gwynneth with her bright head close to Elymas's white one, Senta hand in hand with Reed, Indigo smothering a laugh as Tamarack whispered in her ear. All forms, all customs seemed to have taken wing on this night, when the waxing moon promised fortune and fertility and the only things that mattered were the hawthorn's intoxicating white fragrance and the compelling call of flesh to flesh.

Tonight is a night of joy, for now we bring the summer in. On the other side of the circle, the flute glimmered in the moonlight. The central fire had died to embers, its feeble glow casting a chiaroscuro burnish over the motionless pair who lay beside it, spent in each other's arms. *What were you in your past life? Lovers?* As I stood staring at them, awareness flooded back. I couldn't move. A hand grasped my elbow.

"Shelley?" Archer's eyes gleamed at me from inside his hood; there was a smile on his handsome face. He steered me gently toward the edge of the circle, where the uncut grass stood knee deep. There he freed my arm and lifted a tentative hand to touch my cheek. "How did you like the ritual?"

"Oh . . . it was . . ." I couldn't finish. His hand slipped inside my hood to stroke my hair as he looked into my eyes. I just stood there, still reeling from what I had witnessed tonight, too dazed to register much beyond the fact that the fingers gently caressing my face were very warm. The pair beside the fire drew my attention as irresistibly as if they had been magnetic north, and I a compass needle. My head turned in their direction.

Archer's hand gently brought it back. "Shelley, please. I'm doing my best to sweep you off your feet." He pushed back his hood with his free hand. He was smiling. In the moonlight I could see how handsome he was, the kindness in his eyes—and behind the kindness, a lambent lust. "Would you like to celebrate May Eve with me?" he said softly.

I swallowed and looked away, across the circle, at the lone figure playing her flute in the moonlight. "What about Silkmoth?" I said.

"Silkmoth has made a vow to serve the Maiden Goddess. She celebrates Beltane in her own way, as you see her doing now—by making music all night long." He paused and I could tell he wanted me to look at him, but I couldn't. In my mind I made a picture of myself going off into the meadow with him, the two of us lying together beneath the wise gaze of the white moon. *Tonight is a night of joy . . .* The idea was frightening and appealing at the same time. Romantic. Adult.

"Shelley?"

I still couldn't look at him. But I whispered, "Yes."

He took my hand and led me out of the circle. The tall grass swished around our legs as we walked, catching at the hems of our robes and dragging them open as if by design. It made a soft, thick carpet beneath us when Archer stopped at last and drew me down beside him. Once we were on the ground, the grass rising around us, it was as if we had become a part of the magical night. On every side in the darkness of the meadow I could hear the animal sounds of pleasure, murmurs and moans and arcing cries mingling with the unceasing song of the crickets—a pulsating, irresistible rhythm. The smell of the grass was sweet, the earth warm beneath us. Overhead, the stars were a scattering of white blossoms in the blue-black field of the sky, the moon a beautiful and benevolent Goddess smiling down on her children. *Let my worship be in the heart that rejoices—for behold, all acts of love and pleasure are my rituals.*

I lay on my back and Archer kissed me. His lips were soft and his mustache tickled my mouth. I felt him untie the cord around my waist and part my robe—felt the night air touch my skin and his hands follow. I told myself how romantic this was. Handsome Archer, whom I'd once christened the Prince, with his red lips and dark beard, and his hands so warm on my flesh in the cooling air. I waited, but the pleasure didn't come; I was numb, and beneath the numbness, afraid. I had read too many novels not to know that no matter how gentle he was, this was going to hurt. I didn't really want to go through with it—but somehow, because of what Kip had done, it seemed I must. Because of—suddenly my cheeks were wet with tears. Archer drew back to look into my face, making a soft sound of concern as he released me. I sat up, unable to prevent my stubborn head from turning in the direction of the circle once more.

Archer was quiet. Then I felt his arm gently encircle my shoulders. "Never mind, little one. Never mind. There'll be other May Eves. Let me take you home."

Chapter 20

I didn't sleep. My mind kept jumping from one image to another, unable to hold onto anything for more than a few seconds—and my body was just as uncooperative, ceaselessly changing position without finding comfort anywhere. Had I been more experienced in these matters, I would have recognized the signs of power raised and undischarged, energy restlessly seeking release like a lion circling a cage. My alarm went off at seven. Once I had silenced its insistent buzz I continued to lie in bed, staring at the ceiling. Even though I was certain I hadn't slept at all, the previous night already possessed the outlandish quality of a dream. But I was under no illusions: I knew it had happened. All of it.

An image rushed over me—Snow drawing Kip down on top of her—and I flinched away from its harrowing intimacy. In theory I had understood the significance of the Beltane Sabbat, but I had imagined that the surrogate God and Goddess would perform a purely symbolic joining. As of course they had, but it took me many years to recognize the sex act as itself a symbol. All I understood on that May morning was that Snow had taken Kip away from me, and included in the sum of my misery was the memory of having disgraced myself with Archer—bursting into tears when I was supposed to be in the throes of passion. *Little one,* he had called me. Not a woman but a sniveling child.

Emptiness spread through me. All my efforts, the things I had been forced to do to keep Snow and Kip apart—tattling on him about the love spell, manipulating his jealousy of Jonathan Blackbridge—had failed. This was the shadow I had glimpsed in that dim school cloakroom so many years before: the moment when another's claim would outweigh my own and I would be helpless against it. Against this devastation nothing else mattered; to reverse it I would have done anything, even face the Green Hollow Kidnapper or a hundred more like him. And yet my body persisted in its morning routine. It rose from the bed and washed, dressed and readied itself to head over to the Arms for work. As I left my room I tried not to look at Kip's closed door.

At the Arms only Gwynneth, Silkmoth and Andreas were up, breakfasting on coffee and croissants in the kitchen; everyone else was evidently still asleep. The three at the kitchen table invited me to join them, but the prospect of casual conversation was too daunting. I mumbled some excuse and fled upstairs.

There I started mechanically on my housekeeping tasks, beginning with the tower room where Gwynneth always stayed. Of all the guest rooms, this was my favorite; the bed made me think of some airy ship, its white canopy soaring like a wind-filled sail, and at this time of morning it floated serenely on the tide of sunlight pouring through the windows. Now the charm was wasted on me as I set to work making the bed, concentrating fiercely on my task to keep the emptiness at bay. The sheets were a tangle; Gwynneth was a restless sleeper—or perhaps she hadn't spent the night alone. *Tonight is a night of joy, for now we bring the summer in.* I bit my lip, welcoming the pain's distraction. Flecks of light from the lacy canopy slid over my hands as I pulled the sheets taut, tucking them tightly as Jessica had taught me, bending down to draw up the light blanket and plump the pillows . . .

When I straightened, Snow was in the doorway. She must have just come from the shower; she was wearing a cotton kimono and her hair lay wet and loose over her shoulders. I felt my heart twist in my chest; she was the last person on earth, except maybe for Kip, I wanted to face today. Or ever.

"Good morning," she said. I managed a mumbled response. After that first glance I couldn't look at her. I heard her come into the room, then around to the side of the bed where I was standing. Her presence was like a tight band around my lungs, constricting my breathing. At last I had to look up. As if that was what she had been waiting for, she said, "We need to talk."

To my horror my eyes filled with tears. I ducked my head and blinked furiously, and they retreated. "Talk?" I said. The word emerged in a squeak.

Her gaze sought mine again and I looked away too late. Her kimono was white, patterned with blue, and she was wearing nothing beneath it. I remembered the way her body had looked last night, in the moving light of the fire. I bent down and blindly smoothed the bedsheet, hearing her say, "Shelley, when we take new people into the coven, there's a reason we don't tell them beforehand exactly what the rites entail. The meaning can't be encompassed in words; it has to be experienced in order to be truly understood. And the rites mean something unique to each of us, so that if one of us tried to explain them to you, we would run the risk of depriving you, limiting you somehow."

She hesitated. I knew she wanted me to meet her eyes, but I couldn't, and after a moment she went on. "Of course, the other side of that is the possibility that someone will be shocked or hurt by what happens as part of the ceremony. But we talked about this once before, the morning after you and Kip joined us. Do you remember? About the self of the circle and the self of everyday? When someone takes a role in the ritual, he's not himself any longer. He *becomes* that role."

"I understand all that," I said. Hope had begun to stir inside me; all at once I could look at her. She seemed to be saying that what had happened between them last night hadn't really meant anything—or that it had happened only in some fuzzy, symbolic way that was almost the same as not happening at all. Maybe she didn't want Kip. Maybe that whole business about their previous lives was just what I had always known it was, a little boy's fantasy, and she would laugh if she knew. Like a child who insists on the details of a nightmare solely in order to be reassured that none of it was real, I blundered on. "I understand, but I don't think Kip does. You don't know how he feels about you. His everyday self, I mean. He's got a great big crush on you, Snow. It's so bad he even pretends he used to know you in another life. Isn't that the silliest thing you ever heard?

I hadn't forgotten the exchange I had overheard between them in her office—but there must be some other, less far-fetched interpretation to their words, some entirely different meaning that she would explain to me now, after she laughed and said it was indeed the silliest thing she had ever heard. But she didn't laugh, and she didn't say the words I waited to hear. She said nothing.

"Snow?" My voice was faint and far away, like the last fading thread of an echo. "Isn't it?"

"No." Her face was bleak. "No, he's right. We've encountered each other before."

"You and *Kip*?" I tried to force a laugh, but it wouldn't come. She didn't answer; she was gazing past me as if she had forgotten I was there. "Where?" I said. "When?"

Her eyes returned. "I don't know the details. It's never like that. It's just a feeling—you meet someone, and you know."

I swallowed. "Well . . . what about me?"

"You?"

"Well, if you knew him, you must have known me too. After all, we're twins."

I saw her blink. Then she said gently, "This time. But not then."

The sunlit walls of the room seemed to recede and then rush back with dizzying speed. Past lives, previous encounters—I understood nothing of all this, only that whatever had happened, I had been excluded. But how could that be, when Kip was my twin—when of all people in the world, I knew and loved him best? *Just you and me . . . isn't that enough?* Through my mind flashed a searing image from last night: the two of them kneeling silhouetted against the brightness of the fire while I stood watching from the shadows.

"So three's a crowd?" That high, strange voice—was it mine? "Is that it? Should I just get lost?"

Those two familiar frown lines appeared between her brows. "Don't be ridiculous. What's between Kip and me is just unfinished business, something painful we have to work out."

"But even if it *was* painful," I said in a rush, "you did know each other, and I wasn't part of it. So there's no way I can ever catch up."

"Oh, Shelley!" She was exasperated now. "Why won't you understand that you two are separate beings, with separate lives? You and Kip have one relationship. He and I have another. And you and I, what we have—it has nothing to do with him. Think about it." I could feel her using the work *think* to press on my memory, like a thumb pressing on the catch of a box, and before I could stop it the box sprang open and I caught a glimpse of everything we had shared in the past months. The bond formed not only within the witches' circle, but outside it as well—moments when we had joked together, or she had taught me something, or given me some look meant for only me—moments that formed a pattern unique to the two of us.

"It's pointless to talk about catching up," Snow was saying. "It's not a race! Each encounter, with each person, has something to teach us. Didn't you sing a round when you were little—*Make new friends, keep the old; one is silver and the other gold*—? There's so much wisdom hidden in old songs and rhymes."

To my ear, attuned to any slight, there was a sting even in those words with which she meant to reassure me. The two of them were the old friends, I was the newcomer. *One is silver and the other gold.* I fastened on the first thing that caught my eye: the silver pentacle on its chain around her neck. "But gold is better, isn't it?" I hissed. "So what do you need with silver?"

I snatched at the pendant, meaning to thrust it in her face. I must have used more force than I intended, because the chain broke and I found it dangling from my hand. I saw Snow's eyes darken, but I was past being afraid of her at that moment. I noticed the chain had made a red mark on her neck. She caught hold of my wrist and we stood staring at each other, not speaking. I think I even stopped breathing. My wrist began to tingle, as if a low voltage current were running through it, and all at once the pendant felt hot in my hand. "Don't you work your magic on me," I said. I meant to shout, but I had no breath and it came out a choked whisper. All the same she reddened, and I felt a stab of bitter triumph at having made her summon her power in anger. The tingling ebbed away; she released my wrist. Then, before I could step back, she put her arms around me and caught me close.

I wanted to push her away, but instead I burst into tears. She held me while I cried, choking on the sobs that crashed over me like waves. Everything had changed, and I had a cloudy sense that once this storm of emotion had passed, I would cease to exist. When I had wept myself empty at last, she drew me down beside her on the bed and pulled loose a corner of the sheet to dry my face. The morning sunlight was behind her, dazzling my eyes. From the open window, a warm breeze caught and lifted a few glinting strands of her damp hair.

A jolt of recognition made me catch my breath, and for a moment I couldn't speak. Then: "It was you, wasn't it?" I whispered. "That time I chased the ball across the street . . . ? That was you."

A shadowy smile touched her lips. Our faces were so close that I could see the tiny flecks of gold embedded in her silvery eyes. "Shh," she said. And then she kissed me.

The interlude that followed possessed none of the abandon, none of the fierce urgency of the Beltane ritual. It was a study in tenderness, subtle touches that shivered along nerves I hadn't known I possessed. All else was forgotten as she coaxed from me the secrets of my own body, only suspected until now. The morning sun filtered through the white canopy above us, sending tiny beads of light sliding over her skin and mine in a hush broken only by whispered words and the rhythm of quickened breath. If any magic was worked between us then, it was only the magic of an intimacy in which my shyness was banished by her persuasive and unhurried hands. On the bed I had so often imagined as an airy, light-borne boat, we were two fellow sailors, rocked by tides of pleasure that mounted ever higher until our vessel rode at full flood, slipping its moorings to bear us beyond all known landmarks, out to open sea.

* * *

My first impression, when I woke, was that it had been a dream. It took me a minute to accept my surroundings—to understand that I was fully awake and yet lying naked in the white canopy bed of the tower room at the Arms instead of in my room at home. Around me the house was utterly quiet. Green leaves rustled outside the window, shifting the pattern of sunlight on the floor, and a glint of silver on the other pillow caught my eye. I turned my head to see Snow's medallion anchoring a note.

Come out to the pool when you wake up. I collected my scattered clothing and dressed in a daze. I did not understand, at the time, that the pent-up power of last night's ritual had been skillfully grounded at last, but I was aware of a drowsy contentment suffusing me, body and spirit. Retrieving the medallion I could feel its warmth against my palm. I went to the door and listened. Not a sound anywhere in the house. How can I communicate the quality of that silence? It was a presence rather than an absence: a soundless drifting of light that filled the house and rendered it buoyant as a bubble, barely tethered to this earth.

And I felt myself no heavier as I descended the stairs and crossed the parking lot. As I stepped off the shady footbridge onto the sunlit lawn beyond, I could hear voices coming from beyond the hedge around the pool. The words weren't audible—just someone saying something, someone else answering, and then lazy laughter—but rising behind that green wall of leaves the sound was timeless, mysterious, halting me with the sudden fervent wish that this moment could last forever. I had an inkling that I would never again, in all my life, come so close to knowing peace. *Stay, thou art so fair.* Isn't that the bargain between Faust and the devil—one perfect moment in exchange for one immortal soul? But witches don't believe in the devil; and I was still innocent, then, of the fact that we humans require no such creature to help us renounce our souls.

Nearing the gate I could see them all gathered around the pool in the late morning sun. Newspapers and coffee cups were scattered here and there; some people sprawled in the canvas lounge chairs, others sat at the pool's edge with their legs in the water. Snow sat with Gwynneth and Senta at one of the umbrella-shaded tables; Archer and Andreas stood talking in the shallow end of the pool. At the deep end, a dark head broke the surface.

Kip. I hesitated at the gate, watching him; then Archer saw me and waved. The others turned, calling greetings, and I must have answered automatically as I skirted the edge of the pool and made my way to the table where Snow was sitting. She had put on a sundress and twisted her hair into a loose braid. As I came closer I could see the abrasion where the chain had grazed her neck. When I held the medallion out to her, she looked up, scrutinizing my face. "Sorry," I said.

"Sorry?"

"About your necklace, I mean."

The ghost of a smile touched her lips. I put the medallion in her hand, and her fingers captured and held mine for a minute before releasing them. I doubt anyone else even noticed, but to me the possessive touch seemed a flagrant announcement of our recent intimacy. Overcome by shyness, I mumbled something and retreated to the edge of the pool, where I put my legs in the water, watching the sunlight dance on its surface. A shadow fell across me and I looked up to see Archer standing there. "Morning, Shelley."

"Hi."

He lowered himself to sit next to me. He was wearing only swimming trunks and I glanced sideways at his muscular chest. My infantile behavior of last night seemed very far away, and what I remembered most was how kind he had been. "How are you today?" he said.

"Okay." I could feel my face turning red. Did they all know—had they somehow guessed what had happened? For an uneasy instant I found myself shocked by what I had done. But Archer was smiling at me, and that brief surge of offended propriety faded away in the face of everything I had been taught in the past year. I thought of last night, the random pairings in the meadow, the silver tide of moonlight on which all conventions had been borne away. There was only one law that mattered here. *An' it harm none, do what thou wilt.*

Archer was asking me about the upcoming end of the school year when a blurred shape surfaced suddenly near by, showering us with sparkling droplets.

"Kip! Cut it out!"

Laughing, Archer kicked water at him while I drew my feet up and tried to keep from getting soaked. Kip grabbed Archer's leg and pulled, and good-naturedly Archer let himself be dragged into the pool. There was a tremendous splash as they both went under; then they resurfaced, wrestling playfully. This morning Kip seemed his old exuberant self, released from the doldrums of the past few weeks. Archer ducked him, and as he struggled upright I saw the marks on his back: a crisscross of scratches showing angry red on his tanned skin.

Everything else receded to a far distance as I sat staring at those marks made by Snow's nails, like words written in an unknown language. The images of last night came close once more—the urgent beating of the drum, firelight turning flesh to gold, hissing torches quenched in the cauldron's deep waters. But now, mingling with these images, there were others—of sunlight filtering through a lacy canopy, sighs and murmurs that scarcely ruffled the Sunday morning stillness.

Slowly my surroundings returned: the pool, the friendly faces, the sounds of laughter and splashing water. Kip surface-dived, displaying the gaudy yellow bathing trunks that had been a present from Frog's family, and Archer plunged after him in an explosion of sunlit water. I watched them without knowing what to feel. Things no longer seemed as simple as they had last night or early this morning. My emotions were like a spinning top that strikes an unexpected obstacle and goes careening wildly off course into an unpredictable direction. Had everything changed, or nothing? Had I gained or lost? A quiet voice spoke in my mind. *You have entered a place of power, where light and dark meet and make one.*

I took a deep breath and tried to think. Saw the circle's magical shape circumscribing both moonlit meadow and tower room. Remembered last night's fire and drums, this morning's sunlight and lace, like two halves of a perfect whole. *Where light and dark meet and make one.* The words murmured in my head; I strained to grasp their meaning and felt it slip away. But just for an instant it seemed to me that within the compass of that enchanted boundary Snow had not divided Kip and me at all, only brought our two selves nearer to becoming one.

Chapter 21

Following that Beltane weekend was a period of what everyone said was the most perfect spring weather Green Hollow had ever seen. *For now we bring the summer in . . .* The promise uttered during the ritual was being fulfilled, as a succession of balmy days and gentle night rains transformed the village into a garden. At the Arms there were vases of fresh tulips and irises in all the guest rooms, bowls of floating roses on the dining room tables; a glass pitcher filled with peonies on the kitchen counter caught the afternoon sun. A mingled fragrance wafted through the house, carried on warm currents of air, tickling Shelley's nose as she dusted and swept and tidied, her mind on other matters.

The twins saw Snow only sporadically. She spent long hours behind the closed door of her office, on the phone; or she was off on a trip somewhere, leaving early and returning late. The two frown lines were always present between her brows—a reminder, along with the state police cars cruising the village streets, that the Green Hollow Kidnapper remained at large. But there were still nights when she appeared for supper in the kitchen, blazing with determination to enjoy herself, and on those occasions the table rocked with laughter and raillery like old times.

Or almost like old times. Kip was more pensive than he once had been. The gold glint in his eyes, which Shelley had once dreaded as a sign that she was about to be dragged into some harebrained scheme, now seemed ambiguous—a light glimpsed at a distance, on a far shoreline: elusive and tantalizing. She could no longer guess his thoughts.

Did he share my bouts of uncertainty about what was real in our lives and what was not? Our year's apprenticeship to the coven was moving to a close—a year of astonishing discoveries. And yet there were times when all of it, even the secrets and doubts and fears, seemed like a dream from which I might suddenly wake to find my life diminished to its former narrow scope. At such moments, tallying my memories of the past year like a miser counting coins, I was frustrated by their lack of substance. How could I be said to possess anything so ephemeral? A series of fleeting images glimpsed in the cauldron's black waters, a leaf-crowned face hovering against the darkness of my bedroom, the wise amber eyes of a jaguar. Among these recollections was one of that sunlit interlude in the tower room with Snow—unforgettable but, like all the rest, ultimately intangible.

The middle of May brought an official letter from the State University at Albany, confirming Shelley's acceptance as a freshman for the fall term. It was the only college to which she had applied. Mr. Briggs, the guidance counselor at school, had assured her that her grades and College Board scores would get her admitted wherever she wished, but what she wished was to stay close to Green Hollow—to the Arms. Mother and Marty were delighted with her decision; Dad seemed a little disappointed. "I wish we could afford to send you to a really fine school, sweetheart. Maybe you should have applied to one of the Seven Sisters. I know you could have gotten a scholarship if you'd tried."

Shelley guessed he was remembering his argument with Mother long ago, about what was best for Kip and her, and wondering if maybe his ideas had been wrong. She rubbed her cheek against the shoulder of his jacket. "I don't need a fancy school, Dad. I just want to be able to come home on the weekends if I feel like it."

His hand drifted over her hair. "That'll be nice."

Her graduation ceremony took place in the auditorium at Green Hollow High, where the senior class sat crowded together in folding chairs on the stage, sweating in their hot black robes and mortarboards, assaulted by a blare of electronically amplified voices that uttered all the usual platitudes. At long last their names were called one by one. A smattering of applause, a damp handshake and a roll of beribboned parchment from Mr. Herold, the principal, and finally it was time to sing the school song, accompanied on the piano by Miss Crosby, the Glee Club director.

Guarded by the mountains high
Throned within our hearts
We'll sing your praises to the sky
Green Hollow, ere we part . . .

Jenny and some of the other girls were crying. A couple of the boys too were teary—those very same boys who always infuriated Miss Crosby by altering the last line to *Green Hollow, when we fart,* now appeared overcome with emotion. Shelley was relieved that the tiresome ceremony was over at last, but there was still the aftermath to ensure—kisses and hugs and handshakes from her friends and their parents, teachers' congratulations and good wishes, Marty's tears, and the surprise appearance of a grinning Kate Conklin.

"Kate! Did you come just for me?"

"Just for you, dear girl. I wouldn't have missed it for anything." Planting a resounding kiss on Shelley's cheek: "You look so grown up . . . and you'll be off to college in the fall! I know you're going to be rich and famous. Don't forget I knew you when you were just a dusty little shopkeeper's assistant."

"You mean a shopkeeper's dusty little assistant," Shelley said, and Kate said, "Oh, do I?" As they both started to laugh, Shelley's gaze strayed past Kate's shoulder to light on another familiar face—Benjy, pushing his way toward her through the mob. The sight caused her more discomfort than pleasure. Royce was due shortly, to walk Kip and her over to the Arms; given the circumstances of their last encounter, who knew how Benjy might react to his appearance? She squeezed Kate's hand and turned away, searching the crowded auditorium for Kip. There he was, enduring a tearful hug from Jenny. She reached him just as he extricated himself. "Kip. We've got to get out of here."

"Fine." He was wiping Jenny's lipstick off his cheek with the back of his hand. "Where's Royce?"

"We can wait for him outside."

He looked surprised, but followed her toward the exit. As they emerged into the cooling summer night, the din behind them faded to a hum. "What's going on?" Kip said.

"Benjy's in there. I didn't want him to see Royce."

"Why not?"

Shelley shrugged uncomfortably. Even if he had liked Benjy—*if*—their abortive backyard rendezvous would have been none of his business. "He doesn't like the Arms. Anything about it."

"He doesn't like much of anything," Kip said, and in spite of the fact that she had just gone to some effort to avoid encountering Benjy, her old protective feelings flared into life. "Oh, shut up! That's not true!"

There was a strained pause. Kip looked at his watch and she said, "What time is it?"

"Almost nine. Royce is supposed to meet us at quarter past."

Shelley glanced back at the auditorium doors that stood open to the warm night, spilling light and noise. Had Benjy seen her leave? What if he came looking for her? Suppose Kip said something obnoxious to him, or Royce showed up . . . "I don't want to wait," she said. "Let's just go."

"We'll get in trouble if we show up without Royce."

The light was behind him and she couldn't see his face clearly. He hadn't used Snow's name—but a feeling Shelley could not quite identify made her say deliberately, "I don't care if we get in trouble. Do you?"

I dare you. The unspoken words hovered between them. Abruptly Kip shrugged. "Okay, let's go. I'll race you."

"Race—! I'll kill myself." Mother had made her don high-heeled shoes for the occasion, and just walking in them was tricky enough. Running would be fatal. "Wait." She bent down and took the shoes off. Her nylons—another of Mother's musts—would not survive a run through the streets, but she was past caring. She flourished the shoes at Kip and saw him grin.

"Ready, set, go!"

He took off. Light-footed, I chased him down the shadowy lamplit street, the sound of his laughter floating back to me. I ran without a thought for everything I was leaving behind me, flinging myself eagerly toward what was ahead with no sense that I might ever regret my choice. The skirt of my ridiculously frilly graduation dress—Mother again—kept blowing up around my waist as I ran and I tried to hold it down, laughing at the futility of my efforts, glad it was night and there was no one to see. But just ahead on Main Street there were cars passing: I stopped to put my shoes back on and fix my dress before proceeding decorously to the corner where Kip was waiting. "Slowpoke," he said.

"Cheater."

"What!"

"You had a head start."

He said nothing, but I saw him smile. "Come on, I've got a surprise for you."

"A surprise?"

"A little graduation present."

"What is it?"

"If I told you—" We finished the sentence together: "It wouldn't be a surprise." One of Marty's favorite maxims. Kip motioned me toward the park. "Come on."

"My graduation present is in the park?"

"Yeah, it's in the park. Do you want it or not?"

"Of course I do. But Royce'll be worried about us if we don't head him off. And Snow's going to be mad."

He turned and regarded me steadily. "I thought you didn't care if we got in trouble."

It was my turn to subside. We entered the park. In the leafy silence beneath the trees the air was cool after the heat of our run, and I began to shiver as Kip caught my hand to lead me deeper into the green darkness. "Where are we going?"

"The bandstand."

The center of the park boasted a little bandstand where a group of old men who called themselves the Green Hollow Lads occasionally gave concerts on spring and summer evenings. They wore straw boaters, played a variety of instruments—mandolins, banjos, bugles, trombones—and sang old-fashioned songs like "Ragtime Doll." In the past they had always drawn a good crowd, but because of the kidnapper there had been no concerts this spring.

The kidnapper. I moved closer to Kip. What were we doing here in the dark, all by ourselves, flouting not only Snow's warnings but simple common sense? Leaves rustled around us. The bandstand came in sight, looking spooky in the moonlight, and I shivered again—not from the cold this time—but closer up the spookiness became mere neglect: peeling paint, steps that creaked beneath our feet as we mounted them. I went to the railing and looked out at the silvery open spaces and the shadows crouching beneath the trees. Except for the two of us, the park was utterly deserted. I hugged myself with both arms, trying to keep my voice light as I said, "What's the surprise?"

"I told you. A graduation present."

Curiosity began to nudge my jitters aside. "What *is* it?"

"I said you'll see." He joined me at the railing and I glanced sideways at him, struck by how handsome he looked in the suit he had worn to the graduation ceremony. By rights he should have been up there on the platform with me, receiving his diploma, instead of sitting in the audience with another year of high school to complete. How could I go off to college without him? This separation was something I had resolutely refused to think about; now all at once it bulked huge in my mind, inevitable but impossible. As if he knew, Kip put his arm around me. I didn't move away. Into my mind flashed the image of him in the Beltane circle, radiant with the fiery power of the God. I could feel the heat from his body now, penetrating the thin fabric of my dress like soft fire flowing into me. *I don't care if we get in trouble. Do you?* Kip's arms tightened briefly and then released me. "Wait here. I'll just be a minute."

He went back down the bandstand steps; I could hear him rummaging around beneath them. "What are you *doing*?" I said.

"No fair peeking." He was crouched down, out of sight. There were various incomprehensible noises. Not trusting my own powers of resistance, I retreated to the other side of the bandstand and leaned against the rail, keeping my eyes fixed on the dim ceiling. A breeze stirred the leaves again. But it seemed warm this time: a gentle, calming touch that soothed the last of my fears, leaving me strangely empty for a moment before the whispering of the leaves filled the void. That soft sound said school was over and summer had begun. Kip's and my impending separation shrank to a point on the horizon as I felt the months stretching ahead like a dream, a vast ocean of time in which we would be together every day.

"Almost ready," his voice said, and I came back from that drifting future to the present. Hadn't he promised me a surprise? He was taking a long time getting it ready, teasing me on purpose, and I could hear the leaves whispering that I could turn the tables on him. They were murmuring that I could sneak out of the bandstand and hide now, while he was busy—and when he was finally ready I would be nowhere in sight. I could take off my clothes, and when he came looking for me I could step out of the trees, naked, onto the moonlit grass. Just to surprise him, of course. Just to tease him.

Shhhh, the leaves cautioned me. *Don't make any noise.* In my fancy dress and shoes I climbed awkwardly over the railing and let myself drop silently to the grass below. My high heels sank into the soft ground; I tugged them free and ran across the moonlit grass toward the nearest clump of trees. There, hidden in the shadows, I fixed my eyes on the bandstand and waited for Kip to discover my absence. Even though I'd run only a half dozen yards, my heart was pounding and I was out of breath. The trick I was playing on him struck me as so brilliant, so perfect, that I could scarcely contain my excitement. I saw him go up the steps to the bandstand. A graduation surprise? Any second now I would slip out of my clothes and appear from the shadows and give him the surprise of his life. Laughter rose inside me, threatening to escape; I put a hand over my mouth to contain it as his voice floated across the grass. "Okay, now all we have to do is—Shelley?"

I pressed my hand harder to my mouth.

"Shelley!" His voice was louder now; I could hear panic in it. "Where are you?"

Suddenly my hand was clamped so tightly over my nose and mouth that I couldn't breathe, and with a blinding shock I understood it wasn't mine at all. Not my hand, but someone else's—brutal, gloved, cold as ice beneath the leather I could taste now against my lips. Someone's arm came around my ribs and tightened like a vise. I wanted to struggle, but my arms and legs hung limp, refusing to respond to the frantic messages from my brain as I felt myself sinking into a swimming blackness flecked with colored stars. Faintly I heard Kip's hoarse shout: "Shelley!"

I'm right here, I thought—but I knew he would never find me in this floating blackness, and that was good, because I didn't want him to. If he didn't try to find me, he could still get away. He could run, he could escape—and I knew my captor didn't want that. A faraway voice said silently in the blackness, *Something you know he wants. Your two young apprentices.*

Run, I thought. Above my head I heard a sibilant sound that might have been a laugh, or maybe only stirring leaves, and then the cold hand fell away from my mouth and I found I could move. I was supposed to struggle and scream for help. I was supposed to call Kip's name. I was aware of these impulses being imposed on me by a will outside my own. I wouldn't do it, of course. I wouldn't set a trap for Kip. But in spite of this resolution I could feel my arms and legs thrashing, my mouth opening and my lungs filling with air—

The sky exploded. All at once blinding light was everywhere, accompanied by a deafening bombardment of bangs and pops, sputters, shrieks, hisses and howls. The crushing pressure on my ribs eased momentarily; I squirmed free, stumbled a few yards and collided with Kip.

"Shelley—! Wha—?"

"Look out!"

Against the dazzling brightness of Kip's surprise fireworks display, a hooded shape loomed abruptly over us—dark, menacing, a faceless figment from a nightmare. Kip threw a wild punch, but our assailant simply grabbed his fist and yanked him forward. He stumbled, fell to his knees, and was jerked roughly upright again at the same instant that I felt iron fingers seize my wrist.

Just like that, he had us both. We sagged limply in his grip while pandemonium reigned on every side. My head was too full of bangs and flashes for thought—but some corner of my brain registered the shadow that suddenly shot across the grass, bisecting the whistling, streaking lights and colors of the Monster Snaps and Texas Busters, Golden Bats and Devil's Delights. A swift shadow with a stiff bottlebrush tail, adding its own eerie squall to the din as it crouched and sprang.

Was it only the bursting crazy-quilt of the sky that made Rowan seem to increase in size as his leap carried him through the air? Somewhere in that arc the house cat became a panther, lethal and lithe—and the next instant I had a blurred impression of his shape overflowing its boundaries, changing from familiar to unknown. The light-spangled sky disappeared, blotted out by a darkness in which the eyes remained another moment, twin crescent moons glimmering a baleful green against that boundless blackness, and then were gone.

There was a choked cry, a loosening of the gloved grip on my wrist—I twisted free and tried to run, but my legs were too weak to hold me and I collapsed on the grass, my body instinctively curling into a ball as if trying to shrink and disappear. A hand grasped my shoulder. I moaned and tried to make myself smaller. The hand only tightened cruelly. I waited for the starry blackness—but it was Kip's breathless voice that reached me. "Shelley, it's me! We've got to get out of here! Come on!"

The next thing I knew I was on my feet, running by his side.

They ran all the way to the Arms, arriving sweaty and panting with hearts wildly battering their ribs. Shelley's neck ached from looking back for signs of pursuit—but there were none, only the soft rhythm of crickets in the summer night, disrupted by the racket of their footsteps on the driveway. As they burst into the kitchen, Jessica greeted them with a scowl.

"You two! Where've you been? No, don't tell me, there isn't time. Gentleman at Table Two just now spilled a whole bottle of wine all over his lady friend. Red wine." She thrust a handful of dish towels at them as she spoke. "Don't bother changing your clothes. Just get in there and do what you can with that mess, before it gets any worse." They stood gaping, but their confusion only seemed to exasperate her. "Go!" She gave Shelley a little shove toward the swinging door, sending her through it into the dining room beyond.

There the tables had been drawn together banquet-style. The whole coven was present, seated smiling around the spotless white cloth set with gleaming silver. Grimalkin and Elymas, Tamarack and Senta. Gwynneth, Reed and Indigo. Silkmoth, Archer, Andreas, Snow. At the stupefaction on Shelley's face they raised a cheer that brought Kip and Jessica from the kitchen. Shelley turned numbly to her twin. "Did you know about this?"

He shook his head as Gwynneth came over to take the dish towel from her limp hand. "We didn't tell him. We thought he'd have too hard a time keeping it secret. Are you surprised?"

"She looks surprised." Snow led Shelley to a seat at the head of the table. "But maybe she's just being polite."

She sat befuddled as a fizzing glass of champagne was put in her hand and someone offered a toast. Glasses were raised and emptied; there was applause around the long candlelit table flanked with smiling faces. Jessica and Gwynneth served the soup—Two Melon, Shelley's summer favorite—but to the guest of honor the festive scene was flat and unreal, superimposed upon a quivering darkness like a residue of the horror in the park. If she touched her mouth she could still feel the savage intimacy of that cold gloved hand. Her eyes sought Kip's face: there he was, sitting between Andreas and Indigo, looking as dazed as she was. Their eyes met briefly in mute confirmation of the shock they had so recently shared. *Did that really happen? Yes. It did.*

"Shelley. What's the matter?" Snow was beside her, voice emerging from the incomprehensible hum of talk and laughter.

"N . . . nothing."

"Look at me."

She couldn't meet Snow's eyes. There was a commotion then—Royce appearing in the swinging door, his tense face visibly relaxing as he saw Kip and her. Snow went quickly to him; in the sudden silence that had descended on the room, they conferred in rapid sign language while the others watched. At last Snow turned and addressed the twins, her voice sharp. "Why didn't you wait for Royce?"

They looked down the table at each other. At last Shelley said, "We couldn't."

"Why not?"

"There was somebody at graduation . . . somebody I . . . didn't want to see."

"Who?"

"Benjy Hendricks."

"I thought he was a friend of yours," Snow said softly.

"He is. But . . ." Shelley stopped, overwhelmed by the impossibility of explaining to this roomful of adults why she had wanted to prevent an encounter between Benjy and Royce. How could she talk about the night she had met Benjy in her backyard, and kissed him, and he had wanted her to go for a ride in his truck? Her silence didn't seem to matter, because Snow was speaking again. "Then it may interest you to know he's been picked up by the police."

"*What?*" Shelley found herself on her feet without being aware of getting there. Down the table Kip was standing too.

"Someone set off some fireworks in the park," Snow was

saying. "A patrol car was passing by and the troopers saw Benjy running away. He's being held for questioning."

The troopers saw Benjy running away. Icy fingers clutched Shelley's heart. "But—" It was all she could say; there was no air left in her lungs. The border of darkness around the table began to seep inward, blotting out Snow's face. Benjy. Running away from the park. What had he been doing in the park? Against the darkness she saw a tall, hooded figure silhouetted against the exploding sky. Benjy was tall. As tall as Royce. Was he strong too—stronger than anyone suspected? Impossible. Impossible. But what had he been doing in the park? As her sight came filtering back she heard Kip say, "Why would they pick him up just for setting off a bunch of firecrackers?"

Snow's cool reply. "I don't know."

There was a silence. Then Kip said, "Anyhow, he didn't do it. I did."

Everyone turned and looked at him, then at me. I was reminded of the night we had asked to join the coven—and now, as then, I was seized by a cowardly wish to deny my own part in what had happened, to let Kip take the blame. After all, the fireworks had been his idea. If we hadn't gone to the park—if we'd gone straight to the Arms—we would have run into Royce on the way, and been safe with him. Through the excuses and justifications clamoring in my head, I heard Snow say evenly, "Both of you, sit down."

When we had obeyed she resumed her own seat and I saw, with a surge of relief for which I depised myself, that she was looking at Kip. Her face was pale, her voice scarcely audible. "After everything that's happened, don't you understand the children of this village are in danger? How can we protect you if you won't cooperate?"

He flushed. "I didn't plan to—"

"Plan to what? Go to the park alone, at night, when it's risky even to walk through the streets by yourselves?"

"Royce was in on it," he muttered. "I told him I wanted to set off some firecrackers for Shelley's graduation, as a surprise. He was going to go to the park with us."

"Then why didn't you wait for him?"

"Because—" He bit his lip, and I heard myself unwillingly complete the sentence. "Because I wanted to leave. It was my fault."

Her gaze shifted to me. "You wanted to avoid Benjy."

I nodded. She lifted her hands and let them drop heavily to the table, then sat back with a sigh. Gwynneth said, "This looks like nothing more than a series of unhappy coincidences. Fortunately no real harm seems to have been done."

Snow shook her head, then addressed us again. "Do you understand how lucky you were? If you had—"

"We did," Kip said.

"What?"

"We did run into him. The kidnapper. He was there in the park. Almost like he was waiting for us. The firecrackers surprised him, I guess—and then Rowan came—and—and we got away."

There was one heartbeat's pure silence, and then everyone started talking to everyone else. Snow turned to Archer in the seat next to hers; I heard her say, "Find Rowan," and saw him leave the room, and Elymas take his chair to join her in murmured conference. All around the table my graduation feast lay in shambles, the delicious soup barely tasted, the champagne going flat. In the tense buzz of voices that filled the room, Kip and I sat forgotten.

Chapter 22

"Benjy's been arrested. He'll be formally charged with the two kidnappings later today."

Snow's flat words brought a wordless exclamation from Kip

and a gasp from me. *Formally charged with the two kidnappings.* Suddenly her office seemed stifling, the patches of morning sunlight flat and opaque, like yellow paint slathered on the surfaces of things. When she had summoned us I had been in the middle of replacing the flowers on the tables in the dining room, and now I became aware that I was still clutching the wilted ones in my hands, like a bouquet for the condemned.

"A tall man in a dark overcoat was seen yesterday watching a playground in Pine Glen," Snow was saying. Pine Glen was a village about fifteen miles west of Green Hollow. "The police didn't release the information because they wanted to set a trap for him. But when Benjy was picked up last night, they found a county map in his pocket. Pine Glen was circled. Apparently he couldn't offer a satisfactory explanation. When they found out he drives a white truck—"

A *white truck.* I saw my own surge of horror mirrored on Kip's features. The kidnapper drove a white truck.

But there were lots of white trucks around. Hundreds—and anyway Mister Softee was not a truck, it was an ice-cream *wagon,* which was not the same thing as a truck at all. I imagined myself asking Jenny and Lisa if they thought Benjy Hendricks could be the Green Hollow Kidnapper. Come on, Shelley! Benjy? That's a good one. Remember that time we found a dead chipmunk in the yard, and he cried over it? He acts tough, but he's just an old softy.

Mister Softee. A white truck. A tall man in a white truck.

But Benjy wasn't a man, he was a boy . . . unless of course you were five years old. How many times, riding with him, had I heard kids calling out as we passed? *Hey, mister! Mister, stop!* Benjy's gripe as he stamped on the brakes—*greedy little mutts*—had always made me laugh. Always. Until now. I had a sudden sharp image of Alex Leonard stretching out his hand for an ice-cream bar. *Come on, Benjy, cantcha float me?*

Impossible. But as I suppressed that memory, another one stirred—something I had glimpsed in the scrying cauldron. Benjy with an odd pattern of shadows on his face. A pattern of stripes, or maybe bars . . .

Prison bars?

* * *

When the story broke later that day, the media went wild over what was termed Benjy's "capture." SUSPECT SEIZED IN KIDNAPPING CASE read the enormous headline in the *Albany Times Union,* and from as far away as New York City one of the dailies reported UPSTATE NAPPER NABBED. A blurry wirephoto seemed mainly composed of broad uniformed backs: a pale blur beyond one beefy shoulder might have been the top of Benjy's head.

"Apparently he refuses to explain the map," Tamarack's voice said over the phone, while Snow held the receiver so the twins could hear. It turned out Tamarack was a partner in a big Albany law firm with FBI connections. "When they asked him about it, he just laughed. Now he won't talk at all."

Channel Six in Albany devoted nearly ten minutes to the story on the late news that evening, reviewing the case from its beginnings the previous fall. Photographs of Alex Leonard and Daniel Chaffin were exhibited, along with footage of Alex's distraught parents, who were described as having lost all hope of ever seeing their son alive.

"The suspect, Benjamin Russell Hendricks of Green Hollow, has refused to answer questions about incriminating evidence found on his person when he was apprehended. He is the driver of a Mister Softee ice-cream truck that matches the description of a white truck given by the second young victim, who was miraculously released shortly after his abduction nearly four months ago. Hendricks is currently being held without bail in Albany, charged with two counts of kidnapping."

The reporter's gratified voice was accompanied on the screen by a photograph of Benjy looking sullen, shifty-eyed and friendless. With a start Shelley recognized his senior picture from the Green Hollow High yearbook. She glanced at Kip—the two of them had arrived home to find the rest of the family glued to the TV—and he grimaced in response. No one said a word. The adults were perfectly aware that Benjy was the closest Shelley had ever come to having a boyfriend, and they must have known that whatever they said, it was bound to be the wrong thing.

By the next day, the murder of Alex Leonard had been added to the two kidnapping charges, and the trial set for late September. At the Lockley Arms everyone seemed convinced of Benjy's innocence, but elsewhere in Green Hollow feeling was divided. There were some—Marty, Dad and Mother among them—who reacted to the news with shock and bewilderment that implied a tacit belief in his guilt. Not "He couldn't have!" but "How could he?" Others, like Kate Conklin and Charlie Dietz, were vocal in their opinion that Benjy was merely a convenient scapegoat for the frustrated investigators. Kate kept a protective eye on Benjy's mother, and shoppers at the E-Z Stop were likely to receive unsolicited testimonials from Charlie on his employee's behalf. "They got no evidence, I'm tellin' you! That business about how he won't talk—that's nothin'. They probably got him pissed off. When Benjy gets pissed off, he clams up—that's all. I'm tellin' you, I know the guy. He wouldn't hurt no little kid."

In Tamarack's opinion, the prosecution's case was weak. "For one thing, it's going to be difficult to get a murder conviction without a body. This case has gotten a lot of publicity and they want to look as if they're making headway, but they've gone off half-cocked. Without the Leonard boy's body, their evidence is completely circumstantial. The map alone is meaningless. The truck will have to yield some clear evidence that at least one of the boys was in it at some point. Otherwise they've got nothing."

The twins were riven by guilt. Although the fireworks display had been forgotten in the ensuing uproar, they couldn't forget that it was their fault Benjy had been arrested. If his presence in the park that night had been innocent—

And wasn't that the real question? Shelley was ashamed of the doubts that continued to plague her—but the facts, tainted by the memory of those shadowy prison bars patterning his face, were daunting. He had been in the park that night. He had been running away. He had refused to explain the marked map in his pocket. He was tall. He drove a white truck. *I know all the brats in Green Hollow. Unless there's one that doesn't like ice cream . . .*

And he hated the Lockley Arms. What if, in the course of those childhood invasions of the Arms, he had stumbled across some evidence of the coven's existence? Did he hate them enough to put on a hooded robe and commit unspeakable crimes in some convoluted attempt to implicate them? At last she asked Kip point-blank if he thought Benjy was guilty.

"No."

"You don't? Why not?"

"Shelley. This guy killed the Lockleys. The coven can't control him. You felt for yourself how strong he is. Isn't it obvious he's a witch?"

"But Benjy was there. He was in the park that night."

"Yeah, worse luck for him. But he's no witch, that's for sure." His expression said it all: Benjy was a lightweight, too insignificant for the role. Not a powerful adversary, just a chump who happened to be in the wrong place at the wrong time. She supposed she should have been reassured by Kip's belief in his innocence, but paradoxically the casual dismissal stung and she turned angrily away, hearing him say, "The real guy's still out there. But not for long."

"Not for long? What do you mean?"

"Well, the coven's about to get reinforcements, aren't they? Two more people on their side?" At her blank expression he took hold of her shoulders and shook her, as if to rouse her from sleep. "You and me."

Chapter 23

Midsummer Eve. The summer solstice—longest day of the year, when the power of light reaches its zenith before beginning the slow decline toward darkness. To anyone watching the Davies twins crossing the street to the Lockley Arms that morning, they might have appeared no different than usual. But to themselves they were already transformed by the knowledge that by the time they made the return journey in darkness, they would be initiates of the Green Hollow Coven, full-fledged members of the Craft. A cloudless summer sky arched above the early morning stillness, unbroken except by birdsong and the whisper of tires from cars passing along the shady village street. Behind its emerald hedge the Arms rose dazzlingly white in the sun. As they walked up the driveway, Shelley was irresistibly reminded of that long-ago June morning, twin to this one, when she had defied Mother's rule and crossed Willow Street to retrieve Kip's baseball. Reminded of a longhaired girl who had taken her hand to guide her safely back. *Sometimes the prize can be worth the risk.*

Jessica sent them to Snow's office as soon as they arrived, and she looked up from her desk as they entered. "There you are. Did you eat breakfast?"

When they nodded in bewilderment, she smiled faintly. "I'm asking because that will be your last meal today. You'll be required to remain upstairs, by yourselves. You'll each be given a room. Try to think of this day as like being between the worlds, a space out of time. Do your best to put all your present worries and distractions aside, to think as clearly as you can about the past year, and about the future." Her smile had faded; she looked serious and, Shelley thought, inexplicably sad as she went on.

"I want you to be certain this is what you want. Let me warn you, it'll be a very long day. You'll be bored and hungry; you'll hear the rest of us outside laughing and talking, having a good time while you're stuck inside by yourselves. All your doubts will surface. And I want you to take a careful look at them. Do you understand?"

They nodded solemnly. In silence Snow picked up her ring of keys from the corner of the desk and led the way out of her office and up the stairs. The twins followed, not looking at each other. Shelley was already aghast at the prospect Snow had described, and as they climbed the stairs she began to calculate the hours of isolation ahead. It was not quite eight in the morning now. The banquet was usually served around eight in the evening—but they would be fasting, so that meant no banquet for them—and the rite would not begin before ten . . . Her spirits plummeted. *Fourteen hours.* Fourteen long hours locked in—had Snow said they would be locked in?—a room with nothing to do, no books to read, no one to talk to . . . while the others spent the day enjoying company and glorious summer weather. It wasn't fair.

All your doubts will surface. And I want you to take a careful look at them. Shelley glanced guiltily at Snow's back as they reached the third floor. The ordeal had not even begun, and already her doubts were in full swing. She pushed them away. She could do this. Face a little boredom, a little hunger, a little isolation for the sake of what was to come.

Snow unlocked a door and motioned to Kip. Shelley saw their eyes meet as he stepped across the threshold: the room was the one Jonathan Blackbridge had used during his visit. Was this a reminder to Kip of his folly with the scrying box? He closed the door gently behind him. Shelley noticed that Snow didn't lock it, and in some measure that was a relief. Then it was her turn. The tower room. Was this too a message of some kind? Snow's eyes were unreadable. *All your doubts* . . . And then the door closed behind her and Shelley was alone, with the day stretching ahead like an endless shimmering desert she had no choice but to cross.

It was an instructive experience, in which I had frequent thoughts of Benjy—locked in a prison cell not for a single day, but for what had now been nearly a fortnight—as I went through what I assume must be a more or less standard sequence for prisoners. I paced. I stood at the window. I lay down on the bed and tried to fall asleep, but the sight of the white canopy overhead, pricked by sunlight, made me get up and pace some more.

Snippets of the unattainable outside world intruded to torment me, as Snow had promised they would. I saw familiar cars enter the driveway and disappear beneath the porte cochere. I heard doors opening and closing, the sound of footsteps, voices calling cheerful greetings, laughter close by in the hall and then diminishing down the stairs. I bit my nails methodically, got a drink of water from the bathroom, stared at my own face in the mirror. At one point I heard a scratching at the door and opened it a crack to find Rowan outside. Since that night in the park I had been unable to think of him as just a cat, but I was tempted to let him in; his purring presence would have been a vast comfort. Still, I knew Snow would not approve. "You can't come in. I'm being initiated tonight," I said to the cat, and received a lengthy stare before he turned and stalked away.

Do your best to put all your worries and distractions aside, to think as clearly as you can about the past year, and about the future. A lifeless heap of feathers with one outflung wing. A joyous spiral dance beneath the stars. A young boy murdered, another barely rescued from the same fate. The distant silvery call of a hunting horn. A malevolent shadow menacing the village streets. Broomriders swooping and soaring on the wild wind. A hooded silhouette looming against an exploding sky. Secrets. Danger. Magic. A wheel endlessly turning, its colors now dark, now bright.

I thought of Snow, racked with sobs in Gwynneth's embrace. Elymas's eyes, wise under wild white brows. The poppet surrounded by dazzling light. There was a clock on the mantelpiece, but after the first hour I had turned it to the wall, resolved not to watch the time pass even if I had to hear its ticking. Listening now, I could hear no sound in the house beyond that small, measured beat. On the wall the pattern of sunlight shifted as a breeze stirred leaves outside the window. A breath of warm, flowery air touched my face. I felt my first hunger pang.

What was Kip doing now? Meditating no doubt, with perfect concentration, letting the hours slip past him unnoticed. I sat in a chair and tried to empty my mind, but my stomach kept growling, and each time I succeeded in clearing my head of words, pictures insisted on pouring in to replace them—images of the coven members outside in the perfect summer's day, sitting around the pool. The scene came to me with astounding clarity, as if I possessed some mental periscope that could focus around corners and through walls. There was Silkmoth, chatting with Indigo at the shallow end. Tamarack was doing slow laps through the water while Reed, Grimalkin, and Senta played cards. Gwynneth sunned herself on one of the canvas lounge chairs; Archer sat beside her reading a newspaper. Snow and Elymas walked along the perimeter of the hedge, deep in conversation. Andreas hadn't arrived yet. Or had he? Squinting through my imaginary telescope I could make out someone swimming underwater. Not Andreas; the skin was too light—and then the swimmer surfaced and shook his wet head, and I saw it was Kip.

I became aware of a sensation like some cold, viscous fluid slowly filling the chambers of my heart. Had he simply walked out of his room to join them? Was that the reason for the laughter I had heard? Was I being a fool, a dupe? . . . was this some sort of test to see if I was stupid enough to imprison myself voluntarily for an entire day, without food or company, when I could walk out the door of my room at any time and join the others? Had Kip passed some test that I had failed? The cold spread outward from my heart, chilling my whole body. I stood abruptly—went to the door—hesitated, my hand on the knob. Was this a trick concocted by my bored brain? But the image had seemed so clear . . . and the idea of Kip enjoying himself outside with the others, while I stayed here and proved myself a fool in the process, was too much to bear. I opened the door and peered into the hall. Empty: all doors closed along the shadowy corridor. As I stood listening, poised on the threshold of my room, the unbroken silence in the house convinced me of the truth of my vision—that I was the lone occupant. I started down the hall toward the stairs. But as I passed Kip's room, some faint lingering doubt made me stop and look inside.

There was movement at the window as he turned toward the sound; I had a blurred impression of his astonished face. "Shelley! What are you *doing*?"

I was too stunned to speak. He crossed the floor swiftly and pulled me inside, shutting the door. "We're supposed to stay by *ourselves,*" he hissed.

"I know . . ." My head was whirling; black spots came and went before my eyes. I couldn't think what had made me imagine such an absurdity—that Snow would tell us to remain alone all day and then expect us to violate her instructions. Nothing in my experience of the coven had led me to expect such double dealing. Where had it come from, that bout of temporary insanity? Kip's scowl softened. "What's going on?"

"Nothing. I just . . . I thought maybe you'd left."

His lips twitched. "Left? And gone where?"

"I don't know. Outside, maybe. With the others."

"The others? We're supposed to stay inside, alone. You heard what Snow said. It's part of our initiation."

We were standing close together. I knew I should step back, away from him, but I didn't. The emptiness of the house seemed to swirl around and around and then settle over us like a great billowing cloak. Just the two of us, here on the top floor, the two of us and no one else. I saw Kip swallow. My heart was beating hard; at the edge of my vision the bed hovered, an indistinct shape halfway between dream and reality. Then Kip lifted his hand and the movement broke my trance. "I'm not supposed to be here," I said. "I better go back to my room."

He nodded.

Twenty minutes past one: that was what the clock on the mantel said when I returned to the tower room and peeked at its face. Not even the halfway mark, and already I had come perilously close to ruining everything, not only for myself, but for Kip as well. I returned to my pacing, refusing to think about what had almost happened. Instead I recalled the lyrics to every song I knew and sang them to myself. Recited nursery rhymes, tried to predict the number of cars that would pass on Willow Street while I counted to one hundred. Mounting hunger pangs provided a distraction for a while, taunting me with thoughts of Jessica's bread pudding, duck with blackberry brandy sauce, hot flaky breakfast croissants and plump fruit pies—dozens of individual dishes and entire meals to which I had not done justice in the past. Nor was this review limited to

Jessica's fine cooking: the greasy hamburgers served at the Pig & Whistle, Mister Softee's frozen wares, and even the grim ghost of Marty's mangled pancakes appeared to haunt me. Eventually my stomach subsided into sullen silence while I watched the light change and mellow outside, yielding to green shadow on the lawn below. The sky's blue turned to gold, then to violet, deepening until the treetops showed only in dark silhouette. A few birds called in the shadowy distances. I saw the first lightning bug.

Around me the house began to stir once more with footsteps and voices. Doors opened and closed along the hall; a faint sound of running water came from next door. The tower room lay deep in shadow, but I felt no impulse to light the lamp. I sat slumped in the armchair, more tired than I would have believed possible from a day spent doing nothing, and let time wash over me like warm surf over an exhausted swimmer. At long last I had run out of thoughts—or at least those that would bear inspection—and my mind mirrored the room around me, dim and still.

When the knock came, startling me back to awareness, I was surprised to see it was full dark outside. I had no sense of what time it was. The door opened and a faint qualm went through me as I saw a robed, hooded shape against the light from the hallway. A soft voice said, "Are you ready?"

I swallowed and stood up on legs that prickled with pins and needles. How long had I been sitting? The house was silent. Light from the windows patterned the lawn below. Once the robed figure entered the room, I recognized Grimalkin. "It's time, Shelley." She handed me a soft bundle: my robe, wrapped in its cord. "I'll wait for you in the hall."

As I undressed I thought of last Midsummer Eve, a year and a day ago, when Kip's outrageous prank with the pie had earned us apprenticeship in the coven. Or rather not the prank itself, but his persistence. Snow's words: *This is the third time they've asked.* The number three, a number of power to witches. Found in the phases of the moon—waxing, full and waning, symbolizing the three faces of the Goddess: Maiden, Mother, Hag. In the triple cycle of life, death and rebirth. In the solemn warning to all workers of magic: *Whatever you send returns threefold, good or bane.* Knotting the silky red cord around my waist, I joined Grimalkin in the hall. Two more robed figures waited at the top of the stairs: Kip and Elymas. Together we descended in silent procession. As we passed through the entrance hall I glanced into the dining room, noticing that the tables had not been put together in their usual banquet configuration. So there had been no feast tonight; the others had joined us in our fast.

Outside, the full moon flooded the sky with silvery light. Crickets' song, rustle of leaves, murmur of moving water as we crossed the footbridge above the brook: only these sounds were audible, the gentle breathing of the summer night. The latch on the gate leading to the pool gave a faint metallic squeal as Grimalkin ushered us through, and I caught my breath at the sight within. On the surface of the lit water floated dozens of roses, saturating the night air with their tender perfume. All at once I was keenly aware of Kip standing beside me, both of us naked beneath our robes. My hands shook as I fumbled with the cord at my waist—seeing, out of the corner of my eye, him doing likewise. As I moved toward the water I felt Grimalkin touch my arm and heard her soft warning. "Mind the thorns."

The water slid like cool silk over my skin. I swam out beyond my depth and let myself sink to the bottom, rising only when no more breath remained in my lungs. All around me, roses floated dark on the moonlit water. *Mind the thorns.* I shook back my wet hair and looked around, not seeing Kip; and then the surface rippled as he appeared out of the depths beside me.

"Here. This is for you." A dripping rose: he thrust it into my face. A sneeze took me just as I reached for it, and I felt a quick jab of pain in my thumb. "Ow!"

"What happened?"

"Thorn." I sucked it, tasting blood.

"Let me see." His hand reached for mine.

"It's okay. It's nothing." I could see Elymas and Grimalkin standing like sentinels on either side of the gate leading to the meadow. "They're waiting," I said. "Let's go."

There was no blindfold this time. Our hands were tied loosely in front of us with the cords from our robes, and accompanied by our guides—the coven's oldest members leading its newest—we passed through the gate and made our way to the fire blazing at the center of the meadow. My head was light and buzzy, my body numb except for the throbbing pain in my thumb. The scene ahead, fire surrounded by shadowy figures, wavered and swam before my eyes. I couldn't feel my legs, but they must have carried me forward automatically, because the fire grew steadily closer and then we were there.

We were there. I stumbled, recovered, and looked up to find myself staring straight into the eyes of the Lady, high priestess of the coven. I could find no trace of recognition there, only clear silvery depths continuing forever. Abashed, I lowered my own gaze and saw the point of the athame poised above my heart. In contrast to the wicked, shining blade her voice was soft.

"You who stand on the threshold of the Ancient Ones, have you the courage to enter here? For know it is better to fall on my blade and perish now, than to make the attempt with fear in your heart. How come you to this circle?"

Gwynneth had coached us on the response to this question, and now I heard my quaking voice repeat the required words. "In perfect love and perfect trust."

The blade was lowered. "Who sponsors this candidate?"

Grimalkin stepped forward to stand beside me. "I do."

Snow grounded the point of the athame in the earth, took my hands and drew me into the circle. I waited, shaken by occasional fits of trembling, while she repeated the ritual with Kip. Grimalkin and Elymas untied our hands. We took our places at the stone altar and Snow faced us.

"Have you chosen a name by which you wish to be known to your brothers and sisters in the Craft?"

This was a dilemma that had caused me, over the past ten days, whatever anxiety I could spare from worrying about Benjy. Every name I could think of had struck me as either silly or pretentious, and to make matters worse Kip had apparently selected his with ease, although he had refused to tell me what it was. Now he said, "Strix."

Strix? What did that mean? My lips were numb. Snow's glance flicked over me; she seemed to be waiting. My thumb gave a throb of pain. I whispered, "Thorn."

"Strix and Thorn, a year and a day have passed since you came to us as apprentices. In that time you have learned something of our Craft. Do you still wish to join us?"

"Yes."

"Will you suffer to learn?"

"Yes."

She touched the blade of the athame to my palm. There was a sting, a welling line of blood. Grimalkin stepped forward with the cord from my robe and pressed it against the wound. Elymas, I saw dazedly, was doing the same for Kip. He used the cords to measure us from head to toe, then severed them with the athame and handed them to Grimalkin. Snow was speaking.

"In the name of the Mother, I now renew the marks I gave you, and name you witch, member of the Green Hollow Coven." Swiftly, with annointing oil, she traced the symbols of pentacle and triangle on my skin, then on Kip's. Our hands had already stopped bleeding. "Repeat after me. I do most solemnly renew the vows I made before this gathering, a year and a day ago this night.

"I swear to honor the Goddess and the God.

"I swear to hold the coven workings sacred.

"I swear never to reveal the name of any coven member to anyone outside this assembly.

"I swear to obey the Law of our Craft: *An' it harm none, do what thou wilt.*

"All this I swear of my own free will—on my hope of future lives, mindful that my measure has been taken, and in the presence of the sacred spirits of earth, air, fire, and water."

As the murmur of our voices died away there was only the crackling of the fire. That faint sound seemed all that tethered me to the earth, as if my substance might drift apart like smoke at any moment. I felt Grimalkin strip off my robe, put her hands on my shoulders and press me, naked, to my knees. Snow knelt beside me, putting one hand on my head and the other beneath my heel. Through my daze I was aware of the light pressure of her fingers on my skull as she spoke. "All between my two hands belongs to the Goddess."

A tingling jolt shot through me, bathing every nerve in exquisite fire. I gasped and put my hands on the ground to steady myself. She was doing the same to Kip now, and I saw his eyes widen. Then Elymas and Grimalkin were raising us to our feet, wrapping our robes around us once more. Snow handed us our newly cut cords.

"In the Burning Times, when each member of the coven held the lives of the others in her hand, these would have been kept and used against you, should you endanger others. But we live in more fortunate times—so take your measure and keep it, and be free to go or stay as your heart leads you." When we had retied the cords around us, she took our hands and turned us to face the others.

"God and Goddess in all your guises, Guardians of the Four Directions, witches of the Green Hollow Coven—behold Strix and Thorn, and bid them welcome to our number. On this joyful night, hear the words of the Star Goddess, the dust of whose feet are the hosts of heaven, whose body encircles the universe:

"I who am the beauty of the green earth and the white moon among the stars and the mysteries of the waters, I call upon your soul to arise and come unto me. For I am the spirit of nature that gives life to the universe. From me all things proceed and unto me they must return.

"Let my worship be in the heart that rejoices, for behold—all acts of love and pleasure are my rituals. Let there be beauty and strength, power and compassion, honor and humility, mirth and reverence within you.

"And you who seek to know me, know that your seeking and yearning will avail you not, unless you know the Mystery: for if that which you seek, you find not within yourself, you will never find it without. For behold, I have been with you from the beginning, and I am that which is attained at the end of desire."

There was one moment's perfect silence in which even the fluttering of the fire died away. The moon shimmered in the depths of the night sky. Across the still meadow I seemed to catch a faint drift of melody: *La, la . . . La, la . . .* soundless and wordless, enigmatic as an archaic smile, nonsense syllables that seemed, as I listened, to echo Snow's final words. *I have been with you from the beginning, and I am that which is attained at the end of desire.*

The circle stirred. Suddenly we were the center of a throng of embracing arms, smiles and murmurs of welcome. A cup of wine was passed around; Silkmoth began to play a soft tune on her flute. There were gifts for Kip and me, symbolizing the four elements: an athame for fire, a cup for water, a feather for air, a flat stone chiseled with a pentacle for earth. "Strix?" I said to Kip as we stood together. "What's that mean?"

"It's Latin. A kind of owl."

I stared at him, then winced as Andreas squeezed my hand in congratulation. Surprised, he bent to inspect the cut the athame had made across my palm.

"It's not that, it's my thumb. I pricked myself on one of the roses in the pool."

He peered at my thumb, grimacing. "Part of the thorn's still in there. Hold still while I pull it out."

The sight of the fresh blood brought Snow over to where we stood. "What's this?"

Andreas showed her. Snow looked from the black, wicked point to my face. "Thorn. Now I see." Examining the wound, she seemed distracted, clasping my cold fingers briefly in her warm ones before turning to face the others. "I need your attention, my friends." They quieted at once and she went on. "Tonight is a Sabbat, and as such should be dedicated to celebration and not to business. But this community is facing an emergency. The so-called Green Hollow Kidnapper is still among us, and now an innocent man has been accused of his crimes."

She looked around at the circle of serious faces. Her hood had fallen back and the moonlight spilled its shadowy radiance on her head; her eyes were shimmering pools of silver light. A chill ran over me as I remembered what Elymas had said: *It was obvious from the day Snowden joined us that she was the Goddess's choice.* Looking around at the faces of the others I saw them transfixed as well.

"Tonight, with the initiation of our two new members, the Green Hollow Coven stands at full strength once again. We have tried in the past to end this evil, with only limited success. But tonight we have a full complement of power to bring to the task. It's Midsummer Eve, the longest day of the year. The moon is full. The Goddess is with us." As she held out her hands to us I could see pale light pulsing between her fingers. "The time is right. Let us seize it, to work such magic as we have never worked before."

Chapter 24

Such magic as we have never worked before. The prospect of confronting that terrible faceless assailant who had held Kip and me so completely in his power—even with the protection of the entire coven, I wanted to turn tail and run. But it was too late now. The faces of the others were serious and purposeful and I tried to align my features with theirs. Magic. Not a trick, not a game, but a physical force: pure energy, summoned and shaped at will. A double-edged weapon fully capable of destroying those who wielded it. And in the wrong hands, a tool for deadly harm. *Did you ever think maybe the Lockleys' deaths weren't an accident?*

People were moving into position now, reforming their circle around the fire. I saw Snow remove her robe and let it fall to the ground. All around me, the others were doing the same. Only minutes ago, kneeling naked in front of the group for my dedication to the Goddess, I had been too dazed to feel self-conscious, and now I was too frightened. I bent my head to loosen the knotted cord around my waist, shrugged out of my robe, and looked up to see that the firelight had worked a magic of its own. The scene before me possessed a startling, primitive beauty. Snow had moved to the center of the circle. Around her stood a wreath of nude human figures with hands linked, like a fragment of ancient pottery rendered in tones of umber and flickering gold.

Our breathing rose into the night air, forming a ceaseless rhythm that smoothed the surface of my mind like sand on a glistening beach. For a long time there was nothing but its hissing, hypnotic tide. And then gradually it began to change—almost imperceptibly becoming an eerie, wordless vowel-chant like the hollow moaning of wind that precedes a storm.

Steadily it built, a low *oooooo, ooooooooooooooo* that renewed itself layer upon layer until the air within the circle hummed with tension, until I could feel my bones beginning to vibrate in response—all at once shooting unexpectedly up the scale to a vivid, keening wail. Cold sweat popped out on my skin as my hearing seemed to expand outward to encompass all my senses: each striation of tone and texture registered its own shape and color, smell and taste upon my brain. And still the sound mounted, curdling the air as it swelled, growing ever harsher and more strident—a bedlam of yammers and yelps and howls that suddenly resolved into an unearthly harmony pouring irresistibly into the contained boundary of the circle. And still we chanted, summoning the power.

The air had begun to thicken and take on substance, and suddenly I could see it moving, a luminous spiral surrounding a pale figure with a shining blade in one hand. In my fragmented glimpses of Snow's face I scarcely recognized her: she looked fey and wild, a daemon born of that sizzling funnel of air. It made me dizzy to look at her, but I couldn't tear my eyes away from the whirling brightness. As the voices rang louder and louder in my ears, sound and light merged at last into one vast whirlpool within whose chanting radiance I seemed to catch fragments of words, rising to the surface for an instant before sinking back into the maelstrom.

Conjure . . . I conjure . . . I conjure thee . . . The syllables lingered in my ears, echoing and overlapping, forming a dizzying babble that grew louder, then louder still, finally drowning out the voices of the coven. *I conjure thee. I conjure thee.* My surroundings blurred; the circle of figures grew dim as phantoms. Suddenly afraid, I fixed my eyes on Snow's bright shape—but as I watched, it too began to flicker and fade until suddenly it winked out like a snuffed candle, and I was alone.

But not quite. Kip was with me; I could feel his hand in mine. We seemed to float in an indescribable darkness that might have been purple, or deep blue, or a crimson denser than black. Where were we? What had happened to the others? Somewhere in the darkness there was a distant glow like burning coals, an odor of foul-smelling smoke. Slowly I became aware of a hollow voice speaking as if from a bottomless void.

By the breath within me, by the earth of my flesh, by the water of my blood, by the flame of my desire, I conjure thee. By the hosts of all things celestial, of all things terrestrial, of all things infernal, I conjure thee. Come. Come. Come.

The repeated word seemed to jerk us forward like a rope around our necks. By the red glow of the coals we could make out a crooked opening in the smoky darkness—and within it, the silhouette of a tall, hooded figure. As a shudder of recognition seized me, the voice spoke again.

A feast for fire and a feast for water; a feast for life and a greater feast for death. By the seven seas of the earth, by the four fires of RIL, YUT, SAR and LOD, I invoke and command thee: Show thyselves.

We hovered at the threshold of that jagged doorway. Within it we could see our black-robed summoner standing within a crude circle chalked on the ground, leaning over a brazier of burning embers. He looked up. I caught an avid gleam of eyes far back within his shadowy hood as he flung his arms apart, sleeves unfurling like predatory wings.

Welcome. Have no fear. The sacrifice of blood has always been a part of magic. The weapons of the Magus fulfill the

Wheel: with dagger and cup he preserves and destroys, and together the two make one. One, like the two of you—one spirit divided by flesh, yearning to be whole.

What was this place? How had we come here? We seemed to stand as we had in the circle—side by side, our hands clasped—and somehow I knew our physical bodies remained there still, in the world of flesh and blood. But that world was infinitely far away, overshadowed by the hooded shape before us, with its murmuring, seductive voice.

One perfect whole. Joy and sorrow, light and dark, life and death. Only mortal flesh divides you. Relinquish it, and your spirits will burn as a single flame.

As that last phrase struck through me I felt my whole being shiver like a bell. *A single flame.* The two of us no longer two but one. *A single flame.* The beckoning arms drew us forward. Like a half-forgotten dream I remembered Snow saying, *After everything that's happened, don't you understand the children of this village are in danger? How can we protect you if you won't cooperate?*

Protect us? It was the coven who had sent us here: in a flash I understood that. Hadn't I heard Jonathan Blackbridge say it in plain English? *Why not offer him something you know he wants? Your two young apprentices.* This was their will; they had used the chant to open the way. Words whispered in my memory. *How Witches do Offer Children and Babes to Devils.* Were we being offered as a gift, to appease this apparently invincible enemy against whom they had struggled for so long? Exacted as tribute by a dark power greater than their own? As the winged arms opened wider, we could see his heart pulsing like an ember within those black folds. All his weapons, the secret arts with which he had protected himself until now, he had set aside to welcome us. We would never again see our family, our friends, the coven who had betrayed us on the very night of our initiation. But we would be one. When we crossed the boundary of his circle, the fragile connection between us and the physical world would snap; already it was taut with the strain. He was waiting for us; I could hear the obscene rasp of his breathing. As we reached the circle's edge, his voice rose to a scream.

"NUIT! HADIT! THERION! BABALON! Omnia in duos, duo in unum, unus in nih—"

Without warning the words were obliterated by a deafening, ululating howl that rose out of the darkness. Savagely it swelled—vast, inhuman, relentless. Like a shrieking torrent of flame, a wind of grinding stones, the coven's voices swept through the narrow space between Kip and me to engulf the hooded figure who stood frozen, arms still open in welcome.

Abruptly I found myself standing in the witches' circle, dazed and disoriented, my ears ringing and my hands locked to Kip's and Gwynneth's on either side. What was happening? My gaze found Snow at the center of the circle: I saw her fling both arms suddenly up and out—and as light leaped from the point of the athame to explode against the night sky with a blinding blue-white burst, at the center of that stunning brightness I seemed to catch a brief glimpse of a crooked opening and a dark shape crumpled within it. What was that? Where had I seen it before? For an instant the sense of recognition hovered, then slipped away.

Even though we had eaten nothing since breakfast, neither Kip nor I did more than pick at the supper the coveners offered us before we left the Arms that night. We should have been tired out. After all, we had spent the whole day in solitary confinement, followed by our initiation and our first magical working with the coven. But even though it was past midnight when we got home, we weren't ready to go inside. We sat on the porch steps in silence, watching the lights go out in the windows of the Arms. We knew something extraordinary had happened in the circle—something so extraordinary that our minds, in order to protect themselves, had already hidden it away. Here on the steps of our own house, a few moths fluttering around the porch light, it was just an ordinary summer night.

At last we went in. Upstairs, I undressed and got into bed to lie staring tensely at the ceiling above. Against the darkness I seemed to see a crooked opening . . . I sat up suddenly and the image disappeared, but I found myself drenched in sweat, my nightgown soaked through. I threw back the covers and turned on the lamp. The image was gone now, along with any hope of sleep. Maybe a bath . . .

At this hour no one was around to accuse me of hogging the bathroom and I soaked in the tub for a long time, keeping the water as hot as I could bear. The wound in my thumb was still painful, but at least it had given me a witch name. "Thorn." I repeated it to myself in a whisper that seemed to echo off the tiled walls. I wasn't certain I liked it, but it had come to me of its own accord and I supposed it would do.

At last I climbed out of the tub, cleaner if not noticeably more drowsy than before. My nightgown was still damp, so I tossed it in the hamper and wrapped a towel around me for the journey back to my room. Light was visible beneath Kip's door: he opened immediately to my soft tap. He was wearing a pair of white boxer shorts and nothing else. Seeing his eyes take in the towel, I tucked it more closely around me. "You took a bath?" he said.

I nodded. "I couldn't sleep."

"Me neither. I did fifty push-ups, but it didn't help."

"You did *what*?"

Suddenly the two of us were helpless with laughter we couldn't contain. Afraid of rousing the sleeping household, I fled across the hall to my room and he followed, yanking the door shut behind him just as we exploded into laughter. I clutched at my towel to keep from losing it altogether; my knees went weak and I sat down, spluttering, on the end of the bed while Kip collapsed snorting against the pillow. Afraid of being overheard even with the door shut, we did our best to smother the laughter; tears ran down our faces and we wiped them away, gasping for breath, only to be assaulted afresh by another eruption of mirth.

Gradually, with diminishing tremors, the laughter died away. Kip looked down the length of the bed at me, eyes gleaming behind his damp lashes. Suddenly I was very much aware of being naked beneath my towel. Of the closed door of my bedroom, and the stillness of the house around us. All else seemed to fade from existence in that moment. A strange phrase floated into my head. *Burn as a single flame.* That flame seemed to tremble inside me now, spreading a delicious weakness through my limbs. My heart thudded in my ears. My fingers no longer seemed capable of holding the towel, and I let it go.

I saw Kip swallow. He reached over to the table beside my bed and turned out the lamp, and moonlight poured through the window, a shimmering silver waterfall. From the darkness beyond the waterfall he stretched one hand through the stream of light, his tentative touch burning my skin. I closed my eyes, heard him draw a long quivering breath and softly exhale my name. "Shelley . . ." The bedsprings creaked faintly as he moved closer. I felt him brush the towel aside.

If he had been as impatient as most boys his age, it would all have been over in a few moments, and in that case everything might have turned out quite differently. But he was in no hurry. The May Eve rite had been his first and only sexual experience, and to him this act had been defined as a mystery. *Where light and dark, joy and sorrow, life and death meet and make one.* I suppose, before Beltane, he must have had the same crude fantasies as any other teenage boy. But that night had burned all trace of them away. He knelt before me on the bed. His fingers traced the contours of my face and moved slowly downward to define each susceptible curve and hollow of my body. Those questing, discovering hands aroused in me an expectancy that was almost too keen for pleasure, their every touch evocative of some dreaming darkness we had shared before birth. And his face was a dreamer's, lips parted and gaze blinded by moonlight. We kissed, the merest grazing of our mouths. There was a brief hiatus while he struggled out of his shorts, and then he knelt before me again.

The phallus, sacred symbol of the God, sower of the seed of life, and possessed of a will of its own, beyond Kip's control. As I took it gently in my hand he gasped and bowed his head. He seemed too young, too tender to sustain the pulsing, forceful object in my grasp, and at the core of my own consuming need I felt a kind of pity, a yearning to console him . . .

Marty must have knocked several times, but we were too absorbed in what we were doing to hear her. When my bedroom door opened abruptly, the spill of brightness from the hallway hit us like a bolt of lightning. Kip dived beneath the covers; I snatched up my towel and clutched it in front of me, blinking in shock at the figure silhouetted against the light from the hall and hearing my aunt's outraged whisper. "How dare you, Shelley! How dare you! Behaving like a—a tramp! And under your parents' roof!"

I could not speak. I was aware that disaster had struck, but beyond that my thoughts had jammed. Her quaking whisper continued. "I don't even want to know who that boy is! But if he isn't gone from this house in five minutes, I promise you I will call the police!"

When the door had closed, cutting off that paralyzing illumination, the meaning of her words slowly reached me. The bed lay mostly out of the light's path, in shadow. She hadn't seen Kip's face. He poked his head out from under the sheets. "She didn't know it was me," he whispered.

I was shaking from head to foot. In all the time I had been inhabiting my two very different worlds, the entrancing one of the Arms and the drab one of everyday, they had remained separate until this moment. In the world of family and school, neighbors and proper behavior, there were dozens of rules about what to do and not to do—when to do it and how—what people might think or say. Within the bastion of the green hedge that surrounded the Arms there was only one rule: *An' it harm none, do what thou wilt.* Now, at Marty's unexpected appearance, those two worlds had violently collided, and in the shock of their impact I saw my behavior through her eyes. Here I was, naked in bed with a boy. Good girls did not do that sort of thing. And it horrified me even more than it had horrified Marty—because I knew, as she did not, that the boy in question was my own brother. Kip chose that moment to put his hand on my arm. "It's okay," he whispered. "She didn't know."

I jerked my arm away. Behind his words a tiny singsong

voice inside my head was saying, *A girl's good reputation is her most precious* . . . "Kip, you have to get out of here. Now."

"Okay, but we should make it look like somebody left the house. After I get back to my room, you go downstairs. Open and shut the back door, in case she's listening. You know, like you're letting out Mister X."

I mustered a nod. He found his shorts and pulled them on. "Listen, Shelley, I—"

Her most precious possession. I turned away. "Let's make sure she's not waiting out in the hall."

The hall was empty. At the far end Marty's closed door was like an ostentatiously averted gaze. I nodded to Kip; he dashed across to his room. When he had disappeared inside I fumbled my bathrobe on and started down the stairs. In the kitchen, following his instructions, I opened the back door to let out my imaginary lover, closing it again decisively for the benefit of any listening ears. Then I started back upstairs. I wanted only to go to bed, pull the covers over my head and try to forget I had ever been born—but Marty was lurking on the landing, a shadowy figure in curlers and a quilted robe. "Oh, Shelley, how could you? How *could* you? I thought you had more sense!"

"I'm sorry, Marty."

"I never imagined . . . I just wanted to make sure you'd gotten home all right . . . and then to find you . . . Shelley, this boy—do you love him very much?"

My mouth tasted like glue. I nodded mutely.

"Well, if he loves you, he ought not to take advantage of you. Do you hear me?" It was too dark to read her face, but I could hear from her voice how distraught she was. "Have you—gone all the way with him?"

I shook my head.

"Well, thank God for that. I want you to promise me you won't. Promise me, Shelley. And that will be the end of it. We'll never mention it again."

"I promise," I said dully.

Chapter 25

Exhaustion must have caught up with me at last, or maybe sleep simply offered a convenient refuge from an unendurable situation. In any case, I slept right through my alarm the next morning. When I woke at last, the pattern of sunlight on the wall of my room was unfamiliar. The clock, when I rolled over to look at it, showed nearly eleven. I swore and jumped out of bed. Why hadn't someone awakened me? As I dived for my dresser, my foot caught the bath towel lying on the floor, and the memory of last night returned with shattering force. What had we done? In the light of day the recollection froze me with shame. Not just because Marty had walked in on us, or what she had said to me, but because the standards of the everyday world had cast their shadow over our actions—and in that shadow, what had seemed perfect and right became indecent and disgusting.

An' it harm none, do what thou wilt. The Wiccan Rede, witchcraft's only law. But on this side of Willow Street, where Marty had discovered Kip and me in bed together, there were other laws. Laws that forbade such things. *A girl's good reputation is her most precious possession. She has to look out for herself. One impulse, one little mistake can ruin her whole life.*

What would people say if they knew? My perfunctory dose of Protestant Christianity had given me little real sense of sin, but a conventional middle-class upbringing had left me in no doubt that certain kinds of behavior were unacceptable. Certain things were wrong. And behind those things lurked others, hazy taboos never forbidden outright for the simple reason that they could not be mentioned. One of those taboos was incest.

Another—I thought of the sunlit tower room at the Arms, with its white-canopied bed. Ghostly legions of good girls and nice people formed scandalized ranks around me. Again I saw Marty's hurt, bewildered face. *I don't even want to know who that boy is.* What would she say if she knew? If she knew about Snow and the tower room, or the other things I had done? How I had joined a witches' coven. Lied, both implicitly and explicitly, to my family and my friends. Violated every rule of proper behavior Mother had worked so hard to instill, blithely tossed aside conformity to embrace the occult. Stood naked in a circle beneath the moon and vowed loyalty to forces the conventional world would consider primitive and profane. Sworn to honor the workings of the coven, even while the word *cursing* still rang at the back of my brain—even while I had known that somewhere out there, someone most probably trained in the Craft was murdering children. What had I been doing? Wandering in a fog, blindly following Kip's lead without thinking. Suddenly it seemed I was viewing my own actions clearly for the first time—judging myself as other people, my family and friends and neighbors, would judge me if they knew.

I would be condemned.

Shelley threw on a shirt, shorts and sandals, and dashed downstairs at breakneck speed. Mother, vacuuming the living room rug, looked up as she tore past. "Shelley—?"

"I'm late for work!" she yelled over the horrific noise. "Why didn't somebody wake me?"

Mother gestured feebly with the whining nozzle. "Marty said you worked very late last night. She thought we should let you sleep."

Shelley ran out the front door, letting it slam behind her. The Arms lay quiet in its haze of sunlit green across the street, the stillness absorbing her footsteps as she ran up the drive. A glance into the parking lot showed her the familiar assemblage of cars, but the kitchen was deserted—and the dining room, and the parlor. In the entrance hall she stood still, listening to the silence in the house.

Where was everybody? Here was her chance to escape: walk

out the door, go back across the street and forget all about this secret world with all its risks and dangers. Couldn't she just go off to college in the fall and pretend none of it had ever happened? Even now, the thought was like dropping into a void. A noise from the rear of the house took her down the back hall to find Jessica clumping up the cellar steps with a basket of clean laundry on her hip. The housekeeper greeted her cheerfully. "There you are. You'd best go out to the pool—that's where the rest of them are. You never saw such a sleepy bunch."

"I'll go up and do their rooms," Shelley said.

"No, you will not. You'll relax and take it easy, like they're all doing." There was a conspiratorial flicker in Jessica's eyes as she added, "I know last night was a big night for you and Kip."

Did she see Shelley wince? If so, she probably interpreted it as nothing more than a modest simper. "Really, Jessica, I'd much rather work. I got here so late—look what time it is! Isn't there something I can do?"

"I never saw such a girl for working. All right, if you really want to do something, you can hang these curtains in the parlor for me. Royce got them so filthy while he was fixing that loose window, I had to wash them. I know he did it on purpose just to aggravate me." She handed over the lacy bundle, soft and still warm from the dryer. "Goddess bless, Shelley, we both know I'm not built for climbing. Look in the hall closet. There's a ladder in there."

Grateful for any task, Shelley set up the ladder beside the parlor window, taking care not to smirch the curtains even though she was certain Jessica's imagination had supplied most, if not all, of the dirt Royce had supposedly gotten on them. Clutching them to her chest with one hand, she had reached the top of the ladder when she heard footsteps coming down the hall from the back of the house. She glanced down and saw Kip in the parlor doorway, looking surprised. "Hi. What're you doing in here?"

Shelley turned her back on him and reached for the brass curtain rod above the window. His presence made her whole body feel raw, every nerve exposed. "Working."

"But everybody's out by the pool."

"Then go out there."

"Aren't you coming?"

She didn't answer. She couldn't concentrate with him watching her. Why didn't he just go away? She tried to thread the curtain onto the rod and found her hands shaking too much. A muted note of music made her jump: he had wandered over to the piano and touched a key. "Kip, would you *stop* it?"

She saw him flinch. He came to the foot of the ladder and stared up at her reproachfully. "What's the matter with you?"

"What's the *matter*? You're asking me what's the *matter*?"

He looked down at his feet, then up again. "Look, I know you're upset about last night . . . but Shelley, Marty didn't know it was me. She didn't have any idea."

Upset about last night. Last night. Last night he had come into her room uninvited, turned off her lamp, touched her in ways no decent brother would ever touch his sister, blithely escaped all blame, and now—a sudden surge of fury seemed to rock the ladder beneath her. "Oh, then it's okay! It's okay so long as Marty doesn't know it was you! Well, good. Fine. I feel much better now!"

Kip's face had gone pale. "I didn't mean—"

How dare he look that way—so hurt and confused, when it was all his fault? Not just last night, but all of it—everything, from the very beginning. Forgetting her precarious position Shelley turned violently away from him, lost her balance and flailed out with both arms. There was a sharp crack, a tinkle of falling glass. A searing pain flashed across the back of her right arm above the elbow. She would have fallen if Kip hadn't grabbed her leg with one hand and steadied the ladder with the other.

By the time she was able to grasp what had happened, it was already over—and there were Jessica's freshly laundered curtains, lying in a heap on the floor below. As she watched, a series of bright red drops began to appear on their flawless white.

"You cut yourself," Kip said unnecessarily.

Shelley lifted her arm. The sight of the blood, dripping steadily from the point of her elbow, made her head swim.

"Oh," she said. Awkwardly she descended the ladder to solid ground, trying to ignore the fuzzy black spots swimming busily back and forth in front of her. Kip seized one of the curtains and started dabbing at her arm. "Kip! Jessica just washed these!"

"Well, she's going to have to wash them again anyway." He was holding her injured arm and she snatched it away. "Get your hands off me!"

"For crying out loud, Shelley—"

They were too distracted to hear anyone coming down the stairs, nor did they notice Snow in the parlor doorway until she spoke. "What's going on?"

Both of them jumped. There was a brief pause before Shelley muttered, "I broke the window. I'm sorry. I didn't mean to."

A smile flitted across Snow's exhausted face. "Well, thank you so much for clarifying that." Noticing the blood, she came swiftly toward them. "And you cut yourself. Let me see."

Kip moved out of her way. She blotted the wound—using Jessica's hapless curtain again—and examined it with a frown. "This could be worse, Shelley, but it needs tending. Kip, can you clean up the glass? And let Royce know about the window?"

He nodded silently.

She took me upstairs and we stood at her bathroom basin while she probed the cut for fragments of glass, then dressed it with gauze and tape. We did not talk during this process. When it was over Snow said, "I want you to lie down for a while, and keep that arm up. Come."

As I lay back on her bed, my head swam and I wished I could just keep on sinking—through the bed and the floors below and into the earth itself, down and down and down to a place where nothing mattered. Slowly my head cleared. Snow was putting a pillow beneath my injured arm. Once it was arranged to her satisfaction, she sat on the edge of the bed and said, "I'm going to ask you a personal question. You don't have to answer it."

I slid my gaze away and waited, the way I imagined Marie Antoinette waiting for the blade's swift descent.

"Are you and Kip lovers?"

The tears had been ready since last night. I tried to cover my face with my hands, but Snow caught my right wrist and replaced my arm on the pillow. Then she simply waited. When I stopped crying, she offered me a tissue and I blew my nose awkwardly. "No," I mumbled. "Marty walked in on us. Before anything really happened."

"When was this?"

"Last night."

Snow let out an audible breath. "I see."

"She—she called me a tramp."

Her face did not change, but my good hand was taken and squeezed. "And Kip? What did she say to him?"

"She didn't see who he was. She thought he was just some"—my voice cracked and I tried again—"just some boy I brought home with me." Resentment rose to the top of my general misery. "And it was all his fault, Snow! He came into my room. He—"

"Are you saying he coerced you?"

In her clear gaze I saw myself in a towel, tapping at his door. I bit my lip. "N-no. But—"

"But what?"

"It would have been *incest*."

"That's just a word," she said. "So long as there was no coercion on either side—"

"But it's still wrong!"

"Conventions serve various purposes, Shelley—political, economic, social, psychological—but they aren't absolutes in themselves. Certain acts are intrinsically evil, yes. But for the most part, ideas about right and wrong can change radically with the era, the situation, or the people involved. Use the Rede as a touchstone. If you're in doubt about something, ask yourself what harm it will do."

I squeezed my eyes shut and heard a shrill echo in my head. *How dare you, Shelley! How dare you!* Opening my eyes I faltered, "Marty was pretty upset . . ."

"But it's really none of Marty's business, is it? So let's discount her, and for good measure we'll say no child would have been conceived. Given those conditions, I want you to tell me. What harm?"

What harm? If anyone had found out—our parents, friends, the neighbors—but I knew what Snow would say to that. Suppose Marty hadn't come in, then; suppose things had continued along the course on which they were headed. I thought of Kip's dreaming eyes, the moonlight in his tousled hair. The irresistible longing to mingle my whole being with his, like two streams flowing together. *Have you gone all the way with him?* We had been taught that such things were wrong. But the feeling in those brief moments had been overwhelmingly right.

"Indigo and Reed are sister and brother," Snow was saying. "Did you know that? They've been lovers since they were teenagers."

I swallowed. "But Marty made me promise—"

Her brows went up. "Wait, Shelley. Wait. Please don't misunderstand me. I'm not telling you to go on and do it; in fact, I think it's for the best that it didn't happen. Not because it would have been wrong in itself. But because some situations are simply best avoided."

"But—"

"Please let me finish. Your feelings about Kip are already confused enough without complicating them further. It would be much wiser if you didn't become involved with him in that way." She hesitated and then went on. "Don't blame yourself, or him, for what happened last night. The energy we raise to do magic is so volatile that it's difficult to ground it afterward, so it simply seeks another outlet."

But would other people be so understanding? I clung to Snow's hand and mumbled, "It just made me think about . . . what other people would say . . . if they knew, I mean."

"It's always important to pay attention to your doubts."

"That's what you told us yesterday. But I shouldn't have doubts anymore, should I? Not now that I've been initiated?"

Her face was grave as she looked down at me. "You're going to find the testing never stops," she said. "For as long as you practice the Craft, you will constantly question your commitment to it. Unless you're willing to challenge your belief, you will never learn to trust it. This is not a passive path, Shelley. Not the kind of thing where you make some initial effort and it's enough. If that is what you want, you will never be happy as a witch."

She left me then, with a last squeeze of my hand, and for most of that afternoon I lay drifting in and out of sleep, my drowsy brain reviewing the past twenty-four hours in disordered flashes. My emotions were a tangle. On the whole I was reassured by Snow's calm acceptance of both my doubts and the incident that had triggered them—but the warning in her final words persisted like a faint but ominous shadow across my heart.

When dusk began to fall, I roused myself and went downstairs. Jessica was in the kitchen preparing a summer feast for the coveners, a huge pot of ratatouille and loaves of crusty French bread. Kip was in the dining room, putting the tables together. I still didn't want to be near him, so I hovered around Jessica instead. "Can I help?"

"No, you can't. You need to rest that arm. Sit down at the table and stay out from under my feet."

Having missed both breakfast and lunch, I was starving. The delicious smells from the stove put me into a kind of trance, from which a shout from upstairs abruptly awakened me.

"Mercy!" Jessica stopped, holding the pot lid poised in midair. "What was that?"

"I think it—" Before I could finish, it came again—a hoarse shout that sounded like Archer. From the dining room next door we could hear Kip charging toward the stairs. I jumped up from my chair; Jessica clanged the lid back on its pot, and together we dashed after him. She took the stairs too slowly and I didn't wait for her. Whatever had prompted the shout, I had a vague impression that it conveyed triumph rather than disaster. Reaching the second floor I heard the noise of the television down the hall in the common room, and turned in that direction. Through the door I could see the others crowded around the set, obscuring the screen. An invisible commentator was talking.

"—miraculous break in the Green Hollow kidnapping case, when an apparently routine complaint about a disturbance of the peace led to the arrest of the man who has held this part of New York State in a nightmare grip for the past nine months."

My heart leaped. I craned my neck to see the TV; Indigo noticed me at her shoulder and shifted to give me a better view. Surveying the faces intently focused on the screen, I saw expressions ranging from angry satisfaction on Archer's to deep sadness on Grimalkin's. Snow's eyes were black, her mouth a bloodless line. Jessica appeared in the doorway, panting from her climb, as the newsman on the screen shuffled a handful of papers, adjusted his glasses on his nose and fixed the camera with a solemn stare.

"Near midnight last night, residents at the northern edge of Green Hollow heard what one of them described as 'a god-awful racket' issuing from the woods behind the warehouse of a local mail-order business, Janicot Books. Police, called to investigate, followed the sounds to find an elderly man lying at the entrance of a cave in the throes of a seizure. A search of the cave indicated he had apparently been living there, and among his belongings police found a green T-shirt with the word 'Slim' on it—the T-shirt eleven-year-old Alex Leonard was wearing on the evening he was kidnapped last October. Hidden in the woods not far away was a rusty white van matching the second kidnapping victim's description of his abductor's vehicle."

The newscaster's image gave way to a blurry scene of woods, the camera jerkily panning the trees before focusing on several holes that had been dug in the ground, dirt piled beside them. A shovel leaned against a tree. "Although the suspect has been unable to offer any coherent answers to police questioning," the newscaster's voice said, "less than an hour's worth of digging in the area of the cave revealed a partially decomposed body that medical evidence has identified as the missing boy." The camera moved closer, homing in on a pitifully small hole in the earth, then pulled back to reveal a reporter standing in the foreground. I recognized pudgy, baby-faced George Horn of Albany's Channel Six.

"To those families whose homes adjoin this tract of woods, it will come as a shock to learn that the feared Green Hollow Kidnapper has been living practically in their backyards for months, perhaps even watching their children at play. And the shock will doubtless be heightened by an unofficial statement from the Albany medical examiner's office early this afternoon, to the effect that the young victim's heart had been removed from his body."

I heard Jessica's sharp intake of breath and saw Senta put a hand over her eyes, but the reporter's words scarcely registered on me. I was staring at the mouth of the cave, on which the camera was now unwaveringly focused. In my mind I was seeing a dark hooded outline framed by just such a rough opening. *A feast for life, and a greater feast for death.* The words whispered in my head, turning my skin to gooseflesh and stirring the hair on my scalp. For an instant I seemed to hover in some gray twilight place with Kip, feeling the focused power of the coven coursing through us—and then the memory slipped away and I became aware once more of the TV screen in front of me. The newshounds were gorging themselves on what they termed "the shocking finale to the Green Hollow kidnapping case." The Leonard family was unavailable for comment. Daniel Chaffin's mother broke down and wept when told of the fate her son had so narrowly escaped. Her tearful face was replaced by that of an older newscaster, looking appropriately grave.

"The suspect, whose identity is not yet known, has made no statement since his arrest. He is currently being held without bail in the Albany jail, awaiting medical and psychiatric tests. Meanwhile all charges against Benjamin Russell Hendricks, earlier a suspect in the case, have been dropped and he has been released. Channel Six has been unable to reach Mr. Hendricks for comment." He cleared his throat and rattled some papers in front of him. "In other news this evening . . ."

Around the television we all stirred as if waking from sleep. "It's over," Archer said. "It's finally over." There was a murmur of assent. Someone turned off the television and the group drifted downstairs to the dining room, where Elymas opened wine and poured some for each of us.

"To the Green Hollow Coven." He raised his glass to the faces gathered around him, then turned to Snow and raised it higher. "And to its Lady."

A murmured response came from the others; there was silence while everyone drank. The deep red wine ran smoothly down my throat. Gwynneth lit a few candles along the table and people sat talking in twos and threes. The atmosphere was more subdued than I would have expected; there was a grim satisfaction in the air, but I could detect no real sense of triumph except when my gaze accidentally encountered Kip's and he flashed me a dazzling grin. As I returned a guarded smile, my injured arm gave a throb of pain. All at once exhaustion overwhelmed me; I leaned back in my chair and closed my eyes. When I opened them again, Grimalkin was there. "Are you all right, Shelley?"

"Just tired."

"Yes." She took the empty chair beside me. "I think that goes for us all."

I studied her face, trying to glean some trace of her thoughts. The sudden transformation of that fearsome hooded shape to a nameless old man living in a cave in the woods was somehow anticlimactic. Over the past months there had been moments when, in spite of everything I had been taught, I had thought him a devil, a demonic spirit. Who was he really? A renegade witch, as Kip suspected—a sworn enemy of the Green Hollow Coven, who might even have murdered the Lockleys? If so, and the coven had at last triumphed over him, shouldn't the atmosphere be one of rejoicing? "Everyone seems sad," I said tentatively.

Grimalkin sighed. "That poor young boy—"

"But it's over now."

"Yes, it's over." She spoke absently, turning her glass between her hands.

"Grimalkin? Who is he?"

The glass stopped turning. She didn't look at me. "An old

adversary of ours. You deserve to hear the story, and someday you'll be told, I promise. But not tonight."

My thoughts, heated by the wine, were a muddle. An old adversary . . . so Kip was right. He must have killed the Lockleys. The others had continued to struggle against him—and now, when triumph had come at last, the credit had gone elsewhere. It irked me that the coven had been cheated of the recognition they deserved; I wanted to show Grimalkin that I, at least, grasped the magnitude of what had been accomplished. "It's a shame people don't know the coven is here, protecting them," I blurted. "If they knew, they'd thank us."

I suppose I hoped my clumsy attempt to cheer her would replace her melancholy expression with a smile. And it did, briefly; but not the appreciative smile I had anticipated. Instead her lips twisted in an ironic grimace that chillingly evoked her portrayal of the Hag at Halloween.

"I'm not so sure of that. But in any case, Shelley," and her face softened once more into its familiar gentleness, "in any case, they must never know."

Chapter 26

The remainder of the summer passed with dizzying speed. The annual Fourth of July celebration, it was agreed throughout the village, was the best ever. The parade down Main Street, the bunting and fireworks all seemed to celebrate the capture of the Green Hollow Kidnapper along with national independence—but to the twins the rowdy spectacle could not hope to compare with their first Esbat, a night of full-moon magic between the worlds.

Meanwhile Benjy Hendricks was back at work behind the

counter of the E-Z Stop, just as if his arrest had never happened. Everyone wondered, of course, why he had refused to cooperate with the police, or offer any explanation of the marked map in his pocket—but he stubbornly maintained his silence on these matters. Stopping by the store, Shelley found him barely responsive to her efforts to be friendly. At last he said gruffly that he had appreciated the letter she had sent him in jail. She knew better than to tell him it had been written at Snow's suggestion, but she couldn't resist mentioning, in a vague and roundabout way, that the people at the Arms had believed in his innocence all along.

At that he looked up, scowling. "Oh, can it, Shelley! You know how I feel about those *wonderful* folks at the Arms. It was mighty big of them to think I didn't do it. It cost them zilch. And that's how much good it did me."

"That's what you—" She clamped her tongue down painfully on the *th* in *think* and subsided into silence, but he had already turned away. *It cost them zilch.* Her memory of Snow's exhaustion in the aftermath of the spell brought a hot sense of injustice that Benjy would never know what the coven had done for him. Yet he could never be told. That fact was painfully clear.

The Lammas Sabbat came and went. Shelley's freshman orientation was scheduled for the first weekend in September, and Mother and Marty were already starting to fuss about clothes and supplies. At the Salvation Army store in Woodston, Dad purchased a battered footlocker for her belongings, and she quickly grew to hate its yawning presence in one corner of her bedroom. No matter how many times she might repeat to herself the formula that she would be coming home often, she could not shake off a sense of irrevocable departure.

"But you'll be coming home weekends." As usual, Kip was able to pluck the thought straight from her brain. He was keeping her company while she packed, ostensibly to cheer her up but looking as gloomy as she felt.

"It won't be the same. I won't be working at the Arms . . ." She couldn't help feeling a smoldering envy for him: after all, he had another whole year before he would have to face what she was facing now.

As her final week wound down, there were various farewells—an abortive one with Benjy across the counter of the E-Z Stop, in which he managed to drop something on the floor and bend down to pick it up, thereby rendering himself invisible as he mumbled, "Okay, so long"—a fond but fragmented one with Kate, patched together between customers on a busy afternoon at the shop—and an evening at the Pig with Jenny and Lisa and some of her other classmates from school.

She refused to allow the coven to give her a farewell banquet, as if by doing so she could deny that she was really going away. She would be coming home every weekend, after all. And so there was only the usual late supper in the kitchen with Jessica and Royce, Kip and Snow, and Rowan dozing on the counter. Although Jessica outdid herself with the food, the occasion fell oddly short of its pleasant predecessors: Snow was preoccupied, Shelley too depressed to talk, and even Kip and Jessica managed only a few halfhearted quips before concentrating on the meal. At last it was done. When Jessica and Royce had headed off to the carriage house, the other three lingered uncomfortably in the kitchen and finally said good night. Shelley stood numbly while Snow embraced her.

"We'll see you soon, won't we?"

She could only nod.

The humid September night was warm as breath, the waning moon a crumbling gold coin flung into the blackness of the sky. Crickets and cicadas sang above the ceaseless whispering of invisible trees as the twins walked slowly down the driveway. At the sidewalk Shelley stopped and looked back. The Lockley Arms. A few upstairs windows were lit, but around them the house already seemed to be fading away, its outline flickering like a phantom in the restless shadows of the trees. Her next step would take her beyond its boundaries, out of the magical world of the past two years, back to her old, prosaic existence. As a lump rose in her throat Kip's voice broke into her thoughts. "Hey, Shel. Want to go swimming?"

"Huh?"

"Come on, just a farewell swim. We won't be bothering anybody."

A farewell swim? She seized the suggestion eagerly: any reprieve, no matter how temporary, was welcome. Smothering sudden laughter, the two of them retraced their steps through the darkness—up the driveway, beneath the porte cochere, down through the parking lot. On the footbridge a drift of pine needles muffled their steps. By now the laughter had died away and they went secretly through the singing summer night. Shelley followed Kip, not allowing herself to think too far ahead. A farewell swim. Just the two of them. Across the moonlit carriage-house lawn, the gate to the pool stood invitingly ajar. They looked at each other. All at once Shelley couldn't speak, think, breathe. A farewell swim. Just Kip and her. Because she was going away, and surely she was entitled to take with her some token . . . *I want you to promise me,* Marty's voice said in her mind, and Snow's joined in. *Your feelings about Kip are confused enough already. It would be better if . . .* But she was going away, and Kip was smiling at her, and the whispering leaves blurred and distorted the warning words until they changed into a single phrase repeated over and over.

An' it harm none, do what thou wilt.

He had already started for the open gate, and she ran across the silvery grass to catch up.

And bumped into him just inside the gate, where he had unexpectedly come to a dead stop. My annoyed exclamation died unspoken as I looked past his shoulder. The pool lights had been turned off, and the dark expanse of water reflected a night sky in which clouds now obscured the lopsided gold moon. The unbroken darkness, above and below, had transformed this normally familiar scene into an unknown, measureless stretch of sky and water bordered by huge, shadowy trees. Beneath the throbbing chorus of cicadas I could hear Kip's breathing, and my own. He reached back and took my hand without turning, and together we moved like sleepwalkers toward the pool. As we reached it, the shadowy water stirred and rippled against the tiles at our feet and a voice came floating out of the darkness.

"Shelley? Kip? Is that you?"

The words reached me like a startling image in a dream that brings the dreamer, for an instant, close to waking before sinking deeper into sleep. Kip was still holding my hand. "We thought you'd gone to bed," I heard him say.

"I wasn't sleepy. Too much on my mind."

By following the sound of Snow's voice I managed to locate a pale blur in the darkness of the pool. The water lapped softly against the tiles. Unlit, it was wholly different from the sparkling substance I knew by daylight: a dim, primordial realm. She said, "Are you coming in?"

"Sure," I heard Kip say. "Why not?" His fingers tightened on mine before he released them and moved away. I stood in the darkness, my ears ringing with the insistent calling and answering of the cicadas. A farewell swim. When I heard something clink as it landed on the bricks bordering the pool, I knew immediately what it was. Kip's belt buckle. The small sound went through me with a jolt, becoming a cloudy eagerness that made me fumble at my own clothing with trembling hands until I was free of it, free to join the warm night and the cicada sounds and the invisible, waiting water.

A farewell swim. No longer two, but three. There was a splash as Kip entered the pool, and I followed before I could take time to think. The water was warm as the air; only the change in texture told me I had entered it, and the sensation of being abruptly weightless. A stream of tickling bubbles slid past my face. I touched bottom and let myself rise slowly to the surface. With my head out of water there was more to see, but not much: a night sky like a black plum, the moon a spot of smoldering yellow behind the clouds. Against the sky the shaggy treetops were faintly visible, but closer to earth everything merged into one immense shadow. The air slid softly over my wet skin. Dominating all other impressions was the symphonic song of the cicadas, swelling and fading and then returning in rapturous celebration of the summer night.

Where were the others? The darkness could not prevent us

from converging unerringly through breast-deep water: a meeting of three shadows. No one spoke. But something grazed my left hand in the water, and I caught my breath.

"Shh," came an answering whisper. Gentle fingers twined themselves in mine and squeezed. I swallowed my gasp as another hand fumblingly clasped my right. My heart was thudding; iridescent spots swam before my eyes. Only our hands were touching, but I was so conscious of my own nakedness, and the tantalizing, daunting proximity of theirs, that every random eddy of the water against my flesh was like a teasing caress. No one moved. The chanting of the cicadas seemed to grow steadily louder, filling my head and quivering along my nerves, augmenting the seductive touch of the water. Each shallow breath seemed to loosen my hold on identity, as if flesh and blood were slowly dissolving into the sensuous, fluid matrix of sound and texture around us. My thoughts started to fragment and drift. A farewell swim. Just the two of us. But somehow the two had become three. Three, a number of power. Three. The word repeated itself in my brain. Three. Three.

Three's a crowd.

Two had become three, and I was the third. The thought stung me back to awareness. *Three's a crowd . . .* Abruptly I pulled my hands free and plunged blindly away from them, arms and legs flailing as the bottom of the pool dropped away beneath my feet. All sound vanished as my head went under. When I fought my way sputtering to the surface, the song of the insects nearly deafened me. Behind their racket, and the noise of my own splashing, I could hear voices—but I kept swimming frantically, not slackening pace until I had reached the edge of the pool and pulled myself, panting, from the water. As I crouched there dazed and shivering, someone came quietly along the side toward me, someone whose wet bare feet made scarcely a whisper on the bricks. I didn't turn to look. Someone knelt behind me and whispered my name.

I couldn't answer. Arms encircled me from behind; hands carefully, tenderly cupped my breasts. I turned my head; his mouth was there and we kissed. Droplets fell from his wet hair and ran down my skin. As I leaned back against him I could feel the reckless tempo of his heartbeat matching my own. My shivering had died away; now it began again.

And then other hands were there, gently parting my legs. All that was visible in the water below me was the serpentine swirl of her floating hair, her body hidden beneath the surface as if she were an undine, some elemental spirit only half materialized in human form. Between my unsteady thighs I glimpsed an arrowhead of darkly gleaming water, and then her head moved to fill the gap.

Fire, born of water. On every side the leaves rose whispering to join the soaring crescendo of cicada song. High in the night sky, clouds drifted across the moon. Kip knelt behind me, his erection trembling against my hip, and my fingers closed around it of their own accord while my other hand sought the darkly streaming waterfall of Snow's hair. Enveloped by the sovereign rhythms of the insects, the sighing trees, the ceaseless lapping of the water, we were no longer three, nor two, but one—one at last in the irresistible embrace of the summer night.

Ensure that your actions are honorable, for all that you do shall return to you threefold, good or bane.

——The Standing Stones Book of Shadows

Chapter 1

Shelley scarcely registered her transformation into a college freshman. She was fuzzily aware of the drive from Green Hollow to Albany—of arriving on campus with her family—of their hovering presence and eventual departure—of her new environment of unfamiliar faces and huge impersonal buildings—but all these things seemed mere shadowplay perceived through the lingering daze of that night by the pool. It was only as the memory of that interlude began inevitably to fade, and the present to intrude its demands, that she awoke to her own misery.

What was she doing here, without Kip, away from the coven and the Arms? What was the point of being surrounded by strangers, condemned to a tiresome round of pointless activity, when everything she cared about was located elsewhere? Doggedly she went through the motions of participating in her new existence, but it was like being a ghost, adrift in a featureless gray limbo in which now and then faces floated close to hers and then withdrew, or booming, invisible voices uttered statements she could scarcely comprehend.

"The *Odyssey* simply ignores the historical developments between . . . The chain of circumstances leading to action typically begins outside . . . The Black Death was the most lethal disaster of recorded history, killing about a third of the . . ."

Her roommate was a tall girl named Helen, even more desperately shy than she was; neither could keep a conversation going beyond a few lame sentences. In the dead interval before the dining hall opened for supper, Shelley mimed absorption in her studies while thinking only of the coming weekend, when she could go home. Time had slowed to an unnatural crawl. She had arrived last Saturday; months had passed, yet it was only Wednesday. As she glumly contemplated the prospect of two more endless days, a girl stuck her head into the room. "Is one of you Shelley? You've got a phone call."

In the dormitory corridor she pulled the phone booth door shut, isolating herself from the noise and bustle outside. "Hello?"

"I'm not supposed to be calling you yet," Kip's voice said. "Snow said we should give you time to settle in. But Reed and Indigo got here a little while ago, and she's out by the pool with them, so I sneaked inside." A conspirator's chuckle sounded in her ear. "How's college?"

Unexpected pride made her say, "It's okay."

"Just okay?"

"It's fine. Just tell me what's happening there."

While he obliged she closed her eyes and savored each word, concentrating fiercely until the faint voices outside the phone booth became those of the guests at the Arms, talking and laughing as they gathered in the parlor before dinner. Mouthwatering aromas floated down the hall from the kitchen; the mirror in the entrance hall reflected a silver bowl filled with roses . . . As her homesickness mounted, Kip's cheerful voice became an affront. How dare he sound happy? Didn't he miss her at all? "Listen," he was saying hurriedly. "I'd better go. I just heard Snow in the kitchen, and I don't want her to catch me. She made me promise not to bother you this week. See you in a couple days."

The line clicked and he was gone. Shelley sat staring at the booth's scribbled walls. So quickly, just like that, consolation had been wrenched away. *I'm not supposed to be calling you. She made me promise* . . . The words murmured in her ears, rousing a rush of self-pity. Didn't they care how miserable she was?

When Friday arrived at last, a friendly sophomore who lived across the hall accosted her in the bathroom with an invitation to a party that evening.

"I can't, Mindy. I'm going home right after my last class."

"Going home? You just got here!"

"I want to see my friends."

"Golly, Shelley, what about making some new friends? Listen, you can do both. Go to the party tonight, catch the bus tomorrow morning. Come on—Paul's a good friend of mine, a really nice guy. You'll have a great time. He's a junior, he's got an apartment off campus with some other guys. The party's gonna be really fun."

Refusal on her lips, Shelley felt her pride rally. What kind of figure would she cut, crawling home with her tail tucked, when they didn't miss her, didn't care how she felt? If she were to arrive tomorrow, with some airy reference to her busy social life . . . "Okay," she said.

As it happened, Paul wasn't a nice guy at all. He had a greasy crew cut and a low sniggering laugh, and prominently displayed on a table in his living room was a large pickled rattlesnake in a jar. He spent most of the evening hunched over his elaborate sound system, fiddling with the controls while the speakers blasted an endless succession of deafening rock songs. The party was rowdy and booze was abundant, but in spite of Mindy's glib promise of new friends, the music was too loud for any conversation beyond a few shouted phrases.

"Hi! Name's Bill! What's yours?"

"Shelley."

"Sally?"

"Shelley!"

"Wanna dance, Sally?"

The dancers formed a heaving sea from which some gasping survivor was occasionally cast ashore to stumble blindly for the bathroom. Shelley danced with Bill, then withdrew to a corner of the room to watch, sipping at a gin and tonic someone had handed her.

The drink, and several more, smoothed the harsh edges off the music and lent a semblance of conviviality to the hullabaloo. Another boy asked me to dance and we plunged into the fray, but the deafening thump of the music and the press of sweaty bodies struck me as a kind of pitiful parody of the witches' circle. I imagined the expressions on the drunken faces around me if I were to tell them about the turning of the Wheel, the Horned Hunter, the Triple Goddess who nurtures and slays. I closed my eyes, feeling alienated and extremely sorry for myself, and when I opened them again, Paul was dancing with me.

This was surprising, since he had more or less ignored me since my arrival nearly three hours before. As the music changed to a slower song, couples drifted together. By that time I was feeling dizzy and vaguely sick, and when Paul put his arms around me I shut my eyes and leaned against him. He could have been a tree or a telephone pole for all I cared; my whole body was numb, tongue to toes. My brain had begun to loop and dive like a daredevil stunt plane, and my stomach attempted a series of clumsy imitations. Each time I opened my eyes the stunts grew more daring and complicated, so after a while I kept them closed.

The next thing I knew, I was leaning against a wall. The noise of the party was still going on somewhere, diminished in volume. There wasn't much light. Not too far away I could hear the faint but unmistakable sounds of someone throwing up, then the gurgle of a toilet flushing. A door opened at the far end of a corridor, revealing a bathroom, and a dark shape lurched out. In the spill of light from the open doorway, I discovered Paul unbuttoning my shirt.

"Stop," I mumbled. I tried to push him away, but my arms were rubbery and weak. "Don't," I said. He didn't answer, just continued what he was doing, staring past me and breathing audibly through his mouth. Someone else went into the bathroom and slammed the door, leaving us in relative darkness. Paul smelled like beer, cigarettes and stale sweat. He reached inside my shirt.

Into my fuddled brain came the memory of Larry, my tormentor from the Arms. As Paul's clammy fingers touched me I heard Gwynneth's voice inside my head. *You must know what you want, know you can get it, and focus on it completely. Your desire becomes real by force of will.*

I sucked in a deep breath. My mind felt heavy and sodden as a wet towel, but the image I needed was there somewhere, buried in the towel's thick folds, and I struggled to uncover it. It was difficult to concentrate, because I was distracted by the continuous fumbling battle between my hands and Paul's. Where was the image I needed—the image of my desire? I could perceive its general shape, but the details eluded me. Again and again I almost grasped it, only to feel it slip away. And then I had it. Larry's thick body outlined in dazzling blue-white light.

Your desire becomes real by force of will. I placed my hands against Paul's chest and focused. Nothing happened.

He simply shoved my hands aside and pushed closer, breathing hard, and I was so stunned by my unconditional failure that I just stood there and let him rub against me. I don't know what would have happened if some person desperate for the bathroom had not suddenly started hammering on its closed door with a noise like thunder. Startled, Paul stumbled back and I managed to duck free.

It was the first time I had ever been really drunk. I spent the remainder of that night—Mindy and I got back to the dorm around three—slumped on the floor beside the toilet, racked by spells of vomiting that ended at last in dry heaves. A blurred memory throbbed continually in my head: Paul pawing me in the corridor, and my wretched failure at using magic to repel him. By the time my stomach was willing to call a truce, there was light in the sky outside the bathroom window and I could hear cheerful voices as a group of early risers passed by on their way to breakfast. Breakfast . . . the mere thought sent me diving for the toilet again. At last I staggered to my bed and fell into a fitful sleep.

Just past noon Mother called, wanting to know when I would be coming home. Queasy and exhausted from the short trek to the phone booth, I closed my eyes and concentrated on the sensation of the cool receiver against my cheek. "I can't this weekend. It turns out I've go a lot of studying to do. I was just on my way to the library."

"All right, dear. We'll hope for next weekend, then. Don't study too hard."

"I won't."

On my way back to bed I remembered Paul again, and my abortive attempt to defend myself. What had gone wrong—where had I failed? The paralyzing sense of helplessness came back to me, and with it the nausea. I made a dash for the bathroom.

On Sunday afternoon, when I was finally beginning to feel human again, Kip called. "What's this studying thing? Why can't you study here?"

"I wasn't really studying. I was sick. Don't tell them at home."

"Sick?"

"I had a hangover. There was a party. I got drunk."

A pleased snort sounded in my ear. "You got drunk?"

"It's not funny. It was awful."

"You're telling me! Frog and I got drunk once at Clinton-Monroe, when somebody smuggled in some beer. Did you throw up?"

"Yes." Even after nearly forty-eight hours, the recollection still brought a twinge of nausea.

"Poor thing." Did he have to sound so cheerful? Didn't he possess a heart at all? "You should've come home," he was saying. "Gwynneth and Andreas showed up and so did Elymas and Grimalkin. Jessica made us a special banquet in the dining room after the other guests were done. Cornish hens, wild rice—"

My stomach gave another warning twitch. "Do you mind not mentioning food?"

"Oh, sorry. Anyhow—" His voice rattled on while I listened, willing the queasiness to go away. Gleaming wineglasses and snowy tablecloths, candlelight on faces so familiar I could conjure them as he talked. And he had been there in the midst of them, not even missing me, while I . . .

. . . while I, powerless to defend myself, had been letting

some drunken creep paw me in a dark hallway. Again the flattening force of the memory swept over me. What good had all my training done, all my hours of practice? I had made no magic. I had made a fool of myself, that was all. If I had told Paul what I was trying to do, I would have had more success: he might have died laughing.

"And for dessert Jessica made this incredible cheesecake—"

"Kip, for crying out loud! I just asked you not to talk about food!"

"Sorry, sorry. I forgot about your hangover."

The breezy apology infuriated me. At that instant, when I was lonely, homesick, envious, hollow with failure, his thoughtlessness seemed proof he cared nothing for me all. "Well, call me back when your memory improves!" I said, and hung up on him.

Later, when I felt a little better and consequently less sensitive, I tried to call him back. The telephone provided a link, however unsatisfactory, with home—and I needed that link more than ever now that I had so stupidly condemned myself to another whole week of exile. Next Saturday seemed an infinity away, and my hands were unsteady as I gave the operator the telephone number of the Arms and deposited the proper coins. There were various clicks, a few rings that sounded painfully distant, and then a crisp, cool voice said: "Lockley Arms."

I stammered, "Snow?"

"Shelley?" Her voice changed immediately, took on color and warmth. "Is everything all right?"

"Y-yes." Suddenly I was on the edge of tears. "I just . . . I couldn't come home this weekend because . . . because I had a hangover."

"Oh?" Did I detect amusement in that short syllable? "Are you feeling better now?"

"Yes. Well, not really." Pride had done me no favors so far; I abandoned it and blurted, "I hate it here, Snow. There just doesn't seem to be any point to anything. The classes are boring. And the people—"

"What about them?"

"I don't know, they're just not like . . . well, you know. The people I'm used to."

"Well, I think that's the idea," Snow said. I could hear her smiling. She didn't understand, or didn't want to. *I'm not supposed to be calling you. She made me promise* . . . With an effort I choked back my complaints and changed the subject. "How's everyone there?" I said. "How's Rowan?"

"Rowan and Jessica aren't speaking. She caught him licking the butter this morning."

"And the weather? It's kind of cold here."

"You know Green Hollow. It's been perfect. I swam this afternoon."

"And the others?" I said. "Who's been to visit?"

"Let's see, who's been here since you've been away? Grimalkin and Elymas came last night, along with Gwynneth and Andreas. Indigo and Reed were here, I think it was last Wednesday—"

As she talked, I clung to the sound of her words. Had I really been away only a week? A week of crushing loneliness, boredom, alienation—topped by the hangover and the humiliating memory of what had happened with Paul. "Snow, can I ask you something? Remember what you did to Larry?"

"Larry?"

"That guy who was bothering me that time, in the dining room and then later, outside? You—"

"Yes, okay. I remember. What about him?"

"Well, there was a guy at the party the other night. Paul. And he was . . . well, and I tried to do what you did to Larry. And nothing happened."

There was a pause. Then she said, "What did he do?" The flat menace in her tone brought the image of her across the dining room, one hand at her throat while Larry choked and started to turn purple. Hunched there in the dormitory phone booth I experienced that remembered qualm of mingled awe and fear. "Oh, you know," I muttered.

"Specifically," the cold voice said.

"It doesn't matter, I got away from him. But it was luck, not magic. I . . . tried my best. But—"

"But Shelley, you can't do magic if you're drunk." To my

relief she sounded like herself again. "How could you possibly expect to focus? Now tell me. Are you going to be seeing this Paul person again?"

"I hope not," I said fervently.

"I hope not too."

"There's a big dance next Saturday, but he probably won't go. Anyway, I won't be there either—next weekend I'm not letting anything keep me from coming home."

At the other end of the phone there was a heartbeat of silence. Then I heard her say, "Maybe you should give the dance a try. You might meet someone nice. They can't all be like Paul."

"Go to the dance?" Surprise made me stammer. "B-but next weekend's a Sabbat!"

"There'll be other Sabbats. And you shouldn't skip the chance to do something you might enjoy. You might start having a better time if you put a little more effort into it."

A little more—! How could she possibly say such a thing? All at once I felt betrayed, ambushed. "I don't feel like putting any effort into it," I said.

"That's exactly what I mean."

She sounded almost like Mother. *You shouldn't skip the chance to do something you might enjoy. There'll be other Sabbats.* "Are you telling me not to come home?" I said, still unable to believe what I was hearing.

"Well . . . wouldn't it be wiser to wait?"

Wiser. Her favorite word. A blistering sense of rejection made my voice crack as I said, "Are you *banishing* me?"

I heard her sigh. "That's a little melodramatic, don't you think? All I'm suggesting is that you try to get more involved in your life up there, instead of focusing on what's happening here. It would be good if you could hang on until, say, Halloween."

Halloween—! At her end of the line, there was a familiar squeaking noise and I pictured her closing the French doors to the fading autumn garden. Homesickness flooded me, intensified a hundredfold by the shock of this sentence of exile. Tears stung my eyes. Halloween was six weeks away. "After all, you just got there," she was saying. "You have to give it a chance."

"Why?" I said. "I told you, Snow, it's awful. The people I've met—all they care about is parties and grades and trying to impress each other with how much they've been around. If I tried to talk to them about the things that matter to me, about anything *real,* they'd think I was crazy."

She made a sympathetic sound. "I know it's hard. But you haven't given it a chance, not really. Don't close your mind so soon. You can't just decide, at age seventeen, that you know exactly who you are and what you want from life."

"But I do know."

"You can't possibly. You're too young."

"I'm older than you were when you joined the coven," I said.

The words seemed to speak themselves. There was a pause, somehow frightening, and my heart started thumping as I imagined her eyes going black. Then she said evenly, "Well, I hope whoever gave you that piece of information also told you that, when the time came, Everett insisted I spend four years at a British university. And that however many tantrums I threw at the time, I am now glad he stood firm."

This conversation had somehow gone wrong; but even as I floundered for the words to make it right, I had a satisfying sense of having thrown her off balance. She didn't like the idea of anyone discussing her with me, and her annoyance made her vulnerable. This evidence of shortcoming was strangely exciting; I think it was my first inkling that I was ready to challenge her, although I didn't recognize it then. "But you came back to the coven," I said faintly.

"Yes, I did." The words were clipped. "But I came from knowledge, not ignorance. I knew what I was giving up, and what I was getting. And that is what I want for you."

The phone call ended shortly thereafter, on a distinctly cool note that made it impossible for Shelley to ask to speak to Kip. Nothing further was said on the matter of her return home, but when the following weekend arrived at last, she remained on campus. Most of Saturday she spent in the library with her nose stuck in the *Odyssey,* which she was supposed to finish reading by Monday. Even though she tried not to dwell on what she considered her banishment from Green Hollow, Snow's curt words kept coming back to her. *I came from knowledge, not ignorance.* Her eyes strayed from the printed page to the fading scar the athame had left across her palm. *Will you suffer to learn?* Hadn't she suffered already? It wasn't fair.

She did not go to the dance that night. She told herself she was coming down with a cold, but the truth was that having accepted her banishment, she now took a perverse satisfaction in sabotaging its purpose. The dorm was a ghost town; everyone, even shy Helen, had gone to the dance. Shelley remained in her room, paging doggedly through the *Odyssey*. Before long she had ceased to see the lines of text. Instead she pictured the Sabbat celebration she was missing—laughing faces and leaping flames, flute and tambourine accompanying the dancers as they made merry beneath the waning September moon. Harvest Home, the autumnal equinox, when light and darkness hold equal sway. From now on the days would grow shorter and the nights longer.

And a similar process began in her as well. Over the next few weeks, she brooded over the injustice of what she continued to think of as her banishment from Green Hollow. How could Snow treat her so heartlessly? It was as if the Arms had arbitrarily become once again the forbidden citadel of her childhood, its boundaries closed to her. Kip was her inside connection during this period, and his frequent phone calls were the one thing she looked forward to. Even so they were a mixed blessing, a poignant reminder of what she was missing, and often she felt worse after she had talked to him than before. Once again the two of them had been separated, and this time she had a feeling it was by intention. *You have to find your own direction, not copy everything Kip does. Don't count on him always to be there.*

Some part of her knew she was being unreasonable. There were moments when she resolved to make the best of things. A plan to embrace her new existence was always at the back of her mind, just about to jell. She could—she would—she was going to—but these resolutions never wore the present tense. She began to spend more time sleeping, missing breakfast and often her first class of the day, going to bed early at night. She longed to dream of the Arms, as if she could visit in spirit the place forbidden her in body—but her dreams offered only the bleak present, a scrambled mishmash of trivia that drained and depressed her. Awake, her existence became a fog in which even her cherished memories of the past two years began to slip away.

I am told that many college freshmen undergo a difficult period of adjustment during the first semester. They gain weight, or drink too much—or sink, as I did, into a form of hibernation. Whether my need for sleep would have continued to expand indefinitely I do not know, because on the Friday of Columbus Day weekend I got my wish. I dreamed of the Lockley Arms.

In the dream I took the bus home for Halloween—but where the Arms should have been, I found only a vacant lot overgrown with weeds. No high green hedge, no beautiful white house—only a few stunted trees crouched here and there, the wind rattling their sparse leaves. As I stood devastated, Kate appeared and I tried to ask her what had happened, but I had trouble forming the words; time and again I had to start over because I found myself uttering only disconnected fragments from my college textbooks. While I stammered and babbled, she turned into a series of different people: Miss Cubberly from the library, my ninth-grade algebra teacher Mr. Evans, a boy named Buzzy Spencer who had sat behind me in third grade and later been killed in a car accident. By the time I managed to frame my question coherently it was Maggie, the waitress from the Pig & Whistle, who stood beside me. But she only looked blank, and said the lot had always been there, empty and overgrown.

I woke myself with my own sobbing to find dawn scarcely broken. Gray shadows lay thick in the drab dormitory room. Helen was sitting up in bed, the blanket drawn up to her chin, staring at me. Neither of us spoke. I wiped my tears with the back of my hand; the dream was still close, and so painful that I could barely breathe. At last, with as much dignity as I could muster, I said, "I've got really bad cramps."

Chapter 2

I cut my two o'clock class to catch the bus for Green Hollow that same afternoon. The nightmare had demolished my grievances and resentments, leaving only the raw need to return home and reassure myself that the Arms actually existed, that everything was as I remembered it. *It would be good if you could hang on until Halloween.* But Halloween was nearly three weeks away, and I couldn't wait that long. As the smelly bus lumbered along the Thruway, I found myself leaning forward in my seat as if by doing so I could make the wheels turn faster.

Every mile seemed like ten, but at last we began to follow the twists and turns of Route 23 toward Green Hollow. I counted off the landmarks one by one—the mailbox stenciled with a running horse, the sign for Mr. Hickey's farm, the Janicot Books warehouse marking the village's north border. Route 23 became Willow Street, lined with houses I knew. As the bus neared Main Street I strained ahead for a glimpse of the tower roof above the trees. There it was! We came to a squeaking stop at the red light, and I ran forward to the driver's sat. "Can you let me out here?"

He glowered at me. "You're supposed to get out at the regular stop. That's the Texaco on Main Street."

"I know. But can you just let me out here?"

His grunt sounded like a refusal, but the doors hissed and opened. I grabbed my book bag and bounded down the steps.

"Thank you! Thanks a lot!" As I turned to wave, I saw him shake his head.

I ran across Main Street and down Willow, straight to the Arms without sparing so much as a glance for our house across the street. At the foot of the driveway I stopped. There it was—the house with its every line and angle in harmony, white tower pointing into the clear autumn sky, windows glimmering, the lawn shadowed with gold beneath the autumn trees—all of it protected behind the high hedge that formed a bastion against the outside world. It was here; it was real. As many times as I had crossed this boundary, how could I have doubted the reality of what lay within, or believed its magic could ever fade? I ran up the driveway; the porte cochere returned my footsteps in rapid echo as I passed beneath it to bound up the back steps two at a time—and Jessica, rolling a pie crust on the kitchen counter, looked up in astonishment as I burst through the door.

"Shelley!" She dropped her rolling pin and hugged me with arms that were floury to the elbow. "I never knew you were coming this weekend! Nobody said a word!"

"I didn't know myself until this morning," I said, emerging from her cushiony embrace, laughing as I dusted flour from my clothes. It was here; it was real. I dropped my book bag on the table, just as I always had, and surveyed the kitchen, savoring every detail—the brick floor, glinting copper pans, round oak table, hint of spices in the air. "Where's Snow?"

"Out by the pool. But don't wake her if she's sleeping. She usually takes a nap now, in the afternoons."

"A nap?" I said, laughing again, giddy with relief. "Is she turning into an old lady?"

Jessica gave me an odd look. "She gets tired easy these days."

"Well, I'll just go and take a peek," I said. "If she's asleep I'll come back later."

Crossing the shady parking lot I stopped to savor my surroundings once more—the whiff of moldering leaves in the balmy air, the hazy blue vault of sky above treetops that waved russet and gold. In Albany the weather might be chilly, but here in Green Hollow it was still Indian Summer. The brook murmured lazily as I passed over it; the pine branches tickled my hair as I ducked from under them to head for the pool. Beyond the hedge came the splash of someone entering the water, and I quickened my steps eagerly. Snow was awake.

She must have done no more than jump in to cool off, because when I reached the gate she was already out of the pool, reaching for her cotton robe. She was naked. In the mellow afternoon sunshine the pool looked very different from the last time I had seen it, in sensuous summer darkness; nonetheless the memory made me hang back, eyes averted, until I had allowed ample time for her to put on the robe and tie it. Then I opened the gate and went in. "Snow!"

She glanced up at my call. The length of the pool separated us and I couldn't see her expression. But when we met halfway, she was smiling. "Shelley! What a wonderful surprise!"

As I reached for her, it seemed to me she hesitated a split second. Then we were embracing. I could feel her warm cheek against mine, the dampness of her skin through the robe's light fabric. But I scarcely noted these things, distracted by an unaccustomed thickness at her waist.

"Snow, you—" I released her and took a step back, about to make some crack about her getting fat, and felt the breath drain from my lungs as I stood looking at her, at the shape of her body and then into her face. Her eyes were shadowed and she was no longer smiling. She drew the blue-and-white-patterned robe more closely around her and said, "I was going to tell you."

"You're going to have a baby?"

She nodded, keeping her gaze steadily on mine. The next question came involuntarily to my lips. "Who—whose is it?"

"It was conceived at Beltane. So it's a child of the greenwood."

Around me the autumn trees made a lazy, lopsided revolution. I bit my lips hard, but the words broke through. "It's *Kip's*?"

She drew me down beside her on one of the canvas lounge chairs. At first she didn't speak, and in that brief interval of silence I seemed to hear, across the fall afternoon, a whispered melody. *La, la . . . la, la . . .* plaintive as a lullaby. A phrase whispered in my head: *The age-old cycle shall be renewed.* Snow's hand was on my shoulder, squeezing it gently in reproof. "How many times are we going to have this same conversation? That was not Kip, as Kip, in the circle that night. And I—"

"Why didn't you tell me?" I whispered, not listening, and saw her shoulders sag a little.

"I was going to. I wanted to tell you face-to-face."

"Is this why you didn't want me to come home?"

"Oh, Shelley. You can't possibly believe that. So why say it?"

I bit my lip. "Does Kip know?"

"Not yet. Only Jessica and Royce know, and a couple of the others. It's hardly showing yet. After Halloween I'll go away. Once the child is born, I'll come back here."

"And the child?"

"Reed and Indigo will bring it up," she said. "They've always wanted a child, but because of their relationship they can't risk having one of their own. They'll be wonderful parents. And that way I'll have the chance to know the child."

"The chance to *know* it!" I said, shocked. "You're its mother!"

A look of impatience flickered over her face. "Yes, in the strict biological sense. But my focus is the Craft. Reed and Indigo will have more time and energy to devote to a child."

My focus is the Craft. I thought of the moonlight striking the raised athame in her hand. Her face in the midst of a funnel of sizzling light. *It was obvious from the day Snowden joined us that she was the Goddess's choice.* "I don't understand," I said. "If you didn't want a child, why didn't you keep it from being conceived in the first place? I'm sure you know a dozen herbs that could do that."

"Of course I wanted it. For a child to be conceived at Beltane is a sign of the Goddess's blessing." She shook my shoulder again, harder this time. "I'm not abandoning this baby, Shelley. I'm not abandoning anyone."

I swallowed, but the lump in my throat wouldn't go down. It felt jagged around the edges, like a piece of broken rock lodged there. "You said you were going away."

"Away from Green Hollow, yes." Briefly, amusement lit her face. "I don't think the reputation of the Lockley Arms would benefit from my bearing a child out of wedlock! The official story will be that I've gone to care for a sick relative, but I'll be staying with Grimalkin and Elymas, just over the Vermont border. We'll hold the rites there for a few months." She took my hand in hers. "Archer will bring you, if you like. His home isn't far from the University. Or Senta and Tamarack—they live in Albany too."

"When are you going to tell Kip?" I said. "That it's his, I mean."

She let go of my hand. "The whole coven will be told the next time we are all together. That's Halloween."

"You're not going to tell him specially?"

"Shelley—"

"He's the father, Snow!" I said. "I don't care if the God was acting through him! It's still his baby!"

She sighed. "We're talking on two different levels. The child is no more Kip's than it is Andreas's, or Archer's, or anyone else's. It belongs to itself."

"I doubt Kip will feel that way."

"He may surprise you," she said. "I have a feeling this child may be the reason Kip and I were brought back together."

I stood up abruptly, leaving her sitting there. I hated it when they talked about their previous lives together, like some great enterprise I had not been worthy to join. Never mind if the experience had been a painful one—it was something they shared that I did not. "I have to go," I said. "I want to surprise my father at school. He doesn't know I'm here."

"Are you staying the whole weekend?"

"I'd planned to. Is that all right with you?"

She gave me a long cool look. I dropped my eyes, hearing her say, "What's that supposed to mean?"

"I don't know. You told me not to come home. To focus on my life at college. So I can find out who I am."

She was on her feet more quickly than I could have imagined, and suddenly there was no more distance between us. "Stop it, Shelley," she said softly. "I won't let you do this. Do you hear me? I know I've handled this business badly. I should have told you before you left. But now you know, and that's the end of it. It changes nothing between you and Kip, or between you and me."

She touched my cheek and I choked back a rising swell of tears. I wanted to believe her, to accept the reassurance she was offering. The similarities between this moment and the morning after Beltane were not lost on me, even down to that blue and white kimono whose pattern I can still recall. But already, on that May morning, she had been carrying Kip's child. An image formed in my mind, as mercilessly clear as those I had seen in the Samhain cauldron. A picture of the whole coven gathered together on the green lawn of the Arms, and among them a child with dark hair and silver eyes, running from one to the next while Indigo and Reed beamed proudly. Over the child's head I saw Kip's and Snow's eyes meet in a look from which I was excluded, finally and forever.

I turned away from her and ran. I heard her call my name but I kept going. Even if I had wanted to, I don't think I could have stopped; it was already too late.

Shelley ran over the footbridge, across the parking lot and down the driveway toward the street. On the sidewalk she hesitated, uncertain where to go. Not home—Mother would be there, and her company would be unbearable right now. And not to school to find Dad, because that would mean the chance of encountering Kip. Even this brief inactivity was intolerable: she needed to move, to put distance between herself and the Arms. She started walking toward the corner, turning blindly when she reached Main Street. Her head was whirling. She had no destination, no agenda, and only the sketchiest idea of her surroundings; if she encountered anyone she knew, she must have looked right through them. Certainly she scarcely heard the horn blowing in the street, much less connected it with herself, until the sound of her name broke through her distraction at last.

"Shelley! Hey, Shelley!" A shiny blue pickup truck had pulled over to the curb; Benjy Hendricks was leaning out the driver's side window. "How's it going? Home for the weekend?"

She nodded, staring stupidly at him. Slowly her eyes took in the truck. It looked brand-new. "Nice truck," she said automatically.

Benjy's eyes lit; he patted the dashboard tenderly. "Yeah, I just bought it a couple weeks ago. Hey, want to take a ride?"

Without a word Shelley went around to the passenger side and climbed in. Benjy put the truck in gear and continued down Main Street. In a daze she watched the familiar buildings pass. On the radio Elvis crooned "Love Me Tender" at low volume; Benjy hummed along as they passed the E-Z Stop, the Pig & Whistle, the Texaco station. Gradually the signs of his good mood penetrated her fog. At least somebody was happy. With an effort she roused herself to say, "This is nice, Benjy. You must have been saving a long time."

He shook his head and grinned. "You kidding? I'da never saved enough on what Charlie pays me. No, Shelley. I'll tell you something you're not gonna believe." He flashed her a quick glance. "This was a present."

"A present?" she said blankly.

"Think I'm lying? I don't blame you. I still pinch myself every time I get behind the wheel."

They were leaving Green Hollow, heading west along the road toward Pine Glen, and in spite of herself Shelley couldn't help remembering the map the police had found in Benjy's pocket, and the inked circles he had never explained. She pushed the disloyal thought away. "What are you talking about?"

He laughed. "It's crazy, but I swear it's true. Shelley—I've got a secret benefactor."

"A *what*?"

"You heard me. Listen. In the middle of August I get this

anonymous letter telling me I've been accepted for the fall semester at SUNY Albany. Fees, room and board, everything—it's all taken care of. All I have to do is show up. There was even a goddamn campus map. I couldn't believe it. Me, with a secret benefactor. Ain't that a pisser? I thought for sure somebody was playing a trick on me. But Charlie told me, hey, maybe it's true, man, go check it out. So I—"

His voice went on while Shelley gaped at him, consumed with amazement. A secret benefactor sending him to college, to . . . "You're at the University, Benjy?" Had she managed to miss him in the crowds? "How come I haven't run into you?"

He snorted. "I went up the first day and poked around. Then I got an idea. Why not go to the bursar's office and ask for my money back? Of course, it wasn't really my money, but, hey . . . well, I thought they'd laugh in my face. But they handed it right over—here you go, sir—just like that. I went out and got the truck the next day."

"Wow." Shelley could muster no other response. The idea of Benjy with a secret benefactor, the thought of what a difference his companionship would have made these past weeks—

"Charlie thinks I'm a jerk," he was saying. "He says I should have stuck it out—says my benefactor, whoever he is, is going to be pissed off when he finds out what I did. But hey, I didn't ask anybody to interfere in my life. I was doing okay on my own."

Okay? Shelley thought of his glowering face behind the counter at the E-Z Stop. The way he had skulked around since his release from jail. His bitter animosity toward what he considered the snobs at the Arms. The Arms . . . The memory of her scene with Snow, temporarily ousted by Benjy's revelations, rushed back and she winced.

"What's the matter?" he said. "You think it was a stupid trade-off too?"

"I don't know," Shelley mumbled. The agonizing thought of Snow, pregnant with Kip's child, had filled her once again to the exclusion of everything else. Benjy was silent; for a few minutes there was only the soft growl of the truck's engine as they sped along the road. At last: "You okay, Shelley?"

She meant to nod her head. But she shook it instead, a tight-lipped negative.

"Want to talk about it?"

She didn't. But again she found herself doing the opposite of what she intended. In that instant all Benjy's past hostility toward the Arms and its inhabitants, ill-founded as it was, seemed to make him an ally. "I just . . . found out something really awful." She was staring straight ahead, but peripherally she saw him look in her direction.

"Awful? What . . . is it your family? Is somebody sick?"

The sense of hovering on the brink of betraying the coven took Shelley's breath away. An hour earlier she would have laughed if she had been told she would ever in all her life consider such an act. Now she was aware of a roiling sensation in her chest, the impulse to speak wrestling with her vow to keep secrecy. At last she shook her head. "No. It's something else."

"Something over at the Arms?" he said. White-hot panic flashed through her; she gawked at him. "How—how did you know?"

"Just figures. That's where you spend all your time." His eyes met hers briefly before returning to the road. "What happened?"

But the impulse had fled. Shelley shook her head again, more decisively this time. "Nothing really. Just . . . nothing."

Benjy did not respond. He guided his truck skillfully along the curving road, obviously reveling in the vehicle's quick responses to the slightest suggestion of steering wheel or accelerator. When the hilly fields gave way to woods, he slowed down. A rough road appeared, leading into the trees, and they turned onto it. Benjy brought the truck to a stop, shut the engine off and turned to look at her. "Shelley. A minute ago it was something awful. Now it's nothing. It can't be both, so which is it? Something? Or nothing?"

The engine was making little ticking sounds beneath the hood. Shelley could hear leaves rustling in the autumn trees around them, a jay's strident cry somewhere in the distance. "Nothing."

"Oh yeah? Then how come you look like you lost your last friend?"

She bit her bottom lip, feeling it quivering between her teeth as she willed herself not to cry.

"If they did something to hurt you—" Benjy said. There was cold animosity in his tone. "Did they?"

"No," she whispered.

He slapped the wheel suddenly, making her jump. "You can't admit it, can you—that anything bad could come out of that place? Well, I know different, Shelley. I know so different. I just wish I could prove it to you."

Chapter 3

I turned to stare at him. "What are you talking about?"

"You wouldn't believe me if I told you. So what's the point?"

A silence settled on the truck, as complete as if the two of us had abruptly been sealed off from the rest of the world. My mind was racing. I had wondered before if in his childhood Benjy might have stumbled across the coven's existence. "Believe you about what?"

"I'll tell you—if you'll tell me what happened to get you so upset."

I shook my head mutely.

"Well, then, forget it." He straightened in the driver's seat and reached for the ignition key. "I'll take you home."

"Wait, Benjy. You can't do this. You have to tell me what you mean."

He was silent.

"Benjy—!"

"Will you trust me, Shelley?" His eyes were the color of the sky just before a windstorm. "Will you let me show you something, and then listen while I explain? Without interrupting, or getting mad, or closing your mind?"

"Explain what? Is it something about the Arms?"

He reached out and seized my wrist. "If you promise to listen on my terms, I'll tell you."

The cold from his fingers spread slowly up my arm. My skin was clammy, my mouth dry. I couldn't imagine what he was going to say. Explain what? What was he talking about? *You can't admit it, can you—that anything bad could come out of that place? Well, I know different, Shelley.*

An echo ricocheted off the back of my mind—Snow's voice saying, *You're going to find the testing never stops*—and accompanying the words, a vision of her calm face as she talked about giving away her baby, the baby whose origin stung me afresh each time I thought of it. I was seized with the chilling sense that I scarcely knew her, or any of them, these people I had considered my true family, my closest friends. I thought of Grimalkin, her face painted like a skull to represent the Hag. Of Senta, using the word *cursing*. Of Snow's eyes as she stared at Larry and lifted her left hand to her throat, and a dark hooded shadow beckoning in a dream. Benjy was still holding my wrist. "Okay," I whispered.

"Say you promise."

"I promise."

The chill October twilight had set in by the time the two of us returned to Green Hollow. We went to Benjy's house at the south end of Willow Street—two stories that had once been painted yellow, now peeled and faded until the color was no more than a guess. A balding hedge, like a parody of the luxuriant wall of leaves at the Arms, bordered the front yard.

No lights showed in the windows, but the front door wasn't locked. Benjy held a finger to his lips as he eased it open and led me over the threshold. Inside, I could see dim light coming from the back of the house; opposite the door a staircase led up to the second floor. As children we had never played in Benjy's yard because his mother suffered from migraine headaches. Sometimes when we passed by she would be out on the porch—a thin, frowsy woman who might wave but never tried to engage us in conversation. I remembered giggling with Jenny and Lisa over the fact that Mrs. Hendricks's headaches were actually hangovers. Now a slurred voice called from the back of the house, startling me. "Zhatchu, honey?"

I saw Benjy's shoulders tighten. "Yeah, Mom. I'm going up to my room."

"Doncha want sommen tuh eat?"

"No." His diction had become painfully precise. "I already had something."

We tiptoed up the stairs. Benjy pushed a door open and motioned me into his room. A narrow bed, a rickety dresser, a bookcase on top of which some model airplanes were displayed. The darkness in the room was broken by strips of light from a streetlamp shining through the window blind. There were no chairs; we sat on the bed. There was a lamp, but he didn't switch it on, and as the cold light from outside fell in a barred pattern across his face, a flicker of recognition stirred inside me—a sense of having seen that image somewhere before. "Well?" I said.

His lips tightened into a thin line that added years to his actual nineteen. "Remember, you promised to listen. Not say anything, not interrupt or argue or get mad. Just listen and keep an open mind. Okay?"

I nodded. On one wall was a poster of a French Impressionist painting, speckled water and a blurry church spire. It didn't seem like Benjy's taste; maybe his mother had put it up. I looked from the poster back to his face—

—and felt the jolt of past and present colliding. *Benjy's face, barred with shadow.* There it was, before me now. The image in the scrying cauldron: no longer image, but reality. And the shadow was not of prison bars, but of the slatted blinds in the window of his room, where I had never been before tonight. Sitting there I felt a slow chill creep outward from my heart. I had looked into the scrying cauldron almost a year ago. Last Halloween. Had these events been set in motion even then?

Benjy's voice interrupted my thoughts. "Shelley, I think Everett Lockley was my father." He held up one hand, as if to stifle my unspoken protest. "Don't say anything yet. Just listen. You promised, remember?

"When my mom was young, she used to work for Duncan's Laundry. One of their biggest customers was the Arms. A young guy named Dan Raines drove the laundry truck, and he and my mom were engaged. I know she doesn't look like much now, but I've seen pictures of her when she was young, and she was pretty. Real pretty. Anyhow, whenever she got the chance, she used to ride with Dan to make the pickups. That was how she got friendly with Everett Lockley.

"My mom never really told me all this, not the way I'm telling you. I've put it together from bits and pieces she's dropped over the years, usually when she's drunk. So there are some parts missing. But eventually she broke her engagement with Dan, and he quit his job and moved out West. My mom kept on working at the laundry for a while longer. Then she had to quit because it turned out she was pregnant. With me." His voice shook on the last phrase and I touched his shoulder, but it was like putting my hand on a stone.

"Here's where we skip a few years. Remember how obsessed I was with the Arms when we were kids—how I'd go over there and sneak around until Royce chased me away? I couldn't keep away from the place, and that was because my mom had this crazy attitude about it. When she was sober she'd tell me to stay away from there. She'd tell me it was like a separate country where the people thought they could do whatever they wanted. That they thought they owned the village, and all the rest of us were dirt.

"But whenever she'd had a snootful, she used to get all mushy and talk about how beautiful the Arms was, how perfect, like a house in a fairy tale. How it existed by itself in its own enchanted world. She seemed like she knew an awful lot about it for somebody who just went inside to collect a bunch of dirty sheets. She'd say how, when the sun came through the curtains in the afternoon, the light was like music. I loved the stories, but she'd always end up bawling when she told them, and I hated that. And once she was sober again, she'd go back to saying the Arms was bad. So I didn't know what to think. The bad stuff made me hate the place, but the stories attracted me. I couldn't keep away. I even used to dream about it, and in the dreams it was always beautiful.

"As I got older, I started wondering why she hated the people at the Arms so much. It didn't make sense. I mean, they had nothing to do with us, and we had nothing to do with them. And then one time I was going through her dresser, trying to find her booze stash, and I found a letter from Dan Raines. The guy she'd been engaged to, way back when.

"He must have written it when they broke up. It said something like: you're crazy, he's married to someone else, he's just using you, you'll regret this for the rest of your life. That kind of letter. It didn't say who *he* was, but it started me thinking. Making connections."

"But Benjy—" I had forgotten I wasn't supposed to say anything. "How can you be so sure it was Everett Lockley? It could—" I bit off the end of the sentence, but it hung in the air and he heard it anyway.

"It could have been anybody—is that what you were going to say?"

"No," I whispered.

"My mom's not a whore, Shelley. She made a mistake when she was young, too young to know any better. But *he* should have known better."

"But—"

"Look, I want you to read the letter. It talks about *him* being rich and important, a local big shot. Who else could it be? Read the letter, you'll see what I mean. Come on." He got to his feet.

"Benjy—"

"You promised, Shelley."

I had promised. I followed him into his mother's room, where we eased the door shut behind us. When Benjy switched on the bedside lamp I noted the unmade bed, wrinkled sheets trailing the floor, and the jumble of open cosmetic jars and tubes of lipstick on the dresser. Mrs. Hendricks wore too much makeup—everybody said so. I glanced nervously at the door.

Suppose she decided to come upstairs—suppose she found us in her room, snooping through her things? Benjy had opened the top drawer of the dresser and was rummaging through it. "Dammit," I heard him whisper. "Dammit, where is it?"

"Maybe she threw it away."

"Ha. She never throws anything away."

I registered faint nausea as I watched him paw through his mother's clothing. In spite of my promise, I had already made up my mind about his idea that Everett Lockley was his father. I thought it was farfetched and pitiful, and I was revolted by this whole charade. What I wanted was to be alone, to sift through the ashes of my own misery. And then, as Benjy pushed aside a pile of underclothes in his search, I saw it. Not the letter he was searching for, but something else.

A little cloth bag, tied at the neck with thread. "What's that?" I said. Breath had deserted me; the words were barely audible. I pointed at the bag. Benjy suspended his search to look at me. "You mean this?" He retrieved it from the drawer. "I don't know. She's always had it. I've seen her get it out and look at it a million times, usually when she'd good and loaded." His eyes narrowed as he watched my face. "Why?"

I shook my head. The object in his hand still exuded a tantalizing trace of summery fragrance that stirred a whisper in my head. *I found it in a book. You make a charm and charge it with the power of the four elements. That's all. But the girls were all over him.*

I hadn't touched it. I could still say I didn't know what it was, and leave, and have done with all this. But I did know. It was a charm. A cloth bag filled with certain herbs and talismans, tied with a knotted thread and charged with the power of earth, air, water and fire.

A witch's love charm.

I think Everett Lockley was my father. In the last bleak fortnight, hadn't I wondered at moments if magic actually existed? Here was proof. "What is it?" Benjy was saying. "Shelley?"

"Forget about the letter." I was still struggling to get my breath. "You don't need to show it to me. I believe you."

Back in his room, I sat on the bed again because my legs

would not support my weight. Benjy leaned against the opposite wall, watching me. In the shadows a resemblance seemed to flit across his face like a phantom, now there, now not. The fair skin and light hair, the sharp, sensitive features that might have possessed the hawklike elegance of Everett Lockley if they had not been overlaid by bitterness— "What is that thing?" he asked again.

"Something Everett Lockley made."

I saw his chin jerk up. "You think so?"

"I know so." I rested my forehead on my hands. There was a swelling heat in my chest, as if the fury of emotion sparked by Snow's confession this afternoon had been fanned into new life by this discovery. *There's no harm in what we do. But we may violate some of the conventions you've been raised to believe in.* Had Everett Lockley considered himself above convention—entitled to seduce an innocent girl by means of magic, destroy her relationship with her fiancé, impregnate and then abandon her? Why had he allowed Benjy to grow up fatherless? Because he had needed to keep the knowledge of his irresponsible act from his beloved Emma, and from the coven who looked up to him? *An' it harm none, do what thou wilt.* It seemed to me that the powerful witch Everett Lockley, whose name was spoken with such reverence within the coven, had made a fine mess of the Craft's only rule. I thought his son was entitled to hear the truth; and sitting beside Benjy in the darkness, haltingly I began to speak. To tell him about the Green Hollow Coven.

My own rasping whisper struck my hearing like a stranger's as he listened without a word. Downstairs, footsteps moved around the house and then subsided. Somewhere up the street a car honked its horn in a jaunty signal: *Beep beebeebeep beep.* When I had finished at last, Benjy shook his head. "Witches," he said. "Magic spells. I can't believe I'm hearing this."

"It's true. He used that charm to seduce your mother. It wasn't her fault."

He snorted. "Oh, he used charm all right. But there's nothing magical about the kind of charm he used. Guys use it every day to get what they want from girls. He probably sweet-talked her and bought her presents and told her he'd marry her if he could just shake loose from his old bitch of a wife. And she was dumb enough to fall for it."

"Benjy, you're not listening. She didn't have a choice. Believe me, those charms really work."

He snorted. "Come on, Shelley. I can't believe you buy all this crap about magic. You're smarter than that! How could you and Kip let those people sucker you?"

"It's not crap. It's real."

"Yeah. And Charlie Dietz is the tooth fairy."

His scoffing began to grate on my nerves. "I didn't invent the stuff I told you, Benjy. The healing spell made my dad get better. And you know perfectly well that if the Green Hollow Kidnapper hadn't gotten himself arrested, you wouldn't be sitting here right now."

"Yeah, your dad got better! Lots of people recover from heart attacks; there's nothing magic about it. And that old creep who grabbed those kids—you really think it was magic that made him freak out? He was just some sicko who finally snapped!"

"Well, what about what Snow did to Larry? Kip and I both saw it happen."

"Shit, I don't know how she did it. All I know is, she didn't use magic. Because there's no such thing."

As I opened my mouth to protest I remembered Paul pawing me in the back corridor of his apartment. How I had tried to use magic to send him flying, and nothing had happened. Nothing. Was Benjy right? Was the charm nothing more than a bag of herbs, the existence of magic only foolish fantasy? He had folded his arms and was watching me. "They lied to you, Shelley. They used you for a bunch of mind games and sex games. They're just a bunch of rich weirdos who get their kicks messing with other people's lives, like that son of a bitch did with my mom." A beat of silence for emphasis, and then: "Still think nothing but perfection can come from the Lockley Arms?"

A lump rose in my throat. I was too tired to protest, even to talk anymore. I leaned back against the wall and closed my eyes. A moment later Benjy kissed me.

It strikes me now that there was something doomed in the furtive, desperate way we made love for the first time on the bed where he had probably cried himself to sleep so often that its lumpy mattress had become saturated with his pain. We turned to each other that night out of bitterness and disillusionment instead of the way celebrated by the coven, in mystery and joy. There was no pleasure in it, only a stifling awareness of his mother downstairs, drinking herself into a stupor, oblivious to what was happening above her head. It was an awkward, panting deed in the dark, a single-minded effort to remove the necessary clothing—and then, for me, a red flash of pain followed immediately by Benjy's strangled gasp of release. It could not have differed more from the dreaming magic of my previous experiences—and lying there beneath Benjy, entangled in his lanky limbs, I recalled what his mother had said in her stories about the Lockley Arms. *How it existed by itself in its own enchanted world.*

"Remember how I told you I used to dream about the place?"

Benjy's whisper startled her; she had somehow managed to forget where she was. He had rolled off her and now they lay huddled together on his bed. She found herself whispering in reply. "You said it was always beautiful."

"Yeah. I'd walk around, and everything would be so green . . . There'd be shafts of light slanting down through the trees, and a kind of gold haze everywhere. The air would be so soft I'd feel like crying. And I'd feel welcome, like something was telling me, 'You belong here.' But Shelley, the last time I dreamed about it—it was different."

"Different how?"

She felt him shiver. "The last time, it was night. Cold. The house was dark and it looked really scary, like a haunted house. The trees were bare and there were dead leaves blowing through the air, and a god-awful rotten smell like a dead animal. I wanted to run away, but I couldn't move. I knew something in the house had brought me there. Something that wanted to kill me."

This time the shiver, of uncertain origin, passed through them both. "Benjy—"

"I know. It was just a dream." A bony knee bumped hers as he shifted position. "I wanted to run, but I couldn't. Something kept pulling me closer and closer. The door opened, and inside the house it was pitch-black—darker than anything in the world. I wanted to scream, but I couldn't make a sound. The doorway kept getting bigger and bigger. Or maybe I was shrinking. I could feel myself moving toward it, like I was being sucked in. I couldn't stop. And then . . ."

"What?" she whispered when he didn't go on.

"I'm not sure. You know how dreams are. There was a flash. A burst of light, like an explosion of some kind. Then I woke up."

The ensuing silence expanded around them to fill the room. Only vaguely conscious of her movements, Shelley turned away from him and hid her face in her hands. In the shelter of this darkness the past few hours seemed too horrible to be real. She heard Benjy's voice behind her. "You're only the second person I ever told that dream to. The first was Charlie. He likes to analyze dreams. He's got a book that tells how. Know what he said?"

"What?" The word, muffled by her hands, seemed to come from somewhere outside her.

"Said the dark doorway, and me getting smaller and smaller, could only mean one thing. Guess what it was?"

"I don't know."

The sound he made was too bitter to be called a laugh. "Fear of sex."

Chapter 4

That night in Benjy's room marked the beginning of my intimacy with the Old One, the Hag. In the Craft, no aspect of the Goddess is honored above this dark winnower who fills her Halloween cauldron with harvested souls. She has many names—Hecate, Cerridwen, Kali, Sheila na Gig—but they all imply the same thing. Fate. Darkness. Destruction.

I dreamed of her that night as I lay beside Benjy in his narrow bed. For a long time my cramped position kept me awake. I heard Mrs. Hendricks come stumbling up the stairs very late; I listened to Benjy's breathing and an intermittent scratching noise that might have been a mouse. But I must have slept at last, because I dreamed of the Dark Goddess. In the dream I cast a circle, widdershins, and lit a candle at the center. As I stared into the dancing flame a voice spoke in my head. *Look into a lit candle, and inside the bright flame you will see a dark one. Each of us has a shadow self hidden away, made up of everything we fear about who we are.*

When I glanced up from the candle, she was there. A cold, implacable face: the eyes enigmatic, compelling, lustrous as black jewels. My own distorted reflection in polished ebony. Suddenly her lips curved in a cryptic smile that sent a frisson of terror through me.

You summoned me?

"N-no! At least I didn't mean to—"

But widdershins is the direction of endings, and I can taste your wish for destruction. Won't it be sweet? Revenge for all the wrong that has been done. To Benjy—and to you.

"To me?"

Yes, to you. Because it isn't fair, is it? When love and loyalty and trust are repaid by betrayal . . . when that happens, vengeance is due.

"I—I don't understand."

Don't you? You understood me once. When you were younger. Before you buried me beneath that veneer of good behavior you're so proud of. Can't you remember?

"Remember? I don't have the slightest idea what you're talking about!"

I'm talking about you. And about Kip—the one you love best in all the world. The one who says, Come on, Shelley! The one who leads while you follow. Who takes your loyalty and devotion for granted.

"What's wrong with that? We're twins."

Yes, twins. A pair, two halves of a single whole. But when one half betrays the other . . . vengeance is due.

"Stop saying that. It doesn't make any sense."

No? Yet somewhere inside you that first betrayal still exists, a perpetually resounding echo. In the shadows of the cloakroom they stand hidden by the folds of her coat, and the touch of his soft lips fills her with a wild, squirming excitement she cannot contain. And as that little girl's high giggle echoes forward into the future, becoming a woman's raveled cry of ecstasy, you know this is only the first time. Only the first time, unless—

"Unless . . . what?"

Unless we punish him. Push him into that perilous snowfield where he doesn't belong. Hurt him the way he hurt you. And he deserved it, because now it's happened again, just as you feared. You've been betrayed. And not just by Kip—by Snow, whom you trusted, admired, even desired. When he claimed they'd been lovers in some other existence, didn't she promise it meant nothing? But you saw the way they acted. And so you told her about the spell he'd cast for Frog—manipulated his jealousy of Jonathan Blackbridge to make him take the scrying box—

"I had to! I had to do something to keep them apart!"

Of course you did. But in the end, it wasn't enough, was it? He can never give you a child, but he's given one to her. Can't you see that no matter what you do, her claim still outweighs your own? It's not fair. Not fair at all. But two's company, my dear . . . and three's a crowd.

"Not always! There was the night before I left for college—"

Ah, that wanton little escapade in the pool! Did it really mean anything, or were they just tossing you a few crumbs from their private table? Poor old Shelley, let's give her something to remember us by; it's the least we can do. After all, she's the odd one out.

"No," I whispered. But the eyes held mine and the voice was the voice of my own thoughts, a relentless goading I could not escape.

Think of Benjy, then. Should Everett Lockley escape the consequences of what he did? You know he's guilty! Why not call the coven to account for his irresponsible actions? What does it matter that he's dead? He was their leader; that alone is enough to smear them with his guilt. You must have a reckoning.

A reckoning. I stared into the flame and saw the shadow at its center begin to swell, rapidly expanding until I could no longer see the Dark Goddess. My head whirled; I felt myself sink deeper into sleep, hearing a faint, ominous whisper as I drifted off.

For behold, I have been with you from the beginning . . .

From then until Halloween the days appear to me, in retrospect, shrouded in the somber colors of that dream. I woke Benjy before dawn and he drove me back to Albany. The trip was a blur; by then I was already obsessed with wild, vague fantasies of calling the coven to account for Everett Lockley's misdeeds. The logic of the dream had insinuated itself into my waking thoughts. Over and over I told myself a reckoning was due.

The particulars were hazy at first. But over the next two weeks a plan began to form in Shelley's mind, and at its center was the upcoming Sabbat.

"Halloween." The word dropped like a shadow across the autumn clearing where they lay together on the blanket Benjy carried in his truck. The days had fallen into a pattern in which he drove up from Green Hollow each afternoon and picked her up after her last class. From there they drove out of town to a private spot in the woods where they spread the blanket on the ground and had sex. Their couplings continued to possess the joyless urgency of that first time on Benjy's lumpy bed; he drove himself into her like someone frantically seeking a safe place to hide from unknown pursuers, and however willingly she accepted these grim efforts, she could draw no pleasure from them. "Halloween." She was thinking aloud. "I'll do it at Halloween."

Dazed from his recent exertions, Benjy stirred and blinked at her. "Do what?"

"Confront them. In the circle. At the Halloween Sabbat there are two circles, one for the living and one for the dead. Once we enter the second circle and invite the dead to join us, I can accuse Everett to his face."

Benjy struggled up on one elbow, frowning. "Invite the dead to join you? Accuse him to his face? What are you talking about?"

There's no such thing as magic. He had remained so insistent on this point that Shelley no longer bothered to argue with him, and by now she couldn't have said for certain exactly what she believed. She avoided his eyes, toying with the frayed edge of the blanket. "I mean . . . invite them symbolically. So it'll be the same as accusing him to his face."

He seemed dubious. "You really want to do this?"

"Yes." She prodded her resolve and it sent forth a hot, satisfying burst. "They deserve it. They need to be told what Everett did, to know he made fools of them—that he wasn't the perfect person they think he was. And you should be the one to tell them, Benjy. You should come and tell them exactly what you told me."

He pulled her down onto the blanket, his hands burrowing beneath her clothes. They never undressed for these sessions;

the October air was already too cold, and in any case they would have felt much too vulnerable. There may have been a metaphor in that, and another in the fact that afterward, no matter how closely they huddled together, the meager amount of body heat they were able to generate between them was never enough to keep them warm. On this occasion, as on others, Benjy's need for her seemed insatiable. He had admitted to being a virgin before their night together in his room, and Shelley grew greedy for other confessions.

"Benjy, will you tell me something? That map the cops found in your pocket . . . why *was* there a circle around Pine Glen?"

"Forget about the damn map, will you?" He pulled away from her and sat up.

"You wouldn't tell the cops, okay. I guess you had your reasons. But can't you tell me?"

He didn't answer.

"Don't you trust me, Benjy?"

"Dammit, okay!" He raked a hand through his hair to leave it standing on end, a pale, ruffled crest. "What the hell, I might as well tell you. There was a circle around Pine Glen, and another around Woodston."

"But why?"

"I'm getting to that." His shoulders twitched. "A trucker I was talking to, out in the parking lot at the E-Z Stop—he drew those circles for me. He said . . . he said those were the villages that had hookers. The villages where I could get laid. Okay?"

"Benjy—!"

"Hell, Shelley, after that night in your backyard when we . . . I was so mad at you, and so horny I couldn't think straight. This trucker guy could tell it just by looking at me. He was trying to do me a favor!"

"Did you go?"

"I hadn't gotten around to it yet—then the cops found that map. Just my luck they'd seen some suspicious character hanging around a playground in Pine Glen."

"But why didn't you just tell them—the cops and the FBI? Instead of letting them put you in jail!"

Somewhere in the cold woods around them a jay squawked as Benjy turned toward her, his face an angry, patchy red. "Tell them? And have them blab to the whole friggin' world that I had to go to a hooker just to get laid?"

In that moment he seemed impossibly young to her. Perhaps this touchy pride was one of the things he had inherited from his father, along with the fair skin that colored so easily. For her part, Shelley found it at once tragic and darkly amusing that he had been willing to risk life imprisonment rather than confess the simple if embarrassing truth. *I had to go to a hooker just to get laid.* In any case he seemed determined to make up for lost time; they had intercourse so often it was a miracle she did not become pregnant. At moments she thought this was what she wanted, as if it would even some score with Snow—but lying on the cold earth with Benjy striving on top of her, her body must have received some message from this season of witherings and endings—some warning that this was not a time for welcoming new life.

There were a number of efforts at communication from Green Hollow during this period, and these she met with a surprising knack for duplicity. The first was from Dad, wanting to know when she was coming home. Shelley stared at the scribbled words on the phone booth wall as she made excuses. "I don't know, Dad. I've got a lot of studying to do."

"We'd hoped to see you over Columbus Day weekend."

"I, uh, couldn't get away. Maybe at the end of the month."

So he knew nothing of her abortive Columbus Day visit. Apparently not even Kip had not been told of her brief appearance at the Arms. And it was Kip who was her next caller, his voice brimming with hushed excitement, as if they were still fellow conspirators. As if he had never betrayed her. "Guess who's back."

She had to force a civil tone. "Who?"

"Mister Hoity-Toity Englishman. The high priest himself."

"Jonathan Blackbridge?" Briefly, surprise routed all other feelings.

"He got here this afternoon, along with some of the others.

They're gearing up for something, Shelley. And it's got to be something to do with *him*."

She knew he meant the mysterious old man locked in an Albany jail cell. Once they would have speculated on the possibilities, but now Shelley was too preoccupied by her own plans to spare any interest for the coven's. And the sound of Kip's voice—

"I've got to go," she said. "I'll call you back." But she didn't.

Snow called twice. Both times Shelley asked Helen to take a message, and both times the message was the same. "Please just tell her I called."

Another time she was genuinely out of the dorm, and on her return the sight of the scrawled message tacked to her door gave her pause. *Gwynneth called.* In the abstract it was easy to be furious with the coven—to despise them as dupes, blame them for Benjy's pain and her own, dismiss the whole experience as based on deceit. But seeing Gwynneth's name brought the memory of a jaguar's amber eyes—

She crumpled the note and jammed it into the pocket of her jeans.

Chapter 5

The story appeared in the Albany paper two days before Halloween. Normally I didn't see the *Times Union,* but that day's headline had caught Benjy's eye as he drove into town that afternoon, and he had bought a copy. When I climbed into the truck he tossed it in my lap. "Take a look at that."

I unfolded the paper. The headline was huge; for an instant I saw only a jumble of enormous type, and then the letters settled into words. SUSPECT FOUND DEAD IN CELL. My heartbeat stumbled and then recovered its rhythm. I glanced quickly at Benjy and then back at the newspaper story.

The man known as the Green Hollow Kidnapper was found dead in his cell at the county jail shortly after midnight last night, apparently the victim of a fatal seizure.

"He had been given a number of medical tests, but they showed nothing out of the ordinary," stated Medical Examiner Ron Barry. "We'll have to wait for the autopsy to learn exactly what happened."

As yet unidentified, the suspect in last year's kidnapping and murder of a young boy in Green Hollow was discovered during a routine check by a guard who found him lying on the floor of his cell. Medical experts estimated the time of death at approximately midnight. He was being housed at the jail while undergoing a series of medical and psychological tests which were being administered to determine if he was fit to stand trial . . .

I looked up from the paper to see that we were turning off the road into the woods. Fragments of newsprint seemed to float before my eyes, superimposing themselves on the drab landscape. *Victim of a fatal seizure. Approximately midnight.* As the truck came to a stop in the clearing, a spasmodic shivering seized me. Was there any doubt this death had been caused by the coven? Vaguely I remembered Kip nagging Elymas to curse Alex's killer, and his reply: *Magic is a double-edged weapon that affects the maker of the spell as well as the object. And a curse is no exception.* Elymas, the oldest member of the coven, and the wisest. Was he as much a fraud as Everett Lockley? Other voices mingled with his. Snow's, issuing from the darkness of the swimming pool: *I couldn't sleep. I've got a lot on my mind.* Kip's: *They're gearing up for something.* Senta's: *I won't be party to a cursing. The time may come—*

Evidently the time had come. However much I might waver these days between doubt and belief in the existence of magic, at that instant I knew in my heart that the old man in his prison cell had been murdered by the arts of witchcraft. But why?

Even if he had been a longtime enemy of the coven, responsible for the Lockleys' deaths—surely he had posed little threat locked in jail.

Whatever you send, returns threefold.

A hand touched my arm and I started violently.

"Jesus, Shelley." Benjy was staring at me. "What's the matter?" His gaze dropped to the paper in my lap. "Hey, the bastard deserved to die, you know? Saved the taxpayers some money is all."

I nodded mutely. There was no point in sharing my suspicions with Benjy; he would never believe me. I got out of the truck and shuffled through the drifts of dead leaves underfoot. The chilly air smelled of winter and the sun was hidden behind an iron-gray bank of clouds. I jammed my hands into my pockets. Behind me I heard Benjy get out of the truck; a moment later his hands touched my shoulders. "Hey, Shelley—"

I returned his embrace, but my trembling wouldn't stop. I extricated myself and moved away, seeing him pick up a piece of paper from the ground and glance at it. "Gwynneth called. Who's Gwynneth?"

I remembered cramming the note into my jeans; it must have fallen out just now, when I took my hands out of my pockets. I shrugged. "One of the people from the coven."

"One of the *witches*?" A sudden scowl twisted Benjy's face. "I thought you were finished with them."

"I am. But they don't know it yet."

"Well, why don't you tell her?"

"I didn't talk to her. Anyway, I told you: I want to do it at Halloween. When they're all together. In the circle of the dead." *When they're all together. Even Everett.*

"Yeah? Or maybe you're not finished with them after all. Maybe you decided they're not so bad. Maybe you like playing mind games and sex games and pretending it's magic. Is that it?"

"No!"

"Then why's she calling you?"

"I don't know!" We glared at each other in silence. I was the first to turn away. I knew Benjy would sulk for a while, then want to have sex. For myself, I only wanted to go back to my dorm room and try to stop shaking.

It's like they're gearing up for something.

The time may come . . .

I was only a few yards from the truck when Benjy's shove sent me to my knees on the hard ground. The next thing I knew he was on me. As he yanked my jeans down to my knees and forced himself into me from behind, I loosed a shriek that made the woods ring. And kept on shrieking, breath for breath, while that pitifully brief little exercise ran its course—until Benjy fell away from me, spent, and we lay panting in perfect unison. There was no other sound; the birds, intimidated by my racket, had fallen silent.

"Shelley." A hoarse whisper from behind me. "I . . . I'm sorry."

I said nothing, mesmerized by the twisted shapes of dead leaves inches from my face. A profound lassitude weighted my limbs like wet sand.

"I . . . I don't know what happened. I thought you were lying to me, or . . . or something, I don't know. I just . . . I'm sorry. Do you hate me now?"

"No."

"Shelley—"

"I don't want to talk about it," I said. Whom was I protecting, Benjy or myself, by allowing him to think the obvious? In truth I was afraid to dwell on the release I had experienced just now, in which my profound self-loathing had transformed the pain of his assault into something darkly other. Had I been honest, I would have been forced to confess that my cries had risen not from protest at all, but from some convoluted fulfillment I had not the courage to examine.

A gift from the Dark Goddess.

Chapter 6

The Halloween Sabbat fell on a Friday. Shelley cut her afternoon classes; Benjy picked her up around two and they headed for Green Hollow, the truck radio playing rock and roll that masked the silence between them. If Shelley remembered her last homecoming, it was only with a flash of contempt for an earlier self she now viewed as a fool. She had willed herself to endorse Benjy's version of events, in which she and Kip had been manipulated and seduced by a band of wealthy degenerates. Any memories that contradicted this picture she swept aside, concentrating instead on the upcoming Sabbat.

Reaching Green Hollow they drove straight to the E-Z Stop and parked behind the store, where Benjy led her to the spot in the hedge he had once used as a secret entrance to the grounds of the Arms. Years had elapsed since his last excursion, but he seemed to know exactly where it was. "Here."

Bending down, Shelley could make out a slight concavity in the profusion of leaves. "That's *it*?"

He nodded, hands fisted in his jacket pockets. "Remember, I was a little kid when I used to go through there."

Shelley went first. She had to crawl, keeping her face close to the ground where the growth wasn't quite so dense. The hedge seemed miles thick, every inch of it determined to hinder her as she fought her way forward in a slow, maddening belly-creep through a hostile universe of small cold leaves and stabbing twigs. Finally—it seemed hours later—she poked her head out of the hedge to see an expanse of white clapboard. The back of the carriage house. She dragged herself free and scrambled to her feet on the smooth lawn just as Benjy emerged behind her. The leaves in his pale hair gave him a moment's startling resemblance to the Green Man before he stood up and brushed them off, scowling at her. "You should've let me go first. You scratched your face."

"Who cares? Come on."

They crept around the west side of the carriage house, poised to take cover if the need arose. From not far away came a warning squeak of metal. She stopped Benjy with an uplifted hand and peered cautiously around the corner to see Kip emerge from the enclosure around the pool, carrying the cleaning net. They watched him cross the grass, whistling, and disappear around the other side of the carriage house where the maintenance equipment was stored. Glimpsed this way he was a stranger, an enemy; Shelley had no doubt he would try to thwart her plan if he knew of it. She motioned to Benjy, and together they ran across the grass toward the hedge surrounding the pool. As she put her hand on the gate, she somehow knew that if she lifted it slightly on its hinges as she opened it, it wouldn't squeak. They slipped silently through. The pool, freshly cleared of leaves in preparation for tonight's ritual bath, glinted in the late afternoon light as they hurried past. At the gate to the meadow Shelley hesitated, one hand on its slender iron bars. Benjy insisted there was no such thing as magic. But she could not help remembering the snowfield, the clear stroke of a bell and Kip's voice rising into the cold twilight. *Shelley. I can't move.*

"Come on, what're we waiting for?" Benjy's mutter overrode the echo in her head.

"Shh." Was there another sound, as she stood with her hand on the gate—a sound behind the silence? *La, la . . . La, la . . .* The next moment it had sunk into the hush of the chilly afternoon. Shelley took a breath. Maybe Benjy was right—maybe there was no such thing as magic. But for his sake, she couldn't take a chance. Without looking at him, she took from her coat pocket the athame she had received at her initiation. His eyes bugged. "What the hell, Shelley! You carry a *knife*?"

"It's a ceremonial knife," she said shortly. "It only cuts air. There's a protection spell around the meadow. I need the ath— the knife to cut a doorway through it."

Ceremonial knife. Protection spell. She saw the words strike him painfully. His mouth opened as if to protest, to assert once more his scorn for such foolishness, but no words emerged. He might have been wary of arguing with her while the knife was in her hand.

Standing at the gate she closed her eyes and took a deep breath, struggling to focus her thoughts. Even when she had believed wholeheartedly in its reality, magic had never been obedient to her will—had only sometimes seemed to brush against her in its unpredictable passing. She had failed utterly with Paul. Now, her mind divided about the very existence of the force she was attempting to evoke, she had little hope and even less confidence that anything would happen. Slowly she raised the athame in front of her, its point toward the meadow, and tried to concentrate on sensing the power of the earth, drawing it into her body.

At first there was nothing, only the sound of her breathing and the distant calling of jays across the cold afternoon. Nothing. She was aware of Benjy staring at her, of the pool at her back and the pine trees on the other side of the gate, a line of dark green beyond the tawny meadow. That was all. Nothing else. Nothing but a tingling sensation in the soles of her feet, so faint it might have been the result of what Benjy would call mind games. But as she concentrated, the sensation increased little by little until she seemed to be standing on a host of prickling pins. Slowly it spread to envelop her feet and legs, gradually mounting higher, collecting in her groin and belly. Now it was like heat, a breathless burning suddenly spurting upward to her heart. As she felt that rising rush, Shelley willed the fire out through her arms and into the knife.

The blade quivered. The heat was everywhere inside her now, cycling round and round, seeking release. She kept on sending it toward the knife. The edges of the blade began to gleam. Catching the sunlight? But the sun had gone behind clouds. Vaguely she heard Benjy whisper, "Holy shit."

Deliberately she used the athame to trace an arch in the air in front of the gate, starting on the left, moving up and then down to the right—cutting a doorway in the protective barrier around the meadow. She could feel resistance in the air as she moved the blade. When she had finished, the shape of the arch was briefly visible, flickering against the meadow beyond. Then it was gone. She lowered the athame and turned to Benjy. "Okay. You can go in."

When she pushed the gate open, he stepped through without a word. She noticed he gave her as wide a berth as possible. What must be going through his mind she could not imagine, and at that point she did not care. She shut the gate between them and pointed toward the meadow's far side. "You can hide in those trees. It'll be dark by the time the ritual starts, and then you can come closer without them seeing you. Once we're in the circle of the dead, you can just appear." He gave a curt nod and she glanced at her watch: nearly four o'clock. "You've got awhile to wait. Did you bring something to eat?"

"A couple of Milky Ways." His voice was hoarse. "Where you headed now?"

"Home. To pretend I just got here." Their eyes met through the bars of the gate. "I have to close up the opening I made," Shelley said. "So until later . . . I suggest you don't try to leave."

He nodded silently. She saw the knot of his Adam's apple move up and down in a painful swallow.

Chapter 7

It was a visibly altered group that collected at the Arms that Halloween—so altered that Shelley's own metamorphosis went undetected. In the dining room, where the coveners gathered to fast in preparation for the Sabbat to come, the pervading mood was edgy and somber. Talk was subdued, smiles rare. In spite of herself Shelley was taken aback by how ravaged Elymas and Grimalkin appeared. Had there always been so much gray in Grimalkin's hair? Had Elymas always looked so old and frail?

"What did you do to your face?" Reed asked her. The scratches from that afternoon's crawl through the hedge had become inflamed.

"My botany class had a field trip yesterday. The woods were pretty thick."

Her emotions had hardened into a block of ice. No nostalgia, no regret—nothing inside her but the implacable desire for revenge. On the surface she was happy to be present for the Sabbat celebration, glad to be with the coven again. To their distracted queries she smiled and said yes, school was going well. Did they know she was lying? Did they care? Had they ever cared, or had she just been a toy for them, a plaything now cast aside? She watched Andreas and Gwynneth conversing quietly in a corner. His dark skin had an unhealthy grayish tinge; her eyes were glazed with fatigue. Around these two, as around Grimalkin and Elymas, hovered a kind of miasma that dimmed the room's light and caused the other coveners, no matter how many times they approached them, to spend only a short time in their presence before moving away.

These, then, were the four to whom had fallen the grisly task of cursing the nameless old man in his jail cell. Kip whispered the details in Shelley's ear. "They were in the ritual room for six hours. When they were finished, Grimalkin couldn't even walk; Royce had to carry her downstairs. They—"

"Snow didn't do it with them?"

It was clear, seeing Snow, that she had not. After a guarded greeting Shelley managed to avoid her; but now, listening to Kip's account, she watched Snow covertly from across the room. Except for the shadows beneath her eyes, she looked radiant. For the safety of her unborn child, she would have been barred from the grim work of the cursing. "No," Kip was saying, "it was just those four, and Jonathan. I don't know why."

So Snow still had not told him. It was hard to believe he hadn't noticed—but seeing her every day, he had missed the changes that were so obvious to Shelley. In spite of what Snow had said about the child belonging to no one but itself, she must be nervous about telling him, a little afraid of his reaction. Shelley scrutinized her twin, asking herself what she was seeing. Was this the potent lover of the Great Goddess, sower of the mysterious seed of life? No. This was a boy of seventeen, running blithely, blindly along the edge of a chasm whose depths he had never even suspected. An adolescent who loved mystery and fantasy and expensive cars, who was mentally and emotionally unprepared for the idea of fatherhood, and his part in this whole business was a complete disgrace. At that moment it all seemed very clear.

When it came time for the ritual to begin, it was surprisingly easy to hold herself apart. She went through the motions. She undressed and put on her robe. Around her waist she tied the red cord cut to her height—the cord that in the Burning Times would have been used for vengeance should she betray the coven. She joined the silent procession that made its way down through the parking lot beneath the waning moon. As she shed her robe to enter the heated pool, the biting October air seemed mild in contrast to the cold inside her. She had a fleeting memory of last year, when she had been beset by shakes and hunger pangs and every other torment her body could devise. Now she felt nothing. Nothing at all—until the group was robed again, ready to pass through the gate to the meadow. Then apprehension woke briefly, like something trapped beneath the layers of ice inside her, trying to claw its way free. Benjy was out there in the darkness, awaiting his cue to come forward. Would anyone realize the protection spell had been tampered with? There seemed to be no hitch in the procession ahead, no suspicion that anything was awry. One by one the witches entered the meadow, and then it was her turn.

She passed through the gate.

Halloween. Beltane's somber twin, the greatest festival on the witches' calendar. Of all holidays my favorite. Masked figures flitting like blown leaves through the night, in search of mischief and treasure, the cold October wind carrying distant laughter ending in a shriek, the sense of unseen presences abroad in the darkness.

On this night the gate is open between the worlds.

The beautiful Samhain ritual was wasted on me that night, its words and gestures meaningless. My brain was sluggish, my body heavy as stone. I found myself staring at the waning moon overhead, a gnawed rind in a black sky wisped with cloud. As I lowered my gaze I swayed a little on my feet, and Senta touched my shoulder and whispered, "Are you all right?"

I managed a nod, thinking of Benjy waiting out there in the darkness, watching the robed and hooded silhouettes around the fire, maybe catching a phrase or two of the ritual across the quiet meadow. How did it appear to him? Sinister. Bizarre. A group of cranks gathered beneath the moon to enact perverse ceremonies. As the rite progressed I watched the fire, seeing not the flames but the shadows within them, hearing in their soft hissing the whispering of the Dark Goddess in my ear. Murmuring of reckoning, vengeance, satisfaction hot and salty as the taste of blood.

I came to myself with a start to find people opening their robes and helping one another apply the flying ointment. Pretending to take some of the oily paste for myself, I turned away as if to rub it on my skin. What would happen now? My memories of last Halloween were like a vivid dream, doubtless caused by the herbs in the ointment. None of it could actually have happened. But as I was retying the cord around my waist, making sure the knot was tight, I heard whistles shriek suddenly across the dark air. The wind gusted, moaning across the meadow and flattening the high grass, and in spite of my skepticism I felt the hair rise on the back of my neck. Someone put a besom into my hand, and I joined the dancers circling the fire. I had to keep up appearances, I mustn't give my true feelings away—but my feet were clumsy and self-conscious as I stepped to the noise of shrilling whistles and merrily rattling bones. Around me the others were shouting and waving their brooms, their wild silhouettes showing black against the fire, and again I imagined the scene through Benjy's eyes. A band of eccentrics capering around a fire in a secluded meadow—yet even reduced to these terms, the picture possessed a dark merriment that could not be denied.

Ecstatic cries began to break out as the dancers imagined themselves taking flight, mounting the air on their broomsticks to ride the rushing wind. Of course it was only a fantasy sparked by the flying ointment: to anyone with an unclouded brain, their feet were unquestionably on solid ground. Fools. Contempt tightened my throat; I rejected the memory of the cold Sabbat wind lifting the hair from my scalp as I soared into the night sky. *Tonight we fly between the worlds.* Ridiculous. Anyone could see we weren't really flying.

At last the frantic pace of the dance diminished; one by one the broomriders collapsed, spent, on the ground around the fire. I watched them lift their heads. In their faces was the look of having made a journey. Of having traveled between the worlds. Delusion, nothing more. But the ritual was progressing: the time had come to enter the circle of the dead. Within its somber domain the whole coven knelt, their black robes blending with the darkness, while Grimalkin's husky voice spoke the ritual words.

"We are gathered in the circle of the dead. For these few moments, let us pause and think of loved ones who have passed on. Let us light this place with our memories, as one day we shall want others to do on our behalf. And as these lights burn, so may the light of remembrance burn for our loved ones—for what we shared with them, and what we were to one another."

So may the light of remembrance burn . . . I placed my candle on the ground along with the others. My heart sustained a slow, hard beat, measured and hollow like a drum in a funeral procession. I narrowed my eyes until the candle's flame became a nimbus of dancing gold surrounding the blackness within, and settled back on my heels to wait. Nothing was going to happen, of course. But it was necessary to allow time for the others to imagine that we had been joined by the dead.

I waited. The candles flickered and danced. And then something began to happen.

Shadows and wisps at first. Something that might have been a creeping ground mist. A sound that could have been the wind rustling the dry cornstalks. A sudden simultaneous guttering and flaring of the circle of tiny flames on the ground.

Lifting my head, I saw the circle thick with mist that moved and swirled as if seeking shape. Were there voices not quite audible to human ears, faces just beyond the range of human vision, yearning touches that drifted like vapor over the kneeling coveners? *For what we shared with them, and what we were to one another.* The candle flames burned brighter—and as ghostly figures formed to take their places in the circle, as past joined present to celebrate this hallowed eve, my skepticism began to slip away. Observing the living, I saw their eyes brighten and their lips move soundlessly as if in answer to half-heard questions. Watched their eyes seeking beloved faces in the haze, their hands reaching out to the veiled shapes around them. Rowan appeared out of the darkness and arched his back against the mist and purred as some insubstantial, beloved hand gently stroked his fur.

The dead walk, and to the living is revealed the Mystery.

My focus shifted suddenly. Beyond the perimeter of the circle, there was one dark shape about which there was nothing insubstantial at all. Standing knee-deep in the dry grass of the meadow, waiting. Benjy.

It was time. My legs had no feeling in them, but somehow I managed to stand. The voice issuing from my throat was loud and strong, without a quaver. "If Everett Lockley is here now, let him listen. There's someone who wants to speak to him."

A profound stillness fell over the circle. One by one, heads turned to follow my gaze. I heard indrawn breath, a murmur of shock. Slowly the coveners rose to their feet and stood facing Benjy. No one moved; even the wisps of fog hung motionless in the cold air.

Benjy started forward, but Snow moved suddenly, raising the athame to slash an arc in the air above her head. I saw a dazzle of light run round the edge of the circle, a visible boundary of blue flame splitting the darkness. Benjy came to an abrupt halt. His mouth fell open. Snow ignored him and whirled to face me. "This is your doing, Shelley!" The words were a furious hiss, her face steely. "How dare you bring an outsider here? Have you learned nothing?"

"I've learned plenty," I said loudly, over the heavy thudding of my heart. "I've learned that the only part of the Wiccan Rede that means anything is the second half. *Do what thou wilt.* That's what Everett Lockley thought, isn't it? He did just as he pleased, no matter who got hurt."

The others stirred and I turned to face them. My icy internal calm would stand me in good stead now. If they wouldn't let Benjy speak, I would speak for him. "Yes. There's the proof." I pointed to the mute figure beyond the fiery boundary of the circle. "He's Everett Lockley's son. But Everett never acknowledged him. Never gave him anything, not even the time of day. He grew up without a father. His mother is considered a disgrace in this village. She has a son, but no husband, and she drinks too much. Who wouldn't?"

No one said anything. I had shocked them. The clumsy apprentice, the one they had all secretly pitied—for once I was in command while they were the ones standing tongue-tied and confused. It felt good to accuse Everett in front of his followers; and if his spirit was truly here among us now, it was getting exactly what it deserved. Benjy himself, outside the circle, seemed far away, peripheral to the real action within.

"She was nineteen when Everett met her," I said. "Engaged to a local boy. But she was pretty, and she caught Everett's eye, and so he gave her a love charm. She broke her engagement and the boy left. When she got pregnant, Everett dumped her—and she was so young and dumb, so intimidated by the high-and-mighty Mr. Everett Lockley, that she never dared to demand decent treatment. Her reputation in this judgmental little backwater was ruined, her life spoiled. And what did he do to help her? Nothing." I glanced around at the faces of the coveners, shadowy within their hoods. "*An' it harm none, do what thou wilt.* Look at that boy out there. He belongs inside this circle. He deserves the life of Everett Lockley's son. Not hardship, not people snubbing him because of some social stigma that wasn't his fault. Not a drunken mother crippled by a memory. Don't you think she was harmed? What about him?"

My questions fell into silence. The fog drifted, slowly changing shape. Then Elymas spoke. "You don't know the whole story, Shelley. Benjy was not conceived in carelessness. His existence came out of a contract involving his mother and both the Lockleys. According to an agreement they made, Benjy was to grow up here at the Arms as Everett's and Emma's son."

Contract . . . agreement . . . In my rush of surprise and dismay, the words meant nothing except that I hadn't shocked them after all. "You mean you *knew* he was Benjy's father? All this time—you knew?" No one answered, but that was enough. Their silence infuriated me. "Then why didn't you *do* something?" I shouted.

Finally Grimalkin spoke. "If you intend to judge us, Shelley, at least listen to the facts. Eventually, when we thought you were ready, we would have acquainted you with this bitter piece of our coven's history. But it seems you've chosen to hear it now."

I folded my arms tightly across my chest, making my voice as cold as I could. "I'm listening."

Grimalkin rubbed her hands together as if to warm them, then let them fall to her sides. "The story begins long before Benjy's birth," she said. She sounded exhausted. "It begins with Everett and Emma, who wanted nothing more than what many couples want—a child of their own. Twice Emma conceived; both times she miscarried. A heartbreaking ordeal. But she and Everett continued to long for a child to raise in the tradition of the Craft.

"When they met Barbara Hendricks she was, as you say, very young—only a year or so older than you are now. She used to come to the Arms with her boyfriend, who drove the laundry truck. She and Emma became friendly, and Barbara confided that she and Dan, her young man, wanted to scrape up enough money to marry and move to California. They had plans, she said, for bigger and better things.

"I don't know whose idea it was, or how seriously it was presented at first, but eventually the Lockleys agreed to pay Barbara a large sum of money to bear Everett a child. The plan was that both Emma and Barbara would leave Green Hollow for the duration of the pregnancy. Once the child was born, it would be raised as the Lockleys' own. Barbara would have the money, and she and Dan could proceed with their plans."

"The Lockleys offered to *buy* her baby? Did her boyfriend know?"

Grimalkin nodded. "There was no way to hide it from him. He was against the arrangement, but Barbara was a very determined young woman and she refused to be talked out of it. They quarreled, and Dan left. The Lockleys advised her to reconsider the whole idea, but she was positive that once she had the money, she could make things up with Dan. She wanted to go ahead with it, and they agreed. It sounds cold-blooded, but they all felt they had something to gain.

"None of them foresaw that Barbara would fall in love with

Everett. But once she had conceived, she felt she had a claim on him. She demanded that he divorce Emma and marry her instead. When he refused, she threatened to expose their arrangement—to harm the baby—to kill herself. Eventually she came to understand that her passion was hopeless. But when the baby was born, she refused to give him up.

"The Lockleys were devastated. There was a quarrel. Once Everett saw there was nothing he could do to change Barbara's mind, he began sending her money for Benjy's keep, but she used it only to buy liquor. Finally he saw he was doing more harm than good, and he stopped."

When she had ceased speaking there was silence in the circle. Was this my promised lesson in coven history—this sordid tale, even worse in its way than the scenario Benjy and I had imagined? Grimalkin had said the contract had been a voluntary one, but didn't I know better?

"You make it sound like none of it was his fault, but I happen to know he used magic on Mrs. Hendricks! Benjy showed me a little bag he said she's had for as long as he can remember. It was a charm made by a witch. A love charm!"

"Love charm?" Grimalkin said.

"I saw it myself. A little bag filled with herbs—"

"A blue bag, tied with silver thread? Yes, that is a charm," Grimalkin was saying. "But not a love charm. Shall I tell you what is in that bag? Nine protective herbs—cinquefoil, feverfew, rowan, laurel, vervain, purslane, burdock, motherwort, bloodroot—and a silver coin. The thread was tied with three knots. Emma fashioned it herself. It was a charm for good health. For the baby."

That faded bag in Mrs. Hendricks' dresser—could it have once been blue, like the one Emma had placed beneath Kip's mattress during his illness? A charm for good health. My own mistake only served to fuel my rage. "Well, so what? Even if they didn't use magic, the Lockleys still destroyed a young woman's life! They didn't get what they wanted, but they went right on living in their beautiful house, doing as they liked, while right down the street she was getting drunk every night.

Whatever you send, returns threefold. Is that just like the Rede—nothing but empty words?"

Elymas was shaking his head, but Senta answered me sharply. "Don't disgrace the training we've given you, Shelley. We can never escape the consequences of our actions, and you should know that by now. The Lockleys paid for what they did. A bitter price." She turned away abruptly and Gwynneth, with obvious reluctance, took over the recital.

"What you must understand, Shelley, is that Everett saw in Benjy the only child he would ever have. Because of Barbara's hostility he was denied any contact with his son, and so over the years he began to permit himself what he must have rationalized as a small and harmless indulgence. He began to summon Benjy's spirit to him at night, by magic.

"To Benjy these visits would have seemed no more than vivid dreams. But for a witch of Everett's degree, they were a reprehensible misuse of his magical skill. He used ancient, arcane spells, shunned because they are known to taint the mind and heart of the practitioner. He never told anyone, not even Emma, what he was doing. As the years passed, these forbidden workings caused subtle changes in Everett. Some of us suspected something was wrong—but we refused to admit, even to ourselves, that our beloved, charismatic teacher and leader could be anything less than perfect.

"His equilibrium was deteriorating. For a true witch, elderhood is an honorable state, a period of rest and contemplation. But Everett had begun to fear growing old, to dread the time when his powers would inevitably wane. He threw himself into the study of certain secret arts that promise the artificial prolonging of youth and strength. These arts are the essence of black magic. One of their contentions is that the vital force of one living being can be annexed by another at the moment of death. Obviously this is a transaction no true witch would ever consider, but Everett had already compromised his conscience many times over the years. The spell calls for the sacrifice of a young person in whom the life force is still growing.

"One night while Benjy slept, Everett summoned his spirit as he had so often in the past, intending to kill him. But Emma had been growing increasingly suspicious. She confided in Snowden, who was visiting, and together they managed to keep Everett from completing the spell." As she stopped speaking, I remembered Benjy's nightmare. *The trees were bare and there were dead leaves blowing through the air, and a god-awful rotten smell like a dead animal. I wanted to run away but I couldn't move. I knew something in the house had brought me there. Something that wanted to kill me . . .*

I took a shaky breath. Andreas was talking now, and I forced myself to listen.

"We had no choice but to banish Everett from the coven. He seemed to accept our judgment; at least he didn't outwardly resist. He chose to leave Green Hollow, and Emma chose to go with him. What caused their car to go off the bridge—whether it was a true accident or some design of Everett's—we have no way of knowing. Investigators at the scene reported two bodies in the submerged car. The woman was identified as Emma Lockley, the man as Everett.

"We now know this second identification was a glamour of Everett's working. The man was not Everett Lockley, but some unlucky hitchhiker. Eventually we began to suspect that Everett had survived the accident—to receive signs of his return to Green Hollow. You and Kip wanted to know why the owls were dying. They succumbed to one of the spells Everett used to counteract our protective magic here. An ironic joke on his part."

I remembered the pitiful little corpses scattered through the village. A joke? "So you knew he was out there! Why didn't you have him arrested?"

Andreas opened his hands. "For what? The attempted theft of his son's spirit? He'd committed no crime recognized by our legal system—at least not yet. And you must remember that whatever he had become, he had once been our teacher and friend."

For what we shared with them, and what we were to one another. The words of the rite murmured in my head, but a phrase of Andreas's had caught my attention. "At least not yet? What does that mean?"

He sighed and glanced at the others. In the sickly light of the waning moon their faces were more drawn than ever. The candles commemorating the dead had burned out and the fire from the adjoining circle was a tiny sputtering spark; neither warmth nor light reached the darkness where we stood. When Andreas spoke again, his voice was strained. "Everett's agenda hadn't changed. He still coveted a young life to boost his waning strength. To this purpose, a little over a year ago, he kidnapped and murdered Alex Leonard."

The whole night went black. I could see nothing—not the moon, not their faces or the dim meadow where we stood. I heard a gasping, unfamiliar voice say, "Everett? Everett Lockley was the Green Hollow Kidnapper?"

You can't admit it, can you—that anything bad could come out of that place?

"We put every effort into restraining him by magic. But—"

Vision was coming back to me now, in patches. My voice, interrupting, was still a stranger's. "Why didn't you tell the police?"

"We couldn't risk exposing the coven. We thought we could control him, but he'd gained such strength from sacrificing the boy that we were barely able to hold him in check. We contacted the British coven that had trained both him and Emma, and they sent Jonathan Blackbridge here to Green Hollow to help. He insisted that a cursing was the only real solution, but we weren't ready for such a step. Not then. It was a mistake. But we're only human, Shelley. We've tried many times to tell you that—to share with you a lesson we had to learn under the bitterest of circumstances. We are all to blame for Everett's actions, for refusing to see that he was entitled to be imperfect, fallible, afraid of aging and death."

"But he wasn't entitled to murder children!" I shouted. "And you let him roam around out there, a danger to everyone, until—" A connection lit in my memory. "That's why you took Benjy's side! You knew he wasn't the kidnapper! You let him go jail because you couldn't bring yourselves to turn in your old friend!"

"No," Elymas said. "That's not why we waited, Shelley. We needed to prepare ourselves. Everett is a strong and resourceful witch, and in order to bend him to our will we needed every possible advantage—the summer solstice, the full moon, the coven at its full complement of thirteen. We needed the help of the Goddess. And we needed you and Kip.

"There were some of us, especially Snow, who all along had doubts about involving you. But we knew the intertwined life force of twins posed a great temptation to Everett. There was no question that you needed our protection, and we needed your power. In the end we were able to reach him through his desire for you. We spared his life that night, in order not to risk harming the two of you—but we'd already realized Jonathan Blackbridge was right. A cursing was the only answer."

"So you killed him."

Andreas said, "It was our right. After all, he was one of our own."

His voice shook on the last word. There was an answering quiver inside me, like a glacier about to crack, as I caught a glimpse of the people behind the stylized figures I had constructed to feed my rage. Emma, wanting a child so badly that she was willing to manipulate a young woman's life. Everett, his yearning for contact with his son warped by black magic into a hideous greed. The coven members, trapped in a formidable struggle with their once beloved leader. *One of our own.*

"But what about Benjy?" I said. "He's been nothing but a pawn in all this since before he was born. Is that fair?"

"There is no way we can possibly atone to Benjy for what's happened," Archer said. "That will have to wait for another time, another place."

It was maddening how they just admitted their guilt. They had shamelessly used Kip and me, allowed Benjy to go to jail . . . Why didn't they try to justify what they had done? Accusing them was like striking at air. "You mean you're just going to do nothing?" *Nothing.* As the word left my lips I remembered the anonymous letter Benjy had received—the paid college education that had appeared from nowhere. The wry twist of his lips: *Me, with a secret benefactor! Ain't that a pisser!* Not nothing, but insultingly little, considering the magnitude of the wrong that had been done.

"So you'll make it up to him in some other lifetime, is that what you're saying? Isn't that convenient—like a bill that doesn't come due for a long time! For now, you can go on putting your own desires first, just the way Everett did. Nothing's really changed, has it?" Abruptly I pointed at Snow. "*Do what thou wilt.* Isn't that just what *you* did?"

She was still holding the athame in her right hand. But she spread her left over her belly, as if to shield it from the force of my gesture. "And what harm has been done here?" Her tone was even.

I opened my mouth and tasted its emptiness. Where were the words I needed—words about the abuse of power that would shame her and punish them all? I searched frantically and found nothing. *What harm?* It was wrong, I felt that. But why? Why? Because I had been betrayed. Because they had left me out. But I couldn't say that. In desperation I sought Kip's face among the others; my shaking finger swung to point at him. "He's too young to be anyone's father!" I shouted. "It shouldn't have been allowed to happen! It's wrong!"

I saw confusion in his face. His gaze jumped to Snow; I watched his expression change as he grasped my meaning. He was clearly stunned, but mingled with the shock was something that looked like joy.

"Creating life isn't wrong," I heard Snow say. When I looked at her again, she was shaking her head. "It doesn't do harm. The only harm here, Shelley, is in you. Don't you understand I can't protect you from your own shadow? Over and over I've tried to show you how strong you are, how gifted, how unique, but you have always resisted me. You cling to the idea of yourself as incomplete without Kip.

"Listen to the words of the Goddess: *If that which you seek, you find not within yourself, you will never find it without.* The other half you seek isn't Kip. It's your shadow: the power you possess to create and equally to destroy. Your fear of it has warped you—twisted your strength into envy and mistrust, your capacity for love into jealousy and greed. And until you stop denying it, until you face your shadow and claim it as your own, you will never be able to truly love Kip or anyone else."

I couldn't speak. It was as if she had thrown scalding water over me, or burned me with her fire, transforming my cold scorn into an inferno of rage and pain. Envy—jealousy—greed—how could she use those words when she had pretended to care for me? It was only Kip she cared for—Kip, and the child they had made together. Blood hammered in my temples; my breath came in hot gasps and a shriek burst out of me like some savage thing tearing itself free from a trap. My fingers began to open and close convulsively, clawing the air until it buzzed between my hands. The others stood as if turned to stone. Maybe they couldn't believe I would do anything. How could they? I did not believe it myself—until, without warning, the air erupted from my hands in a crackling stream, arcing across the space of darkness that separated me from Snow, joining the two of us for an instant by a bridge of blinding light.

I heard voices cry out in shock and horror. The athame dropped from Snow's hand and she doubled over to grab her belly. And then I couldn't see her at all, as the coveners rushed forward to close ranks around her. The mist had begun a violent churning; through its swirling vapors I saw Elymas push forward. He had retrieved the athame, and when he raised it high I could see it trembling in his hand. "Shelley, in the name of the Goddess! Have you lost your mind?"

The turbulent fog shifted. Behind him I caught a glimpse of the others gathered around Snow, forming a barrier between us. I could hear them talking in low, tense voices. Alternating heat and cold slapped me in waves; I stood panting and shivering as the sweat trickled down my ribs. "You never wanted me," I whispered. "You only put up with me because you wanted Kip. Snow wanted him in the coven because they were lovers in another life."

"That is your shadow talking," Elymas said. He sounded sad, not angry, and I couldn't bear it. I wanted him to hate me—wanted them all to hate me as much as I deserved.

"I'll tell everyone!" I shouted. "I'll tell the whole village about Everett and the rest of you! That you're witches—that you work magic and do terrible things to people! You won't be safe here anymore. They'll make you go away—they'll run you out of Green Hollow!"

As I shouted I could feel my hands filling with a hot tangle of blue-white light. With my final words I flung it at Elymas, but unlike Snow he was on his guard. He raised the athame; the sizzling lightstream struck it and rebounded in my direction. Everything disappeared; for an indeterminate interval I existed only as a bodiless, colorless dazzle. At last awareness returned in bits and pieces. My ears were ringing. My bones burned. I found myself on my hands and knees on the ground—tried to get up, fell, tried again. Was I lying down or standing up? I couldn't tell the difference.

"I'll tell them!" Was that choked gasp the shout I meant to make? Every nerve in my body sang with white fire, but somehow my feet were under me and I was stumbling out of the circle, starting to run. Dimly I saw a solitary figure in the meadow recoil as I passed.

Benjy. I had forgotten all about him. As I slowed to glance back, I could see the mist flowing through the break I had made in the boundary of the circle, its slow gray tendrils dissipating into the night. *The circle of the dead.* What had I done? There was a shout. "Shelley! Stop!"

Kip's voice. But I could not stop. I ran as if that first desperate flight from the Lockley Arms, seven years earlier—and the second one, from Snow only a few weeks' past—had been mere rehearsals for this moment. I reached the gate, flung it wide and plunged through, my hands stinging from the impact of the bars, bare feet thudding on brick as I ran the pool's glimmering length.

"Shelley!" Kip's voice trailing me. Tears spilled down my cheeks, coating them with a wet salt sting. The second gate squeaked shrilly as I pushed through it and fled across the carriage house lawn. On the footbridge, beneath the darkness of the overhanging pines, the ghosts of other Halloweens reached out for me. Childhood mystery of masks and gusty nights, lit by the glowing curves of jack-o'-lantern grins. *On this night the gate is open between the worlds.* Were there insubstantial shapes stirring among the pine branches—a faint wailing behind the sound of my running footsteps? As I burst out from under the trees into the parking lot, the night dropped over me like a cold black sack.

"Shelley, wait!" Kip's voice drowning out the ghostly ones. He was gaining on me. I ran across the parking lot—past the back steps—beneath the porte cochere—

"Shelley—!"

So close I could hear his breathing raggedly intersecting my own. The gnarled branches of the apple trees on the lawn reached out as if to hinder me, but I put on a burst of speed down the driveway and bolted across the street toward our house, where a carved pumpkin leered from the front step to welcome trick-or-treaters.

I never saw or heard the truck at all. So far as I know, it was not even in sight when I ran across Willow Street; and how it appeared in the brief space between my crossing and Kip's is a mystery. But as I gained the porch of our house, behind me in the street there was a sudden unearthly glare of headlights, and then the deafening bellow of a horn above shrieking brakes.

By the time I looked back, it was already over. Whatever motion was required had run itself out, and all that remained was a still tableau. A huge truck had stopped at a skewed angle in the middle of Willow Street, its headlights spilling brightness. The beams just reached a crumpled shape flung some distance by the force of the impact.

That was the foreground. In the background an elegant Victorian house rose gracefully behind its hedge, and just above the tower roof hung a sickle moon like a rotten, lopsided grin in the dark visage of the sky.

With Kip's death, a curious forgetfulness descended on the village. No one asked questions; no one seemed to wonder about the odd circumstances of the accident. Of course it *was* Halloween . . . but shouldn't someone have inquired why the two of us were naked beneath our costumes, or how Kip could have been so careless as to run right in front of an oncoming truck? I was never questioned about these things. Not, I am certain, out of any wish to spare my feelings, but out of some entirely unnatural lack of curiosity in which I recognized the hand of magic.

The coven had moved swiftly to protect itself. There was no real evidence to connect the Lockley Arms with the accident—but by the following day, any authority wishing to question its inhabitants would have found only a dour Jessica in residence, offering the information that the inn was closed indefinitely while its mistress was away on business. Except for her, and Royce hovering in the background, the house was empty. Later on, they too disappeared.

Nor have any of them ever returned. And I cannot blame them: they had no way of knowing I never intended to carry out my threat to expose the coven. I only wish they had included me in the spell of forgetfulness they cast over everyone else. And this is how I know that Snow survived my attack—because I recognize her touch in my exclusion, as if she wished to leave me with the full knowledge of what I destroyed. Understanding Snow as I do, I would have to guess she meant this double-edged parting gift as both a blessing and a curse.

Along with the coven vanished the spark that for so many

years lit the village of Green Hollow like a candle dancing in a globe of colored glass. Afterward the sunshine seemed duller, the nights less profound; summer did not linger, nor spring come quickly. Stores closed along Main Street—Kate's among them, as she wasted away from cancer. Their windows were broken by vandals and boarded up, and obscenities scrawled on the boards.

Benjy kept out of my way after that Halloween night. Even if he retained no clear memory of its events, he must have experienced a certain uneasiness in my presence. Later he left town and I heard he had gone west, as his mother and her young man had once dreamed of doing. Janicot Books transplanted its business to Kentucky, offering jobs to any employees who wanted to make the move, and many went. The school dwindled and finally closed, and children these days take the bus to Woodston, ten miles to the south. As for the Lockley Arms, it remains beautiful even in its abandoned state, like the last glowing ember in a dying fire.

My father's second heart attack was fatal. After he died I left the village, to wander from city to city before I finally settled in one. The life I lead now is far from unpleasant. I have had some success as a writer, mostly freelance articles for magazines. There have been a few lovers, a few friendships, some other amenities: a neighborhood café where they know me and I can sit with a book and a cup of coffee, a subscription to the opera, a nearby church garden where I enjoy the sunshine and flowers in warm weather. I have never told even my closest friends that I was once a twin. But if in losing Kip I lost some essential part of myself, at least that terrible night gave me, in return, the true measure of my own heart.

Do you still wish to join us? Will you suffer to learn?

Of Snow's child and its fate I know nothing, nor have I ever had word of the others—although I have little doubt that somewhere off the beaten track there exists a small town where fortunes have taken an unexpected upswing in recent years. A place where the sun shines brightly and the buildings are freshly painted, where people bustle along a Main Street lined with striped shop awnings, and a little park with a bandstand resounds with the shouts of children playing . . . where it's suddenly possible to sense the charm of life the way everyone says it used to be. Magic. Is there any other word for the atmosphere of such places? Now and then I even imagine going in search of that little town, although I ought not to entertain such thoughts. After all, I no longer call myself a witch. How can I? I violated the Craft's only law: *An' it harm none, do what thou wilt.*

Yet in the years since then, walking at night in open country or down a poorly lit city street, catching sight of the moon's luminous crescent hanging in the dark sky, I can still hear the echo of an eerie, lilting melody beyond the touch of time or human woe. *La, la . . . La, la . . .* Now it seems to come, not from outside me as I once thought, but from within; and at such moments I recall what Elymas said on that perfect Midsummer Eve when Kip and I asked to join the coven. *Be forewarned: once you have known the Goddess, she will claim a part of you forever.*

And so once a year at Halloween, when the leaves crackle underfoot and the air smells of apples and woodsmoke—when streets everywhere are deserted after dark because parents are afraid, now, to let their children roam unaccompanied on this night of mystery, and a few forlorn jack-o'-lanterns wait in vain for the magic phrase "trick or treat"—once a year at Halloween, I return to Green Hollow. We have supper together, Mother and Marty and I, followed by the usual stilted conversation, and then we say good night. Upstairs in my old room, I lock the door to cast a solitary's circle. I sprinkle salt, light the candles, and remind myself that within this space the opposites of joy and sorrow, light and dark, life and death meet and make one. While the candles flicker against the darkness I say the words I still recall, the words of the Samhain ritual, and discover a kind of comfort therein.

"We gather at the crack of time. On this night the veil is thin between the worlds. The dead walk, and to the living is revealed the Mystery: that every ending is but a new beginning. Here in this time out of time, let us welcome to our circle those we have loved in the past, that we may celebrate with them once more. Let us light this place with our memories, as one day we shall want others to do on our behalf. And as these lights burn, so may the light of remembrance burn for those we have loved—for what we shared with them, and what we were to one another."

As I speak I seem to hear other voices, past and present, familiar and unknown, rising in a murmuring chorus to join my own across the dark:

"Merry meet,
And merry part,
And merry meet again.
Blessed be."